Just Friends

MADISON WRIGHT

Copyright © 2023 by Madison Wright

All rights reserved.

No portion of this book may be reproduced in any form without written permission from the publisher or author, except as permitted by U.S. copyright law.

Cover Design by Sam Palencia at Ink and Laurel

Editing by V.B. Edits

Instagram: @authormadisonwright

My first book was dedicated to my husband because I couldn't have done it without his support. The second was dedicated to my friends because I couldn't have done it without their encouragement. This one is dedicated to you, reader, for giving me someone to write to.

Prologue

HAZEL

"Don't move," someone says from behind me where I've been checking my phone in the corner, his voice deep and smooth. "There's a butterfly on your shoulder."

I freeze at his words and slowly, so slowly, turn my head to see the tiny butterfly perched on my shoulder. Its wings are a vibrant, almost transparent orange, so thin I can see the glint of the sun shining through them.

A large veined hand brushes against my bare shoulder, and a long finger hovers in front of the butterfly, waiting. A heartbeat later, the butterfly flutters from my shoulder and onto the finger. I spin around and finally glance at the man.

He's tall, much taller than me, with rich brown hair, the color so dark it's almost black. It's slightly wavy and slicked back with some kind of matte pomade that must have been applied much earlier in the day, because pieces are rebelling and falling across his strong forehead.

His eyes meet mine, almost as dark as his hair and flecked with bits of green and gold. One corner of his mouth kicks up before the other in the kind of smile you only see in good movies, where the men are British and afraid of their feelings.

The butterfly's wings flap, carrying it away from us, and his smile dims. "I didn't get to make a wish."

"That's a shame, because I hear butterfly wishes are even more powerful than shooting stars or birthday candles."

He crosses his arms over his chest, and I can't help but notice the way his muscles ripple at the movement.

"Is that so?" he asks, eyebrows lifting.

I nod seriously. "Oh yeah. It's quantifiable. Scientific."

"That's too bad," he says, his tone matching mine, although his smile does melt away in the harsh sunlight.

"I—"

My words are cut off by an excited yell from Ellie, my brother's girlfriend, who's making a beeline toward me. Her grin is bright as she nears.

"You met Alex," she says immediately, and I glance back at the man in front of me. A muscle in his darkly stubbled cheek flickers as he smiles at Ellie.

"I did?" I say, although it comes out more like a question.

The man extends his hand, and when I shake it, it's warm and a little rough against my own. "I'm Alex. Ellie's older brother."

Everything clicks into place, and I can see the resemblance between them now. Same pale skin and dark features. Same smile and that energy that feels electric, alive.

"Ah," I say with a nod of my head. "I'm Cam's sister, Hazel."

"I've heard so much about you."

"That's funny," I say, a smile creeping across my lips, "because I've heard almost nothing about you."

A deep chuckle rumbles from his chest, mingling with Ellie's musical laughter. She elbows her brother in the ribs, and he pretends to hiss, grabbing his side. She ignores him and says, "He's the one who's always getting me out of sticky situations with my mom."

My head tilts back in recognition. I only met Ellie in person for the first time two days ago, but we've become easy friends since she started dating Cam last year, and I've heard all about her difficult relationship with her parents.

"Speaking of," I say, daring a look around the bright, green expanse of the country club. "I still feel weird that I'm at their anniversary party since I wasn't invited. I haven't even met them."

Ellie waves me off like she has every time I've mentioned this since she and Cam told me that this party would be smack dab in the middle of my visit to Nashville. I tried to suggest a different week, but except for the party, this week worked best for everyone.

"I told you—they're not even going to notice you're here. Plus, I'm the host, so I can invite whoever I want. And if they do notice, they still won't care."

"I could have just gone exploring by myself," I say.

"They won't notice, I promise," Alex interjects. "They're too busy acting like they're still in love in front of all of their friends."

"It *is* their forty-year anniversary party," I say, catching my bottom lip between my teeth and willing myself not to try to blend into the shadows of the shrubs like I was before he found me.

"Forty years of eating souls," Alex says and places a hand over his heart. "Together."

Ellie elbows him again, but she's holding back a smile. Her gaze darts around us, fixing on my brother, who has a camera pressed to his face on the other side of the area sectioned off for the party. I know for a fact that he would have come with Ellie no matter what, but that he was endlessly relieved when Ellie's parents took him up on his offer to professionally photograph the event free of charge. My brother is always more comfortable with a camera between him and the rest of the world.

"I better go see if Cam needs anything," Ellie says. She looks back at me. "Do *you* need anything? You really don't have to hide away back here."

The thing is, at most parties, I'm right in the thick of it, hoarding all the socialization Cam so desperately avoids. At *this* party, however, for people I've never met, where the only people I know are the photographer and the host, I feel an unfamiliar uneasiness in the pit of my stomach.

"I'm good," I tell her, forcing a smile to my face.

Her brow crinkles with concern, as if she doesn't quite believe me, and I feel guilty for putting that look there. This is her parents' anniversary party, and from what I've heard, they're incredibly picky. I know she's been planning this event for months and doesn't need to be worrying about me.

"You sure?" she asks.

My chin dips in a nod. "Definitely," I say, and with one look in our direction, she disappears.

Alex's gaze is heavy on me, and when I look up, a smirk plays with the edges of his mouth. "You hate this, don't you?"

"I love parties," I tell him, holding my sweating glass tighter in my hand.

"But you hate *this* party," he clarifies.

I don't know what makes me open up to him, but I do. Maybe he just has one of those faces, the kind that's easygoing and nonjudgmental, with permanent laugh lines etched into all the right spots.

"I'm a little uncomfortable," I say finally. With a hand, I gesture at my outfit, a honey-colored sundress with a plunging neckline and wide, fluttering sleeves, embroidered with tiny white flowers around the neckline and down the skirt. "I don't think I quite nailed the dress code."

Everyone else at the party is dressed like they're drinking cocktails on a yacht. There's more Lilly Pulitzer and seersucker here than in the Hamptons. Even Alex matches the aesthetic, although he's easily the most casually dressed person here in the lightest shade of khakis and a white linen shirt with the top four buttons left undone and the sleeves rolled to his elbows.

My skin heats as his gaze dips, assessing my outfit. "I like it."

"I'm also," I say, swallowing, "more than a little nervous about running into your parents."

His eyes glitter with mischief as they meet mine. "I promise you, they will never know. They invited all their rich friends, and their rich friends *had* to bring along their children to show them off. And their rich friends' children had to bring along their significant others or risk getting alcohol poisoning while trying to avoid their parents' disappointment in their life choices. So *my* parents know roughly 20 percent of the people here."

"Surprisingly, that does make me feel a little better."

"Good," he says, his grin widening until it takes over his entire face. "Now, we just need to get you out of this corner. You look like a wallflower in a period drama."

An unexpected laugh jolts from me. "You don't seem like the period drama type," I say, clutching my drink a little tighter.

"Oh, I'm most definitely not. But Ellie likes to watch them when she's sad, and I can never tell her no."

"Sounds like you're a good brother."

"Absolutely not, but I am a great dancer." He extends a hand to me, his head tilting in the direction of the dance floor, where most of the younger crowd has gathered with their significant others, the middle-aged attendees observing with pursed lips.

Alex watches me expectantly, dark brown eyes lighting like crackling firewood.

"Fine," I say, giving him my glass instead of my hand. Pure delight crosses his features, and he quickly deposits the glass on one of the trays of the meandering servers. His hand slides into mine, large and warm, and he pulls me toward the dance floor.

He keeps to the outskirts of the crowd, as though he doesn't want the attention of being in the middle, and when he spins me around, his hand hovers over my waist.

Eyebrows arched, he asks, "This okay?"

At my nod, his fingers curl around the swell of my hip, gently pulling me closer, and his other hand finds mine. Slowly, we sway to the beat of the jazz music coming from the live band in the corner.

"Your parents don't look old enough to be married for forty years," I say, glancing at the couple seated at a table on the other side of the venue.

Alex's shoulder lifts in a shrug under my hand. "They have great plastic surgeons." Dimples pop in his cheeks before he continues. "But they got married pretty young. Right out of college. And they waited awhile to have us. They spent the beginning of their marriage building the family business."

I know from Cam and Ellie that her parents own a large property management company. They own high-end apartments and expensive rentals all over middle Tennessee. From the looks of this lavish party, they seem to have done a pretty good job of building their business.

"Seems to have worked out for them." I don't miss the way Alex's face pinches, a look of displeasure crossing his features before disappearing.

"They've done well for themselves," he says. "But let's not talk about them. It's rather dull when the whole party is dedicated to them."

I can't help but laugh. "Okay, fair point."

One corner of his mouth tips up before the other. "So tell me about yourself, Hazel Lane."

"Well," I say. "I like to watch period dramas, even when I'm not sad."

"What's your favorite?"

"*Emma*," I say immediately. "Most people would probably say *Pride & Prejudice* is better, but there's just something about best friends falling in love that makes my heart melt."

His face scrunches up, as if he's thinking. "I've seen *Pride & Prejudice*, I think. Was the man grumpy and British?"

"They're *all* grumpy and British."

The laugh that slips between his lips makes my hair flutter. "I guess that doesn't narrow it down. Okay, tell me something else about yourself."

I tap his shoulder with an index finger. "It's actually your turn."

"I'm a realtor," he says, and when I roll my eyes, he asks, "What?"

"You can't say your *job*. That's such a boring fact."

"Fine, fine," he says, thinking. His brow wrinkles as he does, his eyes slipping deeper into darkness. "I...like to work out."

My laugh is loud enough to draw glances, and Alex's smile widens.

"What? Is that too boring too? I'm realizing I don't have many hobbies," he says, mirth lacing his voice.

"No," I tell him. "It's just...that's pretty obvious."

His eyebrows lift, and I realize how much of a come-on that sounded like. "I didn't—"

I'm cut off by a regal, commanding voice. "Alex, you haven't introduced us to your friend."

When I turn, Alex and Ellie's parents are standing beside us, his mom's cool blue eyes assessing me. Her white-blond bob is slicked behind her ears, revealing heavy dangling earrings that tug at her lobes. Although she's likely quite a bit older than my own mother, she's almost entirely free of wrinkles and sunspots, making her look almost ageless.

The man next to her is equally striking, and although he still looks remarkably young for his age, he looks to have embraced it. His nearly black hair is peppered with gray, and his eyes and mouth are framed by lines, as though he's spent more of his life laughing than his wife has. He is the exact picture of what I imagine Alex will look like in thirty years.

My eyes widen as I turn to Alex, panic creeping up my esophagus. But he's smiling easily, dropping the hand holding mine but keeping the other pressed to the small of my back.

"This is my date, Hazel."

I try not to glance at him and give us away, but I can't help but feel relief at the lifeline he threw my way.

"Ah" is all she says, completely dismissing me. With most people, it would feel offensive, but I get the sense it's better to be completely off this woman's radar. Her eyes fix on mine for the briefest of moments. "Well, nice to meet you, Hallie. We hope you both have a great time."

I keep my smile fixed in place, but from the way Alex's hand tenses on my back, he's either pissed or holding back laughter. It only takes one quick glance in his direction to know it's the latter.

"Nice to meet you too," I say, even though neither of them actually introduced themselves. When they disappear back into the crowd, Alex presses his lips together.

"Well, Hallie, I think that might have been the smoothest an introduction to my parents has ever gone." The hitch of his lips is infectious, and I can't help but join him.

"That's a terrifying thought," I tell him, and he grins wider.

"Come on, let's get a drink."

The midafternoon sun dips below the horizon as we alternate between dancing and people watching, and as more and more of Alex's parents' friends drift by, introducing themselves and asking questions about Alex's personal life, the date ruse holds in place. With each person, our story gets more and more elaborate, until we're basically on the verge of matrimony and planning to look at potential vacation homes in the Vineyard next month.

It's not until the day has fully dissolved into night that I remember why I was checking my phone earlier—the text I was in the middle of responding to when Alex found a butterfly on my shoulder.

After I've fished the phone from my pocket and responded to the text from hours ago, Alex holds out his hand in front of me.

"What?" I ask, my gaze trailing up from his veiny forearms to the swell of his muscular shoulders and up to his deep brown eyes.

"If we're going ring shopping next weekend, you'll need my number."

I hand the phone to him, biting my bottom lip to keep from grinning. When he returns the phone a moment later, he's saved his name as *Future Husband Alexander*.

"My boyfriend is going to be so disappointed," I say, and his eyebrows lift so high they practically disappear into his hair.

"Boyfriend, huh?"

"Didn't I mention him?" I ask, my fingers tightening on my glass.

"No, I don't think you did." He holds out his hand for my phone once more, and I slip it into his palm.

When he returns it again, it says *Best Friend Alexander*.

I smile faintly at it, and his eyes are warm when I meet them again. "A bit presumptuous, but I like it."

He lifts a shoulder in the kind of shrug that tells me he's sure of himself. "I think we're going to be the best of friends, Hazel Lane. Just you wait."

One

BEST FRIEND ALEXANDER: LONG time, no see

Hazel: I literally JUST left. Have you even made it out of the airport parking lot yet?

Best Friend Alexander: No, but that's just because your brother drives like a grandpa.

Best Friend Alexander: When are you coming back to visit me?

Hazel: I'm coming back for the holidays!

Best Friend Alexander: That's like five months away.

Hazel: Sounds like you're going to miss me.

Best Friend Alexander: No, just figuring out if it's going to be enough time to heal my ears after your karaoke.

Hazel: That's low, even for you.

Best Friend Alexander: A fiancé would never…but we're just friends.

Hazel: Men like you are hard to find.

Best Friend Alexander: And don't you forget it.

BEST FRIEND ALEXANDER: WHAT are you doing today?

Hazel: I'm working on a branding project for a new client.

Best Friend Alexander: On a Saturday night??

Hazel: What? You never work on Saturdays?

Best Friend Alexander: Well, sure. I'm working right now.

Hazel: How is this any different?

Best Friend Alexander: I'm single.

Hazel: You should be out meeting a loose woman.

Best Friend Alexander: I actually laughed out loud at that.

Best Friend Alexander: Where's Sebastian?

Hazel: He had plans tonight.

Best Friend Alexander: With??

Hazel: Idk, I didn't ask.

Hazel: Why aren't you responding?

Best Friend Alexander: Sorry, got distracted. Want to watch a movie?

Hazel: We're two thousand miles apart...

Best Friend Alexander: We can turn on the same movie at the same time and FaceTime.

Hazel: Okay, I'm down. Give me twenty minutes.

Hazel: Just landed!

Best Friend Alexander: Where are you?

Hazel: The plane.

Best Friend Alexander: Okay, smart aleck. What terminal?

Hazel: Getting off now!

Best Friend Alexander: You still didn't answer my question.

Hazel: In the airport!

Best Friend Alexander: I hate you.

Hazel: At baggage claim!

Best Friend Alexander: You'll have to wait. I met a loose woman in the parking garage.

HAZEL: I HAVE A secret.

Best Friend Alexander: Do tell.

Hazel: I'm not allowed.

Best Friend Alexander: This is worse than when you wouldn't tell me what you were sending me for my birthday.

Hazel: It's juicy too.

Best Friend Alexander: That's TMI.

Hazel: Idk what that's even supposed to be in reference to, but gross.

Best Friend Alexander: TELL ME YOUR SECRET

Hazel: CAM BOUGHT A RING

Hazel: He's going to tell you about it tomorrow

Hazel: Act surprised

Best Friend Alexander: Wow, I'm actually really, really happy for them

Hazel: Me too. They deserve it.

Hazel: I didn't tell you the best part yet!!!

Best Friend Alexander: ??

Hazel: He wants to have an engagement party because he thinks Ellie will want to celebrate with everyone as soon as they get back!
Hazel: So…
Hazel: I'M COMING TO VISIT!!!

BEST FRIEND ALEXANDER: HAZEL?? Did you make it home?
Best Friend Alexander: Hazel
Best Friend Alexander: I haven't heard from you in three days, and I'm getting worried.
Best Friend Alexander: Please answer me
Hazel: Sebastian cheated on me
Hazel: He's been cheating on me for a while

BEST FRIEND ALEXANDER: YOU sure you don't want me to fly out there and ride with you to Nashville?
Hazel: I drove here from North Carolina when I moved here.
Best Friend Alexander: Yeah, but…
Hazel: I hadn't just found out my boyfriend has been cheating on me for months?
Best Friend Alexander: Please just let me ride with you.

Hazel: I'll be fine. I'll be in Nashville with everything I could fit in my car in a few days.

    Best Friend Alexander: Are you okay? Really?

    Hazel: No, but I will be.

Best Friend Alexander: What do you want for dinner tonight?

    Hazel: I'm good with whatever. You pick!

    Best Friend Alexander: Can I pick the movie too?

    Hazel: Not after last week.

    Best Friend Alexander: I STAND BY MY CHOICE

    Hazel: I asked you to turn on your favorite Disney movie, and you chose DOUG'S 1ST MOVIE???

    Best Friend Alexander: IT'S A GREAT MOVIE

    Hazel: You're on movie probation for the foreseeable future

Hazel: What should I wear to this bachelorette party tonight?

    Best Friend Alexander: Probably something scandalous

    Hazel: I don't feel like getting hit on

    Best Friend Alexander: You NEVER feel like getting hit on

    Hazel: Men are the armpit of society

Best Friend Alexander: Preach, sis
Best Friend Alexander: But really…do you think you're ever going to date again?
Hazel: One day
Hazel: But not anytime soon
Hazel: I don't need a boyfriend anyway
Hazel: I have you

Best Friend Alexander: So I was thinking. After this wedding is over tonight, we should go get burgers.
Hazel: As long as there's ice cream involved
Best Friend Alexander: I'm not a monster. Of course there will be ice cream.
Hazel: You and me and ice cream
Best Friend Alexander: Always, Lane

Two

HAZEL

THE LIGHTS IN THE diner are harsh and bright. Truthfully, they're the only thing keeping me awake at this point. It's been a *very* long but happy day, and I'm exhausted.

"Two cheeseburgers, double order of chili fries, a cotton candy milkshake, and whatever she's having," Alex says with a nod in my direction.

The waitress, who has been eyeing him appreciatively since we walked through the door, cocks an eyebrow as if to clarify that *all* that food is for him.

Alex gives her a charming smile. The one where one corner of his mouth hitches up first. I roll my eyes as pink stains her cheeks and she completely forgets I'm here.

"I'll have that right out," she says and turns to head back to the kitchen, her dark auburn ponytail swishing against her stark white uniform.

"A Reuben," I say, and she spins back around, finally remembering there's another person at this table—even if my dimples aren't quite as alluring.

The waitress looks at me like I just got in front of her in the ATM line with a big bag of change to deposit. "Anything else?"

I try to give her a sweet smile, but I can tell this woman will only be enchanted by one person at this table tonight. "Mint chocolate chip milkshake."

She doesn't bother to write it down and retreats into the kitchen without acknowledgment.

"Think it's the dress?" I ask Alex sarcastically, motioning to the bridesmaid dress and Alex's borrowed salmon colored tuxedo jacket that I haven't bothered changing out of since my brother's wedding a few hours ago.

His nose crinkles in confusion. "Is what the dress?"

I roll my eyes and press my lips together to keep from smiling. In the little over a year since I moved to Nashville and we became best friends, I've gotten that same jealous look from women everywhere—and Alex has *never* noticed. I swear sometimes I think it's in my head. But then I remember that one time a lady at the movie theater actually curled her lip in disgust, and I figure it's not just me.

Alex takes a sip from the water the waitress brought when we sat down and smiles contentedly at me, his eyes crinkling at the corners. "How do you think the day went?"

I can't help my own grin, thinking of the wedding we just left. My brother, Camden, and Alex's sister, Ellie. A couple who couldn't have deserved this beautiful day more.

"It was perfect," I answer, my voice ringing out dreamily.

"It really was."

"Oh," I exclaim, reaching for my purse on the booth seat next to me. "I almost forgot." I rummage around until my fingers fasten on a cellophane baggie, and I plop it on the counter. "Chocolate penises."

"My favorite," Alex says sardonically.

"Courtesy of Ethel," I tell him, referring to Ellie's elderly friend and tenant at the apartment complex she manages. She has a small business making phallic-shaped candies and desserts and has provided some for every wedding event we've had over the past few months. The bridal shower was a *blast*.

"Only the best," Alex agrees, opening the bag and pulling out one of the candies.

I get one for myself too, letting the dark chocolate melt on my tongue. "She made them for the bridesmaids."

Alex digs in his pants pocket for his phone. Sliding it open, he shows me what's on the screen. "I got some photos of today."

I take his phone, swiping through all the candid shots he got from the groomsmen's room and from the reception. It's a blur of colors, since all the groomsmen and bridesmaids were in varying warm, bright colors of tuxedos and dresses. There are a few photos of me dancing wildly with the hem of my dress tied up around my knees. There's another of Cam's best man and my longtime friend, Wes. He's cheering at something, and beside him, Cam is looking like he's barely containing an eye roll.

"They're nothing like Cam could have gotten," he says, sounding almost abashed.

"No," I say faintly. They're nothing like what my brother, the professional photographer, would have taken. "But they're perfect."

A smile tugs the corner of my lips when I get to the selfie we took earlier in the day. My curls hadn't fallen out yet, and Alex's tie was still around his neck. His arm is wrapped around my shoulders, pulling me into the crook of his neck.

I send it to myself before swiping over to the next photo. It's one of Cam and Ellie during their first dance, eyes only for each other. They were like that all day, and although I'm endlessly happy for them, I can't help the tug of sadness deep in my chest, that pull of longing reminding me just how long it's been since someone looked at *me* like that.

When I look up, Alex's gaze is fixed on me. "Watching them almost made me kind of sad," he says, as if reading my mind. I would think he was saying it just to make me feel better, but I see the way his eyebrows and lips draw down slightly, a look I so rarely see on his carefree face.

"Me too," I agree quietly, knowing he understands exactly what I'm thinking and feeling. It's always been like that, from the very beginning. It's how we formed a friendship so seamlessly, even though we were thousands of miles apart. How it felt like a tether pulling me here when my life crumbled around me last year.

Alex stares at me for another moment, as if searching for something in my face. His eyes are the exact color of freshly tilled soil, with little flecks of green, like plants pushing up from the earth after a long winter.

After a long minute, he seems to find what he's looking for and opens his mouth, words hovering on the tip of his tongue.

"Two cheeseburgers," the waitress says, returning with a tray of food. She puts Alex's plates down in front of him with a lingering smile and even a few light touches on his arm before sliding mine across the table unceremoniously.

For a few minutes, we tear into our food, not speaking. It's not until Alex has finished both of his burgers and pushed his fries in my direction that he talks again.

I look at the fries, one eyebrow raised.

"You never order your own and always want some of mine."

He's right, I guess, so I gingerly pluck one of the fries from the top and pop it into my mouth.

As we work through the mound of fries on the plate, a firm sense of resolution settles in my gut. Today, watching Cam and Ellie, cemented something in my mind for me.

"What's that look for?" Alex asks, motioning to his own eyebrows that he's pinched together, imitating what mine must look like.

Letting out a deep breath, I say, "I want to go on a date."

Alex chokes on his fries and lets out a strangled wheeze, pounding his hand on his chest. I shove his drink in his direction and he takes large gulps, washing down the lodged food. Crimson creeps up his throat beneath the strong fingers he has pressed there.

"What did you say?" he finally asks, blinking back tears.

My hand closes around his water glass, lifting it toward his face once again. "Are you okay? Drink some more water."

He swats it away, his eyes laser focused on mine. "You want to go on a date?"

"You almost died!"

"Hazel," he says, his voice laced with exasperation.

"*What?*"

"Answer my question."

It takes me a moment to remember what we were talking about, my heartbeat still pounding in my ears, but when I do, I almost don't even care to talk about it anymore. With a trembling hand, I reach for another fry and shrug. "I said I think I'm ready to start dating again."

An unreadable expression passes over his face for a split second, there and gone, before I can decipher it. "What do you mean?"

Sighing, I say, "I don't know." I twist my hands together in my lap, trying and failing to make sense of my thoughts. "I feel like it's time, right? It's been over a year since *Sebastian.*"

Alex makes a disgusted face, like he does any time I mention my cheating ex-boyfriend, and I can't help but echo the unspoken sentiment. Fourteen months ago, I returned home to LA from Nashville, where I was celebrating Cam and Ellie's engagement, to find my boyfriend of a year and a half in bed with his neighbor. And after dumping him, eating more chocolate cake than I care to admit, and not leaving my house for five days straight, I realized I had exactly zero ties left to that city. So I did what any mature twenty-six-year-old woman would do. I packed my bags and moved across the country and into my brother's apartment. For the second time in my life.

Living with Cam lasted exactly nine days before I couldn't handle it anymore and we found a new place for me to move into. An upstairs detached garage apartment that belongs to one of Ellie's former tenants. But after the whole cheating fiasco, I decided I should take a break from men and try to piece myself back together. I don't think anyone realized how much Sebastian destroyed me. Not even Alex.

Alex clears his throat, pulling me out of my thoughts. His melting cotton candy milkshake is mixing together to form a pretty shade of pale lavender. It sloshes against the sides of the glass as he stirs it, not meeting my eyes.

"So who do you want to date?" he asks after a long moment.

I clench my hands tighter together under the table, joints popping as I wonder how he's going to respond to the idea I had just minutes ago. "Well, I was hoping you could help me with that."

His gaze shoots to mine instantly, almost searing me with its intensity. "What do you mean?"

"I was thinking maybe we could..."

"Yes?" His shoulders expand, straining against the fabric of his white button-down as he takes a deep breath and holds it.

"Set each other up."

The breath he was holding whooshes out slowly, making his body deflate like a balloon. He pushes a hand through his dark brown hair. "You want to set each other up?"

I grab the hand he has resting on the table and give it a squeeze. "Aren't you ready to start seriously dating someone?"

His voice is a soft exhale, his gaze fixed on mine. "Yes."

"Me too," I say, tucking my legs up under me on the booth seat. My hair falls in loose, limp waves all around my shoulders, getting in my way, so I reach for Alex's wrist and tug off the ponytail holder he always keeps there for me since it wouldn't go with my outfits.

Alex watches as I swiftly braid my hair, the silky strands gliding through my fingers at a rapid, practiced speed. "That's where my plan comes in."

"Your plan?"

"It's just..." I trail off, not sure what I'm wanting to say. One thing keeps running on repeat in my head. Something that's been haunting me since I found Sebastian with his neighbor. "I don't trust myself."

Alex's eyes soften to warm, rich puddles of brown. "Haze, what Sebastian did wasn't your fault."

I sit back in the booth, letting my shoulders slump against the shiny surface. "I know that, and I don't feel like it was. Really. But I'm still scared, Alex. I thought things were good between us, and I don't know how to find something I can trust."

Alex looks away, his jaw flexing.

"I just don't know if I trust myself to find someone good. I want someone I can laugh with. Someone who will take silly selfies with me and tell me when I have paint in my hair. Someone who will get waffles with me at midnight and won't complain when I want burgers for breakfast."

"You should have that," Alex says, and for some reason, his voice sounds a little strange, like the scratch of a match on sandpaper.

"Mostly, I want someone who won't cheat on me." Alex's lips tighten, and I know he thinks I've set the bar entirely too low. "That's where you come in."

You know when you're streaming a show and it freezes, and for a moment, you don't know whether the person has just stopped moving or whether the TV is buffering? That's what Alex looks like right now, still and unblinking.

"What do you mean by that?" he asks slowly, hesitation written in every line of his body.

I pick up a fry from the almost empty plate and throw it at him. It ricochets off his nose before falling into his lap. "You don't have to look so horrified. I'm not suggesting *you* date me. I just want you to find me someone to date."

He pushes a hand through his hair again, and the short dark locks stand on end. He looks like he's been electrocuted. "What, exactly, do you mean by that?"

This plan has been hovering on the edge of my mind all day. It's just now starting to solidify into something worthwhile. "I think we should set each other up on blind dates."

"Blind dates?" I don't miss the incredulity in his voice.

"And we can go together."

"Together?"

I give him a flat look. "Are you going to keep repeating everything I say?"

"Are you going to start making sense?" he shoots back.

I throw my hands in the air, exasperated. "I really thought you were going to like this idea."

He looks away for a moment, studying a spot on the wall across the diner, before turning back to me. His face is resigned, and his shoulders are slumped in what looks like defeat. "Tell me your plan."

The gesture is so unlike him, so at odds with my carefree best friend that I don't even want to proceed. I thought this would be fun for both of us, but I don't want to do it if it's going to make him look like *that*. "No, it's fine. Don't worry about it."

Some of the life returns to his eyes. "Tell me."

"No," I say with a jut of my chin.

His gaze turns devilish. "I know how to make you talk."

He does, and it's not fair. Two months ago, he found the ticklish spot on the back of my knee, and I haven't known a moment's peace since then. "That's not fair."

Alex slides his palm over the table, inching toward the edge. "Talk, Hazel."

"Fine, fine!" I say, and his hand stops. My uneasiness ebbs at his smile, returning at the slash of his white teeth and the crinkles beside his eyes. *This* is how I expected him to react to this idea—with laughter and excitement. Not whatever quiet weirdness he had earlier. "Okay, so I thought we could go on a blind date. Maybe one each weekend? And we could go to the same place, in case either of us wants to bail."

"You want to go on double blind dates?" He sounds so dubious that I almost want to laugh.

"No, not together. Just to the same place. We can be on separate dates, but just close enough to be there if one of us flashes the bat signal."

He presses his hand to his head, his fingers shaped to form an *L* so it looks like he's a middle schooler calling someone a loser. It's a terrible signal we came up with at his office holiday party last year, in case either of us wanted to leave. That's what the *L* stands for in our scenario, although Alex's pervy boss certainly didn't think so when I did it when he cornered me during the party to ask if I've ever dated an older man. Alex caught on, though, and got me out of there like a bat out of hell—no pun intended.

Okay, pun is intended. That's too good to pass up.

"Yes, the bat signal," I tell him.

"So we just go on blind dates?" Alex asks, loudly slurping the dregs from his now fully purple milkshake.

I shrug. "I don't know. The idea just kind of came to me today while I was watching Cam and Ellie together. I just thought that we deserve something like that, you know?"

It's true, seeing Cam and Ellie did spark that thought in my mind, but it was more than that. I watched as Alex danced with one of his cousin's preschool-aged daughters, laughing and spinning her in circles. I watched as he and his brother, Adam, smooshed Ellie in a giant hug that they call an Ellie Sandwich. I watched as he grabbed two slices of cake from the dessert table and gave me the bigger piece. I just watched *Alex* today. And I thought he was too good to be alone. I might be still figuring out what I deserve in a relationship, but I know what he deserves, and I want to help him find it.

"But maybe we should have a more organized plan," I say.

Some of the wariness creeps back into his eyes, but it's gone before I can consider it. "What are you thinking?"

"Maybe some ground rules. Like, we can call it off at any time, no questions asked."

Alex smooths his finger over the rim of his empty glass. "Okay, what else?"

"How does one date per week sound?"

"That's fine."

My shoulders slump at his tone. "We don't have to do this. I don't *want* to do this if you're not on board."

He holds my gaze for a long moment before saying, "No, I'm on board." He scruffs his hand over the dark stubble on his chin, his eyes focused on the ceiling as if he's thinking. "What if we get ice cream after and debrief?"

"You and me and ice cream," I say, a smile tilting my lips. Everything feels right again when Alex returns it, nudging my foot with his under the table.

"And how about if we end up liking the person we get set up with, we can choose to take them out again the next week to see if they have potential?" I ask.

His shoulders tense, the muscles contracting under the stiff white fabric of his dress shirt. "Okay."

I scrunch my nose. "What's wrong?"

"Nothing," he says, and I think his voice may be a little more gruff than before. "Where do we want to do the dates?"

I shrug. "Maybe just dinner for the first one? And then we can alternate picking out the dates after that."

His head bobs in a nod.

"Does this all sound good to you? We really don't have to do it if you don't want to."

Alex hesitates for a moment, drumming his fingers on the vinyl tabletop. "No, I do. Let's do it. Let's set each other up."

Three

ALEX

"You're an idiot," Adam, my older brother, tells me the Monday after our sister's wedding.

It's a bold thing to say, considering I'm currently spotting him as he bench presses. The bar slams onto the rack after Adam's last rep, and he sits up, spinning around on the bench to face me.

"You're actually an idiot," he repeats, his cool blue eyes wide and disbelieving.

"That's super helpful. Thanks so much," I deadpan, fixing him with a flat glare as I push my hand through my sweaty hair.

"Hazel *finally* said she's ready to date again, and you told her you would set her up on blind dates?"

His tone scrapes on my nerves like nails on a chalkboard. I knew telling him was a mistake, but I also knew he was likely to find out somehow. From me. Because I'm terrible at keeping my mouth shut. How I've gone over a year without admitting my feelings to Hazel astounds me.

Instead of answering him, I spin on my heel and walk in the direction of the line of treadmills on the other side of the gym. Adam follows silently, a panther waiting for the perfect moment to pounce on his prey.

"So," he says, right as I'm switching from a walk to an easy jog. "Blind dates?"

I flash him an annoyed look. "I didn't know what else to do. Was I supposed to just tell her I have feelings for her over stale fries and melting milkshakes?"

"Anything seems better than setting her up with other people," he says, his voice drier than burnt toast.

I increase the speed on the treadmill, pushing myself into a hard run. At least then I'll have a valid reason for my increased heart rate. "I have a plan."

Adam, calmly walking next to me, arches his eyebrows. Sometimes I really want to punch him. "Oh, do tell."

My footfalls pound against the rubber beneath my feet as I run faster. "I've given it a lot of thought," I huff out.

"Exactly what you're known for."

Maybe I should try the punching bags after this run.

"I'm just going to set her up with crappy dates so that being with me at the end of it is the best part of her night."

Adam reaches over and yanks the emergency cord, halting my treadmill. I have to grab the edges to keep myself from face-planting from the lack of momentum.

"What was that for?" I pant, propping my hands on my hips.

"*That's* your grand plan? Set her up on bad dates so she thinks you're her best option?"

"What? Do you have something better in mind?"

Adam mirrors my stance, and I know that to anyone watching, we look like reflections of one another. With the same shade of almost-black hair and angled eyes, sharp jaws and crooked noses from when we broke them at different times during our childhood, we've often been mistaken as twins. The only major difference in our appearance is that Adam is about two inches shorter than me, with more of a stocky, sturdy build, whereas I'm lean and toned. He also got our mom's pale blue eyes, while I inherited our dad's dark as night ones. And while my facial hair is trimmed to stubble, he's been sporting a thick beard since college.

"Anything would be better than that," he says with a roll of his eyes.

"Then *help me*," I say, and I hate how desperate I sound. God, I *feel* desperate. Ever since Hazel brought this up two days ago, I've been grasping at straws, trying to think of anything and everything that could get me out of this mess I've created.

"What am I, your therapist?"

I grab my water bottle and squeeze, sending a spray of water droplets over his face. "You're a dick."

Adam wipes his face with the hem of his shirt and follows me off the treadmills to grab a bottle of cleaning solution.

"Do your own workout and leave me alone," I say over my shoulder.

"Fine, I'll help you. But you're going to clean my treadmill first."

I fix my eyes heavenward and head back to our machines to wipe them down. When I return, Alex is talking to Parker, a guy we've met a few times while working out here.

"So he's in love with his best friend," Adam is saying when I walk up to them.

I grab Adam's ear and tug hard. He lets out a loud grunt, trying to pull at my arm.

"Nice to see you, Parker," I say to the very confused man before yanking Adam into the locker room. "What is wrong with you?"

He shoves me in the shoulder and rubs at his ear. "You said you needed help."

"I asked *you* for help," I yell, and the sound echoes in the empty locker room.

"Well, we both know I'm not good at advice."

"But *I* am," a weathered voice says from inside one of the shower stalls, and to my never-ending horror, a completely nude elderly gentleman pushes open the curtain. He strides out without a towel, water droplets glistening all over him. His skin is wrinkled like clothes left in the dryer for days, and everything, and I mean *everything*, sags and hangs in ways that make me nervous to age.

"I couldn't help but overhear your predicament," he says slowly, and I think I detect a hint of an English accent, as if it's dulled over time living away from his home.

"We didn't discuss the predicament," Adam says, focusing his gaze on the lockers above the old man's head.

"You need help," the man says, staring at me with an intensity that is incredibly awkward considering his lack of clothing.

"I think we've got it under control. Thank you, though, sir."

He lowers himself onto one of the benches, spreading his legs wide and resting his hands on his knees. "I was out there," he says, and I'm starting to feel a twinge of annoyance with his cryptic responses.

"Out where?" Adam asks, and I can tell he's done with this whole situation.

The old man ignores Adam's question. "I heard your story, young man," he says, not looking away from me. "I know what you should do."

Maybe it's the confidence he must have to sit naked in front of two strangers, or the wise lilt to his English accent, like a storybook narrator, but I think...I want to hear what he has to say.

The old man pats the bench next to him, watching the indecision flicker on my face, and I find my feet walking in his direction of their own accord.

"What are you doing?" Adam asks as I take a seat. His brows are arched high on his head, his mouth hanging slightly open.

"Do you have a better idea?"

"Many."

"Let me hear 'em," I say, and Adam crosses his arms, looking away. "That's what I thought."

"So you're in love with your best friend?" the old man asks as I sit next to him, leaving a wide berth between us. He's still not bothering to hide anything, although I really, really wish he would.

"Love is a strong word," I say immediately, glancing at Adam quickly. Despite his annoyance, I see a flash of a smile quickly cross his features.

"He's in love," Adam answers. "That's the only logical explanation for why he would be acting this dumb."

My eyes narrow in a glare.

"I agree," the stranger says. "You have the look of love about you." He gestures to my eyes. "It's there, in the depths of your eyes. They're a window, you know."

Maybe listening to this man wasn't my brightest idea. But I can't help the clawing sensation in my chest at that word—*love*. It feels so strong, so powerful and unbreakable, but also strangely...right. Shaking off the thought, I put it on a shelf in my mind and decide to come back to examine it later. Maybe when I'm not sitting next to a naked stranger in a locker room.

"Tell me about her," the man says.

I clasp my hands between my knees, staring at a smudge on the wall. "Hazel is...well, she's sunshine," I say on an exhale, like the thought is a breath I've been holding for two years. "She's got an amazing laugh, and she never fails to light up a room. She's one of those people who's just so easy to be around. She makes everyone feel comfortable. Her nose crinkles when she smiles, and she's always got paint or charcoal somewhere on her body because she's an artist. Her art is breathtaking. It's like she manages to take a piece of her soul and put it on canvas." I pause, my heart beating like a steady drum in my chest. "Sometimes I'm jealous of the people who buy her paintings because they get to keep a piece of her that I'll never have."

When I turn back to my companions, they're staring at me with open mouths. My face heats, an unfamiliar blush staining my cheeks.

"That was beautifully put," the old man says, his accent seeming stronger. "She is obviously very important to you."

I nod, not sure I trust myself not to spill more of my thoughts like a preteen writing in a journal.

"Does she have a best friend besides you?"

"Yes, Lucy. They met at the coffee shop Lucy owns and became pretty fast friends."

"Does Lucy know of your feelings?"

Adam snorts in the corner. "Anyone with eyes knows of his feelings."

My eyes narrow in a glare at him, but I turn back to the old man. "No, she doesn't."

He nods, as if this is confirmation of something he already knew. "I would advise you to talk to her. See how she thinks Hazel feels about you and then proceed."

It's...not the worst idea. Although the idea of baring my soul to Lucy makes me feel physical pain, she's also the only one who would know Hazel as well as I do. She could tell me if there's a chance at all or if I should give up before I get hurt.

I look at Adam, and I'm surprised to see the respect in the lines of his eyes. "What do you think?" I ask him.

"I think," he says and hesitates, considering. "I think that could work."

Turning back to the stranger, I ask, "Did you hear my plan to set her up on bad dates?"

The old man scoffs. "Yes, and that's idiotic."

"What should I do instead?" I ask, ignoring Adam, who just let out a satisfied grunt.

"You're doing both of you a disservice if you make yourself out to be the best of the worst. You have to show her that you are the best of the best. For her. Set her up with men she will like when you go out. But remember to keep showing up for her the rest of the time. You have something that they don't—a piece of her she's reserved for only you. Take advantage of that."

Resolution, warm and heavy, floods through my veins at his words. Now *this* feels like a plan. This could work. For the first time since sitting in that booth with my best friend on Saturday night, I don't feel a sick sense of dread curdling in my stomach.

The old man stands, making his dangly bits level with my face. I push to my feet as well, although that image is firmly seared into my mind like a muddy footprint on clean wood floors.

"Thank you for your help," I say as he starts to walk back around the corner.

"Don't worry about it," he responds with a wave of his delicate wrist.

Just as he's about to round the corner, I call out, "You didn't even tell us your name."

"My name is Destiny, but you can call me Fate." And then he disappears behind the lockers.

Adam moves next to me and crosses his arms over his chest, looking at the spot the small, naked man just vacated. He whispers, "I think we just met a ghost."

Four

HAZEL

It's only two o'clock, and my brain is fried. My blue light glasses have nothing on my workload today. Looking up from my spot in the corner booth at my favorite coffee shop, I stare longingly at the analog clock hanging on the wall. I wanted to paint today, but the freelance graphic design project I just took on is taking much more work than I expected. I honestly love my job, but sometimes doing art for other people drains all of my creative energy.

"Want another matcha?" Lucy, my best friend, yells from behind the counter. She's the owner and loves me enough to let me work from this corner booth every day since sitting at home alone gives me hives.

I smile, my eyes crinkling at the edges. "Yes. Iced, please."

The shop is in its usual after-lunch lull. There will be another flurry of activity before closing time at four, but for right now, she probably has an hour to clean and do inventory.

And make me another free drink.

A few minutes later, she slides into the booth across from me, her overalls scratching against the corduroy upholstery. She pushes one of the iced matcha lattes across the table, taking a sip from the other.

"How's the project going?"

I'm overhauling a fitness start-up's entire marketing strategy. When they started their business two years ago, they skimped on graphic design, and it shows. Now that they're finally starting to make a small profit, they've decided to invest it back into the business by revamping their brand identity.

"Almost done, actually," I say, looking up as she tucks a wild, curly lock of warm, golden-blond hair behind her ear.

"Wait, really?" she asks, stormy gray eyes widening. "I thought it was going to take you weeks."

I shrug, adjusting something on my iPad screen before turning it off. "I've been working almost exclusively on this project, so it's gone quicker. I'll still have a few things I'm working on for them over the next few weeks, but the major stuff—logo, website graphics, promo materials—is almost done."

"Good, I feel like I haven't seen you in weeks with all the wedding stuff going on."

A laugh bubbles from my chest. "Except for the eight hours I spend here every day."

She rolls her eyes. "That doesn't count, and you know it. It's not quality time if we're both working."

"This is true," I say and take a sip of my latte, savoring the creamy, earthy taste of the matcha.

"Let's hang out Saturday," she yells, earning the attention of the only other customer in the shop right now, who must have been able to hear her squeal over whatever he's listening to in his over-ear headphones.

I have to hold back a grin at her exuberance. This right here is why Lucy and I became such fast friends when I moved here last year. We are one soul in two bodies. When I walked into this coffee shop, I immediately knew I had found some place special. The eclectic cottagecore decor and funky drinks called to my free-spirited bohemian heart, and I never wanted to leave. Then I met Lucy, a bundle of joy who's usually dressed like she could be on her way to a Renaissance fair, and I knew I'd made the right decision in picking Nashville as my new home. Friendships like the one I have with her are once in a lifetime.

I'm nodding before I remember I already have plans on Saturday, and my expression turns into a wince.

Lucy's face falls. "You can't?"

"I have a date…" I say, trailing off.

She gapes at me. "*What?*"

I can't hold back my laugh this time. "I know it's been a while, but I *have* been on a date before."

"I tried to set you up with a *pediatric doctor* a month ago, and you told me you weren't ready to date yet." She takes a sip of her drink. "Don't get me wrong, I'm happy about this. Happy for *you*, but what changed?"

My shoulder lifts in a shrug, and I drag my fingers down the condensation on my cup. "I don't know. I guess it was a mix of things, but mostly watching Cam and Ellie this weekend." Meeting her eyes, I say, "They were just so happy. It reminded me that love can be like that, you know? That it doesn't have to hurt."

Her expression softens like melting butter. "No, it doesn't. In fact, it *shouldn't*."

"I know." I bite my lip, trying to hold back the tears that are now threatening.

"So what do you think you're going to try? Apps? Going out? Mail-order grooms?"

My nose wrinkles. "I don't think that's a thing."

She cocks an eyebrow. "I actually just read this book about—"

"Blind dates," I say, cutting her off, because I know if I don't, she'll end up down a rabbit hole of smutty romance recommendations. Lucy loves *love* more than anyone else I know. One time, I caught her googling random name combinations and clicking on the wedding websites that came up so she could read their love stories. When there's a lull at the shop and she's not cleaning or working, she can be found hiding behind the counter with her Kindle, reading free romances, using her Kindle Unlimited subscription.

"Blind dates?" she asks, her head tilting to the side. "Who's going to set you up?"

"I asked Alex to." Lucy blinks, not responding for so long that I ask, "What?"

"You want *Alex* to set you up on blind dates?"

I feel my defenses rise at her tone, although I'm not sure what for. Alex and Lucy are some of the closest friends I've ever had—if anyone is going to set me up, it's going to be one of them.

"What's wrong with that?"

"I just always thought…" Lucy trails off before shaking her head. "Never mind. I think he will be great."

I want to press her, to ask what she always thought, but I know Lucy's attention jumps from one thing to the next faster than I can blink, and she probably doesn't even remember what she was going to say.

"We talked about it after the wedding, and we agreed to set each other up on one date a week."

"You're setting each other up?"

Shrugging, I say, "Yeah, he said he's ready to find something more serious."

"Oh," Lucy says and stops again.

This time I can't resist my urge to ask for more. "What?"

"It's just…you're not worried that a girlfriend wouldn't want you spending so much time with Alex?"

Honestly, no, I hadn't thought about that. But now that she mentions it, fear takes hold in my gut. Whoever I date will have to be okay with my friendship with Alex. It's a deal-breaker. But I can't control what his girlfriend thinks. She could be totally against us spending time together alone, or unhappy with the fact that Alex brings me dinner at least once a week, or annoyed that he texts me first thing in the morning to compare our REM sleep times on our sleep trackers.

"You're freaking out," Lucy says when I haven't responded.

I stare at her, my mind spinning. "Maybe a little."

Her gaze is assessing. "So what are you going to do about it?"

I rack my brain for a solution. "I'll just have to set him up with someone who is okay with our friendship."

"That's one idea." A small smile I can't quite decipher plays on Lucy's lips.

"Do you have a better one?"

She watches me for a minute, that amused smile still on her face. Smoothing back an errant curl, she says, "No, this will work. Let's try to figure out who to set him up with."

"I don't even know," I say, my voice sounding uncharacteristically desolate.

"Hold on," Lucy says, pushing up from the booth. She runs behind the counter and grabs a notepad and a green gel pen before returning. "Let's talk about what kind of girl he needs."

"He needs someone who can make him laugh," I say immediately. "He's got an amazing laugh."

Lucy scrawls it on the paper before turning back to me.

"He's secretly a shy extrovert, so he likes it when other people are the center of attention. He says he can latch on to them and loosen up and be himself. But when he's on his own, he's nervous."

"That's surprising," Lucy says, writing it down. "So someone who can bring him out of his shell."

"Yeah," I answer, smiling. "And he's messy, so he doesn't like people who are always put together."

I watch as Lucy writes *messy* on the paper.

"And he loves creative people, because he's not creative at all. He says he got all of his parents' business genes, and he doesn't want his kids to fail elementary art class like he did."

Lucy gives me a curious look before writing it down. "So someone who is funny, outgoing, messy, and creative?"

I nod as she reads each one off. "Yeah, that's perfect. That's pretty broad, too, so we have options."

"Mm," Lucy hums.

"What? You think it's too broad?"

She shakes her head, looking at the list and then back to me. "No, just thinking of who we can set him up with. You have any ideas?"

My mind is completely blank. It was easy to come up with what he wants and needs, but actually producing a physical woman who checks those boxes seems harder than I imagined.

"What about Chloe?" Lucy asks, referring to one of the shop's regulars. She's got long, long strawberry blond hair and crystal-clear blue eyes, with deep laugh crinkles beside them. And she's an elementary teacher, so I know she ticks the other requirements, but I find myself shaking my head.

"No, she doesn't seem right for him."

Lucy consults the list and says, "*Oh-kay,*" splitting it up like it's two words. "Rayne?"

Rayne is a girl Lucy and I met that one month we tried a cycling class. She was at every single class and was obviously a regular with her muscular thighs and ability to finish the class without looking like she was going to throw up. She's a second-generation Cambodian American with long black hair and eyes that glitter like brown stained glass. And she's a tattoo artist. She did the beautiful, intricate fine-line butterfly tattoo on my forearm last year.

"No, I don't think so." When I look at Lucy, she's smiling. "What?"

She shakes her head. "Nothing. It's just, you have to set him up with *someone*."

I roll my eyes. "Yes, I know that, but I can't just set him up with *anyone*."

"Both of those women fit the description you gave me."

"Yeah, I know," I say. "I just don't think they'd be good together."

"You won't know unless you try."

I stare at Lucy, feeling a twinge of irritation. She's obviously decently acquainted with Alex. He's come to the shop on more than one occasion, and we've all even gone out together a few times. But she doesn't know him like I do.

"Unless there's some reason you don't want him going out with one of them."

"I just don't think he'd hit it off with either of them," I say, unsure of why my heart feels like it's beating harder in my chest. "But fine, I'll ask Chloe."

"Don't ask if you don't think they'd be good together," Lucy says, that frustrating smile on her face again.

"No, no, they'd be great," I say through clenched teeth. "I hope they have beautiful strawberry blond babies with brown eyes and dimples."

Her grin widens. "You don't seem happy about that."

I'm not, although I can't pinpoint why. I guess I just can't picture him with someone like Chloe. I don't know who he needs, but it isn't her.

"I'm fine," I say, standing up and gathering my things. "I've got to go. I think I left my curling iron on."

"Don't forget to text Chloe," Lucy calls after me as I head through the door, her voice as sugary sweet as Pixie Stix.

Five

ALEX

When I let myself into Hazel's apartment later that night, she's covered in paint. She's messy when she's creating. I've always enjoyed that about her, because when she's finished, she looks as much like art as the piece she's working on.

Today is no exception.

She's currently covered in varying shades of orange, blue, beige, and black. Without looking, I know she's painting butterflies. She once told me that every artist has one thing they always gravitate toward when they're making art without thinking, and hers is butterflies.

All over her house are paintings, drawings, collages, and illustrations of butterflies that she's done over the years. When we're at a restaurant waiting on our food, I can almost count on her being hunched over a napkin, doodling a butterfly better than the rest of us could draw given hours and proper tools.

"Hey," I call out, trying not to startle her since she's got her massive headphones clamped over her ears. I can hear the faint melody from an indie folk band we saw in concert last year.

Hazel turns, her mouth lifting in a smile when she sees me. She tugs the headphones off, letting the rest on her shoulders. "Hey, I didn't even hear you come in."

I hold up the to-go bag of Greek takeout from the restaurant down the street. The strong scents of oregano, basil, and garlic fill the tiny apartment. "I brought dinner."

Her eyes flick to the gold clock she has hanging above her pantry. "Oh, good. I completely lost track of time and forgot to make dinner."

A small smile tugs at my lips. "I figured when I couldn't get a hold of you."

She grimaces, reaching for her phone. "I turned it on Do Not Disturb."

"No big deal," I say with a shrug as I retreat into her kitchen. Hazel follows closely behind, heading straight for the sink to wash up.

"I didn't realize how covered in paint I got," she says, and I can't help but look over my shoulder at her. She's got her back to me, lathering soap on her smooth, tan arms and using her nails to pick at the dried paint.

Repressing the desire to keep watching, I turn back to the food, pulling items out of the paper bag one at a time. Hazel loves appetizers more than real food, so when we order out, she usually ends up with a salad and an entire platter of appetizers.

"Did they have the spanakopita?" Hazel asks, still trying to wash away the paint covering her arms.

Our favorite Greek restaurant is known for their spanakopita, so naturally, it sells out by lunchtime most days. But we got lucky today.

Pulling it from the bag, I cross the small distance between us and waft the to-go container beneath her nose. Her deep blue eyes light up, looking like sunshine glinting on the ocean. "They had it?"

I grin, leaning my back against the counter. "Last piece."

"You're my hero."

The water shuts off with a snap of her wrist, and she reaches for a dish towel drying next to the sink. As she dries her hands, she assesses her arms with a pleased look on her face, no doubt proud of herself for getting all the paint off. It's obvious she doesn't know about the burnt orange streak across her cheek.

Looking up at me, she asks, "What are you smiling about?"

My hand reaches out of its own volition, making its own brush stroke against her cheek. "You've got paint right here."

Her eyes widen. "Seriously?" Roughly, she scrubs the hand towel against her cheek, only serving to turn it an angry red. The paint flakes but stays there stubbornly.

"You're going to rub your skin raw," I say, taking the rag from her hand. Reaching around her, I turn on the sink and dampen one of the edges of the rag before turning back to her.

Slowly, I swipe the towel across her skin. Her eyes meet mine, and it's at that moment that I realize how close we are. Her warm breath fans against my face, and the air thickens, spiking with electricity like in the gray moments before a storm.

I step back, clearing my throat, and hand the rag back to her. "There, I got most of it."

She gives me a smile, although there seems to be a weighted look in her eyes. "Thanks," she says, and hangs the hand towel back on the rack. "How was work?"

Hazel moves in a flurry around her kitchen, pulling out plates and utensils.

"Good," I tell her as we load our plates. "I closed on a house today and started working with a new client they referred to me."

After graduating from college, I decided to get my real estate license. I was interested in my parents' field but refused to work for them since I knew it would only put a wedge in our already difficult relationship. I love my parents, but their idea of nurturing leaves something to be desired. I knew looking for a job at a competing property management company would only serve to cause division, so I went into real estate.

"One of these days, you're going to find me a place. I'd like one just like yours." She crinkles her nose. "But, like, with good decor."

I quirk an eyebrow at her. "You don't like my decor?"

"It's a sad, upscale version of a bachelor pad," she says as we walk the short distance to the living room and settle on her soft leather couch.

"I'm a sad, upscale bachelor."

"Not for long, you aren't," she says, dipping a piece of pita in the oily hummus and biting into it, making a sound of pleasure deep in her throat. I wrench my eyes away, digging into my own food.

"Speaking of," I say. "I found your date."

She swallows the bite in her mouth before speaking. "Already?"

I stir my own hummus with some pita, mixing the oils and toppings into the dip.

"Yeah, it's the new realtor who was hired on last month, Deacon. He seems nice." The truth is, I've hardly spoken to the guy. With showings and closings, especially at this time of year, I'm hardly in the office. The few times we have spoken, he was confident and self-assured but seemed nice enough.

And he was on board with the blind date after seeing a photo of Hazel, which gave me enough heartburn that I had to stop at the pharmacy before heading over here.

"Deacon," Hazel says softly, as if trying the name on for size. It makes the food in my mouth turn sour, burning like acid down my throat. I knew, hypothetically, that watching Hazel date other people was going to be difficult, but until this moment, I hadn't considered what it will actually be like to see her laugh and flirt with other guys, wearing those crop tops and flowy pants that drive me absolutely *insane*.

"Who are you setting me up with?" I grit out, and Hazel's eyes snap to mine, questioning the change in my demeanor. I clear my throat, hoping she will ignore it.

Thankfully, she doesn't question it. Instead, she picks at the food in her lap.

"I haven't figured it out yet." Her bottom lip catches between her teeth. "What do you think about teachers?"

"They should be paid more."

When she rolls her eyes, I have to hold back a smile.

"There's a girl who is pretty regular at the coffee shop—Chloe. I was thinking about asking her."

My shoulders lift in a shrug. "Sounds good to me," I say and take a bite of my gyro. In actuality, I'm feeling a little guilty thinking about how I'll be going out with women every week who are spending their time on someone who is only looking for a relationship with one person. I should have asked Destiny what to do about that.

"You don't want to see a picture of her?" Hazel asks, and I realize that I probably should look at least somewhat interested.

"Sure," I say. She pulls up a photo on her phone. It's a selfie on Chloe's Instagram page. She's got pretty light-red hair and a nice smile. Exactly the sort of person I would have gone for if the woman who has become my entire world wasn't sitting next to me with her thigh pressed up against mine and orange paint dried on the tip of her braid.

"Pretty, right?" Hazel asks, her voice soft.

"Pretty," I agree, looking away. I find the remote on the coffee table and click on the TV. "What movie are we watching tonight?"

"*Always Be My Maybe*," she says instantly, and I let out a pretend groan. She snorts. "Don't even play like that. I know you like rom-coms more than I do."

I grumble as I find the movie on a streaming service, but she's right. Not long after we started watching these chick flicks on movie nights—after I subjected her to *Full Metal Jacket*—my disdain for the genre turned into grudging respect, and somewhere along the line, it shifted into actual love. I can't get enough of these ridiculous movies.

I'm a pathetic sap, clinging to fictional love stories, just waiting for my best friend to be ready to start ours.

Six

ALEX

I TEXT LUCY ON Tuesday, asking her if we can meet up and if she would maybe not mention it to Hazel. When she responds, asking if this is about me being in love with Hazel, I choke on my coffee. So when I finally meet her at a cat café midafternoon, it's after heading home to change into a clean shirt.

A spotted calico winds between my legs, and a black cat with beady green eyes sits on the table between us, blocking Lucy's small form from sight. It's staring into my soul with an intensity that makes me shudder, and I can just *tell* this cat has seen some stuff. Exorcisms, exhumations, botched plastic surgery—this cat has seen it.

"So you're in love with Hazel." She waits to say it until I'm lifting my glass of iced tea to my lips, and the black cat hisses when it sprays from my mouth, coating her fur.

I'm definitely going to be cursed by this cat.

"How did you know that?" I hedge, not even bothering to deny it. I'm starting to get the sneaking suspicion that Adam was right, and I've been doing a terrible job at hiding my feelings from everyone but Hazel.

She claps her hands together, a squeal building in the back of her throat. "I'm a witch."

I blink at her, and she sits back, petting the orange striped cat that jumped into her lap.

At my dumbstruck expression, she laughs. It's light and musical, like a melody drifting on the wind. "I'm kidding, Alex. You're incredibly obvious."

My hair is like smooth silk against my fingertips as I push a hand through it. Suddenly, it feels like my skin is stretched too tight, the soft music and quiet murmurings of other patrons too loud in my ears.

"Does she know?" I ask, finally voicing the question that's been buzzing around in the back of my head since Adam called me obvious yesterday morning.

Lucy squints. "Who, Hazel?"

"Yes!" I say loudly enough that the calico near my feet gets annoyed at my volume and walks away.

"No, Hazel doesn't know," Lucy says, and my heartbeat returns to normal. "At least she's never mentioned it to me, but I don't think she'd be putting you through this if she knew."

This, at least, makes me feel somewhat better. If she's known my feelings all this time and just hasn't brought it up to spare me the humiliation, I'd have to start looking up realtor requirements in a remote corner of the world, preferably somewhere without Wi-Fi or phone service.

"So what's your plan?" Lucy asks, waving away the cat in her lap so she can reach into her bag.

I grip the back of my neck with my palm, squeezing hard to relieve the tension building there. "That's why I'm here. I don't really have a plan."

"Mm," Lucy mumbles, not looking up at me as she digs through her bag.

"What are you looking for?" I ask as the still damp black cat stands and moves directly in front of my face. We're nose to nose now, and I'm sure he's memorizing the smell of my soul so he can find it in the afterlife.

"Aha!" Lucy yells, waving a mushroom-printed notebook like it's a white flag. She swats at the black cat, ushering him off the table. "Callisto, get down."

My brows arch. "That cat's named Callisto?"

Lucy rolls her gray eyes heavenward. "No," she says, her voice lowering to a whisper. "They named him something basic like Oreo, but isn't Callisto so much better?"

I have a feeling my opinion doesn't actually matter here, so I just nod.

She flips to a half-filled page and turns back to me, resting her chin in her hand. "First things first. Tell me how you feel about Hazel."

"I'm in love with Hazel," I say, and it honestly feels like a weight being lifted off my shoulders, the first deep breath after being underwater for too long. It's a thought I haven't allowed to take shape in my mind, but it's been burrowing deep into my soul for ages, since a hot summer day with ice cream cooling our hands and sun warming our skin.

It's the first time I've said it aloud, and now that I have, I want to shout it from the mountaintops.

Lucy sighs, her eyes wide and dreamy. "That was lovely. Could you try clutching your chest and saying you burn for her?"

"What?"

She sits back, sliding the notebook across the table. "Never mind. Before we get started, read this."

I stare down at the dainty scrawl on the page, uncomprehending. "*Someone who can make him laugh. Someone who can bring him out of his shell. Someone messy. Someone creative.*" Looking up, I meet her expectant eyes. "What's this?"

"Who does that sound like to you?"

My gaze flickers over the list again, reading through the bullet points. "Hazel."

Lucy's grin is wide, spreading across her face like a flower blooming in the sunshine. "Hazel wrote that list. She said those are the qualities you need in a partner."

A flame of hope catches in my chest, burning through me like wildfire, and I read over the list one more time with fresh understanding.

"Oh," I breathe.

"She wants you," Lucy says, snapping my attention back to her. "Even though she doesn't know it yet."

She reaches for the notebook, pulling it back across the table, and flips to a blank page. Retrieving a pen from her bag, she scribbles *The Plan* at the top.

"Let's figure out how to make her realize it," she says. "Have you watched *Emma*?"

The title sounds familiar, but I know without a doubt that I haven't, so I shake my head.

"Well," Lucy says, sitting back. "That's your first assignment. It's classic friends-to-lovers, and their siblings are married."

I lift one eyebrow, and she nods enthusiastically.

"Right?" She writes *Emma* at the top of the list. "I think you can learn a lot from them. And plus, it's Hazel's favorite Jane Austen movie. We've watched all the adaptations together, but the 2020 version is her favorite," she says, continuing to scrawl all this on the paper.

"2020 *Emma*," I repeat.

"All the *Emma*s, but especially that one." Turning back to me, she asks, "Next, have you ever heard of the female gaze?"

"I don't...think so?" I watch as she writes *female gaze* on the paper.

"We need Hazel to see you as someone desirable." That feels strangely like getting hand sanitizer in a paper cut, but I keep my mouth shut. "In order to do that, I think we need to put you in some situations that will make Hazel see you in a new light."

"*Oh-kay.*" My voice is slow and skeptical.

"Men tend to think women find certain things desirable, when in actuality, what we want is something very different. Have you seen *The Witcher*?"

"No. It's actually been on my—"

"Never mind that," Lucy interrupts me. "We'll just have to strategize without the analogy." I open my mouth to speak, but she keeps going. "Can you put your elbow on the table?"

I have many, many questions, but I do as I'm asked.

"Good. Could you flex your hand?"

My eyebrows quirk of their own volition. "What?"

"Flex your hand," Lucy says, her voice holding a touch of impatience. My hand tightens into a fist on the table, and Lucy shakes her head. "No, open it up and flex."

The veins on my hand stand out, stark raised bumps against my skin, as I follow her instructions. "Like that?"

Her eyes darken slightly. "Perfect. You want to do that when you touch Hazel."

"What? Why?"

"Have you seen the 2005 *Pride & Prejudice* movie?"

"Is that the one with the little girl who likes to play in a secret garden?"

Lucy presses a palm to her forehead, looking distraught. "My lord, you are uncultured swine."

"I'm *what*?"

"Alex, that's *The Secret Garden*." Her hands flail spastically. "Moving on. You need to do this because when Darcy touches Elizabeth for the—"

"Who are Darcy and Elizabeth?"

The sigh Lucy gives is one of a mother whose young child has just pulled out her last straw and has used it to blow bubbles in his chocolate milk.

"It's not important right now, but let me explain. When Darcy touches Elizabeth for the first time, he is overcome. The hand flex represents tension and longing and confusion—all things that *Hazel* will be feeling over the next few weeks as she starts to see you as someone other than her best friend. The hand flex will let her know she's not the only one going through it."

"So I should do this every time I touch her?"

"No, no, no. It needs to be after a particularly poignant moment."

"Poignant, got it. I guess I'll just know it when I get there."

Lucy's eyes soften as she stares at a point over my head. "Have you ever had a moment where time stood still? There were electric currents in the air, zapping and crackling between you and someone else? And you felt like you were standing on a precipice, not sure whether you wanted to fall or not?"

Well, when she puts it that way, *yes*. My heart rate quickens just thinking about it.

"*That's* the moment you want to do the hand flex—when you're right there at the edge of almost, and you back away. Flex your hand so she knows you felt it too."

I nod, starting to understand. "Okay, I can do that. What else?"

Her pen flies over the paper once more. "Do you have a tortured past we can lean into?"

"One time I walked in on my parents having sex. Doggy style. Facing the door. We all made eye contact."

"That's something only a therapist can help you with, honey."

"Don't I know it."

Lucy shakes her head, drawing a line through *tortured past* in her notebook. She taps the pen against her lips, thinking. "We need an excuse to get you dirty and sweaty. Maybe a nature date."

I cock an eyebrow. "Dirty and sweaty?"

"If you haven't seen *The Witcher*, then I just know you haven't seen *Outlander* either, so you won't get it."

"I'll take your word for it."

Lucy writes *nature date* on the paper.

"Is this one of the blind dates?"

"No, this needs to be something for just the two of you. And, *oh*! Bring her favorite snack when you go." She pauses, writing down her ideas. "Do you think stealthily tripping her so you have to carry her back to the car would be too far?"

"You want me to *injure* Hazel?"

"You're right," she says, waving her hand. "Too far."

I'm taking a sip of my tea when she says, "One bed."

The drink hovers a breath from my lips. If she was trying to grab my attention, that did it. "One bed?"

"You need to orchestrate a situation where you have to sleep in the same bed." Lucy writes this on the paper before meeting my eyes again. "Hazel is a cuddler."

Boy, if that doesn't paint a mental picture I want to examine for the next three to five business days. "This seems promising."

Lucy chokes on a laugh. "I bet it does. Do you think you could get your hands on a puppy?"

"Maybe?" I say, and it comes out more like a question than an answer.

She shrugs. "If you can find a puppy to hold, do it. And try to be shirtless."

I'm not exactly sure what situation I'd find myself in half-naked with Hazel and a puppy, but I make a mental note anyway.

"And help her over puddles like she's a Victorian maiden who can't wet her hems."

Nodding, I repeat, "Victorian maiden."

Her phone buzzes on the table, and she reads the screen before saying, "Hazel. She's wondering when I'm coming back from my *errand*. I better get back."

After draining the rest of my tea, I nod. "Thank you for everything, Lucy."

A smile touches her lips, and her gray eyes soften. "I'm glad you're doing this."

Something warms in my chest. Lucy and I have always gotten along, so I didn't think she'd be opposed to me trying to date Hazel, but her blessing is a treat, like cream cheese frosting melting on cinnamon rolls.

One question lingers in the back of my mind, and I hesitate to ask it. "Do you think I have a chance?"

"Yeah, Alex, I do," Lucy says, giving my hand a gentle squeeze. "You and Hazel have always been destined to be more than just friends."

Seven

HAZEL

This is the worst date I've ever been on. When the four of us arrived at the restaurant, things were going well. Alex seemed to hit it off with Chloe, and Deacon was charming. Then, in the middle of the salad course, he asked if I'd ever considered a boob job.

After that, Deacon became *Dickin* in my mind, and I've almost called him that twice already.

"No, I haven't invested in real estate," I say, stabbing a spear of asparagus with my fork.

"You're kidding." Deacon looks actually perturbed at my answer. Then he laughs, one corner of his mouth kicking up. "Right, I forgot you said you're an artist. You probably don't have a stable enough income."

I blink so often that his bleach-dyed blond curls start to form into a golden haze in front of me. "What?" I finally manage to choke out.

"Hey, no shame in it," he says, waving his fork. "Art is a great hobby."

Red creeps into the corners of my vision. "*A great hobby?*"

Deacon looks up from his plate, no doubt interpreting the tone of my voice. His blue eyes widen, and his eyebrows inch up his forehead. "Whoa, don't get emotional. I'm just saying that—"

"Excuse me," I say, standing so quickly that my chair scrapes against the hardwood. My gaze is laser focused on Alex's form disappearing down the hallway to the bathrooms. "I have to use the restroom."

He casts a knowing glance at my empty plate, although I'm not sure what the motion is for. "Ah, that's how you stay so thin," he says, miming a gagging gesture.

My mouth falls open as realization dawns. I don't even have the energy to correct him or try to explain all the reasons his comment is offensive. "Yup, have to go vomit up my dinner. Don't worry, I'll use a breath mint."

He winks, and it physically feels like there are ants burrowing under my skin. Not bothering to respond, I round the table and follow the path Alex took to the bathroom.

Frustration claws its way through me, and before I know what I'm doing, I shove open the door to the men's restroom and plow inside. It swings closed behind me, the heavy swishing sound finally clearing through the indignation pounding beneath my breastbone enough for me to realize I'm *in the men's room*. I mean, obviously, this was my intention, but I hadn't really thought it through. Thank God there are no urinals.

The only sound in the bathroom is the high-pitched *zip* of a metal zipper, and I realize that since I only see one set of feet beneath the stall walls, it's Alex. Heat crawls up my neck, warming my cheeks by degrees, and I call out, "Alex, it's me."

The loud flush of the toilet echoes through the bathroom before the stall door swings open. Alex stares at me with wide, dark eyes. "What are you doing in here?"

My aggravation returns with a vengeance, bubbling in my chest. I close the distance between us, my heeled boots clicking loudly on the checkered tile floor.

Alex steps back, his broad shoulders bumping into the stall door. I don't stop until our toes are pressed together and my finger is digging into his chest. There's no give. Just firm, solid muscle beneath my touch. And he's so warm, sending licks of flame against my skin.

"Alexander Malcolm Bates."

His stubbled throat bobs in a swallow, and I can't stop my gaze from dipping to follow the movement, cataloging the sharp line of his jaw, the fullness of his lower lip. Things I've somehow never noticed before.

"What are you doing, Hazel?" he asks, his rough voice snapping my attention back to his eyes, the deep brown glinting under the dim lights. His chest lifts in a deep breath, making his starched shirt scrape against my knuckles.

It takes me a moment to remember why I'm here, but when I do, fury courses through me once more. I take a step back, putting the barest amount of distance between us, and make an L shape with my fingers before slapping it on my forehead.

His eyes widen. "Oh, not good?"

"*Dickin* told me art is a *nice hobby* and asked if I've ever considered a boob job," I say, each word getting sharper and sharper.

Alex's gaze dips to my chest, making an odd sensation spark through my stomach before meeting my eyes again. His jaw is a tight line. I don't think Renaissance sculptures are this chiseled.

"I'm going to talk to him," he says, moving toward the door.

I block his exit, my palms coming up to land on his chest again. The muscles bunch and tense beneath my fingertips.

"No, don't go talk to him. Let's just leave." My voice drops, tinged with desperation. "Please."

For a moment, uncertainty flashes across his features, and realization courses through my veins. I drop my hands back to my sides. "Oh, right, Chloe. You guys looked like you were having fun."

His back was to me, but I could see Chloe laughing. She's the kind of person who laughs with her full face, like it's bubbling out of her. It made me remember why I liked her so much when we first met, and I made a mental note to ask her for coffee, regardless of how their date went.

Without realizing it, I'm holding my breath, waiting for his answer. Because although I'm desperate to end my date with *Dickin*, I hadn't considered until now that Alex and Chloe probably aren't ready to use their salad forks to slowly extract their eyeballs from their sockets.

Alex's face softens, like butter melting in a pan. "No, I still want to get ice cream with you."

A seed of pleasurable gratification takes root in my chest and blooms, spreading throughout my body. My breath releases in a relieved exhale. "Okay, good. Let's get out of here."

He moves around me, washing his hands in the sink. His eyes meet mine in the mirror. "What about Chloe? Should I invite her to come with us?"

"Oh," I say, thinking.

The truth is, I don't *want* to share Alex right now. Not when I've been on the worst date of my life and I need to review every single detail with my best friend. But I also know it's unfair to leave her when their date has gone well.

"I can wait in the car," I say quickly, not giving Alex a chance to reply as he dries his hands on a cloth towel before tossing it in the bin. "I'll wait in the car until your date is over, and then we can go. Just you and me."

Alex watches me, his expression more intense than I've ever seen it before, and I have to resist the urge to squirm beneath it. The normal mahogany of his eyes turns sable, then ebony. It's utterly fathomless. Like the black hole they've turned into, I feel myself being sucked into their depths.

After a long moment, he nods and moves toward the door, his hand settling on the handle. But then he hesitates, the muscles in his shoulders bunching.

"Is there a reason you don't want to invite Chloe?" he asks, and his voice is soft.

I struggle for a response, unsure of how to explain myself, how to put my feelings into words.

The bathroom door swings open before I can reply, banging into Alex's head. He stumbles back into me, clutching his nose. A large balding man peers around the door, his flushed face creased in shock and concern.

"I'm so sorry," he says, coming into the bathroom, but he stops dead at the sight of the blood gushing from between Alex's fingers. The color drains from the man's cheeks, and I realize a second too late that he's going to faint. His stout form hits the ground with a reverberating *thump*.

"*Ohmahgah*," Alex exclaims from behind his hand, his words mumbling together. Bright red blood seeps between his fingers, staining his starched white shirt. The sight propels me into action, and I step over the unconscious man, rushing for the counter.

The fancy restaurant that Alex picked out is too elegant for disposable paper towels, so I'm forced to grab one of the ornately folded blindingly white hand towels to sop up Alex's blood.

I swat his hands away, and blood drips onto the knotted tie of my mustard yellow top. He starts to wipe it away, forgetting his hands are stained crimson, and leaves a wine-red smear right above my cleavage.

"Sorry," he says, pulling his hand back. His voice is nasal and choked with blood.

"Are you okay?" I ask, gripping his nose more firmly in an attempt to stanch the bleeding.

"Yeah, I'm fine. I think you should get someone for him," Alex says as the man on the floor lets out a low moan. His hand comes up to cover mine, taking control of the towel.

I look down at my body, the red smears on my hands and chest, and the heavy scent of copper coating me. "They're going to think I murdered someone in the bathroom."

A gurgling laugh comes from Alex. "It'll be fine. I'm going to try to wake him up. Go see if you can find a manager or something."

I hesitate, hand on the door handle for a moment, as Alex bends to his knees before the stranger, using his free hand to gently pat his face. "Hey, dude. Wake up, big guy." The tight fist of worry clenched around my chest eases watching Alex cracking jokes, so I crack the door open and slip out.

"They're too fancy for paper towels, but not too fancy to use frozen peas in the kitchen," I say, steering Alex's car out of the restaurant parking lot a half hour later. He's got a bag of frozen peas pressed to his nose and his head tilted back against the headrest.

"I'm very grateful for their frozen peas."

"I think you might have been less grateful if you'd forked out a hundred bucks for your gourmet meal, only to find out the peas cost seventy-nine cents in the freezer aisle."

He grins, lolling his head to face me from the passenger seat. "It was very nice of them to comp the meal."

Stopping at a red light, I glance over at him. Streetlights flicker across his milky skin. His dress shirt, now stained and crumpled, is unbuttoned at the collar, exposing the light dusting of dark hair gathered there.

I'm struck with how *beautiful* my best friend is. It's not that I haven't noticed before, but it's the difference between knowing it's cold outside and feeling the icy wind whipping against your skin. Alex's artistry is undeniable. The way his inky scruff paints his jawline in shadow. How his brown eyes turn from smooth, decadent caramel to rich, dark chocolate depending on his mood. The way his hair looks better as the day goes on, when the pomade starts to lose hold and the waves loosen and tumble around his face.

"What?" Alex asks, snapping me back into the moment.

I shake my head, turning to face the road as the light changes to green. I'm almost back to my apartment when lights from a fast-food restaurant catch my attention.

"Where are we going?" Alex asks when I turn in the opposite direction of my apartment.

"Milkshakes," I tell him. "I think we need milkshakes."

The grin he gives me is bright enough to light the night sky.

I pull into the drive-thru and stare at the menu, checking out all my options.

A voice crackles through the intercom. "Hey, what can I get you?"

"One cotton candy milkshake and…" I trail off, looking through the menu once more. "A mint chocolate chip milkshake with Oreo crumbles and hot fudge drizzle."

Alex's snort prompts me to add another topping. "And whipped cream."

"Sounds delicious," Alex says, a wry tone lacing his voice. Without fail, Alex always teases me about my ice cream order. The man orders *cotton candy* every single time and has the gall to tease my impeccable taste.

"Keep it up and I'll steal your peas."

His chuckle is light and lilting as I retrieve our milkshakes and pass them to him so I can pull into a parking spot.

"Here's your sugar coma in a cup," Alex says, handing me a milkshake. Hot fudge is leaking down the side, and I drag my tongue across it, tasting the rich, warm chocolate.

When I look at Alex, his expression is unreadable. "What?"

He shakes his head and punches a straw through the top of his shake before handing me a spoon.

In the semi-darkness, I can see faint swelling around his nose. Without thinking, I reach out and trail my finger down the slope, checking for lumps. A low hiss escapes between Alex's teeth when I make contact, and I snatch my hand back. "I'm so sorry. Did that hurt?"

His lips hitch up in a grin, light sparking behind his eyes, and I shove him in the shoulder. "You're the worst. I thought I hurt you, you idiot."

"It's fine," he tells me and takes a sip of his shake. I watch the pink and blue ice cream inch up the straw and disappear.

Scooping out a bit of my ice cream, I flip the spoon over and lick it off, tasting rich chocolate and cool mint. "It doesn't hurt?"

Alex's nose scrunches. "No, it definitely hurts, but I'll be fine."

I take another bite of my ice cream and meet his gaze. "I'm sorry. I feel like this is my fault."

"*You* slammed the door in my face?"

"No," I say, rolling my eyes. "But I did charge into the bathroom after you like a bat out of hell."

A light dusting of pink colors his cheeks, like sunrise cresting over the horizon. "I guess I deserved that for setting you up with *Dickin*. I like the nickname, by the way. I was thinking I could buy him new business cards and replace all of his old ones with those."

A laugh shoots out of me. "Please do. It's the least he deserves. When I stopped to tell him we were leaving, he asked if I wanted to meet at his place or mine."

"So I guess you're not wanting to go out with him again next week?" Alex asks, his lips quirking into a smile that makes the lingering tension of seeing him hurt earlier dissolve like mist.

"Hmm, let me see—*no*."

"I kind of figured that was the case, what with you ambushing me in the bathroom and all."

"*Ambushing?*" My voice rises in incredulity.

Alex raises his hands in a placating gesture. "You're right, you're right." He's quiet for a moment, then says, "You just attacked me."

I give his shoulder a firm shove. "You're the worst."

His grin is hypnotic, numbing my senses, and contagious enough to make the corners of my own mouth lift too. This feels *right*. Bad dates with strangers will be worth it if we get to end up in the car together at the end of the night, sugar and cream melting on our tongues.

"New dates next week, then," I say, scooping out another spoonful of my minty concoction. I slide my eyes across the console. "Unless you want to go out with Chloe again."

I hold my breath, unsure of why nerves are creeping up my esophagus as I wait on his response.

"She was nice," Alex says and pauses. My stomach knots further. "But I don't think it was a love match."

"You can't know that after one date." I'm not sure why I say it.

His eyebrows lift. "Do you *want* me to go out with Chloe again?"

"No," It comes out before I can think. Retreating, I say, "I mean, you can if you want to, but *I* don't want you to."

That intensity from the bathroom returns to his face, and I have to force myself not to look away.

"I don't want to go out with Chloe again," he says finally, and I let out the breath I hadn't realized I was holding.

"Okay. New dates, then."

"New dates," he agrees.

HAZEL

I'M PUTTING THE finishing touches on a butterfly painting on Monday afternoon when my phone vibrates on the countertop, the loud buzzing echoing over the sound of the folk band vinyl playing on my vintage record player. I wipe my hands on my overalls and dash into the kitchen, but I still manage to end up with an orange paint smear on my phone case. I'm wetting a paper towel as I swipe the phone open and my mom's face fills the screen.

"Hey, honey!" she yells, loud enough that if I had neighbors, they would have heard it.

"Hey, Mom," I say, trying to wipe the paint off my phone.

"Look who brought me treats." She tries and fails to flip the camera around, and I hear laughter on the other end before two new faces show up on the screen.

My lips split in a smile as I look at my two best friends since childhood, my cousin Stevie and the only neighbor we had within a mile on our old country road, Wren.

"Hey, guys."

"What have you been doing today, Hazel Girl?" Mom asks as I wipe the last bit of paint from my phone case.

The chill of the granite countertop seeps through my overalls as I lean my back against it, holding the phone out in front of me. "I finally finished this big project I've been working on, so I took the rest of the afternoon off, and I've been painting. What are you all doing together?"

"I just brought your mom a slice of cake from this new recipe I tried out," Stevie says.

Wren pushes a ginger curl behind her ear. "And I'm here trying to help your mom do some stocking and inventory before her surgery in a few weeks."

"Speaking of," Mom says, snatching the phone back and setting it on the counter so I can see all of them, "I've decided I don't want to wait to see you until then."

A laugh sputters out of me. "You just saw me at the wedding last weekend."

"But we didn't get to spend any time together," she whines, sounding like a toddler who was just told she couldn't have ice cream before dinner. "And when you come stay after my surgery, you'll be mostly working in the shop for me."

My mom is having sinus surgery in a few weeks and won't be able to run her shop on my aunt and uncle's farm, and since summer is the start of the busy season, she can't just close it while she recovers. I'll be coming down to stay for the first few weeks of her recovery to run the store while my dad takes care of her.

"This is true," I agree, pushing off the counter and moving into the living room. I flop down onto my worn leather couch and tuck my legs up under me. I'd be worried about paint transfer if it weren't already flecked with color, like a disco ball sending shards of light all over it. "Okay, when do you want to see me?"

A grin dances across her face, the same one she uses when she's trying to talk someone into something without them knowing. "I was thinking you could come for Trail Days."

Trail Days. My heart warms just *thinking* about the festival in my hometown. Fontana Ridge is a tiny speck on the map, right off the Appalachian Trail. I spent my childhood riding in the back seat of my parents' station wagon while they picked up hitchhikers to give them a lift to the town square, listening to stories of grand adventures, and writing them down in my notebook so I could look up the images on the family computer at home and paint them.

"Bring Cam and Ellie too," Mom adds.

"I'm sure the newlyweds would just *love* to come spend the weekend with the in-laws."

Mom rolls her eyes. "Fine, then bring Alex."

"Oh, Hazel, how was the date?" Wren asks.

I scrunch up my nose at the question, knowing Mom is going to pounce on it.

"Date?" she asks, looking between the three of us. Wren flashes me an apologetic look, her green eyes blown wide and her bottom lip captured between her teeth.

Sighing, I say, "I went on a date."

"With *Alex*?" Mom asks, her voice rising at the end. She points at the screen with one long finger. "I knew it!"

"What? No, not with Alex," I say quickly. "Well, he was there. On another date."

Mom blinks at me before saying, "I'm confused."

As I explain the situation, Mom's face crinkles more and more, until she resembles tissue paper discarded on Christmas morning. "So you're not dating each other?" Mom asks, looking at me before turning to Stevie and Wren, as if double-checking that this isn't some elaborate prank.

"No, we're not dating each other," I clarify, a heat I can't explain stealing up my neck and diffusing into my cheeks.

Mom presses her lips together until they form a tight line. "Well, I wish you would. He's such a good boy."

That is an understatement. Alex is the definition of good. The brother who is constantly going to bat with his parents when their disapproval hangs heavy over his siblings like a weighted blanket. The best friend who relentlessly pulled me from the dark pit I descended into after Sebastian, when I couldn't trust myself to make sound decisions, when I questioned my own judgment on the most trivial of things, losing myself bit by bit. The man who puts himself last every single time, making the world a brighter, better place for everyone around him.

"He is good," I agree, feeling my features soften as surely as my heart.

Mom nods vigorously, latching on to my concession and soaking it up like a sponge. "Handsome too."

Unbidden, that memory of Alex in my car surfaces, the image so crystal clear it's like I'm right back there, the AC blowing back pieces of my hair, and the rustle of frozen peas melting against his skin. A drop of Alex's blood staining my shirt, the tang of copper tingeing the air. His laugh a husky thing hanging in the space between us, mending the last bits of my broken heart just like he has every day of the last year. I can picture him perfectly, all the beautiful pieces of him I somehow missed, like gold mixed with silt at the bottom of a murky river, always there, even if it's never discovered.

"He's pretty, but he knows it," I say, even though I'm sure he doesn't. Alex is a piece of art, lost for generations and waiting to be found.

I'm saved from thinking of another excuse when Mom laughs, loud and long. "The best kinds always do," she says between gasps, the grooves beside her eyes getting deeper by the second, like a potter is carving them into her flesh.

"Silas doesn't seem like the type," Wren says, referring to my dad.

"He may be quiet, but that doesn't mean he's not confident," Mom says with a wink that makes me wish I could melt into the floor.

"I've got to go." The words shoot out of me like a bullet train racing down the track. "I never want to see you wink when talking about my father again, please and thank you."

"Come to Trail Days," Mom yells before I can hang up. "And bring Alex."

"I'll see what I can do."

Nine

ALEX

Monday nights are movie nights at either my apartment or Hazel's. Tonight, it's at my place, meaning I'm in charge of making a dessert, and Hazel will pick up dinner on the way in. I'm just tossing the brownie box in the recycling and hoping Hazel thinks they're homemade when she walks through my door, paper bags from our favorite taco shop in her hands.

My feet propel me forward, and I take the bags from her arms. Hazel flashes me a bright smile, the one that looks like sunrise cresting over the horizon and never fails to warm me from the inside out.

"Hey," she says. "How was your day?"

"Long. I've been working with this couple that finds something wrong with every single place I show them, even though they're wealthy enough to afford any customizations they could want."

"Oh, so like you," she says, eyes twinkling with mischief.

"Even *I'm* not that rich,"

Hazel swishes past me, the pieces of her hair falling from her loose braid lifting in the air. "You're right. You can't even afford curtains for Mona."

I roll my eyes at the teasing. When I first moved in here, Cam, Ellie, and Adam made fun of me for not putting curtains on the wall of floor-to-ceiling windows that stretches from the kitchen to the living room, saying the missing curtains were like *Mona Lisa*'s missing eyebrows. As much as I didn't want it to stick, it did, and I now have more *Mona Lisa* merchandise than I know what to do with. It's a fan favorite gift in our friend group.

Hazel's hips swish as if there's a melody in her head that only she can hear as she makes her way through my condo. I follow after her like a lost puppy, cataloging every bit of her, the way I only can when she's not looking. Today she's in paint-stained overalls, and there's a smear of purple fingerprints on the side of her neck, like she was pushing back those stray wisps of hair while she worked. There are matching green smudges on her elbows too, and thinking about how they got there consumes my every thought. The cropped tank she's wearing leaves slivers of exposed tan skin on either side of her waist. Little temptations that look like they were carved out just for my hands and will haunt me for the rest of the night.

The paper bags rustle as I drop them on the counter, and my eyes flick up to collide with hers. They're the dark blue of a fathomless ocean that I want to drown in. "How was your day?"

Her fingers tug at the elastic at the end of her braid, and she sifts through the waves, letting them fall around her shoulders. "Good. I finished that big project I've been working on."

"The one for the fitness start-up?"

She nods, sifting through the last of the tangles in her sheet of golden-brown hair.

"And then you painted?"

Her eyebrows pull together like magnets. "Yeah, how'd you know?"

I can't help but reach out and trail my finger over the spot on her neck, the one I've dreamed about tasting. The smoothness of her skin sends my pulse skittering.

"Missed a spot," I tell her, my voice growing a little huskier at the feeling of her skin on mine.

"Man, I really thought I got it all today," she says through clenched teeth, flipping on the faucet.

A smile plays at the edges of my lips as I watch her scrub at her neck with a damp paper towel, and I decide not to tell her about the spots on her elbows. They'll be my little secret, those twin smudges that are more erotic than anything I've ever seen.

I'm in a bad way if paint smudges on skin are getting me hot and bothered.

Shaking my head, I start unloading our food. Fresh garlic, earthy cilantro, tangy lime, and fragrant meat perfume the air, making my mouth water.

"I got that Mexican soda you like too," Hazel says, still wiping stray paint from her skin.

"Want some?" I ask as I pull the glass bottle from the bag.

She waves me off. "I'll just have a sip of yours."

My lips press together to hold back a smile. Hazel always orders one drink and then *has a sip of mine.* Which really means she drinks over half of it.

Filling two cups with ice, I split the soda and pour it into each glass. Hazel sidles up next to me.

"I just wanted a sip."

One of my eyebrows quirks, and a laugh escapes her, more melodic than a symphony.

"Okay, okay, you're right. Thank you." She clinks her glass with mine and takes a drink. "What's the movie tonight?"

With hands loaded up with our food, we make our way to the couch. The white couch gives beneath our weight, cushioning in all the best places. When I moved into this apartment, my first investment was this sofa, and it was worth every penny. I've spent countless nights here sharing a blanket with Hazel and watching her watch the movies because I'm a hopeless sap, and her reactions are better than anything on the screen.

"*Emma*," I say, handing her a taco wrapped in tinfoil.

"Really?" Her tone is incredulous, and okay, I get where she's coming from. *Emma* isn't my typical choice, but Lucy gave me homework, and I intend to put more effort into this assignment than anything I've ever done.

My shoulders lift in a shrug. "I heard it was good."

"Good is an understatement," she says seriously, her eyes lighting up in all the shades of blue: sapphire and cerulean and cobalt and slate. "*Emma* is a masterpiece."

I can't help the smile that tilts my lips at her enthusiasm. Hazel is always beautiful, but when she gets excited about something, she's absolutely *radiant*, like sunshine reflecting on the rippling surface of a cresting wave or light glittering on cut diamonds.

"There's this one scene when they're dancing. You know what? You just have to see it," Hazel says quickly, her words tripping over each other in her eagerness as she searches for the movie. "You're buying this one, not renting. It's too good."

My arm slides over the back of the couch, fingers grazing the smooth silk of her hair. "Yes, ma'am."

Two hours later, the end credits roll, extinguishing the light from the living room. Only the glow of the words on the screen illuminates the happy smile curving Hazel's lips.

"So that's what does it for you?" I ask, stretching my arms over my head.

"Alex, that's what does it for every woman."

I have to bite my cheek to keep from laughing, because although Hazel always says she wants men to act like they do in these movies, if we actually did, she'd think we're crazy. "Okay," I scoff.

Hazel's eyes widen. "You don't believe me?"

I lean forward until we're almost nose to nose, so close that her individual features are blurred. My voice lowers, soft and smooth like fresh sheets or a whisper in the dark of night. "'If I loved you any less, then I might be able to talk about it more.'"

Hazel's intake of breath is quick, a sharp gasp that I feel in the pit of my stomach, like a cord that was tugged, begging me to close the distance between us and taste those lips that have been haunting my dreams for the last year.

I hold her gaze, taking this rare moment and memorizing it, because if this is all I ever get with her, I want it seared in my mind like a cattle brand, a permanent part of me. She smells like citrus today, like a slice of lemon cake drizzled with buttercream frosting. She can never commit to a perfume, so she has a collection under her bathroom cabinet, and she chooses which one she wants based on her mood. But I know, without a doubt, that this is my new favorite. I'll never be able to look at lemons again without imagining the plump curve of her bottom lip, the dusting of freckles across her peachy-pink cheeks, the way her eyes dilate as they dip to my mouth and back up, so fast I'm not sure if I imagined it.

"Try that on a woman, and she'll be putty in your hands," Hazel breathes.

The moment dissipates like dew on morning grass, and I want to reach out for it and pull it back, hold on to it for a moment longer, but I sit back, putting space between us. "Good to know." I clear the knot forming in my throat. "Speaking of—where are we going for our next date?"

Hazel reaches for my soda—since she's already finished hers—and takes a long drink, her throat bobbing as she swallows. "Actually, about that..."

I cock an eyebrow, dangerous hope stirring in my chest.

"My mom called today and asked me to come home to visit this weekend."

The hope catches flame, burning into a pile of ash.

"But she invited you too," Hazel says quickly, and I can't read the tone of her voice. It's hesitant, laced with nerves, and almost desperate. And I don't know what to make of that. Every part of me wants to read into it, to find a deeper meaning where there is likely none.

"Do you want me to go?"

I don't know why I ask it, but maybe I'm a little desperate myself. Maybe I need a little scrap to hold on to, a lifeline to assure me that I'm moving in the right direction by trying to pursue her. Because it's one thing to postpone our dates, but it's another to postpone them to spend the weekend on a trip with *me*. And I really want her to want that.

Hazel blinks those big blue eyes, her head rearing back slightly like she's surprised by my question. "Yeah, I'd love for you to come. Mom told me to make Cam and Ellie come too, but I doubt they will."

"I don't want to intrude on family time." Even to me, the words sound like a paltry excuse, a plea to beg me to come.

"It's not an intrusion," she says. "I'd love to show you my hometown."

Her eyes are sparkling like bits of stardust falling to earth, so mesmerizing I couldn't look away if I wanted to. A pleasurable warmth spreads through me at the sight, an aching tenderness that reminds me of just how tightly she holds my heart in her hands. I am completely at her mercy and happy to be here.

"So it's settled, then," I say, the corners of my mouth lifting. I've never been so happy to cancel a date. In the past, there's never been anything more enticing, but as the faint light from the TV illuminates Hazel curled on my couch, a blanket pulled tight around her shoulders, I can't imagine ever wanting something more.

Ten

HAZEL

"What's up with you?" I ask Alex, nudging his shoulder. We're standing in a truck stop off the highway, getting snacks for our road trip with Cam and Ellie, who, surprisingly, did want to tag along.

Alex is tense as he fills his cup with watermelon slush, harsh fluorescent lighting bouncing off the clear plastic domed lid. His shoulders are a tight line, and I have an overwhelming urge to slide my thumb across the creases between his brows. I shove the thought away. Ever since that night in his apartment when he looked into my eyes and quoted *Emma,* somehow managing to make it sound sexier than when Mr. Knightley himself said it, I've been having some weird urges. About Alex. My best friend.

His brow crinkles even further as he meets my eye. "Nothing." A second later, he jumps back, watermelon slush covering his hand from where it overflowed.

Without thinking, I lean over and swipe my tongue over his thumb and up the clear lid, catching the runoff. When I glance at Alex, his mouth is hanging open, and a pained expression colors his features.

I step back, licking the last bit from my lip. "Sorry, that was gross."

"Yeah, gross," Alex murmurs, voice strained, wiping his cup with a napkin.

"Seriously, what's up with you?" I ask, bumping his hip with my own.

When his eyes meet mine, a slow smile unfurls across his lips, eliciting a strange tingle deep in my belly. "Nothing's wrong. We've been to this gas station before, though."

I tear my gaze from his, looking around the convenience store, but it looks completely unfamiliar. Or familiar in the way that all gas stations look the same. Sticky floors and fluorescent lights, unnaturally bright colors located down white rows and behind chilled coolers. But there's nothing that sticks out to me.

"Really? When? How do you remember that?"

One of his shoulders lifts in a shrug, and he taps a single finger on his temple. "I've got a mind of steel."

"I don't think that means what you think it means."

His brows bunch together as he stabs a red straw into his slushie and takes a sip. "Mind of steel."

"My mind is a *steel trap*," I clarify, following him toward the registers.

"Same thing."

A little laugh escapes me. "No, it's not. Mind of steel means resilience."

Alex looks offended, pressing a hand to his broad chest. "You don't think I'm resilient?"

"Yes, you're resilient," I say with a roll of my eyes. "But you were talking about your memory."

"I have an excellent memory. I've got a mind of steel."

His eyes light up like Christmas lights, twinkling and glittering, and I realize he's messing with me, talking in circles to get me riled up. I shove my palm into his shoulder, unable to hold back my giggle.

"You're the worst."

He leans down until we're almost nose to nose, a brilliant smile playing on his lips. "But you love me."

I bite my cheek to keep from grinning. "Yes, I do."

Something changes in his expression, his eyes turning a deeper shade of brown than I've ever seen them, bleeding into the pupils until they're fathomless.

"Is that watermelon or cherry flavored?" Ellie asks, sidling up next to her brother, breaking whatever spell was cast over us.

My hand presses to my stomach, hoping to stop whatever peculiar sensation is riling there.

"Watermelon," Alex answers. "Want me to get you one?"

Ellie's smile is as bright as his. I think it must be in their genes. A little bit of pixie dust that makes them sparkle a little more than the rest of us.

"Yeah, thanks," she tells him.

Alex's gaze fastens on mine. "Do you want one too?"

"I'll just have a sip of yours."

His mouth hitches, tugging upward. "That's what I thought."

But when he hops in the back seat of Cam and Ellie's SUV a few minutes later, he's balancing three slushies in his hands, one for Ellie, one for him, and one for me.

Fontana Ridge is everything—nestled in the mountains, more idyllic than Mayberry, prettier than a postcard—and I always forget how much I miss it until I'm passing the welcome sign and taking in the way the sun crests over the treetops and glints on the lake.

Today, the town is already decked out for Trail Days. The streets are crowded with more visitors than the town residence year-round, even though the actual festival doesn't start until tomorrow. Time-worn banners hang from streetlights, and shop windows boast sales on hand-painted signs. As we cross over the bridge, a rainbow of tent colors pinpricks against the green backdrop of the campground.

My hand finds Alex's corded forearm, squeezing in excitement. "Welcome to Fontana Ridge."

Alex's nose is almost pressed to the window as he observes our surroundings, a smile playing on his lips. "It's beautiful."

I catch Cam's eye in the rearview mirror. "It's my favorite place in the world," I say, and I can tell he echoes my thoughts.

There's just something about this place that feels a little like magic, and sometimes I get sad I left it so early. I don't regret moving to LA, and I don't have a desire to move back to my hometown, but now that I'm older, I can appreciate all the little things I took for granted growing up. Like knowing my mail carrier by name or having an entire town vote online for my submission in an art contest in California. Like waking up to the same view of the mountains every day, knowing it will never be bulldozed to make room for a strip mall.

Riding back into this town feels like never leaving, like stepping into a fairy tale and finding they were just waiting for me to come back to finish the story. It's everything that no one ever knows they're missing until they're here.

"I can see why," Alex murmurs, eyes still glued to his surroundings.

Lifting up the armrest between us, I scoot into the middle seat until our bodies are pressed together from shoulder to thigh. I press a finger to the window, pointing to one of the buildings painted a pastel pink.

"That's the dance studio," I tell him. "Mom put me in lessons there when I was a kid, but she let me quit after I accidentally knocked a girl off stage during one of our performances."

Alex's laugh is deep, ghosting across the side of my face. "That bad, huh?"

"Not like you and your natural rhythm."

His eyes light up. "I went to a Zumba class one time—"

"And the instructor told you that you have a natural sense of rhythm," I finish for him, and Ellie cackles in the front seat.

The same force that pulls Alex's brows down into a pucker tugs my lips up into a smile.

"I'm very proud of that accomplishment," he says.

My eyes trail down his form, taking in the gray T-shirt pulling tight over his broad shoulders and the blue jeans riding low on his hips, rolled up to hit just above his white sneakers, before focusing again on the hard line of his jaw and the full curve of his lips. I still don't know how I missed that perfect curve, like the smear of charcoal on paper, or that Cupid's bow, like the barest dip of a paintbrush, but now that I've noticed, I can't seem to see anything else.

"I hate to break it to you," I say, dragging my eyes up to meet his again, ignoring the twinge in the pit of my stomach, "but I think she was just trying to get your number, because you have no rhythm to speak of."

The brown of his eyes takes on a challenging glint. One that seems so dangerous I think my cheeks are heating—*um, what's that about?*

"None that you know of," he says, and I swear his voice sounds like sandpaper. It makes my skin feel itchy and tight, stretched too thin, my pulse pounding beneath the surface.

"Gross," Ellie says, spinning around in her seat. "I don't need to know about your *rhythm*."

A smile ghosts across Alex's face, replacing whatever confusing look was there a moment ago. Those faint dimples at the top of his cheekbones hollow out.

"I don't know. I think I'd like to hear about it," Cam says. "Maybe I could use some tips."

Ellie's brown eyes, the exact color of Alex's, blow wide. "*Stop*. You're not taking *rhythm* tips from my *brother*."

"There's this thing I like to do," Alex says calmly, although his mouth is stretched in a mischievous grin. "Where you start at the—"

"No, no, no. Absolutely not. We are *not* having this conversation," Ellie interrupts, and the car goes quiet for a long moment. The only sound is the tires eating pavement as we truck past the outskirts of town and into the country.

I pinch my lips together to keep from laughing, and say, "So you start at the—"

"*No!*" Ellie yells, swiveling in her seat to face us once more, her hair flying all around her. Her eyes are wild as she fixes us with a glare, and any restraint we had on our laughter dissipates.

Gravel crunches under our tires before we can calm down, signaling that we've just pulled into the driveway at my aunt and uncle's farmhouse. My parents live on the other side of the property, a couple of acres away, but somehow everyone can usually be found here.

"Stevie's here!" I squeal, noticing my cousin's old truck parked out front, and jump out of the car before it's fully come to a stop.

Her dark head pops out the front door, a wide smile stretching her mouth. We crash together on the porch steps, hugging and making enough racket to wake the neighbors if there were any. I saw her at the wedding two weeks ago, but Stevie and I always reunite like star-crossed lovers who have just found their way back to each other through time and space.

"You need to come visit more," she tells me, squeezing my body in a tighter hug. "I hardly got to see you in all the wedding craziness, and you haven't been home in months."

"You could always come visit me, you know."

Stevie pulls back, an unreadable expression crossing her features. "Yeah, I should. It's just hard to get away."

The screen door slaps against its frame as my dad steps onto the porch. I move into his arms, gaze still focused on Stevie. "Yeah, you have a terrible boss who never gives you any time off."

Dad grunts. "Stevie can go anywhere she wants and take as much time off as she wants as long as it's not summer or October."

My dad runs a backcountry hiking company, and until a few years ago, he led most of the tours, sometimes spending days at a time leading overnight tours through the Great Smoky Mountains National Park. Ever since Stevie started working for him as a trail guide, he's been able to be home more and mostly run things from the office, even expanding enough to hire another tour guide last year to help out during the busy months.

The creaking of porch steps reminds me that I didn't come home alone for a visit. Cam and Ellie are stepping onto the porch and hugging Dad, Alex trailing behind them. I feel a pinch in my chest at the sight of him. No one else would recognize the tightness of his shoulders or the faint way his eyes dart around the scene as nerves, but I see it. He's outwardly extroverted and outgoing, but inside, he's a little shy. He told me one time that the reason he projects himself the way he does is because he never wants someone to feel the anxiety he does when entering a new social situation. My heart tugs every time I see that barely noticeable strain in his smile that tells me he's struggling on the inside but trying to make things easier for everyone else.

I sidle up next to him, giving his arm a gentle squeeze. A bit of the tension leaves his body, and he gives me a warm smile that feels like honey dripping down my insides.

"Come on," I say, tugging him up the stairs. "Let me show you around." Leaning closer, I whisper, "And no one here is going to hold anything back, so don't feel like you need to put on a show."

I startle at the feeling of his hand on my hip, his fingers squeezing once before he drops his arm back to his side.

"Alex, nice to see you again," Dad says, reaching out a hand to shake.

"Nice to see you too, sir." That easy smile is back on Alex's face, the tension gone from his shoulders, and I know he's relaxed. I wonder if that small touch helped. My skin is still burning from it, and I don't know what to make of that.

"Where's Mom?" Cam asks.

"She's finishing up a few things at the shop with Aunt Jamie, but she'll be here for dinner."

Cam's eyes swing to Stevie, who is leaning up against one of the porch pillars. "Did you make lasagna?"

She grins. "Sure did."

We make our way inside to the heavy scents of tomato and garlic and the underlying smell of the apple candles my mom makes in her shop. The walls are covered in floral wallpaper, and the floors are thin original hardwoods that creak with every step. Shades of azure, rose, periwinkle, saffron, vermilion, jade, and marigold color the room from the wildflower stained-glass window at the front of the house.

Stepping into the farmhouse is like stepping back to a time when my pigtails bounced against the back of my grass-stained overalls, flecks of paint stuck to my skin, and freckles dotted my cheeks from too much time in the sun without sunscreen. It's weird to think about how much I've changed when this house feels frozen in time. A relic to days gone by.

"Hey," Uncle Anthony says from where he's tossing a salad behind the counter when we enter the kitchen, his white teeth bright against his suntanned skin. "Welcome, kids."

The kitchen is too small for all of us, and I find myself pressed up against Alex as Stevie shuffles through the group to get to the stove. We're chest to chest, every inch of exposed skin already turning sticky from the humidity blowing in through the open windows. My gaze drifts up the expanse of his chest and over the strong, lean line of his neck to meet those piercing brown eyes.

"You doing okay?" I ask him, the murmur lost in the sliver of space between us, quiet enough that no one but the two of us can hear.

His head bobs in a nod, and his lips curve in a soft smile that I can tell isn't just for my benefit. It makes something warm beneath my sternum that he feels comfortable here, in this cluttered farmhouse with my chaotic family, when I know that his own childhood was quiet and orderly, filled with exotic vacations and expensive dinners.

"What are everyone's plans for this weekend?"

With Stevie back at the stove and Dad settling into a chair at the table, there's enough room to move around. I plop into one of the squeaky bar stools at the counter and motion for

Alex to take the one next to me. Snatching a grape tomato from the salad bowl, I pop it into my mouth, savoring the rich, sweet taste.

I say, "Well, tomorrow we have to go to the yard sale."

"I'm perfectly fine with missing the yard sale," Cam says, sitting in one of the chairs at the table and pulling Ellie onto his lap.

Spinning around, I pin him with a glare. "You *cannot* miss the yard sale, Camden."

A chuckle escapes him. "And whyever not?"

"It's a town tradition," I tell him, injecting my voice with as much incredulity as I can muster.

"So is running naked through the cemetery on Halloween, so I don't think all traditions need to be enforced."

"Did *you* ever participate in that tradition?" Ellie asks, eyebrows arching.

Cam snorts. "Absolutely not." Then his eyes light up, focusing on me. "But Hazel did."

I can feel Dad's stare hot on the side of my face. "Hazel did not."

Cam laughs, launching into his and Ellie's plans for the next few days. Alex leans over, his breath tickling the side of my face as he whispers, "Hazel most definitely did, didn't she?"

I press my lips together to keep from laughing and drawing Dad's attention back over here. "Oh, absolutely," I say, glancing up at him.

His lips curve in a slow smile, his voice lowering to a deep, honeyed pitch. "I think high school Alex and high school Hazel would have gotten along really well."

Eleven

HAZEL

"No, no, you can't look at that one," I say, trying to snatch the yearbook from Alex's hands, his knuckles grazing mine. We're in my childhood bedroom, and Alex is going through every single memento I accumulated throughout the eighteen years I lived here. The house is quiet, everyone having retreated to their bedrooms for the night, tipsy on too much red wine and stuffed with tangy tomato sauce and creamy ricotta.

His fingers tighten on the book, not letting go. "I'll absolutely be looking at it."

"No," I say, pulling harder, my knees bracing against the quilt-covered twin-size bed Alex is lounging on. "You're not. Seventh grade was the peak of my awkward years."

"Which is exactly why I *have* to see it, Hazel." He gives the yearbook one final tug, and this time, the momentum propels me with it. Alex drops the book, his hands catching me around the waist, and we go down in a tangled heap of limbs.

I land across his chest, our legs twisting together like bed linens. The breath heaves from Alex's lungs, sending my hair skittering away from my face before falling back like a sheet around us. His hands are still on my hips, and I can't tell whether they're pushing me up and away or keeping me pinned there.

My heart is beating hard enough that I know he has to feel it against his chest. Time slows and quivers, not holding its shape around us. Like it's frozen, waiting.

Alex's eyes are solid black as he holds my gaze. "I won't look at it if you don't want me to." His voice is a smooth, buttery whisper.

I don't move for another long moment, unsure why, before finally rolling off and landing on my back next to him on the bed. The lengths of our bodies are pressed together on the twin-size mattress as I reach for the book, flipping through to the pages seared in my memory.

Turning my head, I glance at Alex. "Be gentle."

"Always," he says, fingers brushing mine as he takes the book from me. I watch him as he looks at the photos on the page. My tiny seventh grade class at Fontana Ridge Middle School. There's one of me with my hair falling in terribly styled waves around my head, wearing a coral pink Aeropostale shirt and plaid Bermuda shorts. Assorted colorful bracelets line my wrists, and only the top layer of my hair is crimped. In another, I'm proudly holding up an absolutely terrible butterfly drawing I did in art class. Only my bright yellow rain boots and my painfully awkward soft smile show from above and below the giant canvas.

I expect Alex to laugh, but he just rolls his head across my floral-printed pillowcase, a smile stretching his lips, those dimples peeking out on his cheekbones, his thumb lightly swiping over one of the photos on the smooth paper. "So you've always liked butterflies then, huh?"

A relieved breath startles out of me. "Always," I say, mimicking his soft tone from before.

"I, for one, think that middle school Hazel was incredibly cute."

I reach for the yearbook and look at the pictures once again. "I showed my high school boyfriend this yearbook, and he told me he was glad his family didn't move here until I was hot."

Alex's brow wrinkles, and a muscle in his jaw flutters. "I really hate your ex-boyfriends."

For some reason, this makes me laugh, although it only serves to make Alex frown harder. "I kind of hate them all too." Rolling onto my side, I shut the yearbook and press it tight against my chest. "This is why I need you to find me my next one. I suck at picking good guys."

Alex's eyes leave my face, fixing on the popcorn ceiling. "Glad I can help," he says, his voice sounding flat.

I nudge his thigh with my knee. "Would it make you feel better to chew out my ex-boyfriend? He owns the hardware shop."

He glances back at me. "I think that would, in fact, make me feel better." The faintest grin lifts one corner of his mouth.

Our gazes lock and hold for another long moment before he pushes up from the bed, walking around my room once more. I stay where I am but sit up and lean on one hand, watching as Alex makes his way around my childhood bedroom and pauses to inspect every little thing. His fingers trail across the surface of my dresser, the purple paint chipping to reveal a dark teal underneath. It's been painted every shade of the color wheel at one point or another, and I never took the time to sand away the old layer, meaning every new chip or dent exposes a past life, a past mood, a memory.

Alex points to one of the pictures shoved into the trim around my dresser mirror. "What's this?" he asks, looking over his shoulder at me.

Standing to my feet, my arms still banded around the yearbook and holding it to my chest, I make my way to him.

"Oh, no," I say, pressing a hand to my face as soon as I see the photo he's referring to. It's Stevie, Wren, and me at the public pool, neon swim caps plastered to our heads, circular indents around our eyes from where our goggles had been moments before.

"Swim team?" Alex guesses, his voice lifting with amusement.

"I wish. What you can't see are the mermaid fins our moms let us purchase online."

A laugh rockets out of him, bouncing off the walls. "Mermaid fins?"

I nod from behind my hand, my cheeks hot under my palms.

Alex tugs at my wrist, pulling my hand away. The smile he gives me is wide, unfettered. One corner of his mouth is hitched higher than the other, just like it was that first day we met, when I thought he looked like a British rake stepping out of a period drama.

"That's adorable," he says, his voice tinged with amusement, and something else that sounds a lot like tenderness.

"I was thirteen."

He presses his lips together, trying valiantly to hold back a laugh. He fails the exact second that I do. It's the kind of laughter that takes everything out of you, robbing you of breath and sending sharp pains through your sides. We fall against my closet door. It's the only thing keeping us upright as we try to keep each other from laughing loud enough to wake Cam and Ellie on the other side of the wall.

"*Shh*," Alex whispers, tears leaking from his eyes as he presses a finger to my lips.

"*You shh*," I hiss back, and we dissolve again.

He's holding me up now by the elbows, keeping me from sliding down the closest door to the ground. "Get it together, Lane. What if we wake Cam and Ellie up and they're feeling amorous?"

I press my face into his shoulder to stifle the giggle that rockets through me. "*Stop.*"

My breath comes out in loud gasps, and Alex's shoulder is bouncing. When I finally control myself enough to pull back, Alex's cheeks are a happy pink and stained with tears. He reaches out, freeing the photo from where it was trapped between the mirror and its frame.

"I'm keeping this," he tells me. "I need a photo for my wallet in case you're ever kidnapped."

I snatch it back. "Absolutely not." After fitting it back into place, I turn to find Alex looking at the assortment of pictures again.

He points to one of me at prom. "Hardware store owner?"

My head bobs in a nod, and a displeased grunt sounds from deep in his throat. "I'll keep an eye out for him tomorrow," he says.

I have to bite my lip to keep from smiling.

His finger lands on another one of me with a group of kids standing in front of a movie theater, his brow arching in silent question.

"That's me on my first group date," I tell him, my hand moving against his as I point to the freckle-faced boy standing next to twelve-year-old me, his arm slung around my shoulder. "First boyfriend. My mom didn't know, or she never would have let me go."

"He looks like a punk," Alex says, and I can't help but laugh.

"He *was* a punk. He tried to feel me up on that date."

Alex leans back against the dresser, his hands curling over the edge. "Does he also own a hardware store that we can visit?"

A smile hitches on my lips. "Insurance sales office."

"That's crazy. I've been thinking of pricing out some new policies."

"You know, I'm glad I didn't know you then," I tell Alex, sliding a look his way. "I would have had the biggest crush on you."

He snorts. "I doubt it."

"No, I would have," I assure him. "You would've been the super-hot high school boy, and I would have been that." I jab my finger at the picture, shaking the mirror with the force.

"Well, I'm glad I didn't know you *then*," Alex says, pointing to another photo of Stevie, Wren, and me, this one taken the summer after we graduated from high school. We're once again in swimsuits, although this time we're not at a pee-filled public pool in Fontana Ridge. In this picture, we've got our toes sunk into golden sand in the Outer Banks. It was the first solo trip our parents allowed us to take.

"Why?" I ask, my eyes still fixed on Alex, on the full curve of his lower lip as it lifts in a smirk.

"I would have had the biggest crush on you."

"Once I was hot?" I tease.

His eyes glint, cocoa and moss and bronze. "Once you were legal." His tone softens into something like regret. "I wasn't..." He trails off, looking away before meeting my eyes again. "I didn't treat women the way I should have when I was twenty-three."

"I can't imagine you ever being anything but nice," I say, leaning my hip against the dresser.

That smirk skates across his face again. "Oh, I was always nice," he says, mischief tingeing his voice before turning into something else entirely. "I just wasn't always good."

My heart skitters at his words, at the low timbre of his voice.

"I have a hard time believing that," I say. "You're good now. Right down to your bones."

His gaze is like fire, singeing my every nerve, as he watches me. It's never been like this before. There's an electric current in the air, like seconds before a storm, where before there's only been warmth and sunlight.

One of his muscled shoulders lifts in the hint of a shrug. "Maybe you make me want to be someone good, Hazel Lane."

The feeling burning in my stomach, filling up the space between us, is as terrifying as it is unfamiliar. Unwanted.

Desire. Heavy and desperate and dizzying. Fraying the edges of my reality, infringing on places it shouldn't.

I swallow, taking a small step back. Alex's eyes shutter, the kaleidoscope of colors melting back into earthen brown.

"I'm glad we met each other when we did then," I say, wooden. "Crushes would ruin this."

He nods, a quick dip of his head.

"Our friendship is too special to ruin with something like that."

"Mm-hmm," he murmurs before pushing off the dresser, taking the oxygen with him as he begins to meander around my room once more.

My heart rate returns to normal when, a few moments later, he flashes me a grin from over his shoulder. He reaches for that same butterfly canvas from my yearbook photo, wedged behind my bookshelf.

"That was the first butterfly I painted," I tell him.

One of his eyebrows arches as he studies it. "Really? What made you pick a butterfly?"

I come up beside him, tracing the butterfly with the tip of my finger. "My art teacher told us to pick something from nature. It could be anything."

I shrug. "Growing up, I didn't like change very much," I say with a wry look in his direction. "But butterflies. They were made to change. They were never meant to stay the same. And their change…well, it was beautiful. And I liked that change could be beautiful sometimes. It didn't always mean something was ending or someone was leaving."

I look up at Alex through the fringe of my lashes to find him already watching me. "Pretty insightful for a seventh-grader," he says softly.

"Well, my best friend had just moved away, and my first boyfriend dumped me like two days before I started that project. I was feeling angsty."

Alex leans against my closet door, studying me. "The one who tried to feel you up in a movie theater?"

"One and the same."

"I'm definitely going to need to meet with him to get a quote."

"Adding it to the itinerary for tomorrow," I intone seriously, and then, "Do you want to head to bed?"

He lifts a shoulder in a shrug. "I'm not tired."

"Good. I'm not either," I say, my lips hitching in a smile. After returning the canvas to its spot behind the bookshelf, I wrap my hand around his. "Follow my lead, or you'll step on a creaky floorboard."

The door squeaks softly on its hinges as I open it, the darkness of the hallway swallowing us up.

"Where are we going?" Alex whispers, his breath hot on my neck.

I don't answer. Instead, I lead him past the row of bedroom doors and into the living room, flipping on one of the warm lamps. Dropping his hand, I motion for him to sit on the couch.

He lets out a satisfied hum as I open the cabinet door next to the TV, revealing shelves and shelves of VHS tapes. "What are we watching?" His voice is soft and low.

My fingers trail over the plastic cases until I find the one I want in the dim lighting. "*When Harry Met Sally.*"

Twelve

ALEX

"You know, this isn't really a sunrise hike," I say as the morning sun starts to beat down on us. The pink and orange hues of dawn have disappeared into a golden hue that signals the start of a new day.

"Oh, I know," she says, sounding a little winded as we make our way up the sharp incline. "But hiking The Mountain in the dark is suicide."

A little chuckle escapes me. "It's not that bad of a hike." So far, the trail has been far from easy, going steadily uphill the entire way, but it's been manageable.

Her gaze cuts to mine. "This is the easy part."

A niggle of worry starts beneath my breastbone, remembering my strategizing session with Lucy before we left Nashville. She suggested a nature date, which Hazel planned without my prompting, which worked out in my favor. While her hometown is surrounded by mountains, this particular one is known for its challenging hike and unreal views. Hazel says it's a Fontana Ridge must-see.

But now that we're here, the other part of Lucy's plan is haunting me. Under no circumstances am I going to orchestrate an accident so that I have to carry her back, but looking around at my surroundings—the sharp cliffs to my right, the rocky terrain up ahead, the uneven trail below my feet—I'm worried I won't be able to stop it if something *does* go wrong on this hike.

The trail slowly gets harder and harder to traverse, growing thinner and more craggy until we can no longer walk side by side. With each step, the pack on my back bounces between my shoulder blades, and sweat gathers on my skin, equally from nerves and exertion. I can't even appreciate the view of Hazel in front of me in billowing cotton joggers and the teeniest cropped tank because I'm so sick to my stomach at the thought of her slipping and falling off the side of the mountain.

I'm so wrapped in my thoughts that I don't hear what Hazel says as we near the summit. She spins around, eyeing me with concern. "Alex?"

My hand finds her waist on instinct, pulling her away from the edge. Her skin is warm and damp with sweat beneath my fingertips, setting my blood on fire.

Hazel's palm lands on my bicep, fingers flexing. "Alex, what's wrong?" Her delicate face is etched with worry, and her lips form a slight frown. I have to hold myself back from running my thumb across them until that frown disappears.

I let go of her waist like she's burned me, my hand clenching and unclenching at my side. When her gaze tracks down and fixes on the movement, I freeze, realizing what I've done. The hopeless British sap gesture that Lucy was telling me about.

"Nothing," I grit out. "What were you trying to say?"

Her eyes hold on my hand for a moment longer before swinging up to mine. "I was saying the fire tower is right around the bend."

I mean this in the kindest way possible—I couldn't care less about this fire tower at this point. All I want is to get off this mountain and go back to Hazel's tiny childhood bedroom and try to piece myself back together. I've never felt anxiety like this before. I've never felt less in control than I do at this moment, and I *hate* it.

"Alex, are you okay?" Hazel's voice is soft, concerned.

My chest constricts in a deep breath. "Yeah, come on." I force a smile, knowing she can see right through it. "Let's see this fire tower."

Hazel gives me one last searching look before spinning around and heading back up the trail. It's starting to level out now that we're nearing the top, and some of my anxiety disappears, melting like snow in the sun. With the cinch around my chest loosening, I can finally start to admire the view. Golden brown hair, soft, smooth curves, a butterfly tattoo peeking out with each swing of her arm.

Hazel glances at me over her shoulder, eyebrows bunched together. "What are you looking at?"

Maybe it's the anxiety coursing through my body and numbing my brain, but I speak truthfully and without thinking. "Your ass."

Hazel barks a laugh, spinning around to face me, still walking backward. "You're the worst."

When she gets too close to the edge, my hand finds her hip, guiding her back onto the trail.

Her eyebrows raise at the gesture, and she says, "You're very handsy today."

"I'll keep my hands to myself when you stop trying to walk off cliffs."

A grin lights her face, slow and dazzling. I want to feel it against my skin, taste it and see if it's as sweet as it looks.

She takes a step to the left, coming closer to the edge. "Does it *scare* you, Alex?" she asks, drawing out the words in a taunt.

My fingers circle her elbow, tugging her back. "Yes," I say through gritted teeth.

A giggle escapes her. "I've never seen you like this before."

"Yeah, well, I'm not really a fan of it, so let's just be safe." I spin her back around so she's facing forward again. The look she shoots me over her shoulder is saucy, and I feel a lightning bolt of desire down my spine. I scrub a palm over my face. This trip is going to be the death of me.

Dirt and rocks scuff under our shoes as we round the last bend and the fire tower comes into view, jutting high above the mountains. Early morning sunshine glints off the windows, sending shafts of light refracting across the hills. The view is...breathtaking. It's like standing on top of the world.

"Beautiful, right?" Hazel asks, slightly out of breath beside me. Sweat glistens on her skin, making her shimmer.

"Yeah," I breathe, trying to take it all in.

Hazel's lips curve in a smile, and she points to the top of the tower. "Wait till you see it from up there."

The wooden stairs are rickety beneath our feet, creaking and groaning with every step, but Hazel looks unconcerned, taking them two at a time. Her excitement is palpable, radiating off her in waves. She is always confident, taking on life with the force of a summer storm, but here in her hometown, she's unstoppable, a force of nature.

We're out of breath by the time we reach the top, chests heaving, and the sun has officially crested over the mountains, the purple and blue hues of dawn bleeding into vibrant orange.

Hazel was right. The view from below pales in comparison to this one, like holding an art print up against the original. I can see for miles in every direction, a panoramic view. On one side is the town, tiny buildings nestled in the valley. On the other is miles and miles of uninterrupted mountains shrouded in hazy mist, broken only by the cerulean river flowing into the lake.

Hazel's hand wraps around my bicep, pulling me toward one of the windows. She shoves a palm into the window frame, and it pops out, rotating on its hinges. When she bends down under the windowpane, the breeze whips at the fine hairs around her face.

"Come on," she says, shooting me a glance and patting the spot against the window frame next to her. I match her position, propping my elbows on the ledge and looking out the open space.

The air is cooler up here, drying the sheen of sweat to my skin. My tongue darts across my parched lips, and they taste of salt. With each gust of wind, I can smell crisp pine and cedar, with just a hint of smokiness.

Hazel bumps my shoulder with hers, her hair blowing across my face. "Pretty, huh?"

I make an affirmative noise in the back of my throat, too entranced for words.

"You know what this tower is used for?" she asks, and the windowpane creaks as it gets caught in a gust of wind, knocking against our backs.

"Watching for fires?"

"Nah, it hasn't been used for that in years." Her voice is tinged with something I can't quite read.

I cut my eyes to her, arching a brow.

A grin splits her mouth. "Teenagers use it for sex."

"And how would *you* know that?" I ask. Her eyes twinkle like stars in the night sky, and a strawberry hue lights her cheeks. I shake my head, looking back at the mountains. "Never mind. I don't want to know."

Hazel's shoulder nudges mine once more. "I'm just messing with you."

My gaze snags on her again. She's so achingly beautiful I can feel it in my bones. "So no one has sex here?"

"Oh, they definitely do. Be careful where you put your hands," she says with a nod to where my fingers are gripped around the windowsill.

I release the metal immediately, running my palms down my thighs. Hazel's laugh is bubbly and infectious, and I find my lips curving into a grin of my own.

"You're trouble," I tell her.

"You're not the first man to say that to me in this very spot," she says. When my mouth falls open, a high-pitched chuckle shoots out of her, and I roll my eyes, holding back a smile.

"You should have seen your face." Her shoulder bumps into mine again, but this time she doesn't back away.

"It doesn't take much to rile you up," she says, her voice still tinged with laughter as we stand with our sides pressed together, facing the misty mountains.

"You're not the first person to tell *me* that in this spot."

When I look down at her, her smile is bracketed by the faintest of dimples, little indentations that you could feel better than you can see. I want to memorize those divots with my fingertips, but I can't, so I'll just have to make a little space in my heart for this moment, a memory I can pull back out later when I need a little sunshine.

"Ready for breakfast?"

We set up a picnic on the floor of the fire tower, sitting atop a worn flannel blanket that Hazel pulled from the hope chest in her bedroom this morning and stuffed into the backpack.

It smells of cedar and lavender from the bag of herbs she kept tucked between layers of linens. Hazel retrieves the thermos of strong Folgers coffee and apple donuts that she told me her aunt makes from the apple harvest on the farm.

Crossing her legs at the ankles, Hazel leans back on one arm, taking a bite of her donut. Cinnamon sugar coats her lips and sprinkles across her hands like pixie dust shimmering in the dewy sunshine.

"I could eat these every day," she says around a bite.

I munch into my own donut, the buttery apple flavor sweet on my tongue. "This is probably the best thing I've ever eaten," I tell her.

The grin she gives me is brighter than starlight and just as dazzling. I can't help but stare. Sunrise looks good on Hazel. The early morning light is turning her golden everywhere, making her skin look like soft satin. I want to drag my fingers up the length of her arm and see if she's warm like sunshine, press my mouth to the curve of her neck and see if she smells like apples or something she brought from home. I wonder if the cinnamon and sugar taste sweeter on her lips. If the coffee is stronger. If she makes everything more vibrant like the way I think she does.

"Thanks for coming here with me," she says, pulling me from my thoughts. Cinnamon sugar falls into her lap as she takes another bite. Her eyes are soft on mine, those tiny, faint dimples peeking out as she chews.

I tighten my hand on the thermos to hold myself back from reaching for her, the warmth seeping through the metal to warm my fingers. "I'll go anywhere with you, Hazel Lane."

Thirteen

HAZEL

There's a humming buzz beneath my skin, an energy in my veins, as Alex and I make our way down Main Street. The sun feels like a warm embrace, making sweat prickle on the back of my neck. But the breeze off the river is enough to lift my hair and send it swirling around my shoulders every few minutes.

"Are you going to buy anything?" Alex asks as we stop at another one of the tables lining the street. This one is covered in an assortment of vintage items that remind me of playing at my grandma's house before she passed.

"I'll buy as many things as you're willing to carry," I tell him, my lips curving into a cheeky smile.

His fingers trail across the table, curving over trinkets. "Oh, so nothing, then?"

When I fix him with my sternest glare, a laugh rumbles from his chest. It's the kind of achingly familiar laugh that's almost nostalgic, like ice cream cones on the first day of summer vacation or sleepovers at your best friend's house, where you stay up all night, talking in the dark about anything and everything.

"This is pretty," Alex says, picking up a gold necklace. The metal glints in the sunlight as it gently sways in his hand.

I sidle next to him, our shoulders brushing. Nestled in his palm is a delicate gold butterfly pendant. The wings look brittle, and they're curved, as if in flight.

"Oh," I breathe, gently tracing a fingertip over the dainty pendant. "I love it."

Alex's eyes flick to me. They're not solid brown today. They're flecked with moss green and deep bronze. "Yeah?"

I trail my finger over the wings of the butterfly. It feels so thin and brittle beneath my touch, almost as delicate as actual butterfly wings. "It's beautiful."

"We'll take it," he tells the elderly woman sitting on the opposite side of the table. Deep groove lines appear on her face as she smiles.

"I can get it," I interject as Alex pulls his worn leather wallet from his back pocket.

He waves me off, pulling out a crisp ten-dollar bill and placing it in her withered hand. After the woman returns his change, flashing him that same charmed grin that every woman seems to make in Alex's direction, he makes a swivel gesture with his finger. I spin around so my back is to him and lift my hair off my neck, the light breeze immediately cooling the dampness gathered there.

The tiny, intricate butterfly settles in the hollow of my throat. Alex's hands are gentle, soft, quick brushes against skin that I can somehow feel in the pit of my stomach. It's…disconcerting, yet somehow also exhilarating. There's a tug in my abdomen when his knuckles graze against the smooth curve of my neck, an off-beat thump beneath my sternum when the tips of his fingers slide over the bumps at the top of my spine, a catch in my breath when he skims the shell of my ear.

"There," Alex says, and I think his voice might be raspy.

When I turn, his eyes are focused on the butterfly that has slid from the hollow of my throat to settle above the ties of the floral top I changed into after our hike. "Beautiful," he murmurs.

The husky scrape of his voice sends an unfamiliar pulse through my blood, that same unwanted bolt of desire from last night that threatens to buckle my knees. I swallow heavily, and his gaze tracks the movement. I can feel it as surely as a touch against my skin. When my tongue darts out to wet my suddenly dry lips, his eyes go hazy, like heat rippling over pavement in the thick of summer.

"Hazel!" someone yells, snapping my attention away from Alex and whatever trance we've fallen into. It's like a bucket of cold water being poured over my head, banking the warmth spreading through my middle, leaving me irritated and anxious. My hand presses into my stomach, trying to calm whatever fluttering started there.

A mop of short, curly ginger hair pushes through the crowd, and I immediately recognize Wren. She's clad in an emerald green corduroy overall dress that hits midway down her freckled thighs, and the pale yellow short-sleeve button-up beneath it is covered in bright flowers and birds. I'm not tall by any means, but when Wren throws her arms around me, she barely reaches my shoulder.

"Hey," I say, the breath knocked out of me by the force of her hug.

She backs up, her tiny hands gripping my cheeks on either side. "You look beautiful," she tells me, and a pleasant warmth spreads through me at the compliment, unlike the spiking, pulsing heat I felt when Alex said the same thing just moments before.

"Thank you," I say, fingering a lock of her red hair. "You do too. I'm loving this haircut." For as long as I've known her, Wren and her sister, Rae, have had matching manes of enviable red curls that hang to their waists, but this short bob, cropped to hit just below her jaw, seems to suit her even better.

Twin candy apples appear on her cheeks, lively and bright red. "Thanks. It was getting too hot to keep it long when I'm helping coordinate events at the farm."

It *is* hot today, but it's just shy of too warm instead of stifling like it is back in the city. Spring has only just turned into summer, and the days alternate between sweltering and almost chilly, sunny or gray with rain.

Wren's gaze catches on Alex behind me, and a grin lights her face. Wren has this way of blooming like a springtime flower every time she smiles, like her happiness can't be contained to just her face. It radiates out of her every pore.

"Is this Alex?" she asks, her eyes darting back to me.

For some reason, embarrassment pricks at me like an errant needle, but I can't pinpoint why. Forcing it down, I say, "Yes, sorry. Alex, this is Wren. Wren, meet Alex."

Alex's large hand practically dwarfs Wren's as they shake. "Nice to meet you, Wren. I've heard a lot about you."

"Likewise," Wren responds, her lips still tilted in that breathtaking smile. The one Alex gives her in return makes something in my stomach quiver.

Wren looks back at me. "What are y'all doing for the rest of the day?"

"Mom wrangled us into working a shift at the store, so we're headed there after the yard sale." I gesture vaguely down the street. It's lined with foldable tables as far as the eye can see, with townsfolk sitting or standing around them, laughing with neighbors and bartering with tourists.

"Do you want to have dinner with Stevie and me and then go to the concert after?"

It's basically a town tradition, something Wren, Stevie, and I have done since we were old enough to be let loose on the town by ourselves, and I want to go more than anything, but I'm not here by myself this year. I glance over at Alex, who is already watching me, no doubt seeing my desire written all over my face.

A slow grin curls the corners of his mouth. "We'll be there," he tells Wren, not looking away from me.

Her gaze bounces between us, narrowing slightly before sharpening on something behind us. "It's *Holden*," she says, her voice laced with disgust. "I forked his yard last night and left before sunrise so he couldn't heckle me about it. I've gotta go. See you tonight!" she yells over her shoulder, spinning on her heel and disappearing into the crowd.

"Wren Daniels!" a deep voice bellows from behind me.

"Uh-oh," I say, grabbing Alex by the arm and tugging him into the throng of people.

His breath is warm against my neck as he leans down to whisper in my ear. "Who is Holden?"

"*That* is too long a story for me to try to explain. Plus, we need to get through this yard sale before our shift."

"That's a pretty necklace," Mom says as Alex and I are heading out the door to meet Wren for dinner. We stopped by my parents' house after our shift at the store so I could reapply my coconut perfume and deodorant after a long day in the sun. I'm busy tying my hair up in a knot with the scrunchie I slipped from Alex's wrist when Mom lifts the delicate butterfly pendant off my chest and examines it.

"Thanks. Alex got it for me," I tell her.

Mom's eyes dart to Alex over my shoulder, her bright smile lifting the corners of her mouth. "Is that so? Alex, you truly are the sweetest boy."

"The sweetest boy," I echo, fixing Alex with a mock-serious stare.

His lips twitch, his eyes glittering at me for an instant before he focuses back on my mom. "Thank you, Miss Ava," he says to her.

Mom scoffs, waving a sun-spotted hand. "*Miss* Ava. Your mama raised you right. But you be good to my Hazel now, you understand?"

My eyes widen at her implication, nearly bugging out of my head. "*Mom.*"

"Silas," Mom says, ignoring me. "Ask Alex about his intentions."

Dad doesn't even look up from where he's shucking corn at the kitchen counter for the church potluck they're heading to this evening. "I'd rather not."

"*Silas.*" Mom's tone holds the exact same tone of warning that my own did moments before.

"Don't get her pregnant without a ring, Alex," Dad deadpans.

"That's it!" I yell, tugging Alex by the bicep to the front door. "I'm done with both of you." I point a finger at Mom. "But mostly you."

Alex is chuckling when I finally drag him down the porch and into the driveway, gravel crunching beneath our shoes.

"It's not funny," I tell him, my eyebrows arching high on my head. "They're ridiculous."

"No, no," Alex says, wrapping an arm around my shoulder. "Think of how much they just gave us permission to do just as long as I don't get you pregnant."

I slap his stomach, noting the way the hard muscles bunch beneath my touch with his laughter, and shove his arm off my shoulder. "You're as bad as they are."

His eyes twinkle mischievously, a glint of gold in those dark brown irises. "You have no idea."

I shut myself in the driver's seat of my dad's pickup to avoid the flurry of butterflies taking flight in my stomach. I've never felt so betrayed by butterflies in my life. This is *Alex*, my platonic best friend.

Alex hops into the passenger side, eyeing me suspiciously. "Something wrong?"

The truck revs to life, vibrating the worn leather seats, warm from the sun, and I switch it into gear. "Nope."

"Whatever you say," Alex singsongs, flipping on the radio. An old country song filters through the scratchy speakers, covering the harsh beating of my heart. When he turns on the next station, static crackles, and a smile stretches across my lips.

"You can keep trying, but we only get one station this deep in the mountains."

Alex crooks an eyebrow at me. "You're serious?"

"Well, no. There is a radio preacher on the AM station, but if you want music, it has to be country."

The din of static is replaced by twangy crooning a second later, and I can't help but hum along with the classic. Alex's smooth baritone joins in, singing softly enough that I can barely hear him over the sound of the wind rushing through the open windows. His arm is propped on the window, bright sunlight making the hairs on his sinewy forearm stand out even more starkly against his pale skin. He looks so different here in my hometown, wind rustling his normally styled hair, miles of defined muscles peeking out from shorts and an impossibly thin linen button-up. He looks nothing like the professional Nashville realtor in starched collared shirts and fitted slacks. This relaxed look is doing things to me, and I don't know what to make of that.

The fields slowly disappear as we get closer to the town's center, the roads switching from cracked concrete patched with gravel to smooth pavement. The golds and oranges of sunset crest over the mountains and through the windshield, warming the truck pleasantly.

"Where are we going to park?" Alex asks as we get into the thick of Trail Days traffic. The streets are still lined with tourists, some obviously families who are sunburned and most likely staying in a cabin decorated in bear paraphernalia up on the ridge, while others are clearly hikers, dusty and haggard, with heavy packs that will get discarded in tents or the hostel in town.

"I know just the place," I tell him, making a sharp left in the direction of the river.

Alex says, "Might be a little wet out there," and I roll my eyes.

"There's a little fishing spot down here. My boyfriend and I used to park out there."

"The one who said he was glad you met after you got hot?" Alex asks, one eyebrow lifting high on his forehead.

"One and the same."

He makes a humming noise in the back of his throat before saying, "Didn't realize you were so into fishing." I can see his grin out of the corner of my eye. It's the easy, lilting teasing I'm used to, not diffused with any of the tension I've been feeling over the past few days.

"Oh yes, I love *fishing*," I answer, emphasizing the word.

I back the truck into the dirt parking lot in front of the river, hidden behind trees and big enough for only two or so vehicles. It's darker here than it was on the street, hiding the golden rays of sunset.

"You any good?" Alex's voice has slipped an octave, and I think my calm goes with it, sliding away like water between my fingers. All that's left is a pulsing awareness in my stomach and a thick knot in my throat.

His eyes are dark when I meet his gaze, like looking into a vat of oil. "At *fishing*?"

He nods, not looking away.

My shoulder lifts in a shrug, and I try to lighten whatever tension is forming between us. It's equal parts thrilling and terrifying. "I've been told I'm a good fisher. I'm pretty good at baiting my own hook."

When his eyes slide a little further into darkness, I realize the double meaning of my words. Heat stains my neck, climbing up my cheeks and ears.

"That's *not* what I meant," I tell him.

His voice is still smooth as velvet and thick as honey. "What did you think I meant, Hazel?"

I swallow against the lump in the back of my throat, the one that feels too big for such a tight space. I feel prickly all over, like there's an electric current running beneath my skin, threatening to shock me at any moment. "I don't know," I say honestly.

His eyes clear with his blink, the familiar easy *friend* Alex returning. "I just meant fishing. We should go sometime."

My body flushes hotter at his words, whether he meant them that way or not. I don't know what's happening, where these unwelcome feelings have come from, but it needs to *stop*.

Thankfully, my phone buzzes on the console between us, subduing whatever current was crackling in the air. It's Wren, asking where we are. I shoot her a quick text back with our ETA.

"Ready to go?" Alex asks. He's completely back to normal, cool and unfazed, and I wonder if it was all in my head. That thought leaves a sick feeling in the pit of my stomach.

I force myself to respond normally, willing my heart rate to return to normal. With a nod, I say, "Let's go."

The local barbeque restaurant isn't a far walk and is already teeming with tourists, locals, and hikers alike. The air is heavy with humidity and the smell of sunscreen and unwashed bodies, mixed with the tangy scent of vinegar barbeque sauce as we make our way through the throngs of people waiting outside the restaurant. Luckily, Wren's brother owns the place, so he saved us a table on the patio under the dangling Edison bulb lights.

My thighs slide against the wooden planks of the picnic table bench. Wren smiles at me from across the table, pushing her curly strawberry bangs off her forehead.

"You made it!" she yells over the sound of country music playing loudly over the speakers.

"Did you manage to evade Holden?"

Alex settles next to me on the small bench seat, his thigh pressed against the length of mine. We've sat this close thousands of times before, under blankets and in back seats of cars and in situations *just like this*, so I will the butterflies to stop flapping in my stomach and calm my nerves, forcing my shoulder to relax against his broad one. Instead of feeling tense and heavy like earlier in the truck, it feels calm and normal, and the knot in my stomach loosens further.

"He cornered me at the Hiker Talent Show," she groans, her pale blue eyes rolling.

"And?"

"He told me he was calling the cops if I didn't clean them up by tomorrow morning."

"So what are you going to do?" I ask, taking a sip of the heavily sweetened tea the waitress just dropped off at our table.

"I left the talent show and bought plastic spoons at the market."

A laugh sputters from Alex, and I can't help but grin at him, pressing my shoulder into his. "There's no way she would give up that easily," I tell him.

"Absolutely not," Wren says, her palm smacking against the table and rattling the weathered boards. "You know he sent June over to my house last month when I was working in the garden and had her tell me he was passed out in the backyard. And when I went over to check on him, he ambushed me with a water gun."

"Is June his wife?" Alex asks, looking between the two of us.

"His daughter," Wren answers. "Though how he convinced anyone to procreate with him, I'll never know."

"*Wren*," I scold, and a reluctant grin lifts her lips.

"Okay, you're right. That's too far. But he's a miserable, grumpy old man."

"He's not that much older than us," I say with a laugh.

She waves my comment away. "Enough about Holden Blankenship. How was your shift at the store?"

I lean back on the bench, crossing my ankles one over the other. "We walked in on Cam and Ellie making out in the storeroom."

"Oof."

"Oof is right," Alex grumbles. "His hand was up her skirt."

I nudge his shoulder with my own. "Alex, when a man and a woman really love each other—"

"They go fishing," he interrupts me, his chocolate eyes twinkling like twin stars in the night sky.

My lips twist to keep from smiling.

"Is fishing an innuendo?" Wren asks, her gaze bouncing between the two of us.

"No," we answer in unison, voices blending together as seamlessly as the stitches on the handmade flannel quilt we ate our picnic breakfast on this morning.

Fourteen

HAZEL

We get rained out of the concert. The drizzle starts just before the main act comes out and switches to a downpour sometime after his fifth song. My cream floral top is almost transparent, sticking obscenely to my skin, the ties between my breasts drooping and the bell sleeves heavy with rainwater. My denim shorts are damp, riding lower and lower on my hips as Alex and I run through town, making a mad dash for the truck, puddles splashing all the way up to our thighs. I've got my sandals in hand, my bare feet slapping against wet pavement.

Wren and Stevie, who met us at the concert after we finished dinner, had both found closer parking spots. We lost them in the crowd a while ago, each promising to stop at the farm to say goodbye before we left tomorrow.

When we round the bend to our hidden parking spot, I slip in mud, my legs sliding out from beneath me. Alex's hands are at my waist before I can fall, hauling me against his chest.

His breath is hot on my ear as he asks, "You okay?"

I nod, and after a beat, he lets go of me.

We're both drenched as we shut ourselves into the truck, the wet heat of our clothes making the windows fog in a way that is sure to attract patrolling police officers at this time of night. I crank the engine, turning the AC on low so our sopping clothes don't freeze to our skin.

I glance over at Alex, and my lips stretch into a smile. "You look like a drowned rat."

One of his eyebrows quirks. "You're one to talk."

A laugh bursts from my chest when I pull down the sun visor and catch my reflection in the rearview mirror. I *do* look like a drowned rat. My hair is plastered to my forehead and shoulders in thick clumps, and my once beautifully winged eyeliner is smudged down my cheeks.

Alex is chewing on his bottom lip, humor etched in every line of his face as he watches me under the harsh overhead lights in the ancient truck. His hand finds my face, smoothing a thumb with gentle pressure against my cheek.

My skin burns beneath his touch, no longer cold and damp from the rain but zinging and heating.

When he's satisfied with the state of one cheek, he moves to the other, his full bottom lip trapped between his teeth in concentration. I don't understand the feelings roiling through my body, but it's obvious I'm not affecting him the same way he's affecting me. And thank God for that.

"There," he murmurs, his breath dancing across my face. He grins at me, one corner of his mouth twitching up before the other. "Good as new."

His eyes focus on the goose bumps prickling my exposed skin. "Cold?" He fidgets with the heat settings, making warm air push through the vents a moment later. "Let's get back and get you out of those wet clothes."

"Yeah," I mumble through my lips, hooking my hand around the gearshift. But when I press the gas, the tires only spin, the truck staying firmly in place.

Alex's eyes are wide and glinting in the darkness as they meet mine. "Oh, no."

I press the pedal again, and the tires spin once more. I can just imagine mud spraying against the trees behind us, splashing in big heaps into the river.

"Stop!" Alex yells, and I immediately lift my foot off the gas. "We'll just get deeper in the mud."

"Oh."

A chagrined smile cracks his mouth, making his cheeks light up in a faint pink. "Sorry, I didn't mean to yell."

I shrug off his apology since it's not even necessary. "What do we do?"

Large hands slide down his face, the long fingers tipped with clean, short nails. "I need to think."

"Okay," I say, and for a moment, there's only the sound of the AC and the pelting rain filling the cab.

"Okay," he repeats, breaking the sound machine tropical storm playlist. He clicks on the overhead light, searching the floorboards.

"I don't think you're going to find AAA down there."

The look he gives me is equally playful and scathing, still bent over feeling the floor. "Does this town even *have* AAA?"

"Not a chance."

His grin is roguish, a zap to my system, and I feel like I'm looking at one of the men on the worn covers of the paperbacks lining the shelves in Lucy's apartment. I'm struck with the strong urge to close the space between us and press my lips to the smile, see if it feels as dangerous as it looks.

I shut the thought down as quickly as it flits through my head. *That* absolutely cannot happen, no matter what kind of romantic comedy Upside Down I've landed in with *Alex*, my best friend, trapped in the mud with rain sluicing down the fogged-up windshield.

"That's what I thought," Alex says, completely missing the thread of tension pulling taut between us, and I'm entirely grateful for that. I think.

Alex sits up, pulling up one of the mud-stained floor mats. "I need to put these under the tires to gain some traction."

"Okay," I say, reaching for the one below my own seat. I don't know whether this solution actually works, but it *sounds* legitimate, and that's enough for me.

"Be right back," Alex says, and he hops from the passenger seat. The headlights illuminate his frame as he walks around the front of the truck, bending down to shimmy one of the mats under a tire. Rain is sluicing across his shoulders, making his linen shirt stick to every curve of hard, unyielding muscle. Until recently, I hadn't noticed how much he looks like a piece of art, a statue cut from marble and painstakingly shaped to perfection. His hair is an inky sheet across his forehead, and the harsh headlights make his skin appear even paler, his stubble that much darker.

When his hand pounds against the hood, I jump, snapping out of my trance and hoping he didn't catch me staring. I don't know what's gotten into me on this trip. It's like I visited my hometown and reverted back to the hormone-ridden teenager I was in high school, lusting after any guy who'd give me the time of day. And Alex gives me much more than that. Sometimes his focus is so intense it's like he's cracking my head open and peering inside.

Alex pats the hood once more, motioning with deliberate hand gestures for me to do *something*. I just have no idea what.

Hot summer raindrops splash against my skin as I roll down the window and Alex sidles up next to me.

"Hit the gas." His gaze is focused on the back driver's side tire. "Slowly."

For a split second, when I gently press my foot to the gas pedal, it feels different this time, like the tire had a tenuous grip on the floor mat and lost it, sliding back into the mud.

"Stop," Alex says, his jaw clenching in concentration. His dark eyes meet mine once more. "I think I'm going to have to push. I'll tap the back when it's time to hit the gas and again if we're not moving. Wait for my taps."

I nod, taking in his instructions. If Alex told me the best way to get this truck unstuck was to lie on the ground and let him roll the tires over my prone body, I'd probably listen. That I have that kind of trust in him should probably scare me, but as he taps the back of the truck, there's only a warmth spreading through my chest and dripping down my middle.

My foot hits the gas with more pressure than last time, trying to hurry this along so Alex doesn't have to stand in the rain any longer. But I think I severely misjudged things, because there's a loud curse from the back of the truck, and when Alex appears in front of my window again, his skin is speckled with mud.

I press my lips together to keep from laughing, but it bubbles out anyway. Alex is *covered*. His white linen shirt is splatter-painted, and his face is now dotted with faux freckles.

"You should do a makeup tutorial like this," I say, trying my best to hold in my giggles. "People have spent years trying to perfect the fake freckles look."

His teeth are a slash of white amid the mud caking his face. "Oh, you think this is funny?"

I nod, pressing my fingers to my lips to cover my smile.

"That's it," he says, reaching into the truck and gripping the inside handle. The door swings open, and his hands are on my thighs before I can register what's happening. His fingertips smear mud across my skin, painting me the way I would a canvas, deliberate and messy, strategic and wild. He has the attention of an artist as he covers me in thick, brown mud.

When his eyes meet mine, they're untamed, just shy of feral. "There. Fair is fair." And then he shuts the door and disappears behind the truck once more, his hands propped on the bed.

"Slow, Lane," he yells over the sound of the rain. "Go slow."

This time when I press the gas with just a tiny amount of pressure, Alex's hands and shoulders and thighs straining to push forward, the tires gain the tiniest bit of traction before slipping once more.

"Reverse and then go again," Alex bellows, and I follow his instructions.

The tires grip the mats, and the truck lurches forward amid the noise of Alex's exclamations that sound like a mix of groans and cheering, like when a weightlifter is finishing a snatch.

With the truck safely on the road, I put it in park and jump out. Alex has his fists in the air, a triumphant smile on his face. He's covered in mud, dirty and rugged and so un-Alex-like that I don't stop to pause before launching myself into his arms. His own are around me in an instant, spinning me around in the mire like some backcountry version of a ballroom dance.

I've never felt more like a Jane Austen heroine in my life.

Alex drops me to my feet, my bare toes squelching in the mud, and his eyes travel over my body in a way that makes it flush with heat. "I got you all muddy," he says, a crinkle forming between his brows.

I look down, seeing what he sees—my creamy floral top covered in grime, the front of my light-wash cut-offs caked with mud, my thighs painted brown by his fingertips. We are *filthy*. Like twin street urchins in a period piece. And it makes loud, raucous laughter overflow in my chest and pour out of my mouth into the humid, rainy night.

That crease between Alex's eyes moves to their corners as his lips lift in a smile, his own laughter joining mine. My sides hurt, and my chest aches with the force of it. It feels like something snatched from a movie screen or ripped from the pages of a book and brought to life by pure, effervescent, glittering magic. I want to capture it in a snow globe and shake it on the days that feel dark, the moments that life feels *hard*.

This moment is dazzling and whimsical, a dream I never want to wake up from. It's a sprinkle of pixie dust, smoke billowing from a candle on a birthday wish, wings fluttering as a lucky butterfly takes flight, hope surging as a falling star skates across the night sky. It's enchanted.

THE MUD IS DRY and cracking by the time the truck rumbles over the gravel driveway at my parents' house. All the lights are off inside, meaning Mom and Dad have retired for the night and Cam and Ellie have sequestered themselves in Cam's childhood bedroom.

I put the truck in park and glance at Alex, unable to make out anything but a solidly muscled form in the darkness.

"I can't go inside in these dirty clothes. I'll drip mud everywhere," Alex says.

"Are you suggesting you strip naked and then stroll in?"

"Yes, that's exactly what I was thinking," he deadpans, his arm resting on the back of the bench seat and tugging at a lock of my hair.

I twist in my seat, my wet clothes squelching against the worn leather. "Then what's your plan, if not streaking? I don't know if you've heard, but it's somewhat of a town tradition."

His head rolls against the headrest. "I hear you're a legend. You should probably show me how."

I snort, the sound barely audible over the rain pounding overhead.

"Is there a hose?" Alex asks, his dark eyes darting across the yard.

I sit up straighter, shutting off the engine. "Yes. Good idea."

"Perfect."

The passenger door squeals on its hinges as Alex props it open. When we meet in front of the truck, he eyes me in the pale light of the crescent moon. "Do you think you're clean enough to go inside and get some clothes for me? I don't want to drip water all the way down the hall."

I give him a little salute and lead him around the side of the house on tiptoes. I don't know *why* this feels clandestine, like the times I snuck out to visit my high school boyfriends in the dead of night for some *fishing*, but it does, and I treat this like I'm a world-class spy on a mission to infiltrate the government.

"Quit acting like you're James Bond," Alex says from behind me, loud enough to wake the dead.

Spinning around, I hiss, "Be quiet. You're going to blow my cover!" His laughter rings out over the sounds of the rain and the crickets and the frogs.

With the faint moonlight and glittering stars as my guide, I fumble through the dark until I locate the hose, and it sputters to life beneath my fingertips, gurgling before icy water sprays over my feet, which are caked in mud.

I yelp, and when Alex stifles a chuckle, I spray him directly in the chest.

His breath whooshes out between his teeth. "I think my balls just took up permanent residence inside my body."

My palm connects with his muscled shoulder, shoving. "Oh my gosh, I don't need to hear about your *balls*."

His grin is a flash of white, all bright teeth and wicked intent. "You haven't heard anything yet," he says, and I press my thumb over the mouth of the hose so the spray hits him with more force.

The laugh that rumbles from his chest is music, a movie score playing through my head, as I dash into the house and down the hall, avoiding the creaky floorboards so I don't wake my parents. Mom would be all too thrilled with this turn of events and would most likely bring up baby names around the breakfast table tomorrow morning.

Somehow, my childhood bedroom no longer smells like apples, like the thick wax candles Mom makes in her shop that are always burning around the house and the farmhouse. No, it smells like Alex. Starch and citrus, like clothes left on the line to air dry in the summertime. The scent is so thoroughly caked into the walls and linens that I don't think it will ever smell like apples in here again.

I rifle through Alex's bag, my fingers sliding against a soft, worn shirt and cotton shorts. I know for a fact he will peel this shirt off once the lights are out and he thinks I'm not looking, then slip between the cold bed sheets in nothing but these shorts, but I can't bring myself to leave the shirt. Topless Alex feels dangerous, and I don't think I'm ready or brave enough to consider why.

I fumble through the dark once more, following the sounds of the hose, Alex's clothes gripped in the fist I'm not sliding against the ancient wooden siding. The gurgling of the hose becomes louder and louder until I—

Smack into something hard. And wet. And naked.

Alex's hands are on my shoulders, steadying me, but all I can think about is the feeling of skin against skin, the expanse of my stomach exposed from my wet denim shorts sliding down my hips connecting with the light dusting of hair on his own. His palms on the curves of my shoulders and my empty one pressed against his chest. His—

Alex pushes me back firmly, the space between us filling with darkness.

"You're *naked*," I sputter. They're the only words running on a loop in my brain. Alex is in front of me. *Naked*. And I don't know why, but I'm wishing for the earth to defy gravity and spin a little faster so I could enjoy the view under the champagne and periwinkle shades of sunrise.

The thought makes a hot blush break out across my chest and climb up my neck until it's suffusing my cheeks. Maybe the darkness isn't so bad. Light would give me away, betray whatever confusing feelings are swirling through my brain.

"Well, yes. I did ask you to bring my clothes," Alex says, his voice sounding tight, and in the sliver of moonlight, I can see him covering himself. Suddenly I'm a demure Victorian maiden, and the sight of *all that skin* is making me in desperate need of some smelling salts.

"I still didn't realize you'd be *naked*, Alexander," I say, resorting to his full name in my flustered state.

"Stop saying *naked* like that."

"Like what?" I ask, genuinely curious. To my ears, I'm saying it with reverence, the way you would talk about gelato or Princess Diana.

"Like you just drank one of those nasty juice shots you get from the farmers' market."

I *wish* looking at Alex right now was as unpleasant as the cayenne and turmeric shot I have to hold my nose while downing. It would make things a lot simpler.

"I'm *not* saying it like that," I protest.

"Then how are you saying it?" Alex asks. His voice is rough, like sandpaper against untreated wood or harsh stubble against delicate skin.

"I don't know," I answer honestly. "But not like that."

He holds my gaze in the dark, the brown glinting gold, winking with refracting starlight.

Finally, he asks, "Can I have my clothes?"

Now that he's mentioned them, they're hot coals, burning the palms of my hands. I shove the wad against his chest, my fingers brushing against smooth, velvety skin covering hard, unyielding muscle.

I spin around as he bends down, pulling the shorts over his legs. This moment feels like a lit match, waiting to lap at gasoline and go up in flames.

My heart thumps wildly in my chest, and my blood thrums in my ears, drowning out the sounds of fabric rustling and the hose being turned off. Then we're only left with crickets. Literally and figuratively.

"I could use a drink right about now," Alex whispers, and it cuts through the tension, making my shoulders ease and loosen where they're propped against the side of the house.

I swivel, keeping one shoulder against the siding, and my eyes trail down his form. The shorts ride low on his hips, and that worn tee stretches across his shoulder blades. It's much more comfortable to look at him like this, if not less exciting. All that bare skin was making those confusing butterflies take flight again.

"There's homemade apple juice in the fridge."

The smile he gives me is a slow curl of his lips, and I feel it down to the tips of my bare, dirty toes. "That's not exactly what I meant."

"I know," I say, the corners of my own mouth hitching up. "But it's the best around. Come on."

Fifteen

ALEX

Early morning sunlight glitters through the white linen curtains, and the smell of cooking bacon wafts down the hall. My chest is bare, the shirt Hazel brought me last night lying in a wrinkled heap next to the trundle.

I sit up slowly so the mattress doesn't creak and allow my gaze to travel over Hazel's sleeping form. Her caramel hair is draped across the floral-printed pillowcase, looking like spun silk in the dappled light from the windows. Her lips are parted slightly, and she looks so young like this, like she hasn't changed at all from that girl in the yearbook photos, that my desire to pummel all those boys who treated her badly returns with a searing bolt through my chest.

She doesn't stir as I stand, tugging the worn gray tee back over my shoulders, and let myself out of her bedroom. Things felt *different* between us last night, like a page was turning in our story, and I'm scared to see how she's going to react in the light of day. I don't want to be there if she wakes up and regrets those lines starting to blur between us with flirty remarks and lingering touches.

The wooden floorboards creak beneath my weight as I make my way down the hall and around the corner, the scent of cooking breakfast getting stronger the closer I get to the kitchen. Stevie is at the stove, her long, silky black hair tied in a knot on top of her head.

"Morning," she says when she sees me, lines crinkling around her eyes. Her smile is a slash of white against the dark tan of her skin.

"Morning. Where is everyone?" I ask, looking around the kitchen.

She flips the bacon in the skillet with her spatula. "The farm and store are always crazy busy during Trail Days, but Aunt Ava wanted you guys to have a lazy morning, since apparently, you and Hazel were up so late last night," she says, eyebrows arching high on her forehead.

I palm the back of my heating neck. "How'd she know that?"

Stevie chuckles. It's a little deep, a little raspy, just like her voice. She throws me a look over her shoulder. "Aunt Ava knows *everything*."

"That's terrifying." I lean a hip against the counter.

"Imagine trying to keep things from her in high school. We never got away with anything."

My lips quirk. "I can't imagine. I got away with everything."

The crackling of the bacon quiets as Stevie uses tongs to lift it from the cast iron and onto a chipped plate lined with a folded paper towel. "Uncle Silas may have been shocked to hear about Hazel streaking through the cemetery, but Aunt Ava definitely was not." She turns to face me after pulling the last slice of bacon from the pan, her mouth curving into a smile. "It's how she also knows that you're in love with Hazel."

I swivel around to make sure the hall is clear before turning wide eyes on Stevie. When her smile only grows at my lack of denial, I slide my hands down the plane of my face, my palms barely muffling my groan.

"Am I really that obvious?"

She sucks her lips behind her teeth, not managing to contain her grin. "Only to those of us with eyes."

I sag against the counter, my heart beating in my throat.

"Your secret's safe with me," Stevie says, voice softening, the mirth dissipating.

"I guess," I say. "But it's only a matter of time, right? You're not the first person to corner me about this."

Stevie regards me carefully, and I can tell she sees more than I want her to. I have a feeling Stevie has spent a lot of her life watching, noticing all the things no one else does. "Do you *want* it to stay a secret?"

"No," I say, and it comes out like a moan, like a desperate plea. "No, I don't, but I'm terrified of the outcome of her finding out before she's ready. Of her *never* being ready."

"I don't know how much you know about Hazel's past relationships," Stevie starts.

"I know there's a hardware shop owner and an insurance salesman I'd love to meet in a dark alley."

Her lips twitch again before the serious look returns to her face. "Hazel hasn't had the best luck with men. She's so…" Stevie trails off, searching for the word. "Good. Hazel's so good. She gives everything to the people she loves. And they've rarely given it back to her."

"I won't do that." The vow rasps out of me.

Stevie nods. "I believe you, and I know Hazel does too. Your friendship means more to her than anything, and you have to realize how scary that would be for her to risk."

My throat tightens against the lump forming there.

"Things were so dark for her after Sebastian. I mean, you know. You were there," Stevie says, and my head dips as a flood of memories rushes through me. "She was so lost, so broken. She wasn't painting, and she was hardly working. *You* were her lifeline. You and Cam and your friend group in Nashville. You all brought her back to life.

"And that has to be *terrifying* to risk, Alex. She may feel ready to put her heart on the line again, but I don't know if she's capable of putting you on the line. She can bounce back from another broken heart, but she can't bounce back from losing you. I don't think she's even let herself consider you because that risk is more than she's willing to bargain for," Stevie says, her voice thick.

A door creaks open down the hall before I can respond, and Stevie and I jerk into action, pretending like the conversation never happened. I'm pulling mason jars from the cabinet when Hazel shuffles into the kitchen, her gauzy sleep shorts and tank looking wrinkled, her hair a mess of golden-brown waves.

"Morning," she says, her mouth stretching into a smile brighter than the sunshine cresting over the mountains outside.

"Morning," I echo, pouring her a glass of orange juice from the pitcher on the counter.

Her hands wrap around the jar, and she takes a sip before sidling up next to Stevie. "Can you move to Nashville so you can be closer to me?"

Stevie grins, but it looks strained. "I don't think so. Your dad wouldn't be very happy with me."

"My dad couldn't care less," Hazel says, bumping her shoulder with Stevie's.

"I don't know," Stevie says, cracking an egg over the skillet. "You and Cam ducked out of here. Someone's got to hold down the fort."

"What did I do?" Cam says, rounding the corner, rubbing his eye with the hand that's not wrapped around Ellie's.

"Moved away to chase your dreams," Hazel drones.

"And then you moved away to chase your brother. Twice," Cam says, a smile flickering across his lips.

Hazel scoots next to me, leaning into my shoulder. Her skin is smooth and warm against mine, and having her next to me like this makes everything feel right.

"I was chasing Alex to Nashville," Hazel says. "Don't let your ego get out of control."

Cam sits on one of the barstools. "Then how come you didn't live with him?" he asks, tone teasing.

"Alex never offered," Hazel says, crossing her arms over her chest and fixing me with her best impersonation of a glare.

"He would never make the mistake of giving up the bachelor pad again," Ellie intones, pouring herself a glass of orange juice before sitting next to Cam.

Hazel's eyes dart up to mine. "Alex hasn't even dated in, like, a year."

I swallow, my mouth suddenly dry, because all these hints—not offering to let Hazel live with me, not dating since she moved here—are all bound to add up in someone's mind soon enough.

I see the exact moment it does for Ellie. Her eyes light imperceptibly, fixing on my own. A smile tugs at her lips, and she says, "Maybe he's holding out for someone special."

"A nun who's willing to leave the convent for me," I say quickly, grateful my voice doesn't betray the anxiety roiling inside me.

"Or a mail-order bride," Hazel offers.

Stevie transfers the fried eggs to a plate and says, "Maybe a Nigerian princess you meet online who needs access to your bank account and social security number."

I nod sagely. "That's exactly what I'm waiting for. Something special."

I was worried that in the light of day, without darkness as a safe cover, things would go back to normal between Hazel and me. That this little bud of *different* blooming between us would die out before it got a chance to flower.

But as Cam steers his SUV into Hazel's driveway that evening, the setting sun slicing through the windshield, the tenuous changes still feel present. Hazel's knee bumped against mine somewhere just over the Tennessee state line and stayed like that. And when I told her the design she was working on for a client on her iPad was stunning, a pretty pink blush, delicate as a rose, colored her cheeks.

"Thanks for the ride," I tell Cam as he helps pull our bags out of the trunk.

"No problem, man." He turns to Hazel, holding her bag out in front of him. "Want me to carry this up for you?"

"I can get it. I'm going up," I tell him.

Cam's eyes narrow as he hands me the bag, his gaze darting between me and Hazel's retreating form. "Ah," he says, brows arching, a smug look crossing his features.

"What do you mean 'ah'?" I ask, but I glance over my shoulder to make sure Hazel is out of earshot.

"Ellie told me something was going on between you two."

My irritation is growing, because at this point, *everyone but Hazel* knows, and that's a recipe for disaster, especially with someone as skittish as she is.

"Nothing's going on."

Cam's smile widens. "Okay."

I shove his shoulder, and he laughs. "Get out of here. I still haven't forgiven you for the scene at your mom's shop."

His head falls back now, the laughter growing louder, and I shoot him one more glare before following Hazel's tracks up the stairs.

The door to Hazel's upstairs apartment is open, the cool blast of the AC blowing out into the sticky, humid heat of early summer. The bag she carried up is in a heap on the floor right over the threshold, so I drop the two bags in my arms down next to it and follow her soft humming through the apartment.

I find her in the bathroom, washing her face. A grin, small and almost shy like the ones she's been giving me since last night, curls her lips as I lean against the doorframe.

"I always feel really gross after traveling and have to wash my face as soon as I get home."

I thought I knew everything there was to know about Hazel, all of her little routines and funny quirks, her milk-to-coffee ratio and how she can never stick with one perfume. But I'm realizing there are so many bits and pieces I'm missing, intimate details that no matter how close our friendship is, could never fill in every gap. Like how she washes her face after road trips, whether she flosses before bed like she's supposed to, if she hogs all the blankets or seeks the warmth of the person lying next to her.

"That's cute," I say, and wish I could pull the words back until her blush grows deeper, the exact pink shade of my favorite cotton candy ice cream.

Her back is an arched line as she bends down to rinse. My palms itch to smooth down each bump of her spine, to feel the curves of her hips, the silkiness of her skin.

When she stands back up, face dripping, I hand her a washcloth, then resume my stance against the doorframe, arms crossed over my chest. I could watch all her mundane tasks all day and never get tired of the show.

Her eyes meet mine in the mirror, blue like the deepest trenches in the ocean. "Want to order a pizza?"

I nod, and she turns around, dropping the washcloth onto the counter. She stares up at me, a grin flirting with the edges of her lips. "You going to let me out of here?"

No. No, I'd much rather pick her up by those thighs that have been haunting my dreams and set her on the counter so we're at eye-level. So she can watch how much she's destroying my control. So she doesn't have to stand on tiptoes to reach my lips. So I can run my hands up and down every exposed bit of skin until my mind is a swirling mess and all that's left is *Hazel*.

My feet shuffle back, allowing her the tiniest amount of room to escape, and her body brushes against mine as she leaves. It's an exquisite torture, and hope spears through me at the tiny hitch in her breath as we line up for one instant before she disappears down the hall.

I'm unraveling, but I think she might be too.

The pizza arrives thirty minutes into the movie Hazel picked out—*13 Going on 30*. I pay the delivery guy and settle back on the couch next to Hazel, the open pizza box balanced on my lap.

Her shoulder leans into mine as she lifts a slice from the box, and a warmth spreads through my middle when she doesn't pull away, her body stuck to mine like Velcro.

The pizza disappears slice by slice, but I don't dare move the box and risk Hazel slipping back to her corner of the couch. Sitting this way feels so right, I don't think I'll ever be able to go back to our bodies being on opposite ends with our legs stretched out under a shared blanket.

When the credits roll, Hazel sighs dreamily. "I love that movie. Want to watch another?"

What I want is to press her body into these couch cushions and explore it with my mouth and hands. What I want is for her to look at me like she is right now and never stop. What I want is *everything*. But I know she's not ready for that.

I smile down at her, my fingers reaching up to tuck a stray wisp of hair behind her ear before I can think better of it. I hope she's too tired to remember it in the morning. I know she can't be fully awake with the way she leans into my touch, the hum starting in the back of her throat. There's no way she'd be this responsive if her eyelids weren't drooping. If the busyness of the weekend wasn't crashing over her in waves.

"Better not, sleepyhead," I murmur, and her mouth hitches in a smile at the nickname. "I'm going to toss this." I hold up the pizza box in my lap.

She curls against the couch cushions where my body was the moment I get up, and I know that the way she was snuggled against me was purely for comfort. I can't bring myself to mind. I'll take anything she's willing to give.

When I come back after throwing out the pizza box, Hazel is sitting up, more alert. Her bottom lip is tucked between her teeth, and a furrow is etched in the space between her brows.

"Your phone vibrated, and I thought it was mine, so I checked it," she says, holding my phone out to me. "It's Chloe."

Cold travels up my arm, slicing through my heart at her hollow tone. I grip my neck with the back of my hand, swiping open my phone to glance at the message. "She texted me last week, saying she was thinking about buying a condo."

Hazel gives me a flat look that manages to look even flatter in the milky light of the TV. "Alex, she's not interested in *buying a condo.*"

Irritation crawls through me and seeps out my pores at the unfairness of this situation. I can practically feel Hazel slipping through my fingers over the girl *she* set me up with on the date *she* wanted me to go on.

"Well, that's all *I'm* interested in," I tell her, enunciating each syllable.

Hazel stands, the blanket we were sharing pooling on the floor in front of the couch. She picks up our cups and moves into the kitchen, flipping the sink on. Every move she makes is brisk.

"Why won't you just go out with her again?" she asks, not looking up. She's using a sponge to clean out our sticky glasses, steam rising from the hot water and turning her hands an angry red.

"I don't want to go out with her again." I have to cross my arms to keep from reaching for her, to keep from pulling her against me and showing her with my hands and mouth and teeth exactly who I want to be spending my time with.

Hazel looks up at me, fire behind her eyes. "Then who do you want to go out with, Alex?"

My teeth ache from how tightly I clench my jaw, and my muscles twitch with restraint. She holds my gaze, not backing down, and I see it there, that flicker of fear behind her eyes that melts my aggravation.

I move around the counter, shutting off the water. Her hands are fiery red and hot against my skin as I cup them with my own. "You'll hurt yourself," I say, tracing one finger over her palm, mapping out every line and divot.

"I don't mind," she says, her shoulder lifting in a shrug.

I meet her eyes through the fringe of my lashes. "I do."

She holds my gaze, and her throat works as she swallows. "You don't want to go out with Chloe again?"

"No," I say softly, wondering how much she can read in my eyes, in my pulse pounding against her fingers grazing my wrist.

Her chest lifts as she breathes in, holding it for a heartbeat before stepping back, carving the distance between us as surely as a river wears away rock to form a canyon.

"Okay," she says, and her voice sounds a little shaky. "I'll find someone else for next week."

Sixteen

ALEX

THE LOUD CLANK OF weights smacking against metal grates against my already frayed nerves on Monday morning. I'm at the gym with Adam, my body slicked with sweat from pushing myself hard for the last hour, trying to clear my head and burn away the frustration of the last twelve hours. Everything unraveled so quickly last night. One moment, Hazel was curled against me, and the next, she was picking out women to set me up with on our next blind date.

It feels like one step forward and two steps back. Before, I just had to convince Hazel to see me differently, to consider *me*. But now I'm fearing she *has*, and that scared her more than anything. Square one would be an improvement to being off the board entirely.

"What's going on with you?" Adam grunts from next to me, where he's doing a set with free weights.

"Nothing," I answer. Because I really don't want to talk about it. Adam and Kelsey had the simplest, least complicated love story in history. They met during orientation week of their freshman year of college, became friends, and dated other people. Then, when they were both single at the same time in their junior year, Adam asked her out, and she said yes. There were no worries about ruining their friendship or possibilities that things might end badly between them. Adam looked at his newly single friend across the room at a frat party and knew she was the one. I was shocked when they told us they were planning to get married right out of college, but if they've ever hit a rut in their relationship, I haven't seen it. They've been strong pillars, anchors in a storm, holding each other up and making each other better for over a decade.

"Oh, sure," Adam deadpans, eyes rolling so far into the back of his head that I'm sure he can see another realm.

I ignore him. I don't get frustrated easily. I'm usually pretty easygoing, and despite the anxiety I sometimes feel in new social situations, I can stay unruffled.

But Adam has always had a way of getting under my skin. So I learned at a young age how to burrow just as far beneath *his*.

"Your form is wrong," I tell him, knowing full well that it's not.

"No, it's not."

"It is, actually," I say, dipping into a lunge, my calves burning with the exertion. "I coughed up the money for the personal trainer. *You* were too cheap."

"Oh, with the personal trainer again," Adam groans, his eyes rolling once more.

I swear I don't know how he doesn't get dizzy with how often he does that.

"I was an athlete," he says, voice taut, and I know I'm making progress.

The edges of my lips lift in a smile, and I have to hold it back. All my progress will be decimated if he knows I'm enjoying this.

"Oh, with the athlete thing again," I parrot. "You played tennis in high school."

His eyes flare, and I know I've hit the target. "Tennis is a physically demanding sport," he says through clenched teeth, standing straight up, shoulders tense and workout forgotten.

I keep lunging, ignoring his posture. "I ran cross country."

"Congrats, dipshit. I ran just as much as you *and* played an actual sport."

"And yet you still don't have the correct form when you do a deadlift." My words overlap his, and it takes all my self-control to keep from laughing at the look on his face.

His breath pushes through his nose slowly, his eyes narrowing. The tree trunks he calls arms cross over his chest. "So things went badly with Hazel this weekend, huh?"

Screw him for being so perceptive.

"No, we're actually engaged now. Thank you."

"Ah, so this text she just sent you is a confirmation of the wedding planner she's booked, then?"

I pause mid-lunge and drop my weights to the ground before snatching my phone from his hand. Hazel hasn't texted me since last night, which is a little odd, because I can usually count on waking up to texts she sent me late at night, when I'm already fast asleep, asking if it's okay to eat expired yogurt or if she's supposed to buy toothpaste with or without fluoride when she orders her groceries.

This morning, there was nothing, and it only confirmed my suspicions that things between us are fractured.

The breath heaves from my chest, and my shoulders slump when I read her text. It's two tickets to country swing dancing lessons for Saturday.

Alex looks over my shoulder, and I know I must look like a kicked puppy when his only response is "I'm sorry, man."

I push a hand through my hair, damp with sweat. "It's fine."

"At least you have natural rhythm," Adam says, his normally disinterested expression cracking with a twitch of his lips.

I hold back my smile, not wanting to give him the satisfaction. "You're the worst."

Adam ignores this, bending down (in perfect form) to deadlift the bar and weights again. Through gritted teeth, he asks, "So who are you going to set her up with?"

I sink onto the floor, my back against the mirrors, no longer interested in my workout. My elbows rest on my propped knees, my phone dangling between them. "I don't know. Maybe someone from work."

"Because that went so well for you last time."

I shoot him a flat glare, my jaw ticking. "I don't know why I confide in you."

"I don't either," Adam says. "I've told you so many times that I wish you wouldn't."

"Are you done with those?" Parker, a guy Adam and I have met a few times, asks. He points to my discarded weights on the ground.

I push off the floor. "Yeah, let me wipe them down first."

When I come back a moment later, Adam smiles at me, and it looks a little evil. "Hey, Parker would love to go out with Hazel on Saturday."

It's a good thing I haven't picked up the weights yet, or I would have most likely dropped them on my toes. Parker is decidedly *not* the type of man I want to set Hazel up with. First, he has all his teeth. They're bright white, a stark contrast to the deep brown of his skin. As far as I can tell, he has good style. I've never seen him wear Sketchers or cargo shorts to work out in, unlike some other men in this gym. He's here as often as Adam and I are, and he looks cut from stone, with not an ounce of body fat. His shoulders are so broad I'm sure he has to turn sideways to get through doors. He definitely has to duck, because he's well over six feet. He's nice too. Always offering to clean a machine for the elderly women who read books while walking on the treadmill. And I swear to God, one time he actually fought off a mugger who was trying to steal a woman's purse in the parking lot.

"Oh." It's the only thing I can think to say. My high school English teacher would be incredibly proud of my grasp on the English language.

Parker's gaze bounces from Adam and me and back again, clearly picking up on the tension between us (i.e. me incinerating Adam with my eyes Cyclops-style, and Adam grinning from ear to ear).

"I think they'd be great together," Adam says. "Parker's a high school art teacher, and he's also from a small town. He's watched *Love Actually*."

"My favorite movie," Parker chimes in.

My eyes don't leave Adam's. "How do you know all this?"

Adam's shoulders bounce in a shrug. "Parker and I are good friends."

"You don't have friends. You have work acquaintances and a dog and your barber."

"John?" Parker asks, eyebrows lifting as he glances at Adam. "He's good people."

"Who is John?" I ask, feeling like I've stepped into a black and white episode of *The Twilight Zone*.

"My barber," Adam answers easily.

"How does Parker know your barber?" I have the strong urge to press my thumb and forefinger into my eye sockets until I see spots.

"Adam introduced us." He looks to Adam, brow furrowed. "Brunch at Hallister's, right?"

Adam looks at the ceiling, lost in thought. "No, I think it was drinks at Sparrow."

"Ah, you're right." Parker's gaze swivels back to me. "Great guy, John."

I honestly don't know where to start. My brain feels like it's just taken a turn on the tumble dry setting in the dryer. I have completely *not* followed this conversation, and I think I'm more confused than when we started.

"So, Saturday?" Parker asks.

"I…" Pause. Blink. "What?"

Adam looks to be holding back a smile, and I kind of want to hit him for it. No one brings out the tiny sliver of violence ingrained in me from playing wartime video games at much too young an age the way that Adam does.

"Parker said he would go out with Hazel this weekend. Swing dancing, remember?"

The wet paper towel I'm clutching is starting to make my hand sweat and my fingers prune. I think it's probably the only thing tethering me to reality right now when I swear *nothing* is making sense.

I palm the back of my neck with my free hand, shooting Parker an apologetic glance. "I don't really know you," I say.

"Well, when you tried to set her up with someone you do know, you ended up with a bloody nose in a cloth napkin restaurant," Alex deadpans.

Parker winces visibly.

"Plus," Adam says. "I know Parker incredibly well."

To my knowledge, at least until two minutes ago, Adam has interacted with Parker as many times as I have—which is to say, probably five. But between John and brunch and Sparrow, I've come to the conclusion that my brother is just *really bad* at talking about his personal life. Which, I thought, was mostly spending time with me in the gym on weekday mornings and doing puzzles on his dining room table with Kelsey at night.

"Okay," I say finally, and Parker's mouth stretches in a smile. I pull my phone from my pocket and hand it to him. "Would you mind putting your number in here? I'll text you the details."

"Yeah, man, of course," Parker says, taking the phone from my hand and tapping on the screen. "Hazel sounds great, by the way."

Hazel *is* great, and I don't want Parker anywhere near her. Words like *art teacher* and *small town* and *Love Actually* bounce around in my head. He probably owns a butterfly garden and is too carefree to pick a favorite ice cream flavor. And they're both so beautiful that their kids wouldn't have to work for anything in life.

When Parker flashes me another grin, I notice the dimples winking in his cheeks and feel sick to my stomach.

"I actually don't have time for that last set. I've got to get to work, but I'll see you on Saturday," he says to me before turning to Adam. "See you for dinner at your place Thursday. Tell Kelsey I'll bring dessert."

After he leaves, I stare at Adam, no coherent words forming in my mind. Finally, I ask, "What was *that*?"

Adam plucks the now barely damp paper towels from my hand and uses them to wipe down his bar. "What?"

"All that with Parker?"

Harsh lines form between Adam's brows as he squints. "What with Parker?"

"Since when did he become the godfather to your unborn children?"

"Oh." Adam waves me off, tossing the paper towels in the nearby wastebasket. "He's not. John is."

There's a headache forming in the back of my skull, and I suddenly wish I was back on top of The Mountain in Fontana Ridge so the yell I desperately want to let free would echo across the hills.

"Since when did you become best friends with Parker?"

"About a year ago," Adam answers calmly, pulling the weights off his bar.

"You've never mentioned him."

Adam shrugs, sparing me a confused glance over his shoulder. "You never asked."

How early is too early to start drinking? Asking for a friend.

"Anyway," Alex says, sliding the last of the cast-iron plates onto the storage rack. "Parker is a good guy. I think he and Hazel will get along really well."

That's exactly what I'm afraid of.

Seventeen

HAZEL

I'M NOT PROUD OF it, but I blow Alex off for Movie Monday. In the afternoon, I tell him I have cramps, which he knows is a lie, since I was complaining about them two weeks ago. It's possible I tell him too much.

When he tries to FaceTime Tuesday, I ignore the call and tell him I'm in the bath.

Wednesday, he's showing properties to clients.

Thursday and Friday, I actually do get slammed with a work project.

But the distance is less about the paltry excuses I managed to come up with and more about my need for space. From him, yes, but between *us*. Taking Alex to Fontana Ridge turned out to be a huge mistake, because unlike any of the other guys I've ever taken home, he seemed to fit. With my family, with my town, with me.

And what am I supposed to do with that?

He's *Alex*. My best friend. But friends shouldn't make my skin tingle and desire pool hot and heavy behind my belly button. Friends shouldn't haunt my dreams and snare my gaze from across the room.

Friends shouldn't have such amazing butts.

I considered canceling the dates tonight, and as I sit in my car in a mostly full dance studio parking lot, I'm almost wishing I had, because the thought of seeing Alex wrapped in someone else's arms has me seeing red. And that just won't do. I want him to find happiness. I *need* him to find happiness. I need us both to, with people who are okay with our relationship, who will never ask us to give each other up. Because I can't lose him, and right now, I think the only way to ensure that is to stay far, far away until that 5 percent of me that has been fluttering when Alex is around withers away like a delicate flower left in the harsh summer sunshine without water.

Alex's familiar SUV pulls into the parking lot, taking one of the few available spaces on the other side. My heart races as I watch him, waiting for him to see me parked here. As he climbs out, he tugs down the hem of his short-sleeve linen button-up. The top three buttons are undone, revealing a patch of skin that has just started to turn a light golden shade.

His eyes connect with mine across the mostly full lot, and an electric current zings up my spine. Turns out, whatever weird things I was feeling over the weekend aren't a fluke.

I slide out of the car, and we move toward each other in the slow-motion way that main characters do in my favorite films. It feels like magic, kismet, serendipity. A moment ripped from the time-space continuum and frozen, paused.

"Hey," Alex breathes when he's close enough that I can feel it fan against my face.

I get the sense of being caught in a whirlwind, a tornado sucking up all my emotions and spitting them back out in a jumbled mess, nowhere close to where they safely were moments before.

"Hi," I whisper back.

His eyes search my face, reading me the way you do the back of a book in a bookshop, like you're wanting to get the gist of the thing as fast as possible. He looks like he found one worth taking home in a crinkling plastic bag when his lips turn up at the corners. I don't know what he saw in my expression, but I'm glad he's back, smiling at me the way I think he reserves just for me, the tension between us dissipating like dew in the summer sun.

It makes my heart rate return to normal and my breath come out more evenly. It puts me at ease, the way only he can.

"Ready to dance?" I ask, spinning on a booted heel so my fringe skirt swishes around my thighs.

Alex's eyes track the movement, his smile hitching higher. "Born ready."

There's a bubbling sensation in my chest, like fizzy white wine. "Well, I hear you have natural rhythm."

He glances at me, eyes wide. "My Zumba instructor actually told me that once."

I press my lips together to keep from laughing. "You don't say."

Twangy country music filters through the glass doors before we open them. A blast of cool air brushes against my skin, lifting goose bumps in its wake.

Rayne stands in the foyer, her olive skin covered in intricate tattoos that instantly make me want to book another appointment. She smiles when she sees us, and that smile cracks something inside me, that bit of tension that's slid between my ribs. Alex deserves someone kind and lovely and beautiful, someone who can love him without reservation, and Rayne seems like just that kind of person.

"Rayne," I say, a genuine smile lighting across my face. I wrap my arms around her in a quick hug before stepping back. Alex is right behind me, a solid presence at my back, and I have to step around him, my face warming.

"This is Alex," I say. "Alex, this is Rayne."

There's a twinge in my stomach when they shake hands, but I shove it down and flick my eyes away from the touch.

"Nice to meet you," Alex says. His voice is smooth and deep in a way that he never talks to me. This is his date voice, not the teasing lilt he uses when he's flirting or the gruff tone of his morning voice. No, this holds sensual promise, and I wish I wasn't here to hear it.

A grin splits across Rayne's face, and her body becomes boneless as she sinks into his orbit. "Nice to meet you too."

"Hazel says you're an artist."

My skin pulls tight, and when my jaw screams in protest, I realize I must have been clenching it. I take a step back, my boots clicking loudly on the laminate floors. "I'm going to find a bathroom," I blurt, my voice a little louder than necessary.

Alex flashes me a concerned look, but Rayne doesn't seem to notice.

"Cramps," I tell him, and his eyes narrow suspiciously.

Without sparing him another glance, I swivel and disappear down a hallway I'm hoping leads to a bathroom. I need to splash my face with cold water and give myself a pep talk in the mirror.

The bathroom is cold, raising goose bumps on my overheated flesh, and I sag against the door. I need to get it together. Whatever confusing things I'm feeling for Alex *have to stop*. I won't even entertain the thought.

I wet a scratchy brown paper towel and use it to cool off my neck before returning to the lobby. There's another man in our group, standing a few inches taller than Alex. He's, well, *gorgeous*. Honestly, I have no other words to describe him. His dark, fathomless eyes catch on me and seem to sparkle like they're lit from within. His jaw is a firm, cut line, his nose long and straight. His skin is a deep, rich brown and stretched over miles and miles of taut muscle. His charcoal gray shirtsleeves are straining against the bulk of his biceps, looking like they could rip at the seams at any moment, and his long, long legs are clad in jeans that look perfectly tailored but I bet come right off the rack. His body is the unreal standard that clothing brands design their clothes around.

And he's smiling. Right at me.

Alex turns as the stranger's eyes focus on me, and when I finally look at him, there's a furrow between his brow, a flicker in his jaw.

"Hazel, this is Parker," Alex says, but his tone sounds flat. "Parker, Hazel."

Parker doesn't offer his hand, but instead wraps a single arm around my shoulders, giving me the kind of warm, quick hug that you share between friends. When I glance at Alex, his jaw is clamped so tightly I'm afraid he might break a molar.

I squint at him in confusion, but his eyes dart away, focused on the doors to the studio that are now opening.

"Class is starting," Alex grunts before stalking forward, his long legs eating up the distance before the rest of us have even started moving. I flash Rayne an apologetic look, although I don't know why *I* feel responsible for Alex's behavior. He's *her* date, and I'm here with…

I glance back at Parker, and that dazzling pearlescent smile is still in place. That smile sucks me in like a vortex, stealing my full attention.

"Ready?" he asks, and his low, smooth voice evokes the same feelings as being wrapped in a blanket by a rotating fire, hot cocoa warming your hands.

"Let's go."

Parker is an amazing dancer. He moves with fluid grace, and those strong arms mean he's able to dip and lift me with ease. His body is a firm wall against mine as we go through the movements. Both of us have caught on remarkably well, despite my lack of any dancing skill as a child, adding our own flavor to the basic movements the instructors have been teaching us.

Alex and Rayne, however, have not. It seems that Rayne, like me, wanted to dress the part. But while we were doing our warm-up stretches, she told me that the only cowboy boots she could find at the thrift store this week were steel toed, which meant that when she stepped on Alex's foot halfway through the lesson, I could hear the crunch over the sound of the music. He's still dancing, but I swear he's not putting his full weight on his left foot. Which is impeding his movement even more so than before. Because I was right. Whatever Zumba instructor told Alex he had natural rhythm just wanted his number. Alex is, and I say this as someone who has been to *many* random dance parties with acquaintances in LA, the worst dancer I've ever seen.

His movements are stiff, his body tensely shifting and jerking as he tries to follow the instructors' directives. He looks like a baby foal taking its first steps in the world, not a grown athletic man who spends hours in the gym every week. It's like years of running and strategic workouts have killed his body's natural ability to follow a beat.

I grimace when I hear Rayne's raspy "sorry!"

My gaze drifts back to Parker, who's smiling again. That beautiful grin was replaced only momentarily each time the dance instructors showed us a new move. His brow would crinkle in concentration as he committed it to memory, and then he would turn back to me, that excited smile back on his face and ask if I was ready to try it. The truth is, even if I wasn't enjoying this so much, his natural excitement would urge me on. It's like taking a child to the zoo. You have no interest in standing in the sticky heat with the smell of animal dung soaking into your pores, but when the child's face lights up at the sight of a giraffe's head poking out from around a tree, you can't help but be excited too.

There's a pale blue smudge on the side of Parker's long neck, and when I realize it's paint, my lips curve into a smile. I trail the tip of my finger over it. "You have paint here."

His eyes focus on mine, and a faint pink colors his cheeks. If I were to mix this color up on a palette, I'd use watermelon and chiffon to make the rosewater shade.

"A couple of my upcoming seniors came to my classroom to help paint the walls earlier today," he says, not even winded as we move through the dance steps.

We're going slowly because the instructors are working with a few couples one on one to correct their missteps, but I still feel a pinch in my side that signals I probably need to work out more. Maybe I'll join Alex's gym. I don't have a broad enough imagination to picture what Parker would look like with sweat glistening over those taut abs while he's running on the treadmill.

"I bet you're a cool teacher," I tell him, my own words punctuated by little gasps for breath.

Parker slows our movements so I can catch my breath, his hands tightening on my waist. "I don't know about that."

"Oh, absolutely. My high school art teacher was my favorite person in the world."

"Me too," he says, his grin somehow widening. "She's who made me want to teach."

"I considered it for a while too," I say. "But I don't think I'm cut out for it."

"I don't know. You were really patient with Alex earlier."

I was. I stopped to show Alex one of the moves he was struggling with at the beginning of the lesson. It wasn't until I saw the bright slash of red across his cheeks that I realized I'd embarrassed him. Shortly after that was when Rayne stepped on his toe, crunching bone with steel, and I can't help but feel partly responsible.

"I don't think it's the actual teaching part I would struggle with," I say, working through my thoughts. "I just like the freedom of freelance. I like having a new project to work on every few weeks and the ability to do it from anywhere. I didn't go to college, because the idea of tying myself someplace for four years felt suffocating."

He nods as if he understands, and a bolt of surprise slices through me at the admission. I've rarely told anyone my reasons for skipping college. I told everyone I wanted adventure, or to get out of my hometown. That I missed my brother after he moved away. But the truth was, I didn't want to wait to start my life until I was twenty-two. I wanted to start it at eighteen and not look back. Good and bad came from that decision, but now, ten years later, I'm just starting to see the appeal of slowing down. I don't regret the path I took, but maybe I'm ready to try something new. And that's *really* what prompted my move to Tennessee after Sebastian broke my heart in his headboardless bed in his minimalist apartment that he was actually just too cheap to decorate.

"That's great, y'all!" The dance instructor duo, a tall, tan man and a peppy, blond woman, who are dressed like they're headed to a rodeo-themed party—but not an actual rodeo, please note the difference—take their places back at the front.

"It seems like everyone's got the moves down now," the woman says.

"Or as well as they're going to," the man mutters beneath his breath, eyes dashing to Alex and Rayne in the back corner.

"So we're going to just turn on the music for the last fifteen or so minutes and let y'all test it out, make sure you've got those moves mastered before you hit Broadway tonight."

"We should go tonight," Parker says suddenly, right as the music is starting up.

My hands find their places on his body, one palm curving over his shoulder, the other wrapped in his. "Go where?"

"Downtown," he says, starting to move us through the motions, slow at first, with the tempo of the song.

My muscles move on instinct after almost an hour and a half of practicing, so I'm able to focus on his words instead of the dance. *Go downtown. Tonight.* One part of me immediately shoots the idea down because this night is supposed to end at a picnic table with ice cream dripping down my fingers and Alex's smile warming me more than the sweltering summer heat. But another part of me can't erase the sight of Alex pulling Rayne back into his arms after I tried teaching him the dance move he couldn't nail. Of the way they look with his chin coming to rest against her temple, of the words they've been murmuring too quietly for me to hear.

Dancing hasn't been a good date for Alex and Rayne, but they seem to be hitting it off. So maybe this will be good. Maybe extending my night with Parker will mean shrinking that little bit of me that's still focused on Alex's touch until it disappears like a star winking out in the night sky. Maybe it will give that tender bud forming between my two best friends a chance to blossom.

So I say, "Let's do it."

Eighteen

ALEX

The table is shaking with the force of my knee bouncing beneath it. I'm at a Waffle House, sipping my second cup of stale coffee while I wait for Hazel to arrive, all the patrons waiting for a table shooting me heated glares.

Hazel is twenty-three minutes late, and I haven't heard from her since I sat down and texted her and got a response saying she'd overslept and would be here soon.

In unrelated news, it feels like ants are crawling under my skin and my muscles are pulling tight to the point of pain.

I flip over my phone, checking for the thirty-seventh time to see if Hazel has texted back. When there's nothing on my screen but a notification reminding me to pay my credit card bill, I drum my fingers against the sticky table.

Finally, unable to stand the angry stares of people desperate for my table and a plate of smothered hash browns, I text Adam.

Me: **You up?**

Adam: **Why would I still be sleeping at 10AM?**

Me: **I don't know. I figured you must have had a late night since you REFUSED TO TALK TO ME.**

Adam: **I was on my own date. I can't babysit yours too.**

My heavy breath hisses through my nostrils as I press my lips into a thin line.

Me: **I never ask you for anything**

Me: I thought you might be there for me in my one time of need

Me: My bad

Adam: There hasn't been a day since your birth that you haven't asked me for something. The first eighteen months of my life were so peaceful.

Adam: What do you need?

I push a hand through my hair, some of the tension leaving my shoulders. As much as I want to wring Adam's neck 72 percent of the time, I know I can count on him when I really need him.

Me: Hazel bailed on our ice cream debrief last night

Adam: Yeah, Parker told me.

Me: WHAT

Me: YOU TALKED TO PARKER BUT YOU WOULDN'T TALK TO ME?

Me: WE ARE BLOOD

Me: WE SHARED THE SAME WOMB

Adam: Please never mention our mother's womb again.

Me: You seriously blew me off last night but answered PARKER?

Adam: No, we got breakfast this morning.

Me: Oh

Me: WHAT DID HE SAY

Me: HOW DID IT GO

My phone vibrates in my hand with another text from Adam just as a harried Hazel slides into the booth. I slap my phone down on the table, hoping she didn't see the screen.

Her hair is piled atop her head, short pieces sticking out of her haphazard bun. There's no makeup on her face, just a smattering of pale freckles and a natural pink tinge to her cheeks. She's wearing loose, flowy cropped pants and one of her tiny tank tops that's held by straps thinner than my self-control.

"Hey," she says, sounding a little out of breath, like she's been hurrying since I texted her.

Just the sight of her relaxes me. She may have spent the evening with Parker, but she's *mine* this morning. "Hi."

Her nails are painted white and tap against the plastic menu as she peruses it. I remember how they looked last night, wrapped around Parker's hand, and I want to crush something. Preferably the part of my brain that holds on to memories.

Maybe it's that stab of jealousy the mental image produces that makes me ask, "How was the date?"

I'm not sure I want to know. It was good enough for her to ditch ice cream and go out with him after the lessons. The studio was huge, with bright lights and lots of room to move around. The bars downtown are the exact opposite. They're dark and loud, so you have to get close just to hear. The dance floors are cluttered with bodies jostling you into one another. It's honestly perfect for first dates, when intentional touches can feel too forward, but close proximity forces your hand. It makes everything feel looser and easier, with pressure and inhibitions lowered.

Hazel's eyes flick up to me, dark blue ringed in gold. "It was fun. Did you and Rayne do anything after?"

Rayne asked, and I could tell she was interested, but a weight had settled in my gut as I watched Hazel and Parker slide into his truck, heading downtown. When Rayne asked for my number, I didn't give it out just to be nice, the way I did with Chloe. I learned my lesson, and although it had been awkward to explain that I wasn't looking for a relationship right now, it felt good not to lead her on.

So while Hazel and Parker extended their date, I went home and tried to go over my options. The truth is, I don't know what to do anymore. I almost want to call in an audible and end this whole thing. The blind dates are working against me now, and I can feel Hazel slipping away like water between my fingers.

"No, I just went home," I finally tell her, pushing a hand through my hair. "What did you guys do?"

We're interrupted by the waitress, a woman who could easily be a Dolly Parton impersonator, coming to take our order. But after she leaves, Hazel slides her menu behind the napkin holder and glances up at me before looking away again, focused on the cooks at the grill.

"We went downtown for a while and then ended up at that donut place that has all the board games. We stayed there until it shut down."

There's a lump in my throat, so thick and heavy I almost can't swallow it down. "Sounds fun." Even to my own ears, it sounds dispassionate and flat.

Hazel meets my gaze, her eyes narrowing as she searches my expression. I don't know what she reads there, and I don't think I care. At this point, would it be so bad for her to know? It can't be worse than this—her tromping all over my heart without even knowing she's doing it in those worn white cowgirl boots she wore last night.

Her finger traces circles on the sweating glass of water I ordered her. "It was." She hesitates, meets my eyes. "I think I'd like to go out with him again next week."

I'm not surprised by the comment, so it shouldn't feel like a kick to my gut, knocking the wind out of me. But it does. At least with Sebastian, I already knew Hazel was taken, that she was happy and off the market. But no one prepares you for how devastating it is to watch the person you're in love with fall in love with someone else.

She's still watching me, so I school my features into something I hope isn't a grimace. "Sounds good. Parker is a great guy."

Her lips curve into the barest of smiles, and it's an anvil to my chest, a brutal attack on my emotions. "Yeah, he is. He talked a lot about Adam. I didn't realize they were friends."

"Yeah, me neither," I grumble, shifting in my seat.

Hazel's eyes are still tracking my every movement, noting the way I can't sit still, how my fingers drum against the table, and my foot bounces below it. I fear she can see *everything*.

"Do you want to go out with Rayne again?"

"No."

Her brows crinkle. "Really? You guys seemed like you were getting along well."

"I'm pretty sure she broke my toe."

Hazel watches me for a long moment, spinning her plastic cup around on the worn laminate table. "So she can nurse you back to health, then."

"No, thanks." The words come out more toneless than I intended, but I can't bring myself to care.

"So you want a new date for next week?"

I don't want to go out with anyone ever again. "Yes," I say, and then tack on, "Please."

"Okay," she says, her gaze fixing on my tapping fingers. I stop, shoving them under my thighs. "I'll start looking."

I'm grumpy, and my mother can tell. It's why she's been pestering me all through our monthly family dinner at the most bland Italian restaurant in town. I've been eating soggy chicken parmesan and watery spaghetti noodles here once a month since Adam moved out of the house and into his dorm at college. You'd think I'd branch out and try something else—and I have—but this mediocre entrée is the best thing on the menu.

"Alexander, how is work?" Mom asks. She's the only one who has called me Alexander since I started kindergarten, but I know there's no use in correcting her. She's always said that if she had wanted my name to be Alex, she would have put *that* on the birth certificate.

My knife scrapes against the white porcelain plate as I cut through the last of my chicken. It's so soggy I could probably use my fork, but then Mom would comment on my bad manners.

"Work is busy," I say, ignoring the knowing looks my siblings are shooting each other. "I'm actually leading in sales this quarter."

Mom looks delighted, and I wish I could pull the comment back. Kristin Bates is a piece of work, and it's much more fun to disappoint her and test the limits of her Botox than it is to please her.

"That's *wonderful*, honey," she says, clapping her hands together. "Elizabeth just got a raise at work."

I wait for a snarky comment about Ellie's job situation, but it doesn't come, and the tension in my shoulders eases. Ellie worked for our family's property management company for years, with Mom and Dad as her bosses, which put a ridiculous amount of strain on their relationship. But since she quit two and a half years ago, things between them have slowly been repairing.

"My work is lovely. Thank you for asking," Adam pipes up from directly across the table.

He's eating the scallops, which is a bold choice since I'm pretty sure they come from a freezer bag at the grocery store on the corner, and says this from around a bite, which is even more bold considering Mom still sometimes smacks our elbows if we leave them on the table.

Mom ignores Adam, presumably since his mouth is full, and focuses her attention on Cam and Ellie at the other end of the table. "Elizabeth, when are you and Camden planning on having children?"

I choke on my drink, barely managing to keep it from spraying on Adam, whose mouth is now dangling open, half-chewed scallops inside.

"*Mom*, you can't ask people that," I say incredulously.

She looks genuinely confused, and I think there would be a wrinkle between her brows if her skin wasn't stretched within an inch of its life. "I'm her mother. I can ask whatever I want."

"No, you can't," Adam chimes in, scallops now swallowed.

"Whyever not?" Great, Mom is starting to sound like a Puritan again. This always precedes one of her tantrums.

"Because that's private," I interject.

"Again," Mom says, splaying her perfectly manicured hands out flat. "I am her mother. There's nothing private between family."

This time, Cam chokes. Adam and I hold back matching smiles, our cheeks flushing pink and our lips turning white from pressing them together so tightly.

Dad eyes all of us, always more perceptive than Mom. He's also not so oblivious to believe we haven't kept things from our overbearing mother.

"Let's change the subject," Dad says diplomatically and takes a long sip from his drink.

Mom purses her lips, barely containing an eye roll, and leans back in her chair, almost allowing her spine to touch the backrest. Her hands fold together, resting on the table. "Fine. Adam, when are you having children?"

Adam's mouth falls open again, and Kelsey goes red next to him.

"*Mom*," I say again.

"What?" She looks around the table. "I can't ask him either?"

"No," I tell her, squeezing the bridge of my nose with my thumb and forefinger. "You cannot ask anyone about kids. Ever."

The table goes quiet once more, only the faint sounds of Italian music and chatter from nearby tables breaking the silence. Then Mom asks, "Alexander, when do you plan to get married?"

Dad pushes up from his chair, setting his cloth napkin on the table. His hand falls onto Mom's shoulder, giving her neck a firm squeeze. "This has been fun, kids. We'll see you next month, if not before."

Mom stares up at him from her seat, unmoving, her pale blond bob falling back from her face. "What are you doing? We're not leaving now. We're in the middle of a conversation. Alex was just about to tell us when he plans to finally settle down and marry."

"I've actually been looking up what qualifications I need in order to become a monk," I say, and Mom swivels back to face me, her eyes wide as saucers. "Celibacy is a gift not all people have the chance to embrace."

"You are not going to stay celibate," Mom snaps.

"Does anyone know where I can purchase a chastity belt?" I ask the table, and Mom's cheeks go red with fury.

"Alexander Malcolm Bates. You are not going to remain celibate." Mom's voice is rising, attracting the stares of people at nearby tables. But I'm too delighted by her anger to feel embarrassed.

"Well," Dad says, slapping his hands together, "that seems like a good stopping point. Good night, kids."

He bends down and whispers something to Mom, who flashes me one more icy glare before picking up her Louis Vuitton purse and following Dad out of the restaurant.

"And that's the story about how Mom yelled at me in public about how I need to be having more sex," I intone like I'm finishing the end of a long story, turning back around to face my siblings.

Our server, who is used to our tradition of ordering dessert after Mom and Dad leave, brings us slices of cheesecake before we can flag her down to ask for some.

As I'm pouring the raspberry preserves over the top, Adam asks, "So are you going to tell them about the situation, or should I?" I glare at him, and he grins. "You look just like Mom right now."

That wipes the expression right off my face. "I don't know what you're talking about."

From down the table, Ellie laughs.

A muscle in my jaw ticks. I don't know where this intense irritation with *everyone* has come from, but it's so unlike me, and I'm not a fan. Back before Hazel decided she was ready to date again, I was okay with the way things were between us. But now I want *more*, and every day that passes without it leaves me a little more desolate.

So no, I don't want to talk to my siblings about it.

"So Alex is in love with Hazel," Adam begins and then yelps when my foot connects hard with his shin beneath the table.

"*Adam*," Kelsey scolds, her dark eyes blowing wide as she stares at her husband.

"We all know," Ellie jumps in.

I drag my palms down my face, pulling the skin tight. Suddenly, I am so, so tired. I've been running myself ragged at work to stay busy. And every time I close my eyes at night, I picture Hazel's hair flying around her as she danced with Parker. Her smile stretched wide, her muscles straining as she stood on tiptoe to hug him when they figured out the steps.

"You know," I say, staring pointedly at Adam, "I left you alone when you dated Kelsey."

"I know, which is why I find it particularly unfair that you won't shut up about Hazel," he grumbles. But I ignore him, turning to face Ellie.

"And I didn't bug you about your forbidden love affair with a tenant." My gaze snags on Cam. "No offense, Cam."

He holds up his hands in a placating gesture, as if to say, *none taken*.

"So I would appreciate some privacy on this."

"I'd love to," Adam says. "In fact, let's not talk about it anymore."

"Oh, shut up," I snap. "I'm going to call you to complain whenever I want, and you're going to pick up and act interested."

He rolls his eyes, but I know he'll do it. For all his bluster, he's incredibly loyal. And if I told him how much I was actually struggling, he would be at my apartment with a six-pack in an instant.

The bad thing is, I don't *want* comfort from them right now. I want Hazel. I'm sad and tired and frustrated, and I just want to curl up on my couch with her feet in my lap and a stupid movie playing on my TV.

But things between us feel strained, like tight muscles after an intense workout, and I don't know how to make it better. Do we just push through it, ignore the awkwardness, and keep going as usual? Even that doesn't hold appeal. For so long, I thought I was okay if I at least had my friendship with Hazel. Sure, I wanted more, but if I had her in *some* way, it was enough.

It's not enough, I'm realizing. It's not enough to have pieces of her. It's like trying to do a puzzle upside down. It can be done, but it's hard and time-consuming. But with Hazel, I'm right side up, and everything in life seems just a little easier, a little brighter.

I'm fraying at the seams, not mending fast enough to keep from unraveling, and I don't know what to do about it.

Nineteen

HAZEL

"You're going to get a permanent wrinkle right here if you hold your face like that any longer." Lucy's blond curls pop up over the top of my laptop as she slides into the booth across from me, a finger pressed to the space between her eyebrows.

I accept the strawberry lemonade she pushes across the table and take a long sip. "I've been working on this one design all day and can't get it right. It's driving me nuts."

"Ah," she says, sipping on her own drink—what looks to be a shot of espresso with milk. "Then you probably need a break."

"That sounds wonderful." My back slumps against the booth, my stiff shoulders rolling back and popping.

"How was the date over the weekend? I forgot to ask yesterday."

This is where I should feel the excitement—the butterflies—but I just don't. I *liked* Parker, well enough to extend our date on Saturday, but there was no spark. He was kind and funny, but he didn't make me feel breathless or set my blood on fire. He was warm, steady. Easy.

"It was…" I hesitate, catching my bottom lip between my teeth. "It was fine."

Lucy's blue eyes widen, her eyebrows inching up her forehead. "That good, huh?"

A laugh bubbles out of me, and Lucy's questioning expression dissolves into a smile, one corner of her mouth hooking up before the other.

"Parker was nice," I say when I finally control myself.

Lucy is still grinning as she watches me closely. "Fine and nice. Sounds like a match made in heaven."

My back presses into the shiny booth seat, and I take a long sip of my lemonade, savoring the tangy sweetness as I think of how to put my thoughts into words.

"He *was* nice, and I can't pinpoint any one thing that was wrong with the date," I say finally, trailing my finger up and down the condensation on the plastic cup.

"But…?" Lucy asks, cocking a brow.

I square my shoulders, letting out a breath through my nose, determination steeling my spine. "But nothing."

Lucy's jaw tightens, and I know she's about to lecture me. She takes almost nothing too seriously in life—she's a free spirit like me, and it's what I love most about her—but she doesn't play around when it comes to love. She's been reading romance novels since middle school, bingeing rom-coms every night, and it's given her unrealistic expectations. She loves easily and with abandon, and she's had her heart broken more times than she can count, but somehow, it's never held her back from trying again.

"Hazel Mae Lane, we don't settle for *nice* and *fine*."

I barely contain my eye roll.

"Love should be sweeping and grand and all-consuming. It should make you feel alive and reckless and steal your breath. It should not be *fine*." She says the word with such disgust that it's like it personally wronged her.

I let out a deep breath, pursing my lips. "You just don't get it, Luce."

Her face softens, but I can still see the determination lingering beneath the surface, ready to bubble over, to force me to drop all my reservations and fall deeply in love.

"What do you mean?" she asks.

"You have all these visions of dancing in the rain and kissing on top of the Empire State Building. You think love is butterflies and stardust and the hazy ambience of a nineties film." There's a desperate feeling in my chest, a clawing sensation, and it's choking me. "But it's not like that. It's loving someone so deeply it hurts and then finding them in bed with their neighbor."

Tears prick at the back of my vision, but it's not even about Sebastian. It's about all the times I was so, so close to having it—that love Lucy clings to so tightly—and having it slip through my fingers time and again. Because Sebastian wasn't my first attempt at love; he was just the latest in a long series of deadbeats who let me down.

"It doesn't have to be like that, Haze," Lucy says, and I want to scream. I want to rage. I want to make her understand while also protecting that little bit of innocence and magic that the world hasn't managed to beat out of her yet.

"No, it doesn't have to be," I say finally, sniffing. "It can be nice, and it can be better than fine if I give it another chance."

The look she gives me is pitying. "It can be better than that."

"What if I don't want it to be?" I ask, my voice rising. "What if I want *fine*? What if I want it to be good, but not great? What if I want it to be something I'd be okay with losing?"

The words hit me like arrows, puncturing my armor. I hadn't realized I felt this way, and it settles on me like a too-heavy blanket, smothering.

"Hazel," Lucy says, her voice choking with sympathy. I have to look away from the compassion in her eyes.

"Sebastian almost wrecked me," I say, not meeting her gaze. "And all the ones before him. I just want something easy. Is that too much to ask for?"

"No," she tells me softly, almost a whisper. "It's not too much to ask for. But that doesn't mean you have to settle for fine. That doesn't mean you should want someone who's easy to give up."

My fingers toy with the plastic straw. "It seems less likely to end in heartbreak."

"It doesn't have to end in heartbreak."

I wish I still had her optimism. I wish I could trust myself in love, trust myself to find someone *good*, but I can't. Which is why I started this whole thing with Alex. And it worked—he found someone exactly like what I'm looking for. Someone nice, with the potential to be more than fine.

I really don't want more than that.

I'M PACKING UP MY things for the day when the bell above the door to Whistling Kettle jangles, snagging my attention. When I look up, two familiar figures are crossing the threshold. A smile curves my lips, the first since my conversation with Lucy a few hours ago.

Wes, my longtime friend from LA, and his wife, Lo, who has become a more recent friend, don't even notice me in my booth. They're focused on the menu behind the counter, Wes' arm running slowly up and down Lo's back, his fingers catching in her hair. She smiles at him, and their gazes lock and hold in the kind of gaze that makes me question everything I told Lucy earlier.

I slip out of my booth, and my sandals pad softly on the floor as I make my way toward them. Lo spots me first, her eyes sliding over Wes' shoulder and catching on mine. A smile lifts her lips, making her freckles stand out brighter on the apples of her cheeks.

"Hazel, what are you doing here?"

Wes turns around and grins. When I sidle up next to him, his arm comes around my shoulder in an easy hug. "Hey, Hazel."

"Hey, guys," I say, my words muffled by Wes' shoulder. "This is my friend's coffee shop. She actually just left for a doctor's appointment, or I'd introduce you."

"Is this the coffee shop where you work every day?" Wes asks, glancing around with dawning recognition.

I nod. "Same one."

Lo's smile widens, her blue-green eyes sparkling under the fringe of her dark copper hair. "We'll have to come by more often, then. What's best on the menu?"

I follow them to the counter, rattling off a few suggestions to Lo, since I know Wes gets the same custom drink at every coffee shop he visits.

Her gaze still locked on the menu, Lo asks, "Is the matcha any good?"

"My favorite," I tell her, and she grins.

"Perfect, I'll order that." She nods in the direction of my table. "Do you mind if we sit with you?"

"Of course not," I say as Wes starts detailing his order to the barista behind the counter. "I'll wait for you guys over there."

A few minutes later, Wes and Lo slide into the booth opposite me, drinks in hand. Wordlessly, I hold my hands out for Wes' cup and he passes it over, grinning.

"You know," he says as I take a sip of the iced latte, "you could just order these yourself instead of drinking half of mine every time I'm around."

I scoot it back across the table, licking the cold foam from my top lip. "I can never get it right. There are too many ingredients and steps. Plus, you may be fine with being a barista's worst nightmare, but I'm not."

Lo snorts, covering her mouth to keep her drink from spewing out.

"Oh, you think that's funny, huh?" Wes asks, his green eyes sparking with amusement.

Gathering herself enough to swallow her matcha, Lo says, "I do, yes. I tell you all the time that one day, someone is going to spit in your drink if you keep asking for something so complicated."

"You assume someone hasn't yet," I say, lips quirking in a mischievous grin, and Wes' mouth falls open. A laugh spurts out of me at his expression. "Kidding. I've never spit in your drink. Scout's honor."

"Well, I was going to invite you to the lake house in two weeks, but now you have me reconsidering," Wes says, pushing a hand through his blond curls.

I look between them. "It's done?"

Almost two years ago, Wes and Lo bought an old lake house a couple of hours from here, and they've slowly been renovating it since. I've hardly seen them in the last couple of months as they've been living there and handling most of the final renovations on their own.

Lo tips her head. "Mostly. There's still a lot of cosmetic work to do, and I'd actually love your help decorating. But the big stuff is done."

"That's so exciting," I tell them, a genuine smile lifting my lips.

"We just got off the phone with Cam and Ellie. We invited them too," Wes says. "Want to come? Ellie mentioned you might have plans with Alex."

Surprisingly, the idea of postponing another date makes me breathe a little easier, tension unfurling from my shoulders. I don't have time to examine what that means, so I say, "I do, but it's nothing that can't be rescheduled."

Lo's eyes light up, glinting like a wave crashing against the shore. "Bring Alex."

"Really?" I ask, looking between them. Wes and Lo have met Alex a few times, since he's Ellie's brother and my best friend, but he's not really a part of the friend group, even though he would be a great addition.

"Of course," Wes says. "I don't know why we didn't think to invite him from the beginning."

"I'm sure he'd love to," I say, running my hands over my thighs to warm them against the blast of AC that just kicked on. "Are you sure there's enough room?"

Wes and Lo exchange a look, as if mentally calculating and wordlessly communicating. Then Lo turns back to me, a smile playing on her lips. "Plenty. Please come."

Nodding, I say, "I'll ask Alex."

My keys rattle in the lock as I let myself into Alex's apartment for movie night. After my meltdown to Lucy a few hours ago, she tried to convince me to hold out for more, but it only strengthened my decision.

"Honey, I'm home!" I yell into the vast abyss of Alex's huge apartment, my arms laden down with bags of takeout.

Since the paper bags are tall enough to cover my face, I can only hear his footsteps. They're echoing down the hall because there's not a stitch of carpet in the ultramodern space, only thin, pure white rugs that Alex has to have professionally cleaned every three months because he's clumsy.

When Alex is close enough that I can smell the starched linen scent of his cologne, the heavy load in my arms is lifted. Brown paper is replaced by dark eyes and a messy flop of wavy hair.

"Hey," he says, one corner of his mouth curving.

That smile feels like warm liquid spreading through my stomach, making my body heat and my skin prickle. It's disarming, my reaction, but it's also like hot cocoa on a winter night, comforting and soothing and delicious.

"Hey," I say back, and he gives me one more dazzling grin before spinning on his heel and heading back down the hall.

"How was your day?" he asks over his shoulder, leading us into the kitchen.

His apartment is basically one large living area, with two bedrooms and two bathrooms off the living room. The kitchen, dining area, and living room are all one space, tastefully separated by strategically placed furniture.

The lighting from the floor-to-ceiling windows covering the expanse of the wall is an artist's dream, but Alex wastes it. Everything in here is minimalist and bland, although expensive and high end. I've been sneaking over trinkets and decor to add pops of color every time I come over. Some of it disappears, showing up back in my apartment a week later, but some stays, like the tiny butterfly painting I set on his stark white shelves a few months back and the little cactus I bought that one time we visited the plant nursery last spring.

"It was good," I say, not mentioning my heart-to-heart with Lucy as I slip a colorful boho home decor book from my purse and onto his coffee table.

The paper bags rustle as he sets them down on the counter and starts unloading our tacos from the truck down the street. I wander into the kitchen, pulling glasses from the cabinet.

"Wes and Lo came into the coffee shop today," I tell him.

Alex pulls the last of our dinner from the paper bags. "Oh yeah?"

"They're pretty much finished with the lake house. They invited us and Cam and Ellie to come down in two weeks to check it out."

"Really?" Alex asks, turning around to lean back against the island, his hands propped on the counter at his hips. His eyes roam my face. "You want to go?"

I shrug. "It sounds fun. We'd have to miss that date, though. And then I'm going to Fontana Ridge for three weeks. So we'd miss a whole month of dates," I say, wondering if he can read the ambivalence in my voice.

Alex watches me for a long moment before saying, "I'm fine with it if you are."

A breath of relief escapes me, and I don't let myself examine what that means. "Yeah, I'm fine with it."

Alex smiles, then. It's the one I love—one side first and then the other. "A lake weekend sounds fun."

"I thought so too," I say, moving around him to get my food from the counter. Tacos in hand, I head for the couch. "What are we watching tonight?"

Alex's footsteps echo behind me, and the couch shifts beneath his weight as he settles next to me, his shoulder firm against mine. "*Plus One.*"

Twenty

HAZEL

It's Saturday, and Alex has chosen kayaking as our next date. Not what I would have chosen, but it at least gave me an excuse to shop for a new outfit. And I didn't do it alone. I took Alex's blind date with me.

Marie Smith. She has possibly the most generic name in the English language, but she's spunky and vibrant and fun. And okay, maybe she's not necessarily *Alex's* type, but after I met her at a concert a few months back, I've been meaning to reach out for a friend date because I feel like we would get along really well.

We had the best time scouring the thrift store last night in search of kayaking-appropriate gear. I'm sure either of us could have found something stuffed in the backs of our closets, but I ended up with the cutest little mustard yellow hiking shorts that I paired with a floral bikini top, a white linen button down, and a khaki bucket hat. It's outdoorsy chic, and I ended up taking thirty-seven mirror selfies before Alex walked in on me, shaking his head at my antics.

"Maybe this isn't such a terrible date idea," I say as we turn into the gravel parking lot at the kayak rental location. The windows are down, letting in a steamy summer breeze, and my feet are kicked up on the dash.

Alex arches a brow at me. "I didn't realize it was, but please enlighten me."

"Well, I was thinking we could ask our dates to put sunscreen on our backs. That's hot, right?"

A surprised laugh barks out of him. "No, that's not hot."

"It absolutely is hot," I retort, indignation rising.

"Rubbing sticky, smelly sunscreen all over someone's hairy back is sexy?" Alex props his elbow on his open window, turning his body to face me, the sun glinting in the faded golds in his dark hair.

"*Your* back isn't hairy."

It most definitely is not. It's all gleaming skin stretched over taut muscles. Like velvet covering marble.

His deep brown eyes roll, a smile playing at the corners of his lips. "No, but yours is." My mouth falls open, and his laugh fills the car. He holds up his hands in surrender. "Kidding, kidding."

"For that, you're doing my back," I say, pushing my door open and climbing out.

He meets me at the back, lifting the trunk, his cheeks still tinged with a happy pink, like strawberry frosting on a chilled cake.

Reaching for my bag, I pull out a bottle of sunscreen. "And for the record, my sunscreen smells like a tropical paradise." I shove the bottle in his hand, and he cracks the lid, sniffing.

"It really transports you," he says. "I can practically feel the sand in my ass."

Pressing my lips together to stifle my laugh, I spin around and shrug out of my top. The sun beats down on my exposed skin, warming it. Despite the heat, it pebbles when I feel Alex's breath on the nape of my neck.

I expect the sunscreen to be cold, but it's warm from Alex rubbing his hands together. It's like slick massage oil as he spreads it first across my shoulders and then down my back.

With each pass of his hands, each brush of his fingers, my stomach tightens, heat spreading through me. Maybe this wasn't such a good idea. All the confusing feelings of the past few weeks feel concentrated behind my navel, fire licking up my spine and down my legs.

"Not so bad," Alex murmurs, and I think his voice might be rough. It only makes me more aware of every spot he's touching.

"It's the coconut," I choke out.

He's quiet for a long moment, his hands moving in slower and slower circles over my back, spanning over the flare of my hips. Finally, he breathes, "No, I don't think that's it."

I glance at him over my shoulder, catching his gaze. It's molten, consuming.

"Hey, guys!" a familiar deep voice calls from across the parking lot. Parker.

"Thanks," I mutter to Alex, pulling my shirt up from the crook of my elbows and back onto my shoulders.

He doesn't say anything, wiping his hands roughly on one of the beach towels I packed. Parker jogs up next to us, a wide smile stretched across his face. I force one of my own to match his.

"Hey, Parker. How have you been?" We've texted some this week, especially after my decision Monday to buckle down in my pursuit of him. Our conversations have been ongoing since then, but I couldn't bring myself to respond as quickly as he did. I'd get a text from him while working at the coffee shop in the morning and not respond until I got home in the evenings, only to have my phone ding with his reply a moment later. I need to try harder.

His arm wraps around my shoulders in a quick side hug. "I've been great. Finished painting my classroom. How's the work project going?"

I can't help the way my eyes flick to Alex, who is now applying his own sunscreen to his bare arms with quick motions, leaving streaks of white in some spots and bare, exposed flesh in others. His pale skin is sure to fry in this harsh sun, and it takes everything inside me not to snatch the bottle from his hands and apply it myself. But I'm still off-kilter from the feeling of his hands on me, and that would only exacerbate it. Maybe Marie will help.

I don't know why that makes my stomach twist.

"Hazel?" Parker asks, snapping my attention back to him.

I shake my head, clearing it, and try to remember his question. "Taking everything out of me. Something about the design is just *not* working."

"Maybe I can take a look at it," he says, and his face is so earnest that guilt hangs heavy in my gut.

Parker doesn't seem to notice that my smile takes effort, and I'm glad for it. "That would be great," I say. "Maybe this week?"

"I'd love to. What about Tue—"

"Have you heard from Marie?" Alex interrupts.

I whirl to face him, eyes wide. His jaw is set, a firm line that could cut glass, but his gaze is fixed somewhere above my head, out at the rapidly filling parking lot. Dust kicks up with each car pulling in, clinging to my sunscreen-sticky skin.

"Not since this morning," I say, tugging my phone from my back pocket to check for missed texts or calls.

"Is that her?" Alex asks, his voice holding a hint of surprise.

I follow his gaze, holding my hand to my forehead to block the sun. Marie is across the parking lot, silhouetted in an actual sunbeam. She's wearing ripped denim shorts that make her bronzed legs go on for miles and the bright pink button-up we found at the thrift store yesterday. It's unbuttoned, revealing a stark white bikini top and the dozens of tiny fine-line tattoos that pepper her deeply tanned skin.

"Yeah, that's her," I say, and from the look on Alex's face when I turn around, I start to doubt my previous notion that Marie isn't really his type. Marie is exactly the type of anyone with eyes and a functioning brain cell.

"Want to head over there?" Alex asks, shutting the trunk with a thud.

"Sure thing," Parker says before I have a chance to respond.

Marie smiles when she sees us approaching, a bright, exuberant smile that looks like pure sunshine. "Hey, guys."

Last night, when she hugged me in the thrift store like we were lifelong friends, I'd found it endearing, but when she does the same to Alex, something clamps tight in my chest.

"You must be Alex," she says, her arms around his neck and his settling around her waist before she releases him.

The grin he gives her is my favorite, where one corner of his lips hooks up before the other. "You must be Marie."

"This is Parker," I say a touch too loudly, and Alex's eyes crinkle in confusion as he looks at me.

I avoid his gaze, watching as Marie gives Parker the same quick hug. "I'm a hugger," she says with a laugh. It's deep and raspy, the kind I've always wanted for myself instead of the snort that usually comes out when I find something funny.

"Me too," Parker says, a warm smile touching his mouth.

"You guys ready?" Alex asks, nodding toward the kayak rental building.

"Let's do it," Marie says, bouncing up and down on the balls of her feet. "I'll need someone to help me put sunscreen on my back before we get out there, though."

ALEX'S AND MARIE'S LAUGHTER echo on the breeze. The plan was for us to each get individual kayaks, but the rental place had just given out their last single when we entered an hour ago. So Parker and I ended up in one, and Alex and Marie ended up in the other. They've been behind us the whole time, but I can still hear them every few minutes when the conversation between Parker and me quiets down as we navigate around difficult turns or over quick rapids.

I'm still waiting for that spark to ignite between us. Our chatter has been almost nonstop since we got in the kayak, changing topics seamlessly from art techniques to our favorite movies to the things we miss most about the small towns we grew up in. It's been easy and fun, but it feels like catching up with Stevie and Wren or lounging with Lucy. There are no butterflies, no heat spreading through my middle or skin that feels singed by fire.

It feels safe, like I told Lucy in the coffee shop the other day, but it's also feeling increasingly less satisfying. And that's the scariest of all. I *want* to be okay with no sparks, with gentle friendship and easy laughter, but there's a piece of me that's desperate for the rest, even though it feels like standing too close to a fire, waiting to be burned.

"There are some rapids up ahead," I tell Parker over my shoulder, since he's steering in the back.

"We got this," he says easily, the way he has with each rough patch we've come upon. His encouragement is a balm to my soul, a buoy to my spirit. It's exactly the kind of response I want from a partner, that blanket reassurance. But it doesn't fill that aching emptiness where the butterflies should be.

With each stroke toward the white water, I assess the difficulty of crossing it. It's nothing like the whitewater rafting Cam, Wes, and I attempted one time outside of LA a couple of years back, but it does look like the choppiest patch we've come upon yet.

Adrenaline courses through my veins as I push my paddle into the water, holding firm against the current. Water sprays my skin, wetting my legs and arms that are exposed after shrugging out of my button-up earlier. The droplets cling to my hair and eyelashes, feeling like icy kisses.

Parker and I navigate through the rapids more easily than I expect, working in tandem to cross over the thrashing water. We're nearly through when the front of the kayak snags on a jutting rock I didn't see until the last second, making the kayak pitch dangerously. Parker shouts something behind me, but I don't hear him as I try to stabilize us, shoving my paddle into the water. The momentum sends us spinning, knocking into another large, slick rock.

And then we tip. I know the exact moment we turn too far to come back up, gravity tugging us under. We plunge beneath the cold surface of the water, falling out of the kayak, and we're swept up in the current.

Just as I'm about to plant my feet and break through the surface once more, I hit the rock. Hard.

Pain sears through my head as my skull connects with the slick surface, and stars dot behind my eyes. It hurts worse than the time I got into a car accident in high school and hit my head on the steering wheel. Worse than when I slipped on the boardwalk back in California and my forehead smacked against the wood railing.

No, this is much, much worse.

That's the last thing I think before everything goes dark.

Twenty-One

ALEX

My heart stops when Parker breaks through the water and Hazel doesn't. The seconds feel like hours as I wait for her golden-brown hair to pop through the surface, for her face to be a mixture of chagrin and shock, for her laughter to ring across the water as she surveys the scene.

But it doesn't happen.

By the time Marie and I get through the rapids and pull our kayak off to the side, Marie shoving her paddle into the soft sandy dirt beneath us to keep from moving, Parker is tugging Hazel out of the water. I think I'll be sick at the way her head lolls and blood oozes from a wound to the back of her skull.

I think I yell her name, but I can't be sure with the way my throat is closing up, cutting off my windpipe. Words feel distant and murky, a concept lost in the span of a few gut-wrenching seconds.

By the time I reach Parker, he has Hazel propped on a tall rock, out of reach of the spraying water, although the current rips at both of our middles. My hand slides around her neck, cradling her head so it's no longer resting against the hard surface. Stone scrapes against my knuckles, and it's the only thing tethering me here as my vision tunnels, my eyes scanning desperately for the rise of Hazel's chest, the pulse beating at her throat.

"Is she okay?" Parker asks, his face leaching of all color.

I don't have the strength to answer as Hazel stirs, a moan seeping from between her lips. When she murmurs my name, I almost pass out from the relief.

"I'm right here," I tell her over and over again, leaning close. My hands are everywhere, reassuring myself that she's breathing, that she's mostly unharmed, that she's *alive*.

Her eyes flutter open, the deep dark blue of the ocean, and fix on me. "My head hurts," she mumbles, squinting against the bright sunlight.

I position my body to block the sun, and her face relaxes slightly, although it's still pinched in pain. I want to smooth away the wrinkles, take her pain, and make it my own.

"I know, honey. We're going to get you some help, okay?" Turning to face Parker, who is watching us intently, some of the color returning to his skin, I ask, "Can you help Marie get the kayaks to the bank? I'm going to try to carry Hazel."

My heart is still beating wildly, so fast I don't know that it will ever slow down.

"Yeah, of course," Parker says, snapping into action. His kayak, thankfully, is wedged between two jutting rocks a little way down, so he's able to get to it quickly.

When I start to lift Hazel into my arms, she wakes more fully, blinking at me. "What are you doing?"

"Trying to get you out of the water," I tell her, slipping one arm beneath her knees and the other behind her back. Her damp, sun-kissed skin is warm and slick against my own.

"I can walk."

Not a chance.

The water pulls at me as I carry Hazel through it. Another couple in a double kayak has stopped to ask Parker if we need help, but he waves them on when he sees I've safely carried Hazel through the water.

Wet, sloshy sand squelches beneath my feet as I climb up the bank and set Hazel down, squatting next to her. She looks so small and defenseless that I feel on edge, like a rubber band so close to snapping.

"How are you feeling?" Marie asks, climbing out of the kayak she successfully steered onto the bank. Maybe later I'll feel guilty for not helping her, but right now isn't that time. Not when my entire focus is fixed on Hazel and the way she rests her head on her forearms, which are propped on her bent knees.

"I'm okay, really," she says, and I feel slightly better at the way her voice is stronger, unlike the weak murmur when she was pulled from the water.

I crouch next to her, my hands gently peeling the damp hair away from her skull. The cut is still bleeding, but I can see now that the water was making it look much worse than it actually is. The cut is only about an inch long and not very deep.

"Do you feel dizzy at all?" I ask, trying to recall the questions my cross-country coaches asked every time I inevitably wiped out for no reason except pure clumsiness.

Hazel shakes her head, but then her eyes gloss over for a moment before fixing back on me. "Maybe a little."

"I think we need to go to the hospital and get you checked out."

"I'm fine," she says, but I notice that she doesn't try shaking her head again, and it only firms my resolve.

I lean in so we're almost nose to nose. Her eyes are wide, and I see the panic there, lingering beneath her brave facade. It makes my heart melt. I reach a hand out, cupping the back of her neck. "We need to make sure you don't have a concussion."

She nods, the movement so soft and slow you'd barely be able to see it, but I can feel it against my hand framing her face.

"You're going to be okay, honey. I promise. Do you believe me?"

She nods again, and I press a kiss to her temple, unable to hold back. Not now, when I feel like my terror is a live wire, zapping every nerve in my body.

When I stand and turn around, Parker and Marie are both watching me with wide eyes, and I know they see it. That my every hidden emotion has been exposed like a bright campfire in the dark woods.

"I'm going to get her back to the car. Do you guys think you can finish out the ride and return the kayaks?"

"Yeah, of course," Marie says, her gaze flicking to where Hazel is huddled on the ground. "How are you going to get her back? I don't think she can walk far, and we've gone at least a mile, probably two."

"I'm going to carry her."

Parker's brows inch up his forehead. "Two miles?"

I know he doesn't mean it the way it sounds, but my nerves are frayed, and I have to hold back from snapping. Parker is easily the nicest person I've ever met, and I know I'd regret anything I said later.

"I'll be fine," I manage to get out between clenched teeth.

Parker nods, no doubt noticing the determination in every line of my body.

"Let us know how she is," Marie says, glancing between Hazel and me.

"I will," I assure them, heading back to the kayak to retrieve the small waterproof bags with our phone and my keys that we tucked under and hooked to the strings at the front. I grab both of our shirts, although her linen button-up got soaked in the flip, and tug mine over my tender sunburned shoulders. Stopping in front of Marie, I say, "I'm really sorry to duck out like this."

Her smile is wide, her eyes darting from me to Hazel and back again. "Don't worry about it."

I give Parker one more nod before turning back to Hazel. She's still hunched over her knees, eyes shut against the sun. Crouching in front of her, I smooth a hand over her arm, and she opens her eyes to peer at me.

"I'm going to carry you back to the car. Do you think you can hold on to my back?"

She nods, or the smallest movement that can be considered a nod, just a faint dip of her chin. "Yeah, of course, but I can walk."

I'm already shaking my head before she finishes. "Not a chance. Let's try standing."

Hazel sways on her feet as I help her stand, holding on to my biceps for balance. "I'm okay," she assures me. "Just a little dizzy."

"Are you sure you can get on my back?" I ask.

Her head bobs in a tiny nod, so I turn around, bending down so she can wrap her arms around my neck. My hands slide around her thighs, hitching them around my hips. It feels like actual fire on my sunburn, but I'm just glad she's comfortable as she settles more firmly against me.

"Text us an update," Marie calls out as I start the climb up the grassy bank to the back road that's on the other side of the trees.

"I will," I promise, my heart only slowing its rapid pace when Hazel's face slides into the crook of my neck, her breath warm against my skin.

"Thanks for taking care of me, Alex," she whispers into my skin, and I clutch her tighter, eating up the distance back to the cars.

"SHE HAS A MILD concussion," the ER doctor says five hours later. We lucked out when one of the kayak company's vans passed us on the street on the walk back. They let us climb in the van full of kayakers who had just finished their trip and gave us a ride back to the rental place. We spent more time sitting in the cold, slightly damp waiting room of the ER than we did trying to get back to the car.

"Is she going to be okay?" I ask, keeping one hand on Hazel's knee. I haven't been able to stop touching her since I picked her up on that bank, and luckily, she hasn't pushed me away.

"Yes," the doctor says, and his eyes soften as he seems to recognize the way I'm about to split apart at the seams. "You may have a headache for the next few days," he says, looking between Hazel and me.

My hands shake as I pull my phone from my pocket and start typing in my notes app, trying to get down everything he says.

"You should probably take it easy for a few days," he continues. "I can write you a doctor's note if you need to take Monday off work, although you should be fine to return Tuesday. Try to limit screen time for the next couple of days and make sure you're getting plenty of rest. Avoid any activities that may exacerbate your symptoms."

Hazel nods, her eyes glazing over with the movement once more. It's a good thing that the van came when they did, because I think the dizziness would have knocked her out if I'd had to carry her the whole way back. She spent the entirety of our time waiting in the ER with her head on my shoulder, eyes closed against the bright fluorescent lights.

"Do you have any questions?"

"What happens if she gets worse? Is she allowed to sleep? How much screen time can she have? What activities are too strenuous?" I ask rapid-fire.

The doctor blinks at me before responding. "If she seems to get worse, you guys can come back and we can run a CT scan. Yes, she should sleep. Sleep is an essential part of healing the brain. Some screen time is fine, but I would avoid watching TV or scrolling on your phone for too long." He pauses, brows scrunching. "What was the last question?"

"Activities."

"Ah, yes. Rest up for a few days. You can shower and eat and live normally, but avoid going to the gym or driving or working until you're better."

"Sounds good," Hazel says, her eyes once again closed and her head leaning back against the pillows propped against the elevated back of the hospital bed.

"Any other questions?" the doctor asks, his tone carrying a hint of wariness.

"No," Hazel responds before I can think of anything else.

When the doctor disappears around the curtain, I say, "I had more questions."

The smile Hazel gives me is slow, almost drugged, but it fills me with relief, nonetheless. "I know. I didn't think the poor doctor needed to be heckled any more."

"I wasn't heckling," I say, pushing a trembling hand through my hair.

She grabs the hand I dropped from her folded knee when I started typing my notes and gives it a squeeze. "You were heckling, but it was sweet."

Something calms inside me at her touch, the firmness of it. It's no longer as weak as it was before. I want to collapse under the relief.

"Hey," she says, tugging on my hand, her fingers locking with mine. "Are you okay?"

"Yeah," I say on an exhale. "I was just worried."

"You can't get rid of me that easily."

"I'm glad you say that," I say, and her eyebrows lift in question.

"Why?"

"Because I'm staying with you until you're better."

Twenty-Two

HAZEL

Alex wasn't kidding about staying with me. After we left the hospital, he took me home, got me settled in bed, and then went back out to pack a bag. Which is how I've ended up lying in my bed, darkness creeping in around me, with only the sound of the fan billowing through the room, since I'm supposed to stay off screens for the time being.

And here in the darkness, I can only see one thing—the look of pure terror on Alex's face earlier when I woke up on the riverbank with his large, warm body hovering over mine. I can see perfectly the twin creases between his brows as the nurses took my vitals, feel the imprint of his hands on my thighs as he carried me down the cracked asphalt street.

These thoughts, these feelings, have been swirling through my brain for weeks, and I've shut them down every single time. Because Alex is my best friend, and thinking about him that way makes my skin itch and my heart race. It feels like honey pooling in my stomach and dizziness fogging my head. It makes me *nervous* because I don't know what to do with it, and those illicit thoughts are like standing on a precipice on a windy day, hoping to God you don't get caught up in the breeze.

But right now, I have a brain injury, and so I let myself feel it all. I don't stop my mind from wandering to the way his shoulders stretch the fabric of his shirt so taut it looks ready to rip. I don't make myself think of something else when I imagine the pillowy texture of his lips or how they would feel on my skin. I don't tamp down the heat gathering behind my belly button or the flush rising to my cheeks.

Because hopefully I won't remember this tomorrow. If I'm lucky, when the first rays of sunrise creep through my curtains in the morning, I'll forget all about all the ways I felt about Alexander Malcolm Bates today.

The sound of my door opening snaps me out of my thoughts, and I lock them away, deep in my chest, and make myself a promise to never pull them back out again. Maybe when I inevitably break my own rule, they'll smell like mothballs and dust, mere scraps of memory that no longer hold any consequences.

Alex's footsteps are light as he makes his way through my apartment in the relative dark with only the light over the stove to guide him. When I tried to turn on my lamps earlier, he swatted my hands away, saying he didn't want them to make my headache worse. Which I guess was for the best, because my head was swimming, and walking without leaning on him made my vision cloud at the edges.

My bedroom door creaks open, the old hinges groaning, and a sliver of pale light races through the crack before Alex shuts it quickly but softly behind him. There's a thump, and I have to press my lips together to stifle a laugh as he curses viciously under his breath.

"You okay?" I ask, hoping he can't hear the smile in my voice.

"You're supposed to be sleeping." He sounds grumpy, his tone scolding, and it makes my grin stretch wider.

"I am."

The bed dips beneath his weight, and his usual clean, starched scent is replaced by sunshine, sweat, and river water. It would be bad on most people, and I'm sure I'm foul, but it smells good on him. He's usually so buttoned up—hair slicked back and rebelling against his pomade, stubble clipped close to his face—but he feels different now, like someone else entirely. It makes my guard slip a little.

"How's your head?" His voice rumbles through the darkness.

"Smashed."

I expect a laugh, but when I peek open my eye, his face is illuminated by only a shimmer of twilight seeping through the curtains, but it's clear his brow is creased with concern.

"I'm just kidding," I tell him, keeping my hands tucked beneath the blankets so I don't accidentally reach out and smooth my fingers over the crinkled skin.

His body sags against my headboard, and he looses a deep breath. "I was really worried today," he says quietly, after a long pause.

My foolish hand doesn't heed my mental warnings, slipping out from under the quilt to lock with his. Alex's chin rests on his shoulder, deep brown eyes fixing on me. His thumb smooths over my knuckles, a steady pattern moving in time with my heartbeat.

I try not to focus on the movement, how holding his hand feels so different in the dark in my bed than it does when he's helping me over a fallen branch on a hiking path or into the high passenger seat in his SUV. But my traitorous heart thumps wildly, and my skin prickles with every swipe of his finger.

"I know," I tell him, and my voice comes out as nothing more than a murmur. "I'm glad you were there to take care of me."

Alex's throat bobs in a swallow, and his gaze darts across the room, fixing on a spot on one of the butterfly pictures hanging on my wall. "Parker would have done just fine if you'd been alone."

"Maybe," I say, squeezing his hand with gentle pressure. "But I'm glad it was you anyway."

His eyes snag on mine once more, and I don't know whether it's the concussion or this unfamiliar tautness in the air between us, but my vision blurs at the edges, my focus fixing entirely on him. I want to remember how he looks at this exact moment, and I hope desperately that it doesn't disappear into the hazy memories of today. I don't want to forget the way his hair has become messy, rebelling against the pomade, or the dusting of freckles on his cheeks. I want to remember the pink sunburn on his nose and the look in his eyes, so deep and tender that it feels earth-shattering.

I don't know who moves, or if we both do, but suddenly there's no space between us, and we're touching from shoulder to hip, our fingers still intertwined.

"I'm glad it was me too," he says just above a whisper, his breath fanning against my cheek.

There's an electric current, pulsing and alive. It's like touching a live wire, and it shocks me just as easily. I wrench back, my head spinning at the sudden movement. Alex bolts upright, his hands moving to either side of my face, holding my head steady.

"Are you okay?" he asks, that distress back between his brows. I just know I'm contributing to his early wrinkles. Maybe I'll get him Botox for his birthday.

Whatever tension that was thickening the air a moment ago has dissipated, replaced with concerned urgency. When I nod, his palms scrape against my cheeks, and his lungs finally seem to fill with oxygen again. The last bit of twilight extinguishes, bathing us in darkness, as he sits back, releasing my face.

"Are you hungry?" Alex asks, scrubbing a palm over the back of his neck.

I hadn't noticed my hunger, but my stomach feels hollow as soon as he asks the question. "Yeah, actually."

"Cam made soup for you. I picked it up on the way back over here." Alex shifts off the bed, fumbling for something on the nightstand. The next moment, his phone flashlight turns on, diffused orange from his fingers covering the brightness.

"Mm," I mumble, suddenly ravenous. "What kind?"

"Lemon chicken orzo. But if you don't want soup, I can go get you something. I know it's hot outside." The rambling would give away his discomfort if the shifting from foot to foot didn't.

My stomach feels hollow for an entirely different reason. This is exactly why I've avoided these thoughts for so long, burying them deep to rot away before they can be exposed. If I weren't so equally hungry and tired, I'd let him order takeout just so he could get away from me for longer, like he so desperately wants to.

I wish I could tell if our reasoning is the same, if he's scared like me, worried about ruining something precious, or if he just doesn't feel the same. If I hadn't taken a hard hit to the head today, I'd be able to trust the look I saw in his eyes earlier, add it to the running list of moments between us that I've been cataloging in my head over the past few weeks, waiting to see what they add up to. But I *did* sustain a brain injury today, and so I can't be sure of anything. For all I know, I could be asleep right now, waiting for Alex to return with his overnight bag.

"Soup is fine," I finally say.

He practically bolts out the door, mumbling something I don't quite hear. My shoulders sink against the pillows, my heart beating rapidly. I let my breath out between pursed lips. Everything feels fuzzy and out of focus, and I hate myself for getting wrapped up in a moment when I'm in no state to be making life-changing decisions.

Alex returns a moment later, hissing as he bumps into the bed and spills hot soup on his hand.

"Just turn on the light," I say, sighing.

"No," he says firmly, cursing again as more soup sloshes.

I lean over, flicking on the lamp and bathing the room in a warm golden glow. My head pounds at the sudden brightness, and I close my eyes against the nausea.

"Hazel Mae Lane," Alex scolds quietly, setting the soup down on my nightstand before he turns the light back off. I hate to admit that the barely there glow of his phone flashlight feels much better, settling the pulse beating through my skull.

The bed dips beneath his weight as he settles next to me once more, this time on the sliver of space between me and the edge of the bed.

"Do you need help eating?" he asks. His voice is so smooth and calm, like a gentle purr that feels like a balm against the incessant throbbing in my head.

"No," I say, not opening my eyes, but a moment later, a spoon is prodding at my lips, the scent of lemon, onion, and Italian seasoning wafting up to my nose.

I crack an eye open, taking a bite. The soup is deliciously warm and flavorful. Alex hands me a slice of crusty bread, and I rip a piece off. Tangy sourdough is a perfect combo, and I tear off another bit and stuff it in my mouth before taking the bowl from Alex.

"I can feed myself," I tell him, a smile playing at the corners of my mouth.

"You also said you could kayak," he teases, and the last bit of tension from earlier evaporates.

"You said you can dance," I retort, dipping my spoon back into the soup for another bite.

He leans back on his hands. "Brittney at Zumba told me I can dance."

"Brittney at Zumba lied to you."

He shrugs, his mouth twisting in a grin. "I don't know why she would do that."

"Lying to flatter you."

The usual light returns to his eyes, a twinkle that dimmed the moment my head hit that rock. "You would never do that."

"I don't need to," I say, lifting my pointer finger from my spoon. "I've got you wrapped around my finger."

"That so?"

I raise my shoulder in a shrug. The ease returns to my body now that things are starting to feel normal between us again. "You did leave a date for me today. And it's not even the first time."

In the dim light of his flashlight, his expression is soft, almost tender. "Yeah, I guess you do, Lane."

We're quiet as I finish my soup, Alex pushing off the bed to straighten my room and then helping me to the bathroom to change out of my kayaking outfit and into pajamas. When I open the door, he's situated on my bed once more, scrolling through his phone. He pops up at the sound of the door, but I wave him back down, taking the few steps on my own. His eyes track my every movement, his body tense as I settle back under the blankets.

The quiet descends on me like a thick fog. "I wish I could watch TV."

Alex climbs back out of the bed, moving around to the bookshelf in the corner of my room. "How about I read to you?"

Something in my chest warms, spreading through my veins like the most decadent hot fudge. "Yeah, that would be nice."

When he spins back around, book in hand, there's a broad smile on his face.

"What book is it?" I ask, and he climbs back into bed next to me.

He moves the book closer so I can see the cover in the dim light. *Emma*.

A matching grin curls across my lips. "I actually haven't read it," I tell him. "Lo made me buy it at a garage sale last year. She said Wes would kill her if she brought home another copy."

"Perfect," he says, flipping open the worn paperback, the pages rustling between his fingers. "*Emma Woodhouse*," he starts, his voice rich and smooth. "*Handsome, clever, and rich, with a comfortable home and happy disposition, seemed to unite some of the best blessings of existence; and had lived nearly twenty-one years in the world with very little to distress or vex her.*"

Twenty-Three

HAZEL

The bed is cold when I wake up the next morning. My hand slides across smooth sheets, searching, but only meets emptiness. When I crack my eyes open, Alex is gone. The last thing I remember from the night before is the fluttering of my eyelids and his warm, deep voice lulling me to sleep as he read *Emma*.

My head still swims as I push up out of the bed, but it's much clearer than yesterday. And by the time my feet sink into the plush rug, I know I'll be steady enough to walk on my own. Pain slices through my skull as I make my way out of my room, my fingers gently prodding the bandaged lump on the back of my head.

Hazy morning light filters through my curtains, illuminating Alex's sleeping form on my couch. His body is much too large for the tiny leather couch that I bought when I moved to Tennessee. He's scrunched up in a way that can't be comfortable, his neck tilted at an awkward angle.

But that's not what catches my attention. His shirt is in a pile on the floor next to him, and the chunky throw blanket he has tugged over his hips does nothing to hide the angry sunburn on his back. It's a deep, fiery red, and I cringe, thinking about how the fabric of my sofa must feel up against it.

Not nearly as bad as it must have felt carrying me as my body jostled against it with every step.

I must make a noise, because Alex stirs, and when he rolls over and stretches, his face twists in a wince. Dark brown eyes meet mine, and he shoots up, instantly alert and assessing my condition.

"I'm fine," I say as he stands so fast that I hear his joints pop from being curled up for so long.

It doesn't stop his progress, though. Each step brings him nearer until my vision is a blur of skin. So much skin. His chest and stomach are tinged pink, but they're nothing like the bright red of his back.

"Alex," I say sharply, moving around him and gently skating my fingers across the tender skin covering his shoulder blade. When he shivers beneath my touch, I yank my hand back, scared I hurt him.

His gaze meets mine over his shoulder. "It's nothing," he says softly, his voice like a whisper of silk against skin. "Just a sunburn."

"You should have let me put sunscreen on your back," I scold.

"Yeah, maybe," he says, his lips twitching. He turns around to face me, and one of his hands smooths over the bandage on the back of my head.

With his fingers in my hair and the broad expanse of his bare skin right in front of me, I'm suddenly overwhelmed. He must have showered after I fell asleep last night, because although I still smell like the bottom of the river, that fresh linen scent is back on him, like laundry hung out to dry in the sun. It invades my senses, wrapping all around me until I'm transported to a summer day, clothes draped over the line and swaying gently in the breeze.

My breath hitches, and his eyes meet mine. "Did that hurt?" he asks.

When I shake my head, he drops his hand, taking a small step back. Oxygen flows into my lungs like I've just broken through the surface after being underwater for too long.

"Your skin will peel," I blurt, and he quirks a brow. "That sunburn. We should put aloe on it."

I turn on my heel, heading toward the bathroom, my hand drifting across the wall for balance.

"I don't need aloe," he says, but his footsteps echo behind me.

Ignoring him, I walk into the bathroom and find a bottle of the unnaturally green gel under the sink amid my large perfume collection. When I shut the cabinet, Alex is leaning against the doorframe, one hand propped above his head. It really does wonders for his physique, which I don't think I have ever fully appreciated until this moment.

All those hours in the gym have been good to him, toning every inch of visible skin, carving the muscles beneath into works of art. There are ridges on his abs, and a dark dusting of hair covering broad pectorals. I don't think I've ever noticed how broad his shoulders are, how silky smooth his skin looks.

It takes me a minute to realize he's holding out his palm, waiting for me to hand him the bottle.

"I'll do it," I stammer, motioning for him to turn around.

His gaze locks and holds mine for a long moment, time stretching and expanding in the space of our shared breaths.

"Okay," he says finally, turning to expose his back to me.

The gel is cold on my fingers, but his skin is hot, burning beneath my touch. As much as I tell it not to, my mind flashes back to yesterday, when his hands were moving over my skin just like this. I hadn't let myself think about it then, about the way my stomach flipped, about the hot liquid pooling behind my belly button, about how I wanted to make him feel the same way.

I *wanted* to touch him like this, to see if I affected him the same way he affected me. From the way his body tenses, his hands clenching and unclenching at his sides, I think I am.

It's as terrifying as it is thrilling. Because Alex is *not* someone like Parker. He's not someone I'd be okay with losing. I'd give up almost anyone before him. Not Alex. Never Alex.

I pull my hand back, wiping it clean on the mustard yellow towel hanging on the hook beside me.

When Alex turns around, his face is solemn, his jaw tight, a muscle in it flickering. He's so rarely solemn, but he has been more and more over the last few weeks, like there's a weight pressing down on his shoulders. I haven't let myself consider the reasons for the change, too scared to find out what it meant, that investigating might rock the boat and set us off course.

"Thanks," he murmurs, his eyes cataloging every feature on my face, as if he's committing them to memory. When they fasten on my lips, the pupils dilating, my every nerve springs to attention.

His lips part, words hovering on the tip of his tongue, but he's interrupted by a knock on my front door, smashing the moment into little pieces.

I jolt to attention, slipping past him into the hall, my shoulder brushing against his bare chest.

Lucy is on the other side of my door, two Whistling Kettle to-go cups in her hands. Her eyes dart past me to Alex, who's standing shirtless at my back. My chest heats, and a blush streaks across my cheeks as she turns back to me.

"Alex, lovely to see so much of you," Lucy croons, a grin lighting up her face.

Alex's response is a grumble as Lucy walks through the door and into the living room.

"I take it you didn't see my text," Lucy asks, setting the paper cups down on the coffee table.

I glance at Alex as I say, "Alex locked up my phone the minute we got home yesterday."

His arms cross over his chest, his biceps straining. "The doctor said no screen time."

Lucy's gaze bounces between us before landing back on me. "I just texted that I was going to bring over tea in a bit." She pauses, then says, "Sorry if I interrupted something."

The warmth is back in my neck, creeping up to cover my cheeks.

Alex responds before I have the chance to, picking his shirt up off the floor and tugging it over his head. "I'm actually just going to head out for a bit if Lucy will be here," he says. It's a question for her, but his eyes are fixed on mine.

"Yeah, I'll be fine, even if she needs to go." There's a strange feeling in the pit of my stomach, like after the dip on a rollercoaster. Just minutes ago, Alex and I were in my bathroom, sharing breath, stars and wildfire exploding between us, time and space quivering on a precipice I wasn't sure I wanted to test. But now there's a mask in place that I've never seen before. Something I never expected would hang between us.

"I don't need to go," Lucy replies, and Alex nods once.

"I'll be back in an hour or two," he says, once again to me. And then he's out the door before I can respond, leaving a cold, empty achiness inside me.

"So," Lucy says, drawing the word out as she collapses onto my couch. Her gray eyes are wide, sparking with curiosity. "What happened?"

Slowly, I make my way to the sofa. I was still a little dizzy before the encounter in my bathroom with Alex, but now I'm even more off-kilter. As I lower myself onto the cushions, my breath heaving out of me, I say, "I don't know."

Lucy assesses me. "Is there something going on between you two?"

"I don't know," I say again, wrapping my arms around myself. My heart is racing, and my thoughts are out of control.

"How do you feel about it?" Lucy asks after a long moment.

I pin her with my stare. "I don't know."

Her lips twitch, and it makes relief course through me. Things can't be that bad, not with Lucy here.

"Let's start with something you *do* know," she says.

There's a blip in the universe, a moment where time stands still as I allow the thought to form in my head, as I allow my voice to speak it. "I think I have feelings for Alex."

Lucy's mouth stretches in a slow smile, her eyes lighting up. "I knew it."

"Impossible," I scoff. "*I* didn't know it. I still don't know it. It could just be the concussion talking."

"The concussion finally knocked some sense into your head." When my jaw drops, her smile widens. "Too soon?"

I hug one of the throw pillows against me. "I'm scared."

"I know," she says, her face softening.

"I don't..." I start and let out a breath, gathering my thoughts. "He's not someone I'm willing to lose."

Lucy nods. "I know that too. But, Haze, you could lose him either way. If it's not you, he'll find someone else."

"Maybe that's all this is," I say, latching on to the idea like it's a lifeline in a raging ocean. "Maybe all these double dates have been messing with my head. I'm scared to lose him to someone else, so I'm projecting feelings that aren't there."

Lucy is quiet for a long moment. The only sounds in the room are the ticking of the clock on the wall. "Maybe." My hope soars until she says, "But I don't think that's it."

I clutch the pillow tighter, my fingers sinking into the fabric. "What if he doesn't feel the same way? What if he does and we're a bad couple? What if we ruin it? What if I lose him either way? What if we get together and he…leaves?"

That's the thought that has been haunting me for weeks, a whisper in the back of my head that I haven't acknowledged until now. No one stays. Not for me. There was my best friend in middle school who left when her dad got a new job out of state. The boyfriends in high school who always thought I was too much or not enough. Cam moving away to chase his dreams in LA. And Wes and Cam then leaving again to find the loves of their lives in Tennessee. Sebastian choosing his neighbor over the relationship we'd been building for a year and a half.

Alex hasn't left me, emotionally or physically. And if we're just friends, I get to keep him. If I can find him a partner who takes our friendship at face value, I won't lose him. But if things change between us, if we cross that line, there's no going back if we ruin it. And I don't want to lose him. I don't want him to leave me. Not him. I don't think I'd ever come back from that.

"Haze," Lucy says, her voice so soft it hurts, like a knife to a sensitive, unprotected spot. "Alex isn't going anywhere. You mean too much to him."

I barely hear her words, my resolve strengthening. Nothing can happen. If I want to keep him, I have to *shut this down*. I won't lose him too.

Twenty-Four

ALEX

I HAVE ABSOLUTELY NOWHERE I need to be. I moved around my work appointments yesterday while Hazel napped. I'm way too buzzed for coffee. A grocery delivery will arrive at Hazel's apartment in three hours, with every single thing she could possibly need while she recovers. She won't need to buy food for weeks. Or Tylenol. I probably went overboard with the Tylenol. I bet the delivery person thinks I'm a prepper with the amount of pain reliever and canned soup I purchased.

But I had to get out of that apartment before I did something really, really stupid. For a moment, it looked like she wanted this too, and that's more invitation than I needed. More temptation than I could handle. I almost told her everything, almost *risked* everything.

And now that the idea has wormed its way into my brain, I can't get it out. I want to tell her, screw the consequences.

Without thinking it through, I end up at Adam's house. I don't know if I'm here for advice, to blow off steam, or to pick through his puzzle collection for a non-screen time activity to do with Hazel today, but I quickly realize whatever I choose will have an audience. Parker's truck is in Adam's driveway.

I almost back out, but then the garage opens, and Alex and Parker are there, dressed in gym clothes, a basketball under Alex's arm. He squints when he sees me, raising a hand in greeting, and I know there's no getting out of it. I guess the real question now is how much I want to tell him in front of Parker. Ideally, nothing. But Adam has a way of burrowing under my skin and pulling truths out of me that I'm not ready to reveal.

My breath huffs out of me, fogging up the window before I crank open the door.

"Hey," Alex says when I climb out. "What's up?"

I feel stretched too thin, exhausted in a way I can't quite describe, as my eyes slide to Parker. He's watching me with a pensive, appraising expression.

"How's Hazel?" he asks.

Something inside me snaps at the question. A thread split right down the middle. "I'm in love with her," I blurt, and it feels like aloe gel on a sunburn—instant relief.

His eyes soften, and a grin quirks his lips. I didn't know how he'd respond, but this wasn't it. "I figured that out," he says.

"When?" I ask, suddenly desperate. Because if *he* did, a virtual stranger, there's a good chance Hazel did too.

He shrugs one broad shoulder. "I suspected when we went dancing, but I knew for sure yesterday when she got hurt."

I suck my bottom lip between my teeth, running a hand through my hair. It's messy and disheveled from a night on that abomination of a couch. "Do you think she knows?"

Parker barks a laugh. "Not a chance."

"I don't see how," Adam drawls, bouncing the basketball once against his driveway. "He walks around like a lovesick puppy."

My eyes narrow in a glare at Adam, and Parker says, "She doesn't know."

I glance back at him again, the hope stirring in my chest painful enough that I press a hand against the ache there. "Why do you think that?"

"She wouldn't have gone out with me if she knew," Parker says easily, shrugging once more.

"Oh, so she's stupid and oblivious," Adam says, and despite myself, I laugh. His gray eyes sparkle with amusement, and I know this was his intention all along, to pull me out of the funk that's been dragging me down for weeks.

He holds out the basketball. "We're about to play for a bit, if you want to join."

"I have to be back in two hours," I say, taking the ball from him, the worn rubber smooth against my fingers.

"It won't take me that long to beat you," Adam retorts, smacking the ball from my hand and moving in to make a smooth layup in the basket across the driveway.

I hesitate for a moment, everything in my body screaming at me to go back to Hazel, but my brain holds me back. Temptation is waiting for me at Hazel's apartment, but basketball with my *brother* and *the guy Hazel is dating* will be physically and mentally exhausting enough to drain me. Hopefully. If I'm lucky.

Before I know it, I'm moving, smacking the ball out of Adam's hand. The grin he gives me is wild. It's the same one he used to flash before retaliating against whatever prank I managed to pull on him. With that one expression, I know I'm going to be okay, at least for today. For this next hour or two, I don't have to pretend, and I can *breathe*.

Parker keeps up with us easily, telling us about the three brothers he grew up with, and I have to concede that maybe he's not that bad, especially when he's not pursuing the woman I'm in love with. In fact, I think we could be friends.

My chest is heaving and my pulse is thrumming when we stop for a break an hour later. Wiping my forehead with my arm, I ask Parker, "Did you and Marie end up finishing the whole five miles yesterday?"

The rental company we went with had stops every mile where you could get out and wait to be picked up if you didn't want to do the whole trek.

A light pink suffuses his cheeks, and he takes a sip of the water he pulled from Alex's garage fridge. He walked over there a minute ago, reaching in for a water bottle without looking, which only made me wonder even more how often he and Adam actually hang out.

"We finished it," Parker says, screwing the cap back on his bottle. "And then we got dinner."

A grin stretches across my mouth as his eyes dart my way and obvious relief eases the tension in his shoulders. "Really? That's awesome," I tell him.

"You're not upset?" he asks.

"No," I say. "I'm really, really not. I'm glad some good could come of these dates. They've been instruments of torture for me since the beginning."

A laugh barks out of Parker, and Adam snorts. "Why did you agree to this in the first place?" Parker asks. "I know it couldn't have been *your* idea."

I push a hand through my sweaty hair as the sun beats down on my already too-warm skin. "No, definitely not. I guess I thought I could convince Hazel that the person she was looking for was me."

"She'll figure it out," Parker says, his eyes softening, and my hands tighten on the basketball, the gritty texture biting into my fingers.

"Probably not," Adam says, and I chuck the ball at him. He catches it with a laugh. "You're too easy to mess with."

I ignore him, holding back the smile that threatens to break loose. "What time is it?"

Adam consults his watch and says, "Ten."

Crossing into the shade of the garage to retrieve a water bottle from the fridge, I say, "I better go. Can I borrow a puzzle from your old lady cave?"

"I wish you wouldn't refer to my bedroom that way," Adam says, moving past me toward the heavy metal door leading into the house.

I follow after him with Parker on my heels. "You have an entire cabinet full of puzzles in there, so I wouldn't expect me to stop anytime soon."

Adam's house is a midsize ranch built in the eighties. Unlike so many of the homes on the southeast side of Nashville, he didn't tear this one down in order to build a modern farmhouse on the lot. It retains all the old if somewhat out of style character from the original builders. But it fits Adam and Kelsey, who are more practical than stylish, making everything feel cozy and lived-in.

My shoes scuff against the plush carpets in the hallway leading to his bedroom.

"What kind of puzzle do you want?" Adam asks, opening his bedroom door and going directly for the oak hutch in the corner. When he opens the cabinet door, stacks and stacks of puzzles fill the entirety of the space, organized in a way only Adam himself understands.

"Cardboard?" I say, and it comes out like a question.

Adam glares at me over his shoulder. "How many pieces? Landscape, animal, art piece, movie-themed?"

I blink at him for a moment, processing. "Do you have any butterflies?"

Adam nods, closing the top cabinet and opening the bottom. It's just as full, and he trails his fingers over the glossy boxes until he finds the one he's looking for. Pulling it free, the pieces jostling against the sides, he hands it to me.

The box is green, showing a field of wildflowers. It's zoomed in to display fluffy white dandelions, a couple of yellow and blue flowers, and a swarm of butterflies. A smile tugs at my lips.

"This is perfect. Thanks, Adam."

He grunts. "Don't lose any pieces."

"I'll just lose one. To drive you nuts for the rest of eternity," I say with a wink.

Parker interjects, no doubt seeing the steam pouring from Adam's ears, and says, "Adam and I usually get dinner at that sports bar down the road on Thursdays, if you want to come this week."

I glance between them, my gaze fixing on Adam, who surprisingly doesn't seem to mind Parker inviting me. Nodding, I tell them, "Sure. See you then."

"Bring my puzzle back with all the pieces, Alex," Adam calls after me as I leave, and I can't help but smile.

Hazel is alone when I let myself into her apartment. I've got milkshakes in a cardboard carrier in one hand, and the puzzle box gripped in the other. There's a blanket wrapped around her shoulders and the battered *Emma* paperback lying open in her lap. Hazel's mouth lifts in a smile when she sees me, but it doesn't touch her tired eyes or bring pink back into her pale cheeks. Worry clenches around my chest in a vise grip, cutting off my oxygen.

"Are you okay?" I ask, dropping the puzzle box and milkshakes onto the coffee table with a thud. I drop down into a squat next to her. "How's your head? Have you gotten more dizzy? Nausea?"

Her lips curve as she sits up, and this time, the grin is genuine. "I'm fine, I promise. Lucy only left like ten minutes ago."

The relief punches me in the gut, and I rock back on my heels, pushing my hands through my hair.

"Hey," she says, tugging on my hands. Her own curl around mine, not letting go, and the touch is like smooth, sweet ice cream after dinner. "You okay?"

My breath releases in a huff as I nod. "Yeah, I'm good." I meet her eyes, relishing in the familiar deep blue of them. I could stare at those eyes forever and never figure out how to precisely describe the shade. "I just don't like you being hurt," I say honestly. "It makes me feel on edge."

"I'm okay, I promise. You can't get rid of me that easily. I'm not going anywhere."

Her hand is warm and silky in my own, a reassuring weight, and I squeeze it lightly. "I'm not going anywhere either," I tell her. "You're stuck with me."

Something changes in her face, and Hazel sits up straighter, letting go of my hand. My stomach flips as her gaze darts around the room. When it finally lands on me again, her cheeks are flushed with color, like a ripe peach. The air feels different, charged, and I hold my breath as she watches me for another heartbeat.

"Good to know," she says finally, and I swear her voice is unsteady.

Standing, I squeeze one of the milkshakes from the cardboard carrier and hand it to her. Her face lights up, her eyes twinkling as they meet mine.

"Milkshakes for breakfast?"

I nod, a smile touching my lips. "Sugar coma in a cup."

She cracks the plastic lid off the top, and I hand her a clear spoon, which she immediately dips into the thick vanilla ice cream. A low sound purrs from the back of her throat.

"Sugar comas taste good."

Snorting, I shake my head. "I brought a puzzle too."

Hazel sits up taller, grinning, and the throw blanket slides down her shoulders to land in the crooks of her elbows. "You're allowing me to do something other than stare into the void of darkness?"

"Yes, but keep it up, and you'll lose puzzle privileges," I tell her, clearing off her coffee table—fresh flowers she got from the market last week, a thick hardcover book that serves no purpose other than looking pretty that I returned after she tried leaving it at my condo, and an assortment of colorful coasters that she and Lucy made at one of those boozy craft studios.

She snorts a laugh, sliding off the couch and onto the floor, crossing her legs under the coffee table. The puzzle pieces rattle against the inside of the box as she picks it up, examining the photo on the front.

Her eyes lift to mine under the heavy fringe of her thick lashes, and a slow smile blooms over her lips. "Butterflies?"

"Oh, do you like those?" I sink to the floor across from her, stretching my legs under the table and nudging her knee with my own.

Puzzle pieces in every color clatter against the scarred wooden table as she dumps them out, sending them skittering in every direction. "You know what would make this even better?" Hazel asks, smiling sweetly.

"Hmm?"

"A movie," she says with a sigh.

"Not a chance."

The morning slips into afternoon, the sun arcing through the slits in the curtains, casting slivers of light through the living room that Hazel basks in like a cat as we sift through puzzle squares. We talk little, but even silence with her is better than conversation with anyone else.

It feels like something out of a film, sitting on the floor with her on the laziest of Sundays. It's the kind of day that makes you nostalgic or homesick, like you're already missing the memory, even though it's still happening. The kind of day that carves out a nook in your chest where it will sit, even when you're wrinkled and gray. Like a time-worn fragment of magic you can remember even when everything else starts to fade.

It's the lock of golden-brown hair that keeps slipping from behind her ear that decides it for me. Or maybe it's the faintest hue of pink on her cheeks from hours in the sun yesterday. Or that smile that stretches across her face, making all the colors in the room look dimmer. Or the weight of her knee that's been pressed against mine for an indeterminable stretch of time.

Either way, as the day shifts from morning to afternoon, time stretching and bending like saltwater taffy, I know I have to tell her. The love in my chest has turned into an ache I can no longer ignore. And even if it ends up slicing through me and cutting deep, I can't keep holding on to it like it's a shameful secret.

I can't do it today, on this perfect day ripped from the pages of a book and pressed into the spines of our story, but I have to do it soon. I have to do it before the love eats me alive, devouring every little piece of me I've kept hidden until I'm a shell of who I used to be.

Soon, I'll tell Hazel I love her.

Twenty-Five
HAZEL

The next weekend, my mom calls while we're on the way to the lake house, windows down, the warm breeze snaking around me and whipping my hair into a mess that will take days to untangle.

"Mind if I answer this?" I ask Alex. He's in the driver's seat of my car, steering us farther and farther away from the city. The scenery has turned from glittering high-rises to muted bi-levels to rolling green hills dotted with the occasional dilapidated, burned tobacco barn.

He spares a look my way, keeping his arm propped on the open window, sunshine making freckles pop up over his skin like stars in the night sky. "Of course not. Go for it."

I turn off the radio that has been faintly playing Alex's summer road trip playlist and swipe open the call. "Hey, Mom."

"Hey, hon," she says, and from the way she's slightly out of breath, I know she's working in the shop, probably restocking the shelves. "How are you feeling?"

I shrug, even though she can't see me, and tuck my billowing hair behind my ear. "Pretty much back to normal. The dizziness is gone for the most part, and I haven't felt nauseous in days."

"Are you sure you're going to be okay to come down here on Sunday? I don't know if you should be trying to work in the shop with a concussion."

"I'm fine, I promise. It's been a week," I say. "Plus, the doctor said my symptoms should be completely resolved in ten days, and your surgery is on the ten-day mark."

She huffs out a breath, and it's loud in the speaker. "I still don't like it."

"Sorry," I say, the word catching on a laugh. "But it's your only option. Cam has a bunch of work to do with Wes over the next couple of weeks, and I can take my work anywhere."

"You're not even supposed to be on that iPad," she grumbles, and something clatters in the background.

I sway my hand in the breeze out my open window. "Makes my job a little difficult."

"I don't appreciate that sass," she says, and I can picture her standing in her storeroom perfectly, her free hand on her hip, frizzy locks of hair curling around her head like they do when she gets frustrated and her skin heats.

I have to bite my bottom lip to hold back my smile. "I learned it from you."

"Well, that's just not true," Mom huffs. "Your dad is the sassy one."

"Dad could never be sassy, even if he tried, and you know it," I say, and when I glance at Alex, one side of his mouth hitches in a grin, his eyes focused on the road.

"Fine," Mom says, managing to sound more indignant than a Regency-era mother. "You got it from me. Is that what you wanted to hear?"

A laugh rockets out of me like a bullet, and I can practically hear Mom holding back her own. "Yes, exactly what I wanted," I tell her. "Now, I'm going to go. We're almost to the lake house."

I don't technically know if this is true, but I can see flashes of deep blue between the large houses lining this street, so we have to be getting close. Through the open windows, the breeze carries in the smells of muddy earth, damp grass, musky water. I can practically *feel* the lake, the endless days of summer—damp swimsuits, frizzy hair, grainy sand between toes, and tan lines forming in all the best places.

"Talk to you later, honey," Mom says. "Have fun this weekend."

"Talk to you soon."

When I hang up, Alex flashes me a look, his dark eyes twinkling. "Your mom thinks you're sassy, huh?"

I wave him off. "Not at all."

His lips twitch, but he doesn't say anything else, and I don't feel the need to either. Not with summer coating our skin as surely as sticky coconut scented sunscreen will later. With my feet propped up on the dash and the breeze from the open windows whipping my hair in every direction, it feels like the middle of a teenage summer romance movie, when things are so perfect it's almost unimaginable. So good that it hurts to know it won't ever be this good again.

"We need music," I say suddenly, a song already playing in my mind. My phone has been hooked up to the Bluetooth all morning, so the song starts playing a moment later.

When Deana Carter starts crooning about the boy working on her grandpa's farm, Alex groans. "Not this song."

I crank the song up louder and yell over it. "What's wrong with this song?"

He flashes me a quick look before turning back to the road. "Nothing, but these are *not* the vibes we're going for." Alex holds out his hand, palm up. "Let me pick out a song."

My fingers brush against his as I hand him the phone.

His lips curl and his eyebrow quirks as I watch him. "No peeking."

Rolling my eyes, I turn to look out the window. The scenery really is gorgeous, all greens and blues, interspersed with the pops of color from the lake houses. The early summer sun makes everything look golden, bathed in the magic that only long days and sun-kissed skin and sandy toes and saltwater can bring.

The car fills with music again, and the tune is one I immediately recognize. I press my lips together to keep from smiling, because Alex really did choose the *perfect* song. Keith Urban singing about long, hot summer days with your feet up on the dashboard.

The chorus starts, and I can't hold back anymore. When I turn to Alex, belting out the lyrics, he's already doing the same. We sing along loudly and out of tune, but it feels like one of those core memories that's imprinted on your soul, the kind that an unrelated sound or smell brings back to the surface with startling clarity.

When the final notes fade out, I can't repress my smile. "You win."

Alex's cheeks are flushed, his eyes twinkling, and one of his hands grips the steering wheel in a loose, carefree way that I haven't seen in a long while. It's like whatever tension has been weighing down his shoulders for the last few weeks has burned up in the summer sunshine.

"We're here," he says, turning into a dirt driveway, dust kicking up behind our tires.

The lake house is more rustic than the rest on this street, and much smaller. It's more of a cottage than a lake house, but it only makes it more quaint. The siding is beige, and the front door has been painted a bright orangey-red. As we park, I can see through the windows and all the way to the water on the other side, where the sun is glinting on the surface.

The poppy red door swings open, and Wes stands there, a huge grin stretching across his face. His hair has gotten steadily blonder as spring has bled into summer, and even from here, I can see the sparkle behind his green eyes.

He meets us at the car before we've even put it in park. "You made it," he says, beaming, and I can't help but smile. I bet Lo is inside soaking up the last few minutes of peace and quiet before we descend on her, but Wes looks like he's been counting down the minutes until we arrived.

"We made it," I tell him, climbing out and giving him a quick hug.

Wes is practically bouncing on the balls of his feet as he makes his way to the trunk. "Let me help with your bags." When he opens the trunk, he gives me a conspiratorial look. "You moving in?"

A little laugh escapes me as I assess the pile of my luggage in the trunk. "No, I'm going to my parents' after this, remember?"

"Ah," he says. "I forgot about that. Which bags need to go inside?"

I point out which ones and follow him through the bright red door and into the house. The windows are all open, the scent of pine and cypress blowing in on the breeze that ruffles the white linen curtains.

Lo is curled up like a cat in a patch of sunshine when we come inside, a sweating glass of lemonade on the end table next to the blue and white pinstripe chair she's sitting in, a worn paperback in her hands. Her smile is warm and genuine and so very Lo that I can't help but do the same.

"Hey, guys," she says, pushing out of her blanket cocoon. Lo always sounds the tiniest bit sleepy, like she's just woken up from a nap. It's endlessly endearing, especially to someone like me who has enough creative energy pulsing inside me at all times to power a wind farm.

"How are you, Lo?" Alex asks, giving her a side hug before I move in for a more thorough one. Lo is so much taller than me that hugs with her feel like being enveloped, and I love them.

"I'm good," she says, twisting her long red hair back from her face and securing it with a cream-colored claw clip that was sitting on the coffee table. Her blue-green eyes move behind us. "How was the trip? Did you not ride with Cam and Ellie?"

"No," I tell her, settling on the couch as she sits back in her chair, draping a thin white muslin blanket over her freckled legs. "I'm going to my parents' to help my mom after her surgery on Monday, so Alex is going to ride back to Nashville with Cam and Ellie."

"Ah, right, right," she says, nodding, and wisps of her hair fall from her clip to frame her face with the movement.

"Are there rooms I can put our bags in?" Alex asks, and I notice he's still got a duffel slung over his shoulder. Wes dropped mine next to the couch before settling in the matching blue and white chair next to Lo's.

"Oh," Lo says, her gaze dashing away to look out the window. There's a fiery blush starting to creep up her cheeks. "We only have two bedrooms here, and we told Cam and Ellie they could have it since we asked them first. But I promise the couch bed is really comfortable. We slept on it for weeks before the rest of the furniture was delivered." She says all this to the window, avoiding looking our way.

Lead sinks in my gut as I glance at Wes, who looks like he's trying hard to keep from laughing, his eyes twinkling mischievously. A sick feeling starts in the pit of my stomach, curling up around my ribs to choke off my air supply. I have a sneaking suspicion that it wasn't entirely a coincidence that Wes and Lo stumbled into the Whistling Kettle with a weekend invitation for Alex and me. That chagrined blush and that devious smirk reek of a setup.

When Cam and Ellie arrive an hour later, the four of us are already outside, sun warming our skin, bathing suits damp from our swim in the lake. Wes and Alex are still out in the water, but Lo is stretched out next to me, a white linen shirt unbuttoned over her orange one-piece.

"Hey, hey!" Ellie yells, coming around the back. Cam is walking slowly behind her, hands stuffed into the pockets of his pants, a lazy grin on his face as he watches his wife. It makes my chest hurt to watch them, and I can't help the way my eyes shoot to Alex. A zing slides along every bump of my spine when I find his already on me. Even from here, I can feel the intensity like the burn of standing too close to a flame.

"Stop it right now," Ellie gasps, and I tear my eyes from Alex, heart pounding in my throat. "Where did you get that swimsuit? I *need* it."

When I look down at my daisy-printed crochet bikini, a smile unfurls across my lips. "I'll get you one for your birthday next month."

Her dark brown eyes, so similar to Alex's it feels like looking directly into his soul, light up as she settles onto my towel next to me. She's dressed in a bright floral sundress that spreads over her outstretched legs.

"So Alex mentioned your blind date experiment at family dinner a couple weeks ago," she says almost too casually, smoothing her hand over a wrinkle in her dress. "Tell me all about it. How's it going?"

Uneasiness prickles beneath my skin, and I don't dare look in Alex's direction, not when my confusing feelings for him could be written all over my face. Not when I'm almost positive that this whole trip was set up by the two women across from me, hoping to force our hands.

Letting out a breath, I sit up and cross my legs. "Is this a setup?" At the wild, caught expressions on their faces, I know I've hit the nail on the head. My mouth falls open. "You're not serious."

"Why not?" Ellie asks, her voice sounding whiny and desperate. "We could be *family*."

I give her a flat look. "We're already family."

"But our children could be double cousins."

"That sounds like something out of a documentary about the deep south," I say, and Lo snorts. I fix my gaze on her. "I can't believe she dragged *you* into this too."

Red creeps up Lo's neck and into her cheeks, and Ellie yells, "It was her idea!"

I stare at both of them, wide-eyed. "I cannot believe you two."

"We just want you to be happy," Ellie says, her hand finding mine on the damp, sandy beach towel. "Alex makes you happy."

I can't help it. My gaze snags on him in the lake. Water drips over his skin that's sure to sunburn again since he slathered sunscreen all over himself before I could even attempt to offer, missing major chunks. That's probably for the best, with how things went with the aloe in my bathroom.

Swallowing against the lump in my throat, I turn back to Ellie and Lo, who are watching me with knowing glances. "Alex is my best friend. Of course he makes me happy."

Even to my own ears, it rings hollow, but terror grips at me with sharp claws as I let myself consider the alternative.

Lo's gaze softens. "I think friendship is the most important thing in a relationship. But I understand. It must be scary to consider anything else with him," she says, her voice gentle. Out of the two of them, she would understand what I'm going through; she and Wes were friends for almost a decade before they got together.

"It is scary," I say, and it feels like a confession to say it out loud, to admit that I *have* considered it. That somehow, in the last few weeks, my best friend has transformed into something more, and I don't know what to do about that.

Ellie squeezes my hand. "Alex would never hurt you."

My pulse pounds so loudly I can hear it, a rhythmic beat in my ears that ratchets my anxiety up by the second. "You can't know that."

"He wouldn't," Ellie says, shaking her head, brows furrowing.

I pull my hand back, folding it so tightly with my other that my knuckles strain and pop. Even then, I'm still shaking, but I hope they don't notice. That they can't tell I'm about to fall apart.

"I appreciate what you're trying to do," I tell them, surprised that my voice doesn't betray me. "But I don't want things to change between us. I'm happy with how things are."

My eyes flick between the two of them, the early afternoon sun making them appear golden, wind rustling the ends of their hair. Lo's bottom lip is trapped between her teeth, and Ellie's fingers tap out a rhythm against the sand, but eventually, they both nod, and a frisson of tension releases, making my spine boneless.

"Thank you," I tell them, and a relieved breath slips between my lips. I can feel the sun beating against my skin once more, the gritty sand on my legs, the cooling dampness of the towel beneath me.

Ellie sits up straighter, glancing around. "It's quiet," she says, and Lo's eyes widen.

She barely has time to say "Oh, no," before yells echo across the trees and the surface of the water. I spin to see Alex, Cam, and Wes running for us, and before I realize what's happening, Alex's arms are around me, his wet skin sliding against my own, and I'm being hoisted over his shoulders. His arm bands around my thighs, holding me in place as he sprints across the grass before it turns into wooden dock planks. I bounce against him with each step, my laugh catching in the breeze.

And then we're airborne, time frozen for one instant before water swallows us whole. Alex's hands leave me only for a moment before finding me under the water again, slipping around my waist before tugging me up with him. I feel rather than see when we break through the surface. I feel sun on my skin, Alex's breath against my face, undiluted happiness bubbling through my veins.

When I finally peel my eyes open, Alex is the first thing I see. His mouth hitched higher on one side, his eyes sparking in the sunlight, looking gold and green and brown all at once. He looks the way I feel, like he's a mirror of my soul, reflecting every emotion I have right back at me. If I could freeze this moment in time and keep us *just like this*, I would. Because right now, things are too perfect to ever ruin. Too perfect to bleed and rot away and turn into something ugly. This moment with Alex is flawless, and I hate how scared I am for it to end.

Twenty-Six

HAZEL

THE COUCH BED IS going to be the death of me. Alex and I are staring at it, hands on hips, like we're the disappointed parents of the angsty heroine in an eighties film. We just finished putting the sheets on it, covering the whole thing with a downy white comforter, and stuffing our pillowcases with expensive feather pillows that are nicer than my own pillow at home.

All that's left is to actually *get in the bed*. Despite the heat, I shiver in my button-up mustard yellow muslin pajama set. I normally sleep in underwear and a tank, but I brought this set in case I ended up going over to Wren or Stevie's when I visit home, and thank God.

"Cold?" Alex asks, his eyes confused as he looks down at me. Having his full attention on me is almost too much, making my nerve endings zing to life like I've touched a live wire. I feel tense and on edge—a way I never would have felt about sharing a bed with him in the past. As much as I hate to admit it, things between us *have* changed, and I'm running in circles trying to keep up with stuffing him back into the neat friend box he's supposed to be in.

"No." It's not a lie. I'm on *fire*, and nowhere near cold.

He holds my gaze for a long moment before his eyes dip down, tracing the contours of my face and lingering on my mouth for a heartbeat too long. I feel that stare like there's an invisible string tied to my belly button, tugging hard.

"Want to go outside for a bit? It's nice tonight." His voice is sandpaper scraping against my skin.

It absolutely isn't nice tonight. The pleasant day has turned into a very muggy night. The heat hangs in the air, thick enough to cut with a knife and heavy with the promise of incoming rain. But even the soupy air outside has to be cooler than the scorching heat between us while the tiny couch bed sits like an elephant in the middle of the room.

"Yes," I say, and my own voice comes out squeaky, but if Alex notices, he doesn't say anything. He silently turns and heads out the back door, all long lines and fluid grace.

It's dark as we head for the dock with only the moonlight to guide us, and memories of the day crash over me like waves. We swam in the lake until our skin was pruned, snacking on the charcuterie board Wes and Lo prepared until we needed real food, which was a joint effort between the six of us. We danced in the crowded kitchen, Ellie and me on the countertops, Cam snapping pictures of us on the film camera he's had since high school.

Dinner was skillet pizzas with thick chunks of mozzarella and fresh basil that we ate straight from the pan on the back porch as the sun set, music blaring. The smell of Lo's citronella candle and Cam's heavy-duty bug spray hung heavy in the air, and we made up ghost stories when one of the Edison bulb café lights started blinking. We took turns jumping off the dock as the stars sparked to life in the sky, the sun winking out, not to be seen again until morning.

When everyone finally retreated to the house for bed, our feet were dragging, our eyelids fluttering closed. That is, until

I remembered the couch bed, and then I came to life again, jump-starting like a car battery.

Now it's just us and the crickets chirping in the distance, our friends long since fallen asleep in each other's arms.

The dock groans as Alex and I stop at the edge and sit, sliding our feet into the dark surface of the water. I expected it to be warm, still holding heat from the sunshine, but it's cool silk against my overly warm skin.

"If a water moccasin eats my foot off, I'm blaming you," I tell him, and a laugh huffs out of him, echoing across the water.

"As you should," he says. A smile tugs at my lips, and I don't fight to hold it back.

We fall silent, our shoulders brushing, and it feels like old times. Like before I had this secret attraction growing inside me. Things were simpler when it wasn't there, when I didn't want to know how his skin would feel under my palms and what his body looks like beneath those clothes.

"You okay?" Alex asks, not looking at me. His gaze is still fixed on the inky water in front of us, and that makes it easier to be truthful. Or at least partly truthful.

"I don't know," I whisper, and then he does look at me, his eyes as dark as the sky around us. He holds my gaze for a long moment, his breath syncing with mine, and I feel like I did earlier today, when his hands were wrapped around my waist in the lake and water gathered on the edges of his eyelashes—that he is a reflection of me.

"What's wrong?"

Thoughts spin around me like a tropical storm gaining momentum before it hits shore. How do I explain to him that the stupid bed has made this harmless crush no longer harmless? How do I tell him that since that other night in *my* bed, with him reading to me, his body warm next to mine, I haven't been able to stop wishing he was beside me every night? And now that I have the opportunity again, I am absolutely *terrified* to test my restraint. And even more terrified to leave it all out on this dock, regardless of the consequences.

I *can't* tell him any of that. Not if I don't want to ruin everything.

"Lo said friendship is the most important thing in a relationship," I say, voicing the other thought that's been echoing in my head all day—as Alex handed me the scrunchie from his wrist when I wanted to pull my damp hair off my neck, and when he made my favorite drink without me asking and served it to me as I danced on the counter with his sister, the corner of his mouth hooked in that smile I love so much.

Alex's shoulders lift as he takes a deep breath, and I wish I could better make out his eyes in the darkness so I could know what he's thinking. "Do you agree with her?" he asks finally, slow as syrup dripping down pancakes.

I don't know how to answer, but the truth trips out of me before I can think of something else. "Yes," I breathe, and then, before I can lose the courage, "Are we making a mistake with the blind dates?"

Alex stills next to me, his body going rigid in a way that can only be achieved through all that discipline he has in the gym. "Why do you ask that?"

"It's just that…" I trail off, trying to sort out my thoughts, and press my hands under my thighs on the dock to keep them from trembling. "If friendship is the most important, are blind dates really the best way to do this? Shouldn't we, I don't know, date our friends?"

He's quiet for a long moment. Even his breathing is silent. When he finally speaks, it comes out slowly, like he's chosen his words specifically. "Who do you think we should date?"

I feel his question beneath my skin, burrowing into every one of my atoms. I want to blurt out that maybe we should date each other, just to test it out. But even if he *does* feel the same way, it feels like the edge of a sharp knife, dangerous and with the ability to slice everything I hold dear to ribbons.

So I push the words down and grapple for anything to get out of this conversation before it can swallow me whole. "I don't know," I say finally, hoping I sound more confident than I feel. Then, desperately needing to change the trajectory of the conversation, I ask, "Do you want to swim?"

"You want to swim?" Alex asks, blinking at the sudden change in topic.

I choke back my nerves, feeling on more solid footing the further we get from the conversation. "Yeah, I think it would be fun. It's hot as hell out here," I say, pinching the V of my shirt between my finger and thumb and tugging it to create a small breeze to cool me down.

Alex watches me for a long moment, his eyes glinting in the pale moonlight, and I swear I see stars in his eyes. "Okay, Haze. Let's swim."

I feel a momentary surge of relief that he let the subject go, but then he stands, his muscles rippling with the movement, and pulls his shirt over his head with one hand. His shirt, still warm from his skin, lands in a heap on the wood planks beside me.

"What are you doing?" I squeak out when his fingers slide into the waistband of his shorts, pushing so the curves of his hip bones are revealed.

"I'm not putting wet trunks back on," he says matter-of-factly, and there's an odd lilt to his voice, a challenge.

I swallow against the lump forming in my throat. "So you're going to swim in boxers?" I ask, and I don't know why the thought sends a bolt of lightning through me, because it's not really any different from what he swam in today.

"Nope," he says, and the shorts pool at his feet. "Don't want to get those wet either."

My face heats as his words register, as images take shape in my mind. "Oh" is all I can say.

I can't tear my eyes from his exposed stomach, flexing under my gaze, and from the long line of his neck, the pulse pounding there.

Alex extends his hand, holding it out to me in invitation. "Are you coming?"

This is classic Alex and Hazel. Spontaneous and fun. Like middle-of-the-night Waffle House runs and milkshakes for breakfast, but it also feels different. Like books read in bed under a shared blanket and butterfly necklaces clasped around necks.

It feels the same and different, thrilling and terrifying, and I like the contradictions. So I take his outstretched hand, loving the way his fingers feel curled around mine.

My heart pounds beneath my sternum as I stand to my feet, the top of my head hovering just below Alex's chin. I can feel his stare branding me, and when I meet his eyes, they're dark and depthless, making warmth pool in my stomach, in the hollow of my throat, down the lengths of my thighs, and the tips of my fingers.

"I should probably get my swimsuit," I say, my voice a breathy whisper.

I expect a nod, for his hand to drop mine and to feel his gaze heavy on my retreating form as I head back to the cottage. But instead, he quirks a brow, and one corner of his mouth lifts in a dangerous smile. "You've seen me naked, Lane. Fair is fair."

My mouth falls open. Not at his words so much as the teasing, flirty tone behind them. Alex has never talked to *me* like that, and until this moment, I've never realized what I was missing. Hearing his voice like this is intoxicating, and I have no idea how any of those women I set him up with were able to resist him.

He knows what he's doing too, because I would have gone back inside for anything less than the challenge he delivered.

"Fine," I say, lifting my hand to the button closest to the waistband of my pants. It slides through the hole easily, and Alex's eyes track the movement with startling intensity. I slide up to the next one and free it before moving onto the third. When this one breaks free, Alex swallows hard.

"You okay?" I ask, and my own voice holds that same taunting, flirtatious tone. I'm surprised by it, but when I see how it affects him, the tightening of his jaw, the bob of his throat, the blackness that swallows his eyes whole, it makes my blood spark.

His hands flex at his sides, fingers curling into a fist before spreading wide. "Mm-hmm."

"Good," I say, flipping the next button through the hole. I'm four buttons down, and Alex is consuming every inch of exposed skin like a starving man. It makes me feel heady, powerful, and although I know I should think through this more, ask him what we're doing and what it means, I also don't want to break the spell. Not when he's looking at me like *that*.

Plus, the look on his face when he realizes I'm wearing a sports bra under this is going to be priceless.

His breath catches when I free the last button, and his hands twitch at his sides, almost like he's holding himself back. I pause, my hands at my throat, clutching the thin fabric together.

Suddenly, I don't feel as powerful. I'm equal parts desperate and hesitant, hopeful and scared. My heart pounds in my chest as I ask, "Alex, what are we—"

My words are cut off by the sound of the back door squealing as it slowly opens, followed by a hissed shushing noise. Alex's eyes blow wide, matching my own, and we snap into motion as we see Wes and Lo sneaking across the deck, stripping their clothes as they go.

In every direction, there are flashes of skin in the moonlight as Alex grabs his clothes and Wes and Lo shed theirs. Clothes in hand, Alex pulls me by my arm off the dock and into the dark copse of trees. Wes and Lo would see us if they were paying attention to anyone but each other as they quietly stifle their giggles, tripping across the dirty sand toward the dock half-dressed.

Wes murmurs something to Lo, quiet enough that I can't hear, and I'm glad for it. I think I'd never recover from listening to my friends' dirty talk.

Alex's hand lands on my waist, his fingers curling around my hip bone, and he tugs me a little closer in the dark. My body presses against his, where he's leaning on a wide tree trunk. While he gathered his clothes from the dock, he didn't take the time to pull them on, and I didn't get a chance to button my shirt, so we're skin to skin, our breathing heavy from the adrenaline rush.

Time stands still as we hover in the dark, waiting for Wes and Lo to get into the water, distracted enough that they won't see us crawling back through the dark with our tails between our legs. We weren't doing anything wrong or anything to be ashamed of, but I think we both feel like this is too fragile to let anyone else know about yet.

Wes whispers something about leaving a sock on the dock and Lo's laugh pierces the air, but I'm focused on Alex in front of me, his hand still heavy on my waist, his fingers flexing against my skin.

I expect him to let go, for us to forget what happened or almost happened out there on that dock in the moonlight, so I'm surprised at his hot breath tickling my neck as he asks, "You okay?"

I want to say yes immediately, to brush it all off and act like it was no big deal, but Wes and Lo were a slap of reality. Them specifically, here in the exact spot they risked and ruined their friendship all those years ago. It obviously worked out for them, if the splashing and laughing are any indication, but it took them a *long* time to get there. And I don't know if I'm ready to risk that with Alex, to risk losing him temporarily or permanently just to see if there's a possibility of *something* between us.

So I decide to be honest. "I don't know," I whisper. "I'm...scared."

I feel his nod rather than see it, his facial hair scraping against the curve of my neck. "Me too," he says.

My eyes meet his in the darkness, catching and holding. He looks as vulnerable as I feel. The moment stretches, holding us in its firm grasp, and I feel like we're in a bubble, stardust and magic and dangerous hope crackling in the air between us.

A breathy moan echoes across the water, and our eyes widen together. Alex's hand tightens on my waist, spinning me around so I'm facing the house. "Time to go."

Twigs and fallen leaves crack beneath our feet, but Wes and Lo are too distracted to notice. Instead of risking the squeaky back door, Alex leads me around the front by my hand, and the planks of the porch creak beneath our feet. In the darkness, he pauses to pull his shorts back over his black boxers before we yank the door open and slip inside.

We collapse against the front door after shutting it quietly behind us, stifling our giggles. The room is dark, lit only by the moonlight peering through the windows and the warm dim light above the oven. If Wes and Lo had bothered to look, they would have noticed our couch bed was empty, the blankets untouched.

"They can never know," I whisper between huffs of laughter.

"Oh, I'm absolutely bringing it up at breakfast tomorrow."

I spin around to face him, and we're both still sporting matching crazy grins. "You wouldn't."

One dark eyebrow quirks. "You really think they wouldn't do the same if they had come outside ten minutes later?"

His insinuation hangs in the air between us, and my heartbeat quickens. I'm still pressed up against the door, the wood grain imprinting on the palms of my hands.

I know I shouldn't ask. I know I should let the moment die, protect that last shard over my heart, trust my self-preservation instincts, but I'm also feeling reckless and heady from his full attention fixed squarely on me and the memories of his skin against mine in the darkness. "What would they have seen?"

Alex's throat bobs, his eyes swallowed up by the blackness of his pupils. His own palms come against the door, but they're on either side of my head, caging me in. I don't think I'm breathing as he leans in closer, his breath warm against my already burning face.

"They wouldn't have seen anything," he says after a long pause, as if he's carefully choosing his words. His voice is like gravel. "They wouldn't have seen anything because nothing is going to happen until we have a talk, Hazel. You're too important to me to not make sure we're on the same page."

His words aren't at all what I expected, but they do more for me than any detailed description could have. They're a balm to my soul, filling in all my gaps and warming the places inside me that have been coated with ice for far too long.

My throat is thick as I try to respond, and it takes a few tries, but Alex waits patiently, his eyes never leaving mine, as if he knows how hard this is for me. "Thank you," I finally say. "Thank you for understanding."

Alex leans forward, and his lips brush my forehead, just a whisper against skin, like he can't hold himself back. The gesture is so soft, so tender, I want to cry. "I know you, Hazel Lane."

It's both terrifying and comforting how true that is.

Twenty-Seven

ALEX

Everything smells like Hazel. Not the assortment of perfumes she chooses from on any given day, but the scent that is uniquely her—Herbal Essences shampoo that she told me she can't part with even though her hair stylist keeps begging her to, the apple-scented lotion she stocks up on every time she visits home, and the turpentine and paint that always seem to be faintly clinging to her.

It takes me a moment to remember where I am as I blink awake. The first rays of pale sunshine seep through the windows, and the early morning breeze ruffles the linen curtains, carrying in the smell of a brewing summer storm.

I'm in Wes and Lo's lake house, on a surprisingly comfortable couch bed, a pillowy white duvet thrown over me. Hazel is curled into my side, her deep breaths tickling the space where my neck meets my shoulder. Our legs are a tangle beneath the blanket, and the tips of my fingers tingle, going numb from the weight of her head resting on my bicep. She feels so ridiculously perfect here that I don't want to move a muscle and risk waking her up, risk making her regret the way she migrated toward me in the night like magnets.

A small breath escapes me, and I allow myself one touch, my fingers trailing across the smooth skin of her arm. It's wrapped around my torso like she's holding on to me for dear life. She stirs, tightening her hold on me before her breathing slows again.

I know staying here for another second is a bad idea. Any moment, our friends will wake up and tromp down the stairs to make breakfast, and our day will disappear under the sunshine—loud music and splashing water, sunburned noses and damp swimsuits—and Hazel and I will never have a chance to talk. And I *need* to talk to her. Because as I stood there last night with Hazel on a dock in the moonlight, I realized she held my entire heart in her small hands. It's not fair to either of us to pretend like she doesn't. I need to tell her how I feel and face the consequences.

My chest lifts in a deep breath, and my arm tightens around Hazel's shoulder. She nuzzles closer to me, her nose brushing against the thin fabric of my worn T-shirt.

"Hazel," I whisper, my voice low and crackled with sleep. My gaze drifts over her, marveling at the way she looks drenched in sunrise, lit up in pinks and oranges. Her skin has tanned with all the time she's spent in the sun recently, turning golden. Unlike mine, which has only dotted with pale, faint freckles. Even her hair has changed, bronzing and lightening each day. She looks so different from how she looked last summer. Then, she was a shell of herself, still piecing herself back together after Sebastian. Now, she looks *alive*, and it cracks something in my chest. Love and tenderness seep into every fiber of my being until I'm coursing with it.

Hazel stirs, all her soft curves brushing against me, and her eyelids flutter. In the early morning light, her eyes are impossibly blue, like looking up from the bottom of the lake and seeing the sun glinting over the surface.

I expect her to sit up, pink coloring her cheeks, when she realizes the position we settled into while we slept, but she doesn't. Her hair falls like a golden sheet around her as she tilts her head back, lips stretching in a sleepy smile.

"Morning," she murmurs, and I know right then that her drowsy voice is the first thing I want to hear every morning for the rest of my life. I want her just like this, creases indenting her cheeks, hair a mess, legs draped over my own. I can't imagine anything better than Hazel Lane waking up next to me for eternity.

"Morning," I say back, and her eyes drift in a lazy pattern over my face, pausing on the dips of my cheekbones and the fringe of my lashes and curve of my lips. I wonder if she's cataloging this moment for the same reason I am, because it's the first of many, or if it's because she wants to keep this memory tucked in her back pocket to pull out later, when we're back to being just friends, the blurry lines between us reinforced with steel.

"We should talk," I say finally, and her eyes snag on mine. So many emotions flicker through them, and I want to pull each out to consider them. But her throat bobs in a swallow, and she nods, easing back. She wraps the blanket around her shoulders, hiding the mustard yellow pajama set that threatened all my self-control last night, and I have to force my thoughts back to the moment at hand, my pulse racing.

Hazel stands at the foot of the pull-out bed, the blanket pulled around her like a life jacket. She looks so vulnerable that my heart aches. Without thinking, I rub at the soreness, and she tracks the movement, her eyes softening.

"Outside?" she asks, voice soft as silk, and I nod.

Wordlessly, I follow her out the back door. It squeaks on its hinges, and Hazel's blanket drags across the worn, weathered wooden planks of the back porch. Just last night, we followed this same path, but things were different then.

Hazel sits on the top porch step, and my shoulder brushes against hers as I squeeze myself down next to her. The morning air is heavy with the humidity of incoming rain, but it's surprisingly cool, and I wrap my arms around myself. Whether to keep for warmth or to keep myself from reaching for her, I'm not entirely sure.

We're quiet as we stare out at the lake. The muted sunrise peeks through the heavy gray clouds and glitters on the water, sending every shade back at us like a disco ball. There's only the sound of the wind rustling the trees, their branches waving in a slow dance, sending leaves skittering to the ground and across the dock.

It's peaceful, the way only nature can be. It's so much bigger than us, making all of our problems seem infinitesimal by comparison. Amid the grandeur, I almost convince myself to keep quiet. But that clawing sensation is back in my throat, words begging to break free.

My eyes drift over the planes of Hazel's face. A lock of sun-bronzed hair catches in the breeze before drifting back across her forehead. Her cheeks are dusted in the palest constellation of freckles, ones you can only see if you're a breath away, everything but her features blurring at the edges. She's got one of those noses people pay for, short and curved at the tip, just like the corners of her mouth, like she's always just a heartbeat from smiling.

She makes my chest ache.

I know I should be eloquent. I should ease into it and explain myself, but watching her like this, it just slips out. "I'm in love with you."

Hazel's gaze snaps to mine, her eyes wide and depthless, the exact color of the lake beyond. "What?" she asks, lips parting.

My heart rate ratchets up behind my sternum, my pulse pounding in my ears loud enough to drown out the wind rustling the trees. It's not the response I wanted, but the vise around my chest eases when I see it there behind the shock clouding her eyes—the fear. It matches my own, and I feel such a visceral need to blot it away.

"I'm in love with you, Hazel." My voice comes out in rasp, sounding as desperate as I feel. "I have been for so long."

I shove a shaking hand through my hair, tugging it from the roots, and Hazel tracks the movement with wide eyes, clutching the blanket tighter around herself. The gears in her head are working so loudly I can practically hear them searching for a response.

"You don't have to say anything," I tell her before she can respond. "I just needed you to know, just once."

"Alex," she says, and I feel myself shattering like broken pottery at the pity I hear in her voice. Bits of my heart scatter so far I know I'll never be able to piece it fully back together again.

My gaze rips from her, fixing back on the water out of self-preservation. Like maybe if I imprint the memory of the sunrise cresting over the lake on my mind, I won't have any more room for that look of regret on her face.

Hazel's cool fingers wrap around my forearm, squeezing. "Alex, please look at me."

Her voice is sandpaper, heavy and rough. Tears are gathering in her eyes when I force myself to look at her, and this time when my heart breaks, it's for *her*. For how scared and unsure she looks, wrapped in a thick white duvet on a peeling porch, the gathering storm tugging at stray wisps of her hair.

"I'm scared of what I feel for you," she manages to get out, her voice cracking, and I slide my hand over hers, linking our fingers together. "You're my best friend, and if something goes wrong, I don't think I could handle losing you."

My thumb makes a pass over her knuckles as I try to figure out what I want to say. "I can't promise anything, Haze. I can't promise it will work out, but I can tell you that I spent the first year of our friendship trying not to love you. You were happy with Sebastian, and I thought this piece of you was all I'd ever get. And then I spent another year trying to convince myself that risking what we have wasn't worth it, but I could never quite manage it. You're worth it to me, Hazel."

Tears fall unchecked down her cheeks, and she sniffs, tugging her hand free to wipe her face. I ask, "Would it help to know I'm scared too?"

A wobbly laugh huffs out of her. "A little, yeah." She's quiet for another heartbeat. "I don't want everything to change."

My knee bumps against hers, or what I can feel of it under the heavy duvet. "Change can be good, Haze. Like butterflies."

"Like butterflies," she echoes, then says, "What if you decide you don't want me?"

Everything inside me softens, and tenderness sweeps through me with the forcefulness of a tidal wave. "Nothing could make me not want you, Hazel. Trust me, I've tried."

"I just need some time," she says after a long moment. "To figure out what everything I've been feeling means."

Her words make my breath hitch. Dangerous hope ignites in my chest, the single careless match that starts a wildfire. "What have you been feeling?" I ask.

Pink tinges her cheeks, and when she shifts, the wooden steps groan beneath her. "Well, there was the sunscreen," she says, and a groan escapes me.

"The sunscreen," I repeat on a huff of air, and her lips twist in a reluctant smile.

"I know you were trying to torture me."

"Not even a little," I tell her, completely serious. "I was barely keeping myself together."

Hazel leans back against the railing, tucking the blanket more securely around her shoulders. "Well, you did."

"Torture you or keep myself together?"

She shrugs. "Both, I guess."

"I didn't want to," I say, stretching my legs out on the stairs in front of me, my knees popping from sitting in the cramped position for so long.

Her lips quirk, and I want to bottle up that smile and keep it in case she says this thing between us is too vast, too scary to consider. "Torture me or keep yourself together?"

"Keep myself together," I say.

"I don't think I wanted you to either," she says after a moment, and my mind spins. The kind of swirling you feel when you get off a Tilt-A-Whirl, where everything is upside down and shaken up.

"I didn't want to read to you that night in your bed." My voice is sandpaper, scratchy and rough, grating against this fine line of friendship I'm so desperate to buff away.

She watches me carefully, throat bobbing in a swallow. "What did you want to do?"

A million things flash through my mind, but I feel too vulnerable to say that, most of all, I wanted to hold her. That I was so wrecked when I saw her blood on that rock that I needed to feel her skin against mine just to reassure myself she was still there. To make sure she was whole and safe and with me when she so very nearly wasn't.

I end up saying, "A gentleman never tells."

Hazel's bottom lip catches between her teeth, and her eyes are heavy on me. "Time," she says, and it comes out scratchy. "Can I have some time? To think about everything."

"Yeah, Haze," I say. "Take all the time you need. I've been waiting a long time. It won't kill me to wait a little longer."

Her eyes dart across my face, never landing on any one spot for too long. "How long have you been waiting?"

A knot forms in my throat, but I'm too embarrassed to tell her. To let her know just how long I've pined for her. So I just let a small smile slide across my lips and sidestep the question. "A while."

"You love me," she says softly, and it comes out like a question.

I lean forward until my lips are at her ear and whisper, "I love you, Hazel Lane."

A shiver races up her spine, and her breath comes out in a heavy exhale against my neck. I want to dip my face into her shoulder, drag my lips up the column of her neck until I can *taste* that shiver, until it's as much a part of me as it is of her. I bet she'd be sweet like ice cream on a hot summer day and warm like sitting beside a crackling fire. She'd be better than any wish I could make on the flap of a butterfly's wings.

"Alex," Hazel says into the curve of my neck, and I have to flex my hands at my sides to keep from threading them in her hair, to keep from breaking her request for more time.

"Yes?"

"Everyone is awake and watching us through the window right now," she whispers, and my head falls onto her shoulder, muffling the groan deep in my throat. Her laugh rings out, echoing off the trees. It sounds like music, the kind you can only get in nature, and feels like peace.

Twenty-Eight

HAZEL

When it's time to leave the lake house and drive to Fontana Ridge, I don't want to. The day was just as perfect as the one before it. The rain that felt like a promise never broke through the clouds, and the sun made its appearance just as we finished eating a huge salad topped with fresh peaches and pecans from the farmer's stand down the road.

Alex let me put sunscreen on his back, and we kept sharing secret glances every time Wes yawned or Lo mentioned that she was tired. We tracked sand through the house and got the jitters from drinking too many of Wes' homemade iced coffees on the dock. Our skin pruned and our hair frizzed, and by the end of the day, we smelled like sunscreen and bug spray and sweat and lake water, but we were happy.

It was the kind of perfect day you never want to end, the kind that makes everything else in your life melt away like popsicles in sunshine.

But now, as I'm pulling out of the driveway while the rest of my friends load their belongings into the trunks of their cars and Alex waves in the reflection of my rearview mirror, everything comes rushing back. That crippling fear has the kind of grip on me that makes my stomach hurt and nausea roil in my gut.

I can still hear Alex's whisper perfectly, feel it against my skin. *I love you, Hazel Lane.*

With each passing mile into the mountains, it echoes in my mind. For the first half of the drive, I have to talk myself out of picking up my phone and calling Alex to tell him I love him too. For the second half, I have to convince myself that Alex isn't Sebastian, or Oliver the hardware store owner, or Noah the insurance salesman, or any of the other guys who have come and gone from my life without realizing they left damage.

The sun has just set when I pass the Fontana Ridge welcome sign, lit only in the faint blue hue of twilight. Alex's ghost is all over this town now, and I can't tell if that makes me infinitely happy because he's here with me in my favorite place, or desperately sad because he's *not* here, and my hometown will never feel the same without him.

I pass the turnoff for my parents' house, driving farther up the hills and deeper into the woods before steering my car down a dirt road you'd probably miss if you weren't looking for it. Dust kicks up behind my tires as I drive through the twist of trees, the smell of moss and earth blowing in through my open windows.

Up ahead, nestled in a copse of trees, is a silver Airstream, reflecting the deep violet and inky blue of quickly falling night. Wren's old yellow Volkswagen Beetle is parked behind Stevie's beat-up pickup, and I come to a stop right behind them, dust settling behind me. Just seeing their cars here, the same ones they've had forever, makes something settle in my chest and the tight knot of anxiety ease.

When I climb out of the car, seventies rock music filters out of the vintage record player Stevie found at a garage sale when we were in high school. This whole piece of land feels like nostalgia. It was formerly owned by a kind elderly man with waist-length white hair who never minded when high schoolers would sneak up here to smoke joints on his property on weekend nights. Stevie bought it from him a few years after graduation, when she'd saved enough money working for my dad. Then she found the most decrepit motor home on Craigslist and somehow made it feel homey before she finally upgraded to the Airstream two summers ago.

Stevie and Wren are laughing at the weathered, rain-bent picnic table, café lights illuminating the whole space in a warm, golden glow. At the sound of my footsteps, their heads swivel in my direction.

"What's wrong?" Stevie asks immediately, her dark eyes filling with concern.

I throw my legs over the bench seat, sliding down next to Wren. The table is covered in an assortment of colorful dishes. "Who said anything is wrong?"

Wren props her chin on her hand. "You texted the group chat saying you needed to have dinner with us tonight," she points out.

"I just wanted to see you," I say, unsure of why I'm deflecting. Maybe I'm scared that if I tell them about Alex, if I try to explain my reasoning out loud, they'll tell me I'm being irrational. Maybe I'm worried that I *am* being irrational. But even if the fear is irrational, it's real, and it's suffocating me.

Stevie holds my gaze, and I think she can see every thought going through my head. She's like Cam in that way, often quiet and on the sidelines, watching everyone until she knows the secrets they're keeping from even themselves.

"What happened?" she asks, and my breath comes out shaky.

I have to sit on my hands to keep them from trembling, the worn wooden seat biting into my palms. "He told me he loves me," I say.

"Parker?" Wren asks, eyes wide.

"Alex," Stevie says before I can get the chance. "Alex loves her."

Wren looks between us. "Why is this a bad thing? We love Alex." She puts a hand to her chest. "At least, *I* love Alex."

"I love Alex," I whisper, and it feels like relief to say it out loud, like finally pulling out a splinter that has burrowed beneath your skin. Tears crowd into my eyes, blurring my vision. "I love Alex, and I'm so scared."

Thin arms wrap around me—Wren. And a moment later, stronger, leaner arms follow suit—Stevie. We all crowd on that picnic bench, like we did in the back of my mom's SUV so many times as kids, whispering secrets to one another after school or singing too loudly to songs we probably shouldn't have been listening to.

There, with their arms around me, I finally let myself go. I tried not to fall apart with Alex today. Not when I could see how much his admission was costing him, but now, the fear claws through me, ripping and shredding, fighting against the warm, glowing bundle of love that wants so desperately to be let free.

"Alex isn't Sebastian, honey," Wren says after long moments of holding me, rocking slowly.

"I know," I say into the damp air between us, heavy with tears.

"He's not Oliver either. Or Noah," Stevie tells me.

I sniff, and it echoes loudly. "I know that too. He's better than all of them combined, and he means so much more."

They nod in unison against me, words not needed, giving me space to say what's on my mind if I want to. "Losing him would be so much worse," I whisper.

"But having him would be so much better," Wren says, and it feels like rainwater seeping down into drought-parched soil, filling in all the cracks and soaking into deeply buried roots.

Sitting back, I run my hands under my eyes. "I need to get it together," I say, glancing between them. "How do I look?"

"Like you've been hit by a bus," Stevie says.

Wren adds, "But in a cute way."

A laugh rockets out of me, wet and choked, but real and genuine too. Wren smooths a hand down my arm, squeezing my elbow before gripping my hand.

"You're going to be okay," she tells me. "And we're going to be here for you, no matter what."

Tears threaten again, ones that feel like gratitude and the kind of happiness that aches. "Thanks, guys. I love you both."

Wren smacks a kiss on my cheek. "You know I love you. Always."

"I love you too," Stevie says, bumping her shoulder with mine. "Now, let's eat before the gazpacho gets warm." She stands, moving back over to the other side of the table.

"Gazpacho, huh? I don't think you've made that for me before." I say, examining the dishes on the table. The deep red chilled Spanish soup sits in the middle of the table in a matte black serving bowl. A bright green salad topped with avocado slices sits beside it. On the other side, there's garlic bread on an acacia wood serving platter and some sort of eggplant dish. At the very end, next to several types of dipping sauces, are cinnamon and sugar dusted churros.

"You sure it's going to be enough?" I ask wryly, and Stevie smirks at me.

She passes us each a bowl. "Get your food and leave me alone."

Wren and I stifle giggles, filling our bowls before doing the same with the matching black plates. We will never be able to eat all this food, and a good amount of it will probably end up with the sweet old lady who lives in a tiny cottage at the bottom of the hill, but I'm glad for this bit of familiarity. Everything else may feel like it's changing, but at least I can be here with my best friends since childhood with way too much food and oldies rock music playing through the speakers.

The stars wink alive in the night sky as we eat, and the cicadas chirp in response to our laughter. Dinner with them feels like medicine to my soul. We stay at the picnic table until our butts go numb on the hard seats and the vinyl stops playing, humming on the needle. Then we haul vintage handmade quilts from the Airstream and turn off the café lights before hiking to the clearing in the trees and spreading the blankets on the ground.

We lie down, shoulder to shoulder, watching for shooting stars, and hit each other's shoulders like we're playing Punch Buggy every time we think we see one. After the third time I punch Stevie for an airplane, she says, "That's enough of this game."

I have to press my lips together to keep from laughing, but it spurts out anyway, and before I know it, they've both joined in.

Finally, Stevie says, "Fine, we can keep playing. But if you punch me for an airplane again, I'm punching you back."

"Deal," I say, holding back laughter once again.

We're quiet for a long time after that. So long that the night seems to stretch on forever, as vast and endless as the sky itself. Then Wren says, "Tell us why you're scared to start something with Alex."

Right now, I'm not scared. Right now, I don't think I could be scared of anything. Under the never-ending night sky, my problems seem unimportant. My fears are like stars that will disappear come morning, fading out in the sunshine.

But I force myself to face the dark part of myself, the one that has scars that were patched but never healed. The part that is raw and hurt and trying so hard not to feel or get too close to that pain again.

"Everyone leaves me," I say.

"*You* left," Stevie says, and I almost get the sense that she didn't mean to. I turn my head to the right to look at her. Her dark hair falls all around her, looking like ink against the pale blue of the quilt.

"I did leave," I say. "I went for Cam. I was hurting after Oliver broke up with me after graduation, and I was *still* hurting after Cam moved away, so I just…left too. It felt good to be someplace new, to *be* someone new, I think."

"What do you mean?" Wren asks softly.

I let out a breath. "Being far away from the things that hurt me back home made it easier to forget them. But then my friends in LA slowly started moving back to their hometowns or out to the suburbs, or they started hanging out with other friend groups, and I saw them less and less. The same happened with the few guys I dated. Then it was mostly just Wes, Cam, and me. And then they…"

"They moved to Nashville," Wren fills in for me.

"But I still had Sebastian," I say. "And for a while, that felt like enough. Maybe my family and friends lived on the other side of the country, but I had *him*. And I loved him. Gosh, I loved him so much." My voice cracks.

Wren slips her hand through mine and Stevie nestles closer.

"And then you know what happened there," I say, sniffling. "And I ran again. I followed Cam, who is probably sick of me at this point."

Stevie lets out a small laugh, and I do too, thinking of my brother, who welcomed me into his new apartment in Nashville with open arms—literally. He let me cry on his shirt for two days before he finally said he needed to get some work done.

And then Alex was there, wiping my tears and bringing me cartons of ice cream to binge.

"What if Alex figures out what everyone else has?" I whisper into the night sky. "What if he realizes I'm not worth sticking around for?"

Stevie sits up, her hair falling around her like a sheet. "Hazel Lane. Tell me right now that you don't believe that."

I stare up at her and Wren, who is now sitting up next to her. They wear matching expressions of disbelief and hurt that I can barely make out in the moonlight. I sit up so they're no longer staring down at me and wrap my arms around my bent knees.

"I don't know," I say, my voice choked. "I know I *shouldn't* believe it, but it doesn't mean I don't."

Wren sniffles next to me, and I look over to see tears falling down her cheeks. "Honey, why haven't you ever mentioned this?"

My shoulders lift in a shrug. "It's a terrible thing to think. A terrible thing to *feel*, and I don't know…" A shaky sigh slips from between my lips. "I don't want anyone to see the ugly parts of me if the pretty parts aren't enough to keep them around."

"Hazel," Wren breathes, and for the second time that night, two sets of arms wrap around me, holding me tight. They feel like the anchors keeping me steady in the midst of this storm.

A heavy knot forms in my throat at their murmured *I love yous*, and I think I might break apart because of it. *This* is the secret piece of me I've kept locked up and hidden, desperate for no one to find or else they might turn away from it. But my two oldest friends are here, weathering it and telling me they love me in spite of it. *Because* of it.

A tiny bud of hope blooms in my chest.

Twenty-Nine

ALEX

Adam knocks on my car window on Monday morning, jarring me from my texts with Hazel. I was unsure of what the next three weeks would look like between us after the confession I made yesterday, but this morning, she texted me first thing, saying she had a dream that she was a dairy cow who befriended a time-traveling dragonfly and asked if that would make a good children's book. I actually laughed out loud into the quiet of my apartment, somehow missing her, even though she's only been gone for a day.

It's been good, but also slightly nerve-racking. I meant it when I said I'd give her all the time she needed to figure this out, but I can't deny that the waiting feels like standing completely naked in front of a crowd—exposed and vulnerable. Hazel knows all my soft spots now, and even though I know she'd never purposefully hurt them, she has the power to.

Turning off the car, I swing the door open. Adam quirks a brow. "What were you smiling about?"

"Scientists have found a solution to global warming."

He rolls his eyes, falling into step beside me as we walk toward the gym. "What are you doing today?" he asks when the blast of cold air from the AC hits us in the face.

I know he's asking about my workout, but as my phone vibrates with another text from Hazel, I have a better idea. "I'm finding Destiny."

"Not again," Adam groans.

Since the last time we talked with Destiny (or Fate?), we haven't run into him again, but I have a sneaking suspicion he's a ghost that haunts the men's locker room, and all we need to do is summon him, and he will come.

The locker room is thankfully empty when we enter. It also smells like a foul mixture of sweat, feet, and Lysol.

"He's not here," Adam says, the lockers rattling as he leans against them.

"He's a ghost. He's always here," I say, letting my voice sound airy, like an underpaid actor playing the villain in a children's Halloween movie. "Destiny," I call out. "It's Alex and Adam. We need to talk to you."

I pause, waiting for an answer from the spirit of a nude elderly man, but nothing comes. Planting my hands on my hips, I try again.

"Fate, are you there?"

The locker room door swings open, and Adam and I both spin around to look, our wide eyes briefly meeting each other's. A familiar man walks in, although it's not Destiny.

It's Parker.

He stares at the two of us for a moment, confusion crossing his features. "What are you guys doing?"

"They're here to talk to me," a rattling voice says from behind me, and I turn around to see Destiny standing there, although he's thankfully clothed in a velour tracksuit this time. His sun-spotted, transparent skin sags, and blue-gray eyes twinkle with mischief.

Adam sputters from his spot near the lockers, his mouth opening and closing but not making any intelligible noises. Honestly, if I weren't just as shocked as he is, I'd be pulling out my phone to take a picture of that face. It would be perfect on my Christmas card this year.

Destiny clicks his tongue in disappointment at Adam before swiveling to face me once more. With a wrinkled hand, he motions to the red aluminum bench we sat on last time. "Take a seat, young man."

"What's going on?" Parker asks, sounding wary. His dark eyes dart between the three of us, trying to figure out the puzzle that is this unlikely group.

I settle on the bench, motioning in Destiny's direction. "This is Destiny," I tell Parker. "Destiny, Parker."

"Nice to…meet you," Parker says slowly, and it almost comes out like a question. "How do you guys know each other?"

Destiny props his hands on his bony hips. "I gave him some advice weeks ago about how to get his best friend to fall in love with him."

"Ah," Parker says, glancing at me knowingly.

"And you must be one of the men Alex set her up on a date with?" Destiny says, his faint English accent sounding stronger as he looks between Parker and me with raised brows.

My head whips his way. "How did you know that?"

Destiny winks and sits beside me. "I'm a ghost, remember? I hear everything." With a wave of his hand toward the benches, he says to Adam and Parker, "Take a seat, boys. Let's chat."

As if in a trance, Parker and Adam sit on the bench across from us without a word. Only the sound of their shoes squeaking against the linoleum floor breaks the silence. After Destiny proclaimed himself a ghost, I don't think any of us feel like we can ignore what he says. Our eyes catch and hold on one another's before we turn back to Destiny.

The air feels charged, like the moments before a storm, and we're all waiting for the lightning to strike. Without meaning to, I'm holding my breath. Even my heart seems to slow.

"You did the blind dates for a while now," Destiny says, his voice cracking the heavy silence in the room, echoing off the lockers. "But you took a trip over the weekend, correct?"

My skin prickles, all the hair on my body standing to attention. This man really must be a ghost. I can feel Adam's eyes heavy on me, as if trying to wordlessly ask if I told the old man about my plans, and when I shake my head slightly, his throat bobs in a gulp.

"Yes, we went out of town," I say carefully. There's no use lying when the man already knows *everything*.

"Ah," Destiny says, his chin dipping in a nod. "And did you tell her your feelings?"

Heat creeps up my neck and spills onto my cheeks, and I avoid looking at Parker and Adam now. Instead, I focus on the wetness pooled around the drains in the floors. On an exhale, I say, "Yeah, I did."

"You actually did it?" Adam blurts, and I flash him a glare.

My voice is hard when I say, "Yes, I actually did it."

Destiny watches the two of us, and I know he can see everything. "And it didn't go well?"

I shove my hands under my thighs, trapping them there to keep them from shaking. "No, it went okay. She said…" I pause. "She said she needs time."

"How much time?" Parker asks, his voice sounding even deeper in the quiet of the locker room.

"I don't know," I answer, my shoulders lifting in a shrug.

I can feel Parker's eyes on me. "And things are just going to stay the same between you guys in the meantime? What about if she ends up saying she…" He stops, as if searching for the right words. "If she says she doesn't feel the same way?"

That's what's eating at me, the thought of continuing how things are going for days or weeks or months, only for her to decide she can't date me, that it's too big a risk. I don't know where that would leave me. My friendship with Hazel is the best thing in my life, but it's also the thing that's slowly deteriorating me. I don't think I can be *just* friends with her anymore, not after everything that has changed over the past few weeks. I think if she were to tell me she couldn't love me the way I love her, I'd have to back off. The thought makes me physically ill.

"I don't think things can stay the same," I say, and my gaze connects with Destiny's. "Is that selfish? To be all or nothing?"

The words hang in the air between us for a long moment. Only the distant clack of weights and the pounding of footfalls on treadmills in the gym outside mar the silence.

Finally, Destiny says, "No, it is not selfish. But I have to ask, will it hurt more to give her up completely or to only get to keep the part of her that she's willing to give you?"

That is the million-dollar question, the one that has been going on an endless loop in my head for so long. All along, I knew it would come down to this one day, and I've managed to make it this far. Surely, I could keep going, hold on desperately to whatever pieces she can give. But even as I think it, I know it's not true.

"You can't do it," Parker says softly. "I've seen you two together. You'd never be able to watch her fall in love with someone else."

He's right, of course, and I feel it all the way down to my bones. It's like there are strands of my DNA written entirely just to love her, and I know that parts of me would shrivel up and die watching her fall in love with someone else. The past few weeks have been eating me alive, and she hasn't even hit it off with anyone yet.

My shoulders sag as the breath leaves my body. "I'd have to let her go," I say, hating how my voice sounds like fresh sandpaper, rough and scratchy.

"Are you prepared for that?" Destiny asks.

A storm brews in my gut, roiling and churning. "No, not at all."

"Maybe while she's on this trip—"

"How did you know she's on a trip?" Adam cuts Destiny off, the pale blue eyes he inherited from Mom turning hard and glinting under the fluorescent lights.

Destiny looks at Adam, white brows raised on his sun-spotted forehead. "I told you I hear everything." Turning back to me, he says, "Maybe while she's gone, you should figure out what you will do if she says she doesn't feel the same way."

The thing is, I *know* she does. I could see it all over her face yesterday, read it in her body language as easily as words on a page. Hazel loves me, even if she's too scared to do anything about it.

And that's a very real possibility. One I need to prepare myself for. Or else it will feel like hurricane-force winds ripping me to shreds.

"I can do that," I tell him, resolution settling firmly inside me.

Destiny nods, his lips pursing. He looks at the three of us in turn before saying, "It's been good chatting with you, kids. I won't hold you up any longer. Thank you for indulging an old man who loves gossip."

Adam watches Destiny warily before pushing off the lockers and heading for the door. Parker follows a second later after flashing me one more confused look. When I stand to go, Destiny says, "Wait, Alex."

I spin to face him.

His blue eyes are warm, and he looks at me like a concerned grandfather would, tenderly and sympathetically. "Let me know how things go, would you?" he asks, and I can detect that faint English accent, the one that can only be heard in certain words.

"I will," I promise, and I then head for the door before turning around once more. "Destiny, are you really a ghost?"

A smile touches his lips. "No," he says after a moment. "I own the gym, and the security cameras are always playing in my office. You'd never believe the juicy gossip I hear."

Laughter punches out of me with the force of a cannonball.

"Don't tell your brother. I want to keep him guessing," he says.

My grin spreads wider. "Your secret's safe with me."

Thirty

HAZEL

Mom is a terrible patient. For the first week after her sinus surgery, she could do almost nothing on her own, but now that we've hit the ten-day mark and she's finally on the mend, we haven't been able to keep her in bed. Whenever Dad disappears into his home office to get some work done or retreats into the kitchen to cook her a meal, she sneaks off in the golf cart and drives to the shop.

I'm restocking a shelf when the bell above the door jangles and I turn around to find her trying to slink in, her house slippers padding softly on the thick white-washed floorboards.

The smile I'd pasted on my face in preparation for a customer slides off. "Mom, there's a bell above the door. How did you think you were going to get past me?"

Mom shrugs, looking like she's happy to be caught. "I was going to sneak into the back and do inventory."

"You're not supposed to be lifting boxes for another two weeks."

Mom snaps her fingers and slides onto the bench stool behind the counter, watching as I continue to fiddle with the weekly special display. "Well, shoot. I guess I'll just have to talk to you instead."

When I glance at her over my shoulder, she looks way too pleased for this to be a coincidence. My shoulders sag, and I spin around, propping my hands on the table behind me.

"Okay, what do you want to know?"

Mom leans her elbows on the table, the sun slanting through the windows catching on the light gold highlights in her hair. "Tell me about Alex," she says, a knowing smile curving her lips.

I consider lying, but it's futile. Ava Lane knows *everything*. One time in high school, I thought I'd managed to succeed at sneaking out to meet my boyfriend, but then Mom texted me and told me to bring home milk and not to bother trying to climb back in my bedroom window because she didn't want me to drop it. No matter what tricks Cam and I think we have up our sleeves, Mom always knows more.

My cheeks puff out as I exhale. "He told me he's in love with me," I say.

Mom doesn't look the least bit surprised. She just nods, as if she's been waiting for this to happen. "Did you say it back?"

A knot forms in my throat, choking off my words, so I shake my head.

Mom's eyes soften, topaz deepening to sapphire. "Why not?"

The words are gentle, the way she would talk to me when I was sick or hurt, when my boyfriend broke up with me or when I got into a petty fight with my best friend. It feels like an embrace, like pushing my head into her chest and letting her hold me until everything is okay again.

"I don't know, Mama," I whisper, my voice cracking.

She's around the counter in an instant, her arms coming around me. For just a moment, the fear dissolves like an Alka-Seltzer fizzing in a glass of water. That suffocating anxiety that's been humming in my veins banks to a simmer and everything feels clear.

It's *Alex*. My best friend. The person who, arguably, has seen the worst parts of me and still chose to stick around. The person who would show up at my new apartment those first few weeks after I moved to Nashville and force me to shower and take me to lunch so I actually got fresh air and sunshine. The person who always carries a scrunchie on his wrist so I can pull back my hair, who orders an extra drink because he knows I'll want one even if I say I don't. The person who went on double dates with me, even when it had to be killing him, because he knew I didn't trust myself enough to go alone.

Alex, Alex, Alex, my heart beats.

Mom's hands smooth over my hair, down each bump of my spine, holding me tightly to her. "I know you're scared," she whispers into my hair.

I nod against her shoulder, too teary for words.

"The best things in life are always a little scary," she tells me.

Pulling back, I wipe under my eyes, sniffing loudly. "I thought the best things in life take time?"

A smile touches Mom's lips, and her smooth, suntanned hand comes up to pat my cheek. The gesture is so familiar it makes me ache. There are so many little things that your parents do when you're small that you never realize you miss until they repeat it when you're grown.

"Good things *do* take time," she says, smoothing away the last of my tears. "So you take all the time you need, and don't feel bad about it. There's nothing worse than being with the right person at the wrong time."

"What if…" I start to ask and trail off, unsure if I want to voice my fear, if I want this dark part of me to be exposed to the light of day.

Mom dips her head so she can look into my eyes. "What if what?" she asks.

Swallowing, I say, "What if I wait too long and he decides he doesn't want me?"

"Then he's not the right one, Hazel Girl." She nudges under my chin with her knuckle, the smile returning, a flower blooming in spring. "But I don't think that's going to happen. I think that boy has been waiting a long time already."

Dangerous hope takes root deep in my belly, but I'm cut off from responding when my phone buzzes on the wooden display stand. I snatch it up, expecting a text from Alex, but my heart stops beating when I see the name on the screen.

Sebastian.

"What is it?" Mom asks, sensing the shift, like the air has dropped in temperature. A shiver races through me, and my throat works on a swallow, sucking air through my nose. "Hazel," Mom says, her tone sharp enough to draw my attention this time.

"It's Sebastian," I say, staring at the phone in my hand. The image on the screen has me frozen. It's one of us together, a selfie we took while lying together on a picnic blanket on one of those perfect days in LA. The sun was shining, and while I was looking at the camera, Sebastian's attention was fixed on me. That perfect smile was on his mouth, the one that always seemed to drug me a little, the one that made me believe him even when things didn't quite add up.

I'd forgotten I made this his contact photo, that even though I deleted it from my photo album and social media, it still lives on forever right here, waiting to come back and haunt me when I'm already on uneven ground. That photo makes me feel like the rug is being ripped out from under me, like I've been turned upside down, all the painful memories hitting me with their full force again.

The screen goes blank again before I can even decide what to do. Like there *is* a decision to make. I'm certainly not going to answer.

"Hazel," Mom says, her voice cutting through the fog in my brain. "Are you okay?"

"Yes," I say, but I'm shaking my head *no*, and I'm not even sure what the correct answer is. I can hear my pulse thrumming in my ears, feel myself shutting down. I can taste the copper tang of blood in my mouth that means I bit my tongue, even if I hadn't noticed the sharp sting of pain.

I step back, bumping into the display, and Mom steadies me with her hands on my shoulders. Her face is creased with concern. "Hazel," she says again, this time sharper.

"I think I need some air," I say, and Mom nods.

"Let's go outside." She starts to lead me toward the door, but it opens before we can get there, and three women enter. From their Smoky Mountain T-shirts and brand-new hiking boots, they must be tourists.

Mom shoots me a pained look, but I wave her off. "It's fine, really. I think I just need a few minutes alone," I say, quiet enough that only she can hear. "Can you handle them?"

At her nod, I remind her to take it easy, and then I slip through the door, taking in deep breaths of the fresh mountain air. It's bright today, and the sun immediately warms my suddenly chilled skin, making sweat prickle on my hairline and the back of my neck. The light breeze ruffles the hem of my skirt as I walk around the building, my hand sliding along the siding like I used to when I was a kid, sneaking out to climb onto my handmade wooden swing and watch the stars.

The swing is still there, swaying gently in the breeze from the gnarled limb of an old towering weeping willow. I push aside the dangling branches, sliding under the shaded canopy, and wrap my hand around the stiff fraying ropes. The swing groans as I settle my weight against it and push off, dust kicking up beneath my feet.

It's hot today, the kind of sticky heat that clings to your skin and requires a shower morning and night, but the breeze as I swing is enough to soothe my frazzled nerves and cool me down. Slowly, my heart rate returns to normal in shades, the same way the sun slowly sinks below the horizon each night, until I'm finally breathing normally again.

When my phone vibrates in my skirt pocket once more, I drag my feet in the dirt, halting the swing. My pulse pounds in my throat as I pull out the phone, braced for that photo again.

But it's not there.

This photo is of Alex. It was one he sent me early on in our friendship, back when I was still living in LA and our main mode of conversation was texting and the occasional phone call or FaceTime. In the photo, he's holding up a cotton candy ice cream cone the size of his head, a wide grin splitting his mouth. He'd said *the only thing I'll ever love more than you*, and I laughed it off, but now I'm wondering if he knew, all the way back then.

The FaceTime call almost clicks off before I remember to answer it. When my shaking fingers slide it open, he's there, his real grin replacing the one snapped so long ago. But as soon as he sees my face, it dissolves.

"What's wrong?" he asks. "Is it your mom? Do I need to come down there?" He pushes up off his white couch, his apartment a blur in the background as he moves around. "I just need to pack a bag."

Something warms inside me, like honey dripping from my heart and down into my chest. It's tenderness like I've never felt before. A living, breathing thing that's growing and taking shape. It's overwhelming.

"Alex, everything's fine," I say, and at the sound of my voice, he slows. His apartment gains clarity behind him again, and his eyes focus on me.

"Something's wrong," he says, and he sounds so concerned that I wish he was here so I could wrap my arms around him and assure him I'm okay, that I'm always okay when I'm with him.

Swallowing, I say, "It's Sebastian. He just called."

Alex slumps onto his couch, the phone jostling before the camera sharpens on his face again. "Oh, what did he say?" His voice is strained, tight, and I suddenly wonder how often it's been like that in the past, how many times I didn't notice. It's like now that he's told me he's in love with me, I can see the evidence everywhere, in everything he does, and I don't know how I missed it for so long.

I kick off the ground again, setting my swing swaying. "I didn't answer. I kind of freaked out."

Concern replaces the dismay on his features. "Are you okay?"

"I'm okay now," I say, and I want to tell him it's because of him. That in the same way that just seeing Sebastian makes me anxious, just seeing *him* makes me calm. Alex is the rays of sunshine peeking through Sebastian's storm.

Alex is quiet for a long moment, studying me, and I take the opportunity to do the same. He's dressed in that same threadbare gray tee that I gave him the night we were here in Fontana Ridge, when I ran into him naked. I can practically feel its softness against my skin, and I have the desperate desire to know what it feels like against his. To see what's softer, the shirt or him, to see if it still holds his warmth after I peel it off.

Clearing my throat, I ask, "Is there a reason you called?"

Alex's eyes dash away from the phone, and his hand palms the back of his neck. I want to know what he was thinking as he watched me. If his mind drifted to where mine did. The thought sends an illicit thrill through me, and heat pools behind my belly button.

"This is going to sound ridiculous," he says, the words drawn out like they're being pried from him.

I let my feet drag in the dirt, scuffing against the bottom of my sandals until the swing slows. "What is it?"

His gaze meets mine and holds, warm chocolate fudge on the top of vanilla bean ice cream. "I just had a feeling like maybe you needed me." Pink colors his cheeks, creeping up his ears. It's like when he's standing in a group of people he doesn't know, trying desperately to look unaffected, but inside, he's nervous and fluttery.

"It was stupid," he says quickly.

But my heart has stopped, and that tenderness is back, threatening to consume me. The tenderness has a name, if I'm brave enough to give it one.

I cut him off before he can say more. "It's not stupid. I think I did need you," I say quietly, unsure if I'm meaning in this exact moment or in the grand scheme of life. "I was kind of freaking out after Sebastian called. It sent me spiraling."

His eyes soften around the edges, like charcoal being smudged on canvas. "But you're okay?"

"I'm okay," I tell him, and some of the tension leaves him.

He's quiet for a moment before asking, "So are you going to call him back?"

"What?" I blurt, my fingers gripping the rough rope until it chafes. "No. No, I'm not calling him back."

Just the thought gives me hives, makes me feel like there are insects burrowing under my skin. After I walked out of Sebastian's apartment that day, him chasing after me, a hastily wrapped towel around his waist and his neighbor still naked in his bed, I haven't spoken to him. I couldn't bring myself to block his number, though, and the texts and phone calls poured in for days. Apologies, so many of them that I was honestly too heartbroken to read, that I deleted before I could give myself a chance to read them. I was so *fragile* back then that I didn't trust myself not to accept his apology and forgive him.

But then one night, he called, the night I was at my very lowest. And I answered. I didn't speak, but he did. He grasped on to that one bit of leeway I'd allowed and put everything into it.

I remember how desperately I wanted to believe him, that it was a mistake, that he didn't know how it happened, that he was scared of how much he loved me and was self-sabotaging. I wanted so very badly to believe that was true that I almost convinced myself it was.

And then Alex texted. Something short and silly, an idea he had for a car wash commercial, but it snapped me out of it. I hung up, and when Sebastian called again, I sent it to voice mail and messaged him to stop trying to contact me.

The next day, I decided to move to Nashville.

"You don't at least want to know what he has to say after all this time? For closure?" Alex asks after a long moment.

I shake my head firmly. "No. I don't." The words come out clipped, and Alex nods.

When Alex speaks again, his voice is soft, gentle. "Maybe you should paint. Painting always helps you feel better."

The thought of painting feels like slipping into a warm bath, the water closing around me. It eases all the tension built up around me like brick walls, and more than anything, I want to. I want to lose myself in acrylics, messy droplets and smudges drying on my skin.

"Yeah, I think I'll do that," I say, and a smile breaks across his face. It's beautiful and unhurried, the kind of smile reserved for lazy mornings in bed, the kind you feel pressed against your lips and exposed slivers of skin.

"Call me if you need me," he says, and as soon as he hangs up, I feel the urge to dial again. Without my realizing it, Alex has maneuvered so deeply into my hierarchy of needs that being without him feels like missing a limb.

And for the first time, that revelation doesn't feel all that scary.

Thirty-One

ALEX

Hazel FaceTimes me on Monday night. It's been two weeks since I watched her drive away from Wes and Lo's lake house with my heart in her hands, and she still has another full week in Fontana Ridge before she comes home.

Which means I have another week of dinner alone on my couch, staring at the slightly indented cushion where she usually sits. I've gotten increasingly more pathetic as the days have gone on. Yesterday, I bought a bottle of her laundry detergent and washed my sheets in them so they'd smell like hers. And then I realized how creepy that was. So I washed them again in my own detergent and threw that bottle out. And then I felt bad for throwing away a perfectly good bottle of detergent, so I bought fifteen bottles and donated them to the homeless shelter across town.

Basically, I'm losing my mind.

Sitting up on the couch, I swipe open the call. Hazel is in her tiny twin-size bed in her childhood bedroom, that soft, worn floral quilt tucked up around her bare shoulders. I want to tug it down and press my lips there instead.

She grins, bright as a lighthouse on a stormy night, and everything inside me calms. "Hey," she says.

"Hey," I say back.

Just the sound of her voice grounds me, stills the part of my brain that's been spinning since that morning on the porch, sunshine glittering on the lake.

"It's Movie Monday," she says, and I chuff a laugh.

"I know," I say and flip the camera around so she can see the messy spread of takeout containers on my coffee table. I ordered enough Chinese food to feed a small village, or in my case, enough for two meals.

The TV is on but muted in the background, playing some action movie that Adam wanted me to see with him in theaters last year. I blew him off that night to go to a concert with Hazel. It's the kind of movie we would never watch on Mondays, so I figured now was the perfect time, but I haven't been able to focus. I don't know when my preferences changed from wars and aliens and well-dressed spies to cozy nineties rom-coms, but I don't even think I'm mad about it.

"Are you watching a movie without me?" Hazel asks, sounding indignant, and I have to force back a smile when I turn the camera around.

I press a hand to my chest. "I would never."

"I just watched someone be beheaded."

My eyes flick back up to the TV screen, and sure enough, a severed, bloody head is rolling around on the white marble floors. "Gross," I mutter, my face scrunching in disgust as I search for the remote.

"You deserved that," Hazel says.

I nod gravely, pressing the power button. The glow of the TV disappears, leaving me only in the warm light of the table lamp. "I really did. It's what I get for trying to watch a movie without you."

"And on a *Monday*, Alex. Our sacred day."

I laugh, sliding down into the couch cushions once more. "It was despicable of me, I know."

"I'll forgive it this one time," Hazel says, tugging the blankets more securely around her shoulders, effectively hiding the thin strap of her tank top.

That thin, flimsy strap will haunt my dreams tonight.

"How was your day?" I ask. This has become our routine since she's been too busy at the shop and helping with her mom to text much most days. But at night, when the sun is gone and the moon and stars wink alive for the night, it's our time. After her parents go to bed, we talk on the phone for hours, like we're teenagers, too obsessed with each other to hang up even for sleep.

It's been the only thing keeping me sane over the past two weeks. I can't deny that I'm ready for it to be over. I'd rather have her voice in my ear, her body pressed up against mine on my couch than hundreds of miles away, one Wi-Fi glitch away from disappearing.

"It was good," she says. "The shop has been crazy busy the past few weeks. It's a really good thing I came. There's no way Mom would have been able to handle it on her own, even now that she's up and moving more. She actually worked the entire morning with me and then spent the afternoon resting."

"And by resting, you mean heckling your dad about how his butt looks in his jeans while he tries to get work done?"

"Exactly." She pauses for a moment before saying, "Sebastian called again today."

I sit up straighter on the couch, my shoulders squaring on instinct. "Did you...answer this time?"

When Sebastian called Hazel last week, I didn't *want* her to talk to him. In fact, if he suddenly lost the ability to speak, I'd be pretty happy. Everything that came out of his mouth was a lie or a manipulation—something I'd always thought but didn't mention in case it was my feelings for Hazel talking.

But I wanted her to answer if that's what she needed to do. I think she thinks I haven't noticed the way he still haunts her, a ghost she can't shake, but I *have* noticed. I've noticed every single day. In the way she distrusts herself. In the seemingly light-hearted digs she makes at herself about her poor choices in men. In the way she questions whether she will ever be lovable enough for someone to stick around for.

I've done my best to show her how *I* feel about her, but most of those things are how Hazel feels about *herself*. And Sebastian is a big majority of the reason she feels that way. So if she needed to answer that call to chew him out or hear whatever lame excuse he tried to come up with, I'd back her up.

"I let it go to voice mail again," she says, and her voice splinters. "I just froze again. It makes me so…angry that he still has this effect on me. He shouldn't still be able to hold this much power over me."

My heart breaks, shattering into a thousand tiny pieces, when I see the tears lining her eyes, when I hear the ragged tone of her voice, usually so smooth and bright.

"You could always block his number," I say, tilting the camera toward the ceiling so she won't see me trying to rub away the ache forming beneath my sternum.

She sighs. "But then he wins. Then it feels like he's so dangerous to me that I have to block his calls."

It takes everything inside me not to hang up and call Sebastian myself. I don't remember how I got his number so long ago, but like her, I've never been able to delete it. I saved his name in my phone as *Piece of Trash*, and whenever I got tipsy, I'd compose long-winded, angry text messages to him that

I always deleted before sending them. It was therapeutic, to tell him the things Hazel never would, even if I also never hit Send.

"I'm sorry, Haze. I wish I could do something to help you," I say, and it's true. That frazzled tension is building beneath my skin, the one I always feel when Hazel is in pain and I can't fix it. "If Sebastian lived closer, I'd break into his house and put glitter on his ceiling fans and put green hair dye in his shampoo."

Hazel spurts a laugh that brings a smile to my face. "He'd never fall for that. He only uses dye-free products."

"Of course he does," I say with an eye roll.

"He's allergic to red dye number seven." Her lips twitch, holding back a smile, and some of the tension leaves me again.

"Oh, good. I'll Amazon Prime him some Kool-Aid pouches."

She shakes her head. "Wouldn't work. He doesn't consume processed products."

"I'm going to have to google how to poison someone with red dye," I say. "I won't be able to let this go."

"I'll write down that quote for your memoir," she vows, and my lips crack into a smile. Snuggling farther into her pillow, she says, "What if we watched the same movie at the same time for Movie Monday?"

I reach for the remote, flipping the TV back on. The blue glow casts shadows across my face once more, and when I look back at my phone, Hazel is watching me, her bottom lip trapped between her teeth. Her eyes are heavy-lidded and warm, like sugar being heated into simple syrup on the stove.

It sends a jolt of desire straight down my spine.

When I clear my throat, she blinks. "What movie?" I ask. My voice sounds like the scratch of a match on sandpaper.

"What If."

"I'M LOSING STEAM," I mumble into the phone hours later. We switched from FaceTime to a phone call over an hour ago, when she needed her phone flashlight to walk down the hall to the bathroom. Since then, we've made it halfway through our third movie, and even though I'm going to be an actual zombie at work tomorrow, I haven't been able to hang up.

"Me too," Hazel says. Her voice is quiet and hazy, drugged with sleep. I want to hear it like this every single day for the rest of my life. Late nights wrapped in sheets together, skin to skin. Early mornings when neither of us can manage to get out of bed.

Groaning, I force my mind to change course. "Let's go to bed."

"I'm already in bed," Hazel grunts, and if I weren't so tired, I'd laugh.

"I'm on the couch," I moan, barely able to lift my head. I peel my eyes open, staring down the ever-elongating hallway to my bedroom. "My bed is too far."

"Sleep on your couch," she murmurs. "It's comfier than my bed at home."

"I love your bed."

Hazel must have loosened her grip on the phone because when she speaks again, she sounds farther away, her voice faint and tinged with sleep. "You've never slept in my bed."

"Yes, I have. That night you were sick," I say, nuzzling farther into my sofa, the cushions molding to my body, cocooning me.

"You were on my couch when I woke up," she mumbles, her words running together, like she's too tired to open her mouth all the way.

"I left in the middle of the night."

"How come?"

I'm in that sleep-drenched fog, where you're not sure if you're awake or asleep, when your guard is down and your words come without thoughts. If I were fully awake, I wouldn't say it, because although I told Hazel I love her two weeks ago, we haven't mentioned it since. I'm giving her the time she asked for, and that doesn't include foisting my love on her like a last-minute dinner invitation.

But I'm not thinking clearly, and my guard is more than down; it's obliterated. So I say, "Because I woke up and I never wanted to leave."

She's quiet for so long that my words start to break through the sleepy haze around my brain, waking me up, even if just slightly. Panic creeps in like an unwanted houseguest, unpacking its bags in my chest.

"You should have stayed," she says finally, and my heartbeat settles, the breath heaving from my lungs in a rush. Her words, the tone of her voice, feel like waking up in that sofa bed at the lake house to find her wrapped around me. Like waking up from a dream to find out reality is better.

"Why?" I breathe, unable to keep from asking the question. Maybe it's wrong for me to ask when we're like this, half-asleep and not thinking through the answers, but that's what makes me do it. I know she's scared, that she's weighing every possibility between us all the time, but I *have* to know what she's feeling when she's not thinking, when sleep is blurring the edges, and dreams and reality are mixing together.

"Because I like sleeping next to you," she says, and then her breath evens out, and I know she's asleep.

It takes me much longer, her words echoing through my head, but eventually I drift off too, wrapped in a butterfly throw blanket Hazel left at my house months ago.

I DON'T KNOW WHAT time it is when I wake up, whether it's real or a dream, but I hear her voice, whisper soft and sweet as ice cream on a hot summer day. "I love you too, Alex."

Thirty-Two

HAZEL

Wren's sunshine-yellow front door is unlocked, and I let myself into her little cottage. The scent of her jasmine trellis hangs heavy in the air, like expensive perfume. Medieval tavern music is playing on the speakers, and when I round the corner into her tiny kitchen, she's got a floral-printed apron tied over her denim shorts overalls.

Sunset slants through the open windows, and the gentle breeze ruffles the gingham curtains. Wren's tiny kitchen is one of my happy places, with its sage green beadboard and bee-printed wallpaper. There's a table in the center that she uses as both a dining table and island, and a fresh bouquet always sits in its center. Today, it's an assortment of daisies that I'm sure she picked from the farm.

At the sound of my footsteps, she spins around, a bright smile cresting over her face. "You're here!" she yells, and I can't hold back a grin.

"I'm here," I say, setting a bottle of chilled white wine and a container of Mom's homemade cinnamon buns on her scarred kitchen table.

"Stevie's running late," she tells me, turning back around to stir something on the vintage white stove, flames flickering under the pan. I can detect the faint scent of basil and garlic.

I walk over to where she's standing and glance down at the stove. It's some kind of pasta, with cherry tomatoes and bright green asparagus. "That smells amazing. What is it?"

"Pesto chicken tortellini," she says, and I hum excitedly.

As I pull out three mismatched jars from the cupboard beside her, she says, "I'm sad you're going back tomorrow."

"Me too," I tell her, and it's the truth. As much as I miss Alex and the cozy comfort of my apartment and the bustling familiarity of Lucy's coffee shop, this trip back home has felt like it's existed outside of time. Back in Nashville, I'll have to confront my fears about Alex, but here, I've been in a safe bubble.

Wren looks at me over her shoulder as I rummage through a drawer for a corkscrew. "Are you excited to see Alex?"

Butterflies swarm in my stomach, and I have to press a hand there. I *am* excited to see Alex. Missing him has felt like a physical ache beneath my breastbone. Things between us have seemed the same while I've been gone, but I have to wonder how long that will last when I'm back. When he's flesh and blood in front of me, temptation personified. I've been waking each morning from dreams of what he'd taste like, how his lips would feel against the sensitive spot below my ear.

But I can't deny the prick of anxiety that still lingers, even if it is fading. Being back home hasn't helped that either. Not when I crawl into bed each night, haunted by memories of crying there when my ex-boyfriends inevitably broke up with me, or calling Sebastian when I was here for the holidays, only to have it go to voice mail because he was with *her*.

"I'm excited," I say, finally finding a corkscrew.

Wren smirks. "You sound like it."

I busy myself uncorking the bottle and pouring some in each glass so Wren doesn't see my hands shaking. I'm so tired of saying I'm scared. I'm so tired of *being* scared. But wanting something to go away doesn't make it happen.

"Hey," Wren says, turning around when I haven't responded, concern etched in every line of her face. "What's wrong?"

I set the wine bottle back on the table with a thud. My hands are trembling, and there's no hiding it now, so I don't bother trying. Wren watches as I wrap my arms around myself, hugging my elbows.

"I'm just so sick of feeling like this," I admit, my voice cracking. I feel that crack go all the way through me, like I'm being cleaved in two. The part of me that's happy and whole sliced clean from the part of me that's damaged and hurting.

"Like what?" Wren asks softly.

"Like I'm *broken*," I say, and I feel the prick of tears at the back of my eyes, like I have so many times over the past few weeks. "I thought I was past this. I thought I was ready to get back out there, but I wasn't ready to love him, Wren."

She nods like she understands, her ginger waves bobbing. "But you do love him."

"Yes," I say, and it feels like equal parts relief and terror. "But then Sebastian won't stop calling me, and every time I see his name on my phone, it feels like I'm back at square one, sobbing alone in my crappy apartment in LA."

Her eyes widen, green as a spring meadow. "Sebastian's been calling you?"

I sag against the counter, all the fight leaving me. "Yes, and I didn't mention it to you guys because I've been trying to forget about it, but I *can't*. It's always there at the back of my mind."

"What's he been saying?" she asks, leaning on the counter next to me, her shoulder brushing against mine.

I stare at the bee-printed wallpaper until it all starts to blend together and the bees actually look like they're flying on a creamy white backdrop. "I haven't answered him. I can't talk to him."

Wren is quiet for a moment. "Maybe it would help. It seems like not talking to him isn't making you feel any better. What's the worst that could happen? You can hang up at any point."

I could, but the damage could already be done, tiny cuts that seem insignificant but get infected. Or it could be like alcohol poured over the wounds, painful in the moment but helpful in the long run. Cleansing.

"I'll think about it," I say, and then the front door squeaks on its hinges, alerting us to Stevie's arrival. "Let's just have dinner and forget about Sebastian for a while."

Wren picks up a mismatched jar, tilting it in my direction. "Hear, hear."

IT'S LATE WHEN I finally let myself back into my childhood home, using the back door since it's quieter and won't wake Mom and Dad. Muscle memory guides me around the creaky floorboards and into my old bedroom. I flip on the lamp on the bedside table, and warm light fills the space and casts shadows on the walls.

I catch my reflection in the mirror. My cheeks are tinged pink with the faintest sunburn from all the time I've spent outside over the past few weeks, and my hair is up in a messy bun on the top of my head, a remnant from earlier in the night when Stevie, Wren, and I decided we were finally going to learn the Hoedown Throwdown from the *Hannah Montana Movie*. My mascara is smudged from laughing until we cried.

My eyes snag on the photo Alex pulled from the mirror frame when he was exploring my bedroom, the one of me on my first group date. Next to it is the one of me at prom. I look so happy in them—my smile wide, my eyes bright, my cheeks rosy. Just looking at all the photos from my childhood and teen years lined up around the frame makes my heart ache for that girl who used to love without fear of being hurt.

I can't go back to her. I can't make myself forget what it feels like when sweet, tender love turns rancid, rotting away all the soft, vulnerable pieces inside.

But I can face my demons. I don't think I'll ever be able to move on without confronting that shattered piece inside me once and for all, even if I can never put it back together the right way again.

Last fall, Alex and I spent a lazy Saturday morning wandering through a flea market. We stumbled upon this booth full of broken pottery that has been glued back together. Each work of art was an amalgamation of the others, a kaleidoscope of colors compiled together until the broken bits of all the shattered pieces formed one creation. Just looking at the mosaics felt monumental.

Maybe I'll never be able to get back to the person I was in those photos on my mirror, but I can be something new, a coalescence of all the bits of goodness people have given me.

My hands tremble as I pull out my phone and dial the one person I thought I'd never speak to again.

It's the middle of the night, but Sebastian answers on the third ring. "Hazel?"

Swallowing, I say, "Hi, Sebastian."

I can hear rustling on the other end, like he's sitting up in bed, and I can picture him there perfectly. In his shoebox of an apartment, his mattress on a platform I once thought was different and unique. In reality, it was the hipster version of a mattress on the floor.

"I didn't think you were ever going to call," he says, his voice rough and tinged with sleep. I thought hearing his voice would send me into a panic, but although my hands are shaking and my heart is beating loud enough for him to hear through the phone, I feel almost…calm.

"I wasn't planning to."

He's quiet for a long moment, and I can imagine him pushing a hand through his always-tangled shoulder-length black hair. "Why did you change your mind?"

"Why did you do it?" I ask before I lose my nerve. When it happened, I couldn't bear to ask. I was too scared of the answer. But it has haunted me for over a year now, the question of *why*.

"Hazel." He sighs. "I can't give you a good reason. Not one that will justify it."

Obviously, I knew this. I knew he could never give me a reason to explain away cheating on me, but it still stings. I guess I've been holding out hope that there'd be a logical explanation or some kind of misunderstanding. Like his neighbor was suffering from hypothermia and he had to cuddle her naked to share body heat.

I grip the dresser to stay steady, my fingers biting into the wood. "I just want the truth, Sebastian."

"I was scared, Hazel," he says after a long moment, one where I can *feel* my pulse thrumming, waiting for his answer.

It's not the answer I expected, and I blurt out my surprise before I can think better of it. "What?"

Sebastian blows out a breath, and it rattles through the phone. "Before you, I'd never been in a serious relationship, and I wasn't looking for one when we met."

This is news to me. I remember the exact moment I saw Sebastian for the first time at a music festival in the desert a couple hours' drive from LA. We spent the night talking and dancing, and I thought I'd never see him again. But then two days later, he randomly walked into the coffee shop where I spent my days working on freelance projects, and it felt like a sign.

I sidled up next to him, and he looked as surprised as I was. He ended up at my table and stayed there until the place closed down. We went on our first date the next night and never looked back.

"What's that supposed to mean?" I ask.

"Everything happened so fast," he says. "Before I knew what was happening, you became this intrinsic part of me, an extra limb, and it terrified me."

My mind is spinning, a top set loose on a table. "So because I was so important to you, you cheated on me?" I know I sound incredulous, but I can't bring myself to change it.

"No." He sighs, sounding defeated. "But loving you felt too vast and scary, and I wanted something—someone—easier. Someone who wouldn't overwhelm me and feel so utterly necessary to my existence."

I hate how similar the words are to the ones I spoke to Lucy weeks ago when I told her I wanted to go out with Parker again because being with him felt manageable. Loving Parker wouldn't have consumed me.

Worst of all, I hate that I understand how Sebastian felt. Now that I've been confronted with this undeniable, all-encompassing, terrifying love for Alex, I know exactly what it must have been like for him.

"That doesn't excuse your actions, Sebastian. What you did"—my words cut off, choked with tears—"it *hurt*. You wrecked me," I finally manage.

He's quiet for so long that I think he's hung up. Then he says, "I know. I know that, Hazel. And I've spent the last year reliving it over and over again and trying to come to terms with the reality that I ruined us. I'm so, so sorry, Hazel. You have to know that."

Until this moment, I didn't. It felt like Sebastian had been playing me the whole time we were together, pretending he felt the same love for me that I did for him. That he didn't mind when we broke.

But even if it was his fault, and he was so very wrong, I know it shattered a little piece of him too.

He exhales. "Well, that's what I've been trying to call to say. To be honest, I've been trying to call since the day you walked out of my apartment, but I could never figure out the right words."

Even though he can't see me, I nod, everything he said playing on a loop in my head.

"I'm really sorry, Hazel," he says again. His voice has lost all tinges of sleep. It's no longer rough, but soft as silk. He sounds like the Sebastian I knew, even if that man turned out to be a stranger.

I don't think Alex could ever be a stranger to me, even if things turned sour between us. He's the other half of my soul. A poem scratched on paper that I've memorized until reciting the words is as easy as breathing.

"Thanks for telling me," I respond. I can't bring myself to tell him it's okay, because it's not. But I am glad I heard it. Because for the first time, I'm realizing that maybe the problem was never *me*. He was the broken one, and it was his shrapnel that embedded in my skin.

"Well," Sebastian says. "I'll talk to you later, Hazel."

"Goodbye, Sebastian," I say and end the call. His contact photo watches me in the dim light, the long-ago photo we took together, back when we were happy and whole. It doesn't hurt to look at it as much anymore. It no longer feels like a knife slicing through my chest.

Scrolling down to the bottom of the contact, my finger hovers over the delete button. I could block him, but I don't think I'll need to. This phone call is the last I'll hear from Sebastian Castellanos.

It's easy to press the *Delete* button. It doesn't feel like letting him win or running away. It feels like letting go and running toward something new. I'm ready to begin again.

Thirty-Three

HAZEL

"I talked to Sebastian last night," I tell Mom over breakfast the next morning. It's Monday, and I'm heading home this afternoon. She insisted on making a full breakfast, with sausage, eggs, and Belgian waffles topped with whipped cream, just like we used to have on those special occasion mornings growing up.

Mom swivels to face me from where she's flipping sausage in a pan on the stove, holding her spatula in the air like a magic wand. "Why? What did you say?"

As much as she's driven me nuts over the past few weeks with her inability to follow doctor's orders, I'm going to miss her. She was officially cleared to go back to work at her follow-up appointment on Friday, so I'm surprised she even made time for breakfast this morning. She's like a horse chomping at the bit to get back into her shop—without me hovering and restricting her activities.

"I guess I needed closure," I say slowly, turning the words over in my head. "I needed to know why he did it so I could figure out how to keep it from happening again."

A divot forms between Mom's brows, and she flips the stove off, the flames dying beneath the grate. "Honey, it's not your fault he cheated."

"I know that," I say, leaning against the counter for support. "But it's one thing to *know* it, and a different thing to *feel* it. To believe it."

Mom watches me, her face solemn, and I know the words hurt her. That she wishes she could take my pain away and heap it upon herself like she would do with my backpack in the airport on family vacations.

"Do you believe it now?" she asks after a long moment, searching my face for the truth.

I shrug one shoulder and let out a breath. "I'm starting to," I say, and then after a moment, I add, "I'm still scared about Alex."

A small, tender smile touches Mom's lips. "Love is scary, kiddo. No matter what you've dealt with in the past."

"I just don't want this to end badly," I say, the words caught in my throat. Tears prick the backs of my eyes.

Mom hands me a dish towel, and I dab it under my eyes, breathing in the lemony scent of her laundry detergent. It's the same kind she's used for as long as I can remember, and it feels familiar when everything else around me feels like it's on the brink of changing and evolving.

"I can't promise that it won't," Mom says after I finish wiping my eyes. "But you might miss out on something very special if you let your fear get in the way." She pauses for a moment. "And you may still lose him."

That has always been the fear. The thing that's been twisting and writhing in my head for weeks now—that no matter what I choose, I may still lose him. We can't go back after that morning on the porch, after he told me he loved me. And I can't go back to when I didn't feel this way about him. I have a feeling it's always been there, a piece of me reserved only for him.

We can't go back, and I have to decide whether I'm brave enough to move forward.

My phone vibrates on the counter, making a loud buzzing noise against the butcher block.

Best Friend Alexander: **Will you be back in time for Movie Monday?**

A smile tugs at the corners of my mouth as I type my response, and Mom says, "Alex?"

When I look up at her, there's a softness in her eyes that wasn't there before, and it makes my heart pinch. Maybe I've been oblivious to how I feel about Alex, but it's obvious that no one else has. And they're happy for me. They're happy that it's *Alex*.

It strikes me that I am too. That for the first time, thinking about a life with Alex fills me with more joy than it does fear. It will be a life with ice cream and movies, lake days and sunshine, bad dancing and whatever drink I'm in the mood for. It will be butterfly wishes and stardust and the magic of simply being with my person, the one who makes my soul sparkle.

And I want that. I want it so badly it hurts.

"Yes," I say, and it feels like a benediction, a wish come true, and an answered prayer. "It's Alex."

THE DAY SIMULTANEOUSLY PASSES in a blur and stretches on like the miles and miles of open road that will lead me back home. To Alex.

I'm still terrified of the future and the heartache it could bring, but I'm also buzzing thinking about seeing him tonight, about telling him what I've decided, and everything that will come after.

Those lips of his that I've been daydreaming about will be a reality, and I intend to find out what his skin feels like beneath my fingertips. I know so much of him, and yet there's so much left to be explored.

The zipper on my duffel sends an echo through my room as I close up my last bag. I perch on the edge of my bed, looking around at all the mementos of my childhood, the pieces that made me who I am. I'll be back here soon, probably as soon as apple season starts, but this also feels like an ending. This will be the last time I sit on this bed brokenhearted and too scared to reach out into the universe and grasp on to the things I want.

My eyes catch on the pictures on my mirror once again, a record of all the memories I made in this town, all the things I've loved and lost and felt and dreamed of. Pushing off the bed, I walk down the hall, the floorboards creaking under my weight. The door to my dad's office opens easily, squealing on the hinges, and I head right for the printer on his scarred walnut desk.

It takes me just a minute to connect to the Bluetooth and print the photo before I turn back around and head into my room. With steady hands, I fit the photo into the sliver between the frame and the mirror.

A smile curls over my lips as I look at the photo, mixed in with all the other ones, on plain printer paper instead of the glossy prints like the rest. It's the selfie of Alex and me from Cam and Ellie's wedding, the night everything was set in motion for us. Looking at it now, I can see the love in his eyes, his happiness to just *be* with me. I don't know how I missed it before.

I don't think I'll ever be able to look at him again without seeing it.

Mom and Dad are in their matching white-washed rockers on the porch when I carry my bags out. Dad jumps up from his seat and grabs the duffel bags from each of my shoulders, leaving me with just my faded canvas backpack bumping between my shoulder blades.

"You heading out?" Mom asks as Dad unlocks my car and carefully arranges the bags in my trunk.

I nod, looking out across the mountains, vibrant green and drenched in the bright yellow sunshine of the early afternoon, before fixing my gaze back on her. "Yeah, I want to get back before it gets late."

A smile touches her lips. "It's movie night."

Dad climbs back up the stairs and pulls me in for a hug. I breathe in the familiar scent of him, like pine and cedarwood and lemon laundry detergent. Hugging him feels like being transported back in time, and I have a hard time letting go. I didn't realize when I followed Cam to California at eighteen that I'd never be back here again with them the way it had been. I would never *live* here again, but being back here for the past few weeks has been like watching a movie you haven't seen in years, only to realize you loved it more than you remembered.

Leaving this time, *knowing* this, is harder than it was back then. But I have someone waiting for me back home.

"Let us know when you make it home safe," Mom says when I release my hold on Dad and wrap my arms around her. Her hands smooth down my hair and over the bumps of my spine, one, two, three times. It's the smooth, reassuring gesture she's always given me, and I sink a little further into it.

"I will," I promise and give one more squeeze before pulling back. The wind rustles the trees and catches my hair, making it blow around me.

Mom tucks a strand behind my ear and grins, her eyes sparkling. "And bring Alex next time."

Dad looks between us. "So you *are* seeing him?" he asks, like he's just now putting the pieces together. And also probably regretting not pulling out the air mattress with the tiny hole we've never been able to find when Alex came home with me for Trail Days. It will probably haunt him for weeks thinking about what may or may not have happened in my tiny twin bed.

A laugh punches out of me. "No, I'm not. We're just friends."

But hopefully that will all change after a few hours and a couple hundred miles.

He nods, relieved, and Mom and I hold back matching smirks, our cheeks coloring. I'll call him tomorrow and tell him the news if things go according to plan. If I can muster up enough courage to tell Alex how I feel. Dad will be thrilled, but I know that next time we visit, the deflating air mattress will be set up in the living room.

"I better hit the road," I say, letting my eyes roam over them one more time. Mom looks good. The bruises across her cheekbones from the sinus surgery have faded, and freckles now dot in their place. There's a light behind her eyes, glowing with something like joy. Dad looks like he always does, a little rough around the edges, callused and leathered from spending all his days in the woods with no sunscreen. There are wrinkles around his eyes that have been there since I was small and deepen with every passing year.

"I'll miss you," I tell them. Their arms come around me again, and they whisper in my ears that they will miss me too, that I need to visit more, and that my room will always be ready with fresh sheets whenever I want it.

We're all sniffling when we pull back, and I vow to visit more. This town is as much a part of me as they are. The mountains are written in my DNA, and the trees and grass and sun have left their little marks all over my skin.

Wiping my eyes with my knuckle, I say, "I'll be back for apple season, if not sooner."

"Okay, honey," Dad says, patting my shoulder with his large, rough hand. "We'll be here. Hit the road so you make it home before dark."

I nod, giving them one last quick hug before making my way down the porch steps and across the dirt driveway, dust kicking up beneath my feet and coating my leather sandals. When I climb into my car and look out the window, they're standing right where I left them, Dad's arm around Mom's shoulder, soft smiles lighting their faces.

The farm disappears in my rearview mirror as I pull out of the driveway and steer my car toward town, swallowed up by the trees and mountains. I follow the winding roads, rolling down the windows to let in the smell of wildflowers and pine. Over the whir of the engine and the wind whipping past, I can just make out the sound of the babbling creek leading toward the river in town.

Afternoon sun glistens on the windows of the shops in town, busy with tourists and hikers milling about. My gaze catches on a wooden sign hanging above a door, swaying in the breeze. *The Ridge Hardware Store*. I have an urge to walk in there and tell Oliver that I hope no one ever tells his daughter he's glad he met her once she was hot, that even the small things can stick with you.

But I have better places to be. A high-rise apartment in the middle of downtown. With way too many windows and not enough curtains. Monochromatic furniture and a colorful throw blanket strewn over the back of the couch. A butterfly painting interspersed with the black and white artwork.

And Alex, in the middle of it all. Gray sweatpants and the thinnest, worn tee. Messy hair and a smile that hitches up on one side first.

I can't get home fast enough.

Thirty-Four

ALEX

I'M ON THE COUCH when my front door opens and shuts with a click. Before Hazel can make it down the hallway, I'm up and moving. It feels like when you walk into a restaurant at the end of a long day and realize you've forgotten to eat. You knew you were hungry, but it's not until you're being seated and perusing the menu that you notice you're *ravenous*.

Missing Hazel has been like that. Being without her was lonely and sad, but now that she's here, I feel it like the ache of a missing limb.

Hazel rounds the corner at the exact moment I do, and then we're chest to chest, careening into each other too fast to stop. My hands find her forearms, steadying her, but I don't step back. And neither does she. Time blurs at the edges, like we're slipping between universes. I'm desperate to find the one where we're together, to hold on to it for dear life and make it our reality.

"Hey," I say, soft as a whisper in the dark. I'm scared to talk too loud or move too suddenly and break this trance we've fallen into.

But then I don't have to move, because Hazel is. Her arms come around my middle and her face tips up into the crook of my neck. I respond immediately, hugging her tighter, like I'm worried she'll change her mind and pull back, end the embrace before I have my chance to soak it in.

My head dips into the curve of her shoulder, breathing her in. She's wearing something rich and floral today, and I want to drag my nose along her collarbone and up the line of her neck to find where it's strongest.

"I missed you," she says into my shoulder, her words muffled, but they still seep into my skin like fragrant oil.

My arms tighten, pulling her tighter against me until I can feel every dip and swell, every curve and jut of bone. When she breathes in, I take advantage of the sliver of space until there's nothing left.

"Three weeks is too long," I say into her hair, letting my hand that's been planted on her shoulder blade travel across her back. Down the length of her spine. When she shivers against me, I feel it everywhere. The tips of my toes, the palms of my hands, behind my navel, at the base of my spine.

Hazel's breath is hot against my skin as she says, "Three hours is too long."

I pull back without thinking, needing to see her face. My gaze trails over her features, the slope of her nose, the dark fringe of her lashes, the curve of her lips, the spark behind her eyes.

She's looking at me like she never has before, all soft eyes and parted lips, heavy breaths and blushing cheeks. That look feels like honey dripping inside me, warm and liquid, pooling in all the places I'm desperate for her.

"I forgot food," Hazel says, and it takes me a moment to register her words. "It was my week to bring dinner," she clarifies, and I nod, my mind shifting gears.

"That's okay," I say.

She pauses, her gaze dipping before it lands on me again. This time she looks shy, hesitant, twin roses blooming across her cheekbones. "I just wanted to see you."

A kaleidoscope of butterflies takes flight in my stomach. "I wanted to see you too," I say. Then, "We can order food."

Hazel's head dips in a nod. "Yeah, let's do that."

She slips past me, disappearing into my apartment, and I stare at her for a moment before following. She's wearing high-waisted linen shorts and a cropped white tank with those teeny tiny straps that always drive me crazy. For the rest of the night, I'm going to want to hook a finger through that strap and tug.

Temptation in the form of thin straps. I'm officially pathetic.

Hazel glances over her shoulder at me, raising her brows at the way my feet are rooted to the spot. I don't know what she expects, walking in here and acting like *that*. Maybe if I stay here all night, she'll come back, and we can pick up where we left off.

"What do we want to eat?" Hazel asks, sinking into the couch and tucking her legs up under her. I guess that ruins my plan to stay fixed to this spot.

Slowly, I make my way into the living room. All my senses are amplified. I can feel the air conditioning blowing on my skin, and I can smell Hazel's sex goddess perfume from across the room. Even the lights seem brighter, flaring at the edges of my vision.

"I'm good with whatever," I say, lowering myself onto the couch next to her. She shifts, and her knee presses against my thigh. My every nerve ending singles down to that exact spot.

What kind of place am I in that *knee touching* is making it difficult to breathe? Maybe it's just Hazel. Maybe everything feels bigger with her. The small moments are magnified, and the things that have never mattered before feel like they're being written into my DNA.

If Hazel doesn't want me, my new Bumble profile will have to be *really into knees*.

"Indian food?" Hazel asks, snapping me out of my thoughts.

I nod in quick succession before realizing that's not how normal people behave. "Indian is good," I say on an exhale.

Hazel watches me for a long moment, and I wonder what she sees. I wonder if she knows I'm falling apart, cracking at the seams. I thought I'd be able to handle waiting with more grace, but I feel like I'm on *fire* with the need to touch her. Now that she knows how I feel, any last barrier I had of holding my feelings in check has been obliterated, and I'm left trying to piece myself back together until she gives me an answer.

"You want your usual?" she asks, dragging her eyes from mine and to the phone she's pulled from her shorts pocket. She pulls up the restaurant's online ordering feature, scrolling through the menu options.

"That's fine," I say, and it sounds hollow in my ears.

If Hazel notices, she doesn't show it, dragging her finger across the screen and adding items to the cart.

Pushing up from my seat, I head for the kitchen. "Can I get you something to drink?"

I need something to do with my hands, even if it's just chugging liquid until I piss myself.

"No, I'll just take a sip of whatever you have," Hazel says, and amusement cracks through the fog. A smile curls across my lips as I open the fridge and pull out two cans of Hazel's favorite probiotic soda.

When I return to the living room and extend the can to Hazel, she looks from the soda to me, and her mouth twists into a grin. "Thanks," she says and pops the can open.

I sit back down next to her, feeling lighter than I did before. I still want to find out how durable those tiny straps are, but *this* feels normal. Hazel and me on my couch, the setting sun slanting through the windows and casting my monochromatic living room in shades of color.

"Did you order the food?"

She nods, taking a sip of her soda. "Yeah, should be here in, like, thirty minutes."

"We can start a movie," I say, reaching for the remote on the coffee table.

"Or we could talk."

The words hold weight that wasn't there before, and it sends lightning crackling down my spine, lighting up my insides. When I let my gaze travel up the length of her to meet her eyes, they're dark, like the very depths of the ocean. Blue fading into black.

"Okay," I say, and it comes out like a whisper but deeper.

Hazel shifts on the couch, and when she tucks a sun-streaked strand of brown hair behind her ear, her hand is trembling. She lets out a breath slowly between pinched lips.

I want to reach for her, but I don't know if it will be welcome, despite our hug in the hallway. I hate that I don't know how to translate it, that what felt like a beginning to me could have been an ending for her—a goodbye.

"I talked to Sebastian," she says, and my world narrows, my vision closing in tight. I don't know what I expected her to say, but it wasn't *that*.

But despite it, I can't help but feel a tug of pride in the middle of my chest. That had to be like facing demons for her, to talk to him when he so thoroughly wrecked her. She's spent the last sixteen months piecing herself into something new and different. Something *stronger*, if not more scared.

Willing my heartbeat to calm, I ask, "How did it go?"

Hazel lifts her shoulder in a shrug. "About as well as could be expected, I guess. There's no justifiable reason for what he did."

"Then why did you talk to him?" I ask gently.

Her eyes dart away from me, fixing on some point on the floor. Her exhale is shaky. "I just needed to know if it was me."

When her voice cracks, so does my heart.

My hand finds hers without thinking, trailing up the length of her forearm before sliding back down to link our fingers. She watches the movement, and her skin pebbles beneath my touch.

"It wasn't you, Haze," I say, trying to keep my voice soft but firm. I don't know how to make her *believe* it, but I'm frantic to. "I *hate* that he made you feel like it was."

My free hand slips beneath her hair, cupping her jaw. Her skin is so warm, and she's so impossibly soft that my head swims.

Her eyes focus on me, and I can see the anguish there, the hurt that might never fully go away. But I also see something else, something I can't quite name but that I desperately want to find out.

"It was not you," I say, emphasizing each word. "You are everything, Hazel. You are sunshine and butterflies and ice cream. You are kind and gentle and you make magic with a paintbrush. You are everything, and if he didn't see that, he's blind."

I'm panting now, my words coming out faster than I can think. I'm raw and on edge and unfiltered.

"He's blind, Hazel. And maybe you'll forgive him one day, but I won't. I'll never stop hating him for making you feel like anything but the kinds of dreams you never expect to come true, the ones that feel too silly to even wish for. Wishes on butterfly wings, Haze. That's what you are."

Her gaze holds mine for so long that I start to come back to myself. That I finally realize I shifted my legs beneath me, and that I'm practically horizontal as I lean over Hazel, my hand tangled in her hair. I can feel her shallow breaths against my skin, her pulse thrumming against my palm. She's so real to me right now that it hurts.

But then she leans forward, and the gap between us closes. Inches that feel like miles dissolve until there's nothing, and her lips are on mine.

The kiss is soft, tentative. The barest whisper, like she's testing it out. And I want to devour her, to pour all my love into this kiss, but I don't. If this is all she can give me right now, I'm not going to push it.

Then her hand fists around the collar of my shirt, tugging me closer, and I almost lose all my restraint. Hazel is the water I've been deprived of while wandering in the desert, and I have to hold back from drinking her in too fast.

Her lips part, and I stifle a groan when her tongue trails across the seam of my mouth, parting me. The first taste of her is sweet, like the whipped cream on top of a decadent cake. I want to tilt her face for a better angle, but I let her lead.

When she sighs against my lips, I know I've made the right decision.

I've imagined kissing Hazel Lane more times than I can count, but the daydream pales in comparison to the real thing. I feel overwhelmed, my every nerve ending standing at attention, in tune to the barest of touches. Her knuckles against my collarbone. A knee pressed to mine. Nails curling against the back of my neck.

Hazel pulls back, her head sinking into the throw pillow below her as she looks up at me. Somehow, during the kiss, we slid farther and farther down so I'm almost propped over her, our hands still intertwined and pushing into the couch cushions. Her chest rises and falls with heavy breaths, and her gaze moves all over my face before fixing on my eyes once more.

"That was nice," she says after a long moment, and a laugh shoots out of me.

I sit back on my heels, dragging Hazel up with me. "Yeah, nice is one word for it."

Her bottom lip catches between her teeth as she watches me, and I want to ask what that kiss meant. If it was a one-time thing or the first of many. If it was a test or a goodbye. If we can do it again. If this means she's willing to try with me.

"Maybe we should start the movie," she says, and I nod. At this point, she could ask me to run naked through the grocery store, and I'd probably say yes.

Flipping on the TV, I ask, "What do you want to watch?"

"*Just Friends*," Hazel says, and my heart stops for an instant before resuming its beating, if not at a faster rhythm. I open the search bar and begin typing in the title.

"Is that the one with Ryan Reynolds and Effie Trinket?"

Hazel snorts a laugh. "No, that's Elizabeth Banks. This is that one girl," she says, trailing off and patting her knee with the tips of her fingers, thinking. "You know, what's-her-face."

"Ah, yes," I say. "Best Actress last year went to What's-Her-Face. And her co-star, What's-His-Nuts, won Best Actor."

A high-pitched giggle escapes her lips, and I look at her, sidelong, holding back my smile. "What do I get if it's Effie?"

my voice drops to something reserved for late nights and bed sheets.

Hazel watches me through heavy lids, her gaze only straying from my eyes to dip to my mouth. "What do you want?"

I wonder if her heart is beating as fast as mine, if she wants to kiss me again as badly as I want to kiss her. It feels impossible, after all this time, that she would feel the same way. But I want it so much that I'm willing to take her scraps until she's ready.

"I want to kiss you again," I say, deciding on honesty.

Her throat bobs in a swallow, and her eyes drop to my lips again, holding. "You know what?" she says, and her voice is thick as maple syrup. "I think you're right. It is Effie. We don't need to look it up."

My pulse skyrockets, and she comes closer, this time crowding into my space. I can't breathe as she swings one leg over my hips, settling her weight into my lap. My hands find her hips on instinct, sliding against the curves to rest there. It's like the hollows of her hip bones were made with my hands in mind, like they were always destined to land right here.

When I try to pull her closer, Hazel stops me with a hand on my chest. Her hair falls around her in a curtain, blocking off the rest of my view of the apartment. But I don't need to see it. Not when my entire world is sitting right here, her hands sliding over my collarbones and up the length of my neck until they stop on either side of my face.

Her palms scrape against my stubble, and I wonder if it will leave a friction burn on her skin. I want to tug her hands away and inspect them, press kisses against the redness, but she holds tight.

"Alexander Malcolm Bates," she says slowly, as if tasting each name. "You said a lot of things earlier."

I swallow. Nod. Words are beyond me right now, with her so close, her knees hugging my hips and her hands on my face.

"I wanted to say some things of my own, but I got distracted." The corners of her lips twitch before settling back down. "You said I'm everything," she says, her voice cracking.

Again, all I can do is nod. I'm worried that if I try to speak, the words will tumble out again, not making any sense, an outpouring of love that's been locked behind a cracking dam for too long.

"You said *I'm* everything," she says again, enunciating the word. "But to me, it's you who's everything. You're safety and friendship. Forcing me to get sunshine when my mind goes dark. Always having a scrunchie and ordering me a drink because you know I'll end up wanting one. You're movie marathons and reading to me until I fall asleep. Taking care of me when I'm hurt and calling me when you have a feeling I might need you."

She stops, her words choked with tears, and I reach up, trailing my thumb across her cheek to catch them.

"You're everything, Alex, and I love you so much it hurts."

My heart careens to a stop in my chest, wheels squealing on pavement. "What did you say?"

A bright, dazzling smile crests over her face like a sunrise, and she lets out a wet laugh. "I said I love you, Alex."

I want to close the distance, taste her and touch her until we're both bleary-eyed and not thinking clearly. But I don't. Not yet. There's one more thing I need to know.

"And you'll be with me?" I ask, scared of the answer.

Her eyes shutter for just a second, but she doesn't try to hide it from me, doesn't pull back and disappear. "I'm still scared," she says, and my pulse skitters. "I'm scared of losing you, but I'm more scared of not trying." Her eyes hold mine, fire dancing behind them, and I can feel the flames licking at my soul, threatening to set me ablaze. "Yes, Alex. I want to be with you. Be with me. Let's be brave together."

I don't need further encouragement.

If the last kiss was tentative and testing, this one is bruising and accepting. A clash of teeth and tongues, hands against skin and bodies fusing together. It feels like lighting a match against tinder and watching it go up in flames.

Hazel's hand slides into the collar of my shirt, and my eyes roll to the back of my head. Her skin against mine is the stuff of dreams, ones I never imagined would come true. She sighs against my mouth, and I take advantage, kissing her harder, until we're both gasping.

My lips trail across her jawline, learning all the places that make her gasp or squirm, saving them away for later. When my tongue traces a line down the slope of her throat, she moans my name, and I have to let go of her hips and bury my hands in the couch cushions.

I let my mouth slide along her collarbone. Not kissing, but just feeling, memorizing. When I get to that tiny strap, I nudge it down with my nose, pressing a kiss to the little indentation where it used to be. Hazel's breath comes in loud, panting gasps, and when I look up at her, I think I'm coming undone. I don't know how I ended up here, but I never want it to end.

"Say it again," I rasp, my voice like sandpaper.

Hazel's face softens, her eyes lightening like the last tinges of night fading into the sunrise. Her hands come up around my face once more, thumbs swiping over my cheekbones. She's got a beard burn on her neck, and it sends a pulse of desire straight through me, a want so visceral I think I'll die if I don't touch her again.

I let my hands settle back on her hips, tugging her closer until she's blurred around the edges. Until the only thing I can see is Hazel. My Hazel.

"I love you, Alex," she says and presses her lips to mine once more.

This kiss is slow, our lips swollen, our tongues tasting. I think I could do this forever and never get sick of it. Kissing Hazel feels like stealing magic that never belonged to me. A wish on butterfly wings that was never meant to come true.

But it did, and my chest aches from the force of it.

I grip her tighter, deepening the kiss, and I see stars when she rocks against me.

A knock on the door jars us apart. We stare at each other with wide eyes, our lips bruised, and our clothes rumpled. It takes a minute for me to figure out who's here, to remember the dinner order we placed.

"Dinner," I pant, and Hazel's head hangs, her shoulders sagging.

I push to my feet, carrying her with me toward the door, and she squeals. "Let me go!"

"Not a chance," I say, holding her tighter, and her thighs squeeze against my hips. She's laughing into my shoulder when I swing open the door. The delivery driver, for his part, doesn't comment on the woman wrapped around me, clinging like a barnacle on the bottom of a ship.

"Thanks, man," I say, and he nods, not even acknowledging the situation.

When the door snicks shut, I set Hazel down, propping one hand on the wall beside her head.

"I hate you," Hazel says, but her eyes are sparkling.

"No, you don't," I say and dip my lips to that spot on her neck that I now know makes her shiver.

She shakes her head as I press my lips there, goose bumps erupting on her skin. "No, I don't," she breathes. "I love you, Alex."

Thirty-Five

HAZEL

Nine Months Later

I'm going on a blind date today.

Warm hands come around either side of my face, and a blindfold covers my eyes. Alex's breath dances across the back of my neck as he says into my ear, "No peeking."

"I wouldn't dare," I respond, even though I'm trying to peer through the crack in the bottom.

A laugh rumbles out of him, and he spins me around, bending down to look up at me from under the blindfold. "I'm serious, Lane."

"Fine, fine," I grumble, a heavy sigh slipping from between my lips.

"This is supposed to be fun." His hand folds through mine, leading me forward. Months and months later, and I still haven't gotten over the feeling of his hand in mine. How his fingers thread through my own, and his thumb never stops making lazy passes over my skin. When I squeeze his hand, he squeezes back, a wordless message.

Alex pauses to open the front door of his apartment and leads me through it. I hear it snick shut behind us, and then he's leading me down the carpeted hallway, my high-top Chuck Taylor's padding softly.

"So was that camping trip in the fall, and we both know how that went," I say as Alex turns me around a corner, stopping to press the elevator button.

I can hear the smile in his voice when he says, "So I'm not the best planner. You knew that already."

The elevator button dings, and he pulls me inside, his hand leaving mine to circle around my waist, fingers indenting into my hips.

"I still don't understand how you forgot *food*, Alex."

Instead of answering, he presses me against the wall, his lips finding mine. I don't need to see him now to know where to touch him. His body is familiar. I know he likes it when my nails scrape against the base of his scalp. I know he gets frantic when I kiss his throat. I know that he will never stop a kiss first, and that if we ever want to get anything done, I have to be the one to pull back.

"Where are we going?" I ask against his lips.

He lets out a long-suffering sigh. I've asked him no less than ten times since he told me about this cryptic date idea two weeks ago. Blind date, just for old times' sake, and ice cream after. That's all he gave me. And honestly, I'm fine with whatever we do, but he's been so flustered with my questions that I've kept going just to elicit the reaction from him.

The elevator dings again as we reach the ground floor, and I hear the doors slide open, letting in the quiet sounds of the lobby. Alex's fingers tighten on my hip once, then slide into my hand again, tugging me gently forward.

As soon as we're out in the lobby, he announces loudly to his doorman, "She's not in distress." A laugh snorts out of me, and I have to stifle it behind my free hand. "It's a blind date, sir," Alex says, even louder this time.

The doorman, who could not care less about our antics, grunts in our direction, and I have to press my lips together to hold back my giggles.

"No laughing," Alex whispers in my ear. "He might think it's a nervous tic and that I actually *am* trying to kidnap you."

"I really wish I could see his face," I murmur back.

"He's not even looking," Alex says, leading me through the side door into the parking garage. "I think I should report him. I could totally be a kidnapper, and he doesn't even care."

"You're wearing a knit polo," I say.

Alex keeps walking us toward his parking spot, our footsteps echoing in the cavernous space. "I don't see how the two are related."

"Men in knit polos do not kidnap women. They commit tax fraud."

We stop at Alex's car, and it beeps as he unlocks it. "Where'd you get that information?" he asks, and I can't see, but I know from how close his voice sounds that he's got one hand propped next to my head, his face hovering inches from mine.

"Oprah, I think."

His ability to hold back his laughter slips, and he presses a kiss to my nose. "Okay, I'll make sure to let the cops know that if I'm ever accused of kidnapping."

"I would like to know what kind of situation you'd be in that would make you a suspect.

"Maybe I stumbled upon a dog fighting ring and there were children present, so I got them out of there," he says, swinging the passenger door open and helping me inside.

"Sounds plausible."

He leans in, adjusting my blindfold so it's more secure. "But as long as I'm in a knit polo…"

"Hey, Alex?" I say, letting him hear the smile in my voice.

"Yes, Hazel?"

"Where are we going?"

The door slams shut, and my laugh bounces through the otherwise empty car. When Alex climbs in a minute later, I say, "So we're going to the drive-in."

He lets out a sigh and begins backing out of the parking spot.

"A picnic!" I shout. "How romantic."

Light shines through the cracks in the blindfold as we turn out of the garage and onto the street, and I can feel the bright sunshine warming my skin. "It's fifty-five degrees outside."

"Life's a beach if you make it one."

"That's not a saying," Alex says, and I can practically *hear* the furrow in his brow.

I lift my shoulder in a shrug, blindly feeling for the radio buttons. "If you get to make up sayings, then so do I."

Alex swats my hands away from the radio. "What do you want to listen to?"

"Something good," I say, and a few moments later, even though it's barely spring, soft music from Alex's *Summer Anthems* playlist filters through the speakers. It reminds me of warm days in Fontana Ridge, of driving with the windows down, my hair catching in the breeze. It reminds me of muddy tires and washing off with a hose on the side of the house. It reminds me of sleeping beside Alex in a too-small trundle bed. It reminds me of all the little moments with Alex that I never realized would become core memories.

"Did I tell you Lucy wants me to paint a mural in the coffee shop?" I ask after the first song ends. Last weekend, we drove to a huge indoor flea market an hour away and spent the whole day wandering booths, picking up pieces of homemade pottery and vintage jewelry. When we got to the back, there was a woman running an apothecary booth, and she had a giant mural painted on her portable wall. It was stunning, and Lucy immediately asked me to do one for her.

"Really?" Alex asks, his turn signal blinking softly in the background. "That's amazing, Haze."

"I've never done anything like that before, but I think it will be fun," I say. "I'm thinking I'll really lean into her cottagecore vibes. Make it look like a witch's cottage in the woods."

"Wait," he says, voice perking up. "Did I ever tell you about the time last spring that I met with her when I was trying to figure out how to make you fall in love with me?"

Laughter crackles through me, splitting my face in a smile as I say, "No, you just told me she was giving you advice."

"Hazel, she's a witch."

His tone is so serious that I can't hold back my barking chuckle. "Oh, I definitely have to hear this now."

For the rest of the car ride, he tells me about the time he met with Lucy in a cat café. I know exactly the one he's talking about, since I've gone with her many times. I even recognize the precocious black cat from the story.

We have to start and stop many times as I ask for details in some places and laugh so hard I have to clutch my side in others. By the time he's finishing up, his voice is animated, and even though I'm blindfolded, I know he's waving his hands madly as he tries to get his point across.

"She's a witch, and you can't convince me otherwise," he says, ending the story.

I have to press my lips together to hold back my grin. "I'll make sure to tell her that."

"*I* tell her that all the time," he says. "I'm not positive she hasn't cursed me. You know I haven't been able to get a good haircut in a year."

"It did make your family Christmas card photos look insane," I acquiesce.

"*Mom* made our Christmas photos look insane," he grumbles. "I still don't understand why we have to do a Christmas card now that we're grown adults." His voice goes high as he mimics his mother. "'Adam represented a famous client, *who shall remain nameless*. Alexander sold a six-million-dollar home, and Elizabeth is now managing a second property. We're holding out hope for a wedding and grandchildren next year.'"

"Christmas was something else." I brought Alex home to Fontana Ridge for Thanksgiving, but we spent Christmas together at his parents' house. The theme was formal Nutcracker ballet, and while I showed up in a gauzy white dress, Ellie wore a huge tulle skirt that Alex had to spend the entire evening distracting his mother from commenting on.

We drank eggnog milkshakes in the burger drive-in parking lot after, and when we'd finally stopped laughing, our throats were sore and our voices were hoarse. Despite the craziness, it was my favorite holiday. Although I already knew I was in love with him and never wanted things between us to end, *that* was the night I knew I wanted to spend every holiday with him. I wanted to spend all those precious, sacred days laughing at our families' antics, eating ice cream so sweet it makes our teeth hurt, and falling asleep on the couch twenty minutes into a movie, wrapped in each other's arms.

The turn signal clicks for a moment before Alex steers the car left. A moment later, we slow, and he pushes the gearshift into park.

"Are we here?" I ask excitedly.

"Yes," Alex says, and I hear his door crack open. "But *no* peeking."

My door opens a few moments later, but instead of Alex's hand wrapping around mine, he settles his hands on my waist, brushing against my exposed midriff. Gently, he pulls me from the seat and lowers me to the ground. My hands land on his shoulders, fingers curling around the curves. A year ago, I wondered what it would feel like to touch him like this, but now it feels as natural as breathing.

Alex's lips brush against my ear, and I shiver as he whispers, "If I didn't say it already, you look beautiful today."

My skin heats, and goose bumps skitter across my skin. It's been nine months—nine months of slow kisses and easy touches, of heated glances and frenzied lips on skin, of Alex and me and our friendship changing—but it hasn't stopped feeling like the first taste of an ice cream cone on a hot summer day, like the perfect mixture of sweetness and relief and goodness and magic.

Alex's hands drift up from my sides to frame my face, slowly lifting the blindfold, the brightness reaching my eyes by degrees. I blink against it when he pulls the blindfold back, and when I see where we are, I have no words.

When I glance back at Alex, his lips are pressed together, mirth dancing in the browns and greens and golds of his irises.

"We're at a gas station," I say, my voice flat as I take in the building in front of me. Dilapidated and in sore need of a paint job. Cracking pavement and one of the lights on the sign blinking as it battles against dimming completely. Cigarette ashes littering the ground and the heavy scent of gasoline in the air.

I gesture at the building. "*This* is our special blind date?"

"And don't you forget it," he says, his fingers slipping through mine. He pulls me toward the steel and glass front doors, leaving his SUV parked beside one of the pumps.

It's a warm spring day, but the gas station air conditioning chills me as soon as we walk in, a blast of cold air hitting us in the face. Alex walks with purpose, leading us toward the back, as if he knows exactly what he's doing. When we stop in front of a brightly colored milkshake machine, a smile curls across my lips.

"Ah, I see," letting my gaze trail over him as he confidently presses the button on the screen and scrolls through the options. "Although, I don't know that the blindfold was necessary for milkshakes."

He smiles down at me, an unreadable expression hidden behind his eyes. "I didn't say this was the *only* part of the date."

Something warm and liquid bubbles inside my chest as I watch him. I don't know how I went two years without seeing him the way that I do now, without noticing how objectively beautiful he is. He's a work of art, the kind that I would stand in a museum and stare at all day, trying to decipher what makes it so breathtaking. The sharpness of his jaw contrasted with the soft flutter of his lashes. The dark stubble that blends into the creamy lightness of his skin. The pink that colors his cheekbones when he's nervous in social situations, that everyone assumes is merriment. The way his hair looks better at the end of the day, after it's rebelled from the styling products.

Every bit of him is a masterpiece, something I've never been able to capture, even though I've made him sit for me as I tried to paint him. I'd get frustrated and he'd try to make me feel better, and we'd both end up covered in paint and breathless.

The machine finishes mixing a peanut butter cup milkshake, and Alex hands it to me before ordering a cotton candy for himself.

"I don't even get to pick my own flavor?" I ask, lifting an eyebrow, a smile hitching up one corner of my mouth.

He shakes his head as he finishes his order. "Not today."

I suck hard through my straw, and overly sweet vanilla and rich peanut butter and chocolate bits coat my tongue. "It's a good thing I like peanut butter cup."

Alex doesn't say anything, waiting for the machine to finish his milkshake, but a smile plays at the corners of his mouth. While the machine whirs, I look around the store. It's almost...familiar, like I recognize the peeling paint on the yellowing wall near the register or the slightly crooked sign on the women's restroom.

"Have we been here before?" I ask Alex, my brain still trying to place details.

Alex pulls his milkshake out from the machine, holding it in front of me. He ignores my question, asking instead, "Want a sip?"

My face scrunches up, my nose crinkling. "I still don't understand how you think *cotton candy* is an acceptable ice cream flavor after the age of four."

"A tiger can't change its spots, Hazel," he says calmly, walking toward the register.

I blink at his back. "Alex, you know that's not the saying."

"What are you talking about?" he asks, glancing at me over his shoulder. "That is the saying."

"It's 'a tiger can't change its stripes,'" I tell him. "Or 'a leopard can't change its spots.' Tigers don't have spots, Alex."

He shakes his head, setting his milkshake on the counter, and I follow suit. "I'm pretty sure tigers have spots."

My eyes blow wide, and the woman behind the counter watches us, scanning our treats. "*No*, they don't."

"*Yes*, they do," he says and turns to face the woman checking us out. He gives her a winning smile, the same one that convinces me to let him choose the movie on Monday or leave the dishes in the sink and cuddle with him on the couch. "Do tigers have spots or stripes?"

With that one stupid smile, I know he's winning this argument, even though he's wrong. The woman looks caught up in the snare that is Alexander Malcolm Bates, and I simultaneously want to laugh and strangle him for it.

The woman's eyes flick to me for one second before fixing back on Alex. "I think spots," she says slowly, and Alex's grin widens, his eyes lighting up in triumph.

The look I give him in return is withering, and this makes his smile deepen, the lines at the corners of his eyes blinking to life. I should be angry at him, but instead, I'm breathless, my heart squeezing tight like a vise in my chest. Sometimes when he looks at me like that, I don't know how we got here, how I ever found him, and it makes me grateful for all the terrible experiences before him that led to this moment of pure, undiluted happiness.

Alex's hand slides around my waist, squeezing with the barest amount of pressure, the kind that would have me leaning in to kiss him if we weren't in a gas station, a stranger's eyes watching our every move.

"That was unfair, and you know it," I say as we walk out of the gas station, Alex lagging behind me. "You did that ridiculous smile that's irresistible. You could have asked her if the sky was brown, and she would have agreed with you."

"Hazel," Alex says, and his voice is different, not the teasing I expected, but something more soft and serious.

I spin on my heel, but he's not right behind me like I expected. He's a few feet back, halfway between the doors and the car, right in the middle of the parking lot. And he's on one knee, his milkshake on the ground next to him.

The smile is back on his face, but this one is different, more gentle and full of adoration. So tender it makes me ache. "Last year at the lake house, you asked me how long I've loved you."

My heartbeat dies, and my breath hitches.

"I didn't tell you," he continues.

It's true, and I finally gave up asking after he refused to tell me for months. Instead, I came up with elaborate stories, like we were at a masquerade ball and I lost my shoe, so he carried me out to his horse-drawn carriage, and we took it through the ice cream shop's drive-thru. As he wiped ice cream off my bottom lip, *that* was when he knew. Every time I would come up with one of these ridiculous tales, Alex would play along, adding details, until the actual moment he knew didn't seem to matter so much. All that was really important was that he *did* know, and I did too, and we were happy.

"It was here," he says, not looking away from my eyes, and I think I see silver lining his, peeking over the edges to fall down his cheeks. "We stopped here for milkshakes one day. I don't even know where we were going, but it was soon after you moved here. You were so sad then." His voice wavers, like the memory is both treasured and painful for him, and although I can't recall it, I know what he's talking about, can still perfectly imagine that fog of sadness that hung over me for months.

"But we were out somewhere, and you saw something that reminded you of Sebastian, and I just...I wanted to make that haunted look disappear from your eyes. So I pulled over right here and told you we were getting something sweet."

The memory takes shape in my mind, although the details are as hazy as mist.

"You got peanut butter cup, and I got cotton candy, and you told me that cotton candy ice cream is gross," he says, his lips twitching. "And when we came back outside, you were smiling. You looked at me over your shoulder and said you'd like to eat ice cream with me forever." This all comes out in a rush, and when he stops, he lets out a breath, his eyes locked on mine. "And that was the moment I knew."

There's still so much space between us, and he suddenly looks so earnest and sincere, there on his knee in the middle of the parking lot, vulnerability written in every line of his face. My feet propel me forward, closing the distance between us.

When I'm close enough, Alex takes my milkshake from my hands, setting it on the ground next to his. The melting ice cream glistens in the sun. His right hand slides around my left, holding my fingers.

There's still tears in his eyes, and that devastating smile plays on his lips as he says in the most professional tone he can muster, "You're probably wondering why I've brought you here today."

A tear-choked laugh bubbles out of me, and I press my free hand to my mouth.

Without letting go of my hand, he reaches into his back pocket. The moment stretches, my heartbeat pounding in my ears. Alex's eyes widen slightly, and he drops my hand, pushing to his feet. He pats both of his back pockets before moving to the front.

"Alex," I say slowly when his searching becomes more frantic.

But then he smiles, one side of his mouth tipping up before the other, and pulls something from his back pocket. "Just messing."

His hand opens, and nestled in his palm is a gold ring, its diamonds refracting with sunlight, sending rainbows of color all over us.

My eyes dart up from the ring to his face. His eyes are glimmering brighter than the ring, his grin wide and heart-stopping.

"What do you say, Haze, want to eat ice cream with me forever?"

Tears are falling unchecked down my face, and Alex reaches up with his free hand to wipe them away., There is such reverence in the gesture that an ache builds inside me, the kind you get when everything is so good it doesn't feel real.

But he's real, and he always has been. My best friend, although he was always more than just that, even when I didn't know it.

It makes it easier than breathing to say, "Yes."

Epilogue

HAZEL

Three Months Later

"You know," Mom says, meeting my eyes in the mirror from over my shoulder. "There's no shotgun."

I roll my eyes. "I'm *not* pregnant, Mom. How many times do I have to say that?"

"Well," she says, clicking her tongue. "You only got engaged three months ago."

We did. Three months ago to the day, Alex slipped the gold oval-cut ballerina ring on my finger in the middle of a gas station parking lot. When we called our families an hour later from the courthouse parking lot and told them we were eloping, *both* of our mothers popped blood vessels in their eyes.

"This was the compromise," I tell her. "*You* threw a fit when we wanted to elope, so we're doing the wedding thing."

She huffs, buttoning the last of the tiny buttons on my dress. "*The wedding thing.*" I can't help the smile that curves my lips at the snarky tone. "I'm *so sorry* that I want to see my only daughter marry the love of her life."

"Yes, yes, I know. I've heard it all before," I say, smoothing my hands down the front of my off-white dress. It's a mixture of layered lace and tulle, and the fluttering sleeves are entirely transparent. When I tried it on in the bridal shop, I felt like I'd walked out of the pages of a fairy tale.

Despite my tone, Mom starts tearing up as she watches me in the mirror. "You're getting married today."

My smile is shaky, and I have to hold back my own tears to keep from ruining my makeup. After Sebastian, I wasn't sure I'd ever even *want* to get married, not when I felt so precarious, so unable to trust. But with Alex, I can't imagine anything less. I want it all with him.

The door to my childhood bedroom cracks open, and Ellie's grinning face peers through the gap. "Hazel," she breathes. "You look stunning."

I do a little spin, the skirt of my dress twirling around me. Out in the meadow, surrounded by the wildflowers and butterflies, I'll look like a fairy, which is exactly what I was going for.

"Alex is going to love it," she tells me with a wink, and my own smile widens.

"How much time do we have?"

"Cam should be ready for photos in just a few minutes, and we have about a half hour before the ceremony starts. He told me to have you head out to the meadow."

"Perfect," Mom says, reaching for the hem of my dress, although I'm not sure why she's bothering. The hem is going to be covered in dirt and dust by the time the night is over.

The photos don't take long since Alex and I decided to forgo bridesmaids and groomsmen because of the small guest list. As I peer through the shop doors, I can see everyone important to us, dressed in varying earth tones to match the colors of summer in the meadow. The ceremony will be short, the music will be loud, and there will be ice cream instead of cake.

Alex is already at the front, his hands shoved into the pockets of his rolled-up khakis. His white linen shirt is a little wrinkled, and there's a lipstick stain under his collar from where I snuck out when Mom was greeting guests earlier. I unbuttoned the top three buttons and slipped my hand inside, pressing my lips on his pulse point, and when he groaned, I laughed into his skin, urging him to be quiet.

He left the shirt unbuttoned, and when his eyes snag on mine and a smirk crooks his mouth, I know he's remembering that moment too.

"Hazel," Mom yells from behind me, sliding the cracked barn door shut. "You can't let Alex see you. It's bad luck."

I refrain from telling her that Alex saw *all* of me in the downstairs powder bath a half hour ago when he slipped free every button down the slope of my spine and let my dress pool on the floor at our feet.

"What's wrong with your dress? "Mom asks, and I freeze.

Slowly, I ask, "What do you mean?"

Her hand presses into the base of my spine. "These two buttons are undone."

"Oh," I say, my pulse jumping in my throat. "Must have come unbuttoned."

She begins fastening them. "I don't see how. These holes are so tiny."

"Mm," I mutter noncommittally.

Mom halts her movements, looking at me more closely over my shoulder. "Hazel…"

The shop door opens, and Cam peeks in with Dad right behind him. "Mom, you can go sit down. We're about to start."

Mom's lips brush my cheek, and she whispers in my ear. "I'm on to you, Hazel Girl."

The grin I give her is wide, and she smiles back, but before slipping out the door she says, "Wait, family hug."

Cam groans, and Dad looks like he's holding one back, but they both slip through the door, and then their arms are coming around me, all three of them enveloping me. I have to hold back the tears that threaten to fall.

"I'm glad you found Alex," Mom says, her words muffled.

"You just can't let me have anything of my own, can you?" Cam asks, and I press my lips together to keep from laughing.

Dad stays quiet, but his hand squeezes the back of my neck gently, his large hand enveloping me.

My sniffle is lost in the press of their bodies. "Time for a wedding."

"Do you need witnesses for signing the marriage license?" Ellie asks as she and Cam follow us into the shop after the ceremony. Alex and I exchange a glance, and Wes, who got ordained just to perform the ceremony for us, watches us with raised eyebrows.

Alex's hand squeezes on my waist, and my mouth splits into a grin as I meet our friends' gazes.

"Well, no," I say. "Because we got married three months ago."

Cam's eyes widen, and Wes barks out a laugh. Ellie just grins, her face brightening with delight. We weren't sure if they'd be mad, but their reactions are even better than I hoped for.

"I can't say I blame you for not wanting to have my mother at your wedding," Ellie jokes. Looking at Alex, she says, "I can't believe you kept it a secret."

He shrugs, pulling me tighter into his side, and I melt against him, his skin warming mine through the thin layers of our clothing. The day we got engaged, after we talked to our families and agreed to a wedding, we got back in the car, but Alex didn't pull out. Instead, he turned to look at me and said, "I don't want to wait."

And I didn't either, so we climbed back out, grinning like idiots as we raced each other through the parking lot. I had a dent in my hair from the blindfold, and his tongue was purple from the cotton candy milkshake, and we were both sweaty from chasing each other, but it was perfect. I wouldn't have had it any other way.

"We knew it was important to everyone to have a wedding," Alex says, and when his eyes meet mine, they're full of a warmth that makes butterflies take flight in my chest. "But we didn't want to wait."

Wes grins, his smile a white flash in the dimness of the chapel. "I understand."

The shop door opens again, and there's a flash of copper hair and freckles. Lo's face lights in a smile as she sees us. "What do you understand?" she asks, coming to stand next to Wes.

He presses a kiss to her temple and says, "Alex and Hazel secretly eloped three months ago."

"The day we got engaged," Alex clarifies.

A grin splits across her face, a happy pink tingeing her cheeks. She looks so genuinely happy for us that warmth spreads through me like wildfire. "You know I love an unconventional wedding," Lo says, and envelops us both in a hug. "I'm so happy for you both."

"Thanks, Lo," I say into her tangle of thick hair, my arms tightening around her, holding on for a long moment before I let go. Turning to my brother, I meet his deep blue eyes, the exact color of my own. "Are you mad we didn't tell you?"

"Of course not," he says, his lips twisting in a smile. "You going to tell the parents?"

I glance at Alex, and find he's already watching me, a tender expression on his achingly familiar face. I can never look at him without feeling it like a shot of adrenaline to my bloodstream. Sometimes I have to actually pinch myself to see if it's real. If *he's* real. Whenever Alex catches me doing it, he presses a kiss to the spot, his lips lingering until I'm shivering, assured that he's flesh and bone and *mine*.

No one makes me feel like Alex does. I knew from that first kiss that everything was going to be okay, that I'd made the right decision in trusting my heart to him. It was flawless. Fearless.

Still holding Alex's eyes, I say, "One day," and he nods. "But not today. Today is for celebrating."

WE DANCE UNTIL THE sun disappears and the stars come out to play. The ice cream turns to liquid in the buckets of melting ice, and we drink from the cartons with glow in the dark straws. Alex and I slip off again, but this time, we're more careful with the buttons, even if he does leave a hickey somewhere hidden. My garter is embroidered with the words *Just Friends*, and instead of tossing it into the crowd, Alex rockets it into the lake under the moonlight, our friends cheering loud enough to wake the dead behind us.

The night is perfect. It's everything I didn't know to wish for when a butterfly landed on my shoulder three years ago. Everything and more.

Also By

NASHVILLE IS CALLING SERIES

Just Go With It
Wes + Lo's Story

Just Between Us
Cam + Ellie's Story

Acknowledgements

ALL BOOKS ARE CHALLENGING to write, and this one was no exception. It took me months to finally start it. For the longest time, these characters were so clear in my mind, but I couldn't get their story to work. One day it just clicked, and it may have become my easiest book to draft from that point on.

But it took a long time to get there, and a long time to make it into the version that it is right now. And for that, I have many people to thank, starting with Graeter's Ice Cream. Just kidding. Kind of.

Always first is my husband, Josh. I couldn't write books if you don't keep our world together for me so I can slip off into the one I've created in my head. You make everything brighter, and I hope one day I can write a character as complex and loving and special as you are.

My Pancakes—I don't know how I wrote a book without you. I know it was much, much harder, and I never want to do it again without you all by my side. Thank you for encouraging me endlessly and also reading my 2AM paragraph-long text messages working out a plot hole that's keeping me awake. You guys are the kinds of friends people write about.

Jamie, I'm so glad we met online, just like our mom's always warned us against. You've proven that sometimes internet strangers aren't murderers. Thank you for being one of my very best friends and treating my characters like real-life friends. Thank you for helping me through every little plot hole and also listening to my random tangents and reading all my drafts. You're the best. Never stop sending voice memos.

I have the best beta readers in the world. Melissa and Myra, thank you for reading this book as it was being written and not judging my bad grammar and overuse of words because I don't edit as I go. Seriously, you guys are saints, and this book would not be what it is today without you.

Beth and Sam, you make my books shine in all the best ways. Sam, you bring my characters to life, and I will never stop squealing about it. You deserve all the love and happiness in the world. Beth, you continue to edit my books even though I misspell the same words and never learn. One day I'll remember that blond doesn't have an *e*. Thank you for being the best editor in the world.

Readers, I want to thank you. *cue tears* When I started writing *Just Go With It*, I had this little idea of a group of friends leaving LA to come to my little slice of the world, and I never thought anyone would read it. For so long, these characters existed only in my head, and sharing them with the world was so, so *scary*. I never could have expected that people would resonate with these characters or love them the way that I do. I never could have imagined that there would be people out there eagerly waiting to read more of my words. It's incredibly humbling, and it's a dream that seemed too extravagent to wish for. I hope you know that each and every one of you that pick up one of my books mean so much to me. Thank you for sticking with me and with this series. I can't wait to write something new for you.

Above all, to God, who lets this sweet dream of mine keep coming true.

About The Author

MADISON WRIGHT IS A rom-com writer living her own happily ever after in Nashville, TN! After falling in love with reading at a young age, she always dreamed of being an author.

Madison spends most of her time with her head in a book—whether that be in the car, at the grocery store, or in her reading chair. When she's not reading, she's probably watching The Office, eating excessive amounts of chocolate, or spending time with her husband and dog.

Follow Madison on Instagram @authormadisonwright